LIVING JUST A LITTLE

A NOVEL

GUY A. SIMS

Published by BCE Pressworks: Blacksburg, VA
A subsidiary of Big City Entertainment

First Edition

Front and Back cover design by Dawud Anyabwile

Library of Congress Cataloging-in-Publication Data is available upon request.

ISBN 10: 0615695418
ISBN 13: 978-0-615-69541-9

For Ed, Deanna, and Michael

I'll read it to you later.

Also by
Guy A. Sims

FICTION

The Cold Hard Cases of Duke Denim (series)

Brotherman:
Dictator of Discipline comic book series

The Kwanzaa Kids Learn the Seven Principles

NON-FICTION

The Kwanzaa Handbook

OTHER

Living Just A Little: The Conversation (Blog)
www.ljalnovel.wordpress.com

I is the Future (Blog)
http://iisfuture.wordpress.com

Living Just A Little Pinterest Page
http://www.pinterest.com/livingalittle/boards

LIVE!

The wind blows us
Like sand, leaves, trash
Down long stretched streets and winding boulevards
Trapping us in alleys where we spin forever between dumpsters and
dreams
Casts us away into rivers, down sewers, or out to the horizon between
seagulls and sunfish

The sun shines
Bathing us in light, warmth
Growing us tall or drying us out
We spread our arms like petals or fold in the cold shadow of stones and
trees
And when night comes we wonder where did it all go?

Life has no friends
Each one begins as another
Our hands hold on to what's precious
Love, Anger, Happiness, Jealously, Strength, Pain, Joy
Fear not!
Open your hands and live! Open your hands and live!

-GAS-

Living Just A Little

PROLOGUE:
A TWELVE PACK OF LAMENTATIONS

-1987-

THE SMELL OF sweat was deep in his clothes as the A & P grocery sack swayed to the slow rhythm of his gait. He no longer felt how tired he was. Neighbors watched him from the corners of their eyes. One or two shouted words of encouragement...*It'll work out Mr. Parker* or *The insurance should help you Carl* but most remained silent--out of pity--out of guilt. He was numb as he approached the corner. His house was now in sight but he didn't want to see it. He wished he would die. Drop dead right there on the spot so that he didn't have to go inside--to answer questions--to look at their faces. Dread was the residue crusting in his throat. What else could he do?

Stopping at the steps, he slowly pivoted to face the street before sitting down. Opening the bag, he retrieved one of the cans of beer. He looked to what should have been the heavens. He used to believe it was there he would find the answer to all of his questions but now it was only sky. With three strong swigs, he knew there were no answers to come. His mind had nothing to do but wander, wander back to a different day. A day when things were happening but he couldn't see or understand. A second beer conjured memories with the clarity of a hall of mirrors.

It was 1981 or sometime near there, his recollection was vague. During those days he really wasn't paying any attention. The store was still holding on, as best he could keep it. The neighborhood was changing again with drugs and gangs choking the life out of the residents. With the community facing an increase in crime and

1

weekly gun fights, he didn't have the time to think about the group of people moving in on the next street over from his Pine Street home.

"I hear it's them MOVE people." Mr. Parker's neighbor, Smitty, blabbered as he swept his front steps. "I wonder what the city's gonna do with them this time."

It was a warm summer afternoon in the city of Philadelphia. Mr. Parker watched his neighbor sweep his walk as he dabbed his forehead with a small towel.

"So far I hear they've been pretty cool. Should mean more customers for me."

"You don't remember the Powelton Village thing back in the 70s? They moved in and then next thing you know, cops gettin' killed and they arrested the whole bunch of them. Ugly scene man! Go on over there and you'll see what I'm talkin' about...if anything's left." Smitty put the broom down, taking a seat on his steps. "Now they're over there on Osage Avenue, settin' up shop."

"Smitty, please! They're people just like you and me...just trying to eek out a life for themselves." Mr. Parker unfolded a lawn chair and sat down.

"Like you and me?" Smitty exploded with disgust. "Get with it Parker. They're over there wearing their hair in those Jamaican braids. The kids are runnin' around all half naked...and none of 'em go to school. They even got animals livin' in the house...goats...chickens. Hell, if they want chicken they can go right on down to the Kentucky Fried!" Smitty paced back and forth, flailing his hands as he talked. "If things start buggin' out over there, I'm going to have to move. Property values are dippin' as it is anyway. I'm lookin' at Jenkintown."

Mr. Parker's mind drizzled back to the present. He had dismissed Smitty's words. He tried to believe there was something for him in this neighborhood. He held fast to his dream of building a chain of stores, sadly the daily receipts told a different story. He refused to see his store for what it truly had become, a hangout for the time-wasting young men of the neighborhood, including his two older sons. All he ever wanted to do was to prove that he could make something of himself. All he wanted was a chance to realize his dream.

He started on a fourth beer as his mind drifted back to a conversation he had with Smitty in 1982. The U-Haul truck was backed up to his neighbor's steps. Mr. Parker caught him as he carried a box.

"You need to be thinkin' about movin' out Parker. Thems over there are doing exactly what they did back in the day and I'm not waitin' around for any casualties and calamities." Smitty dropped the box in the truck and started back into the house.

"I heard that people on the block have kept the city informed. I'm sure they'll handle it." Mr. Parker leaned on his fence. Smitty stopped.

"C'mon Parker! My man who lives across the street from them says he called the city fifteen times and he ain't got a single return call. You can keep your head in the dirt but I'm tellin' you...somethin's gonna jump off." With that, Smitty continued inside and by the end of the day, he was gone.

By 1984, Smitty's words rang true for Mr. Parker. Reflections of those days mixed with the fifth and sixth cans of beer. His line of thinking was blotted with momentary points of clarity. He could again hear the scripted and repetitious messages from MOVE's bullhorns and loud speakers: Anger, vulgarity, conspiracy, disdain, and distrust--so many messages to be interpreted in so many ways.

People were scared, the city was unresponsive, the media ate it up, and the Parker family suffered. There was such a tension in the air, even those who used to hang out in front of the store moved their inactivity to the next block, just to see if something would happen. Sales dropped, revenues dropped, hopes dashed.

Mr. Parker rifled the inside of the bag. One left. With a crack of the pop-top, the day in 1985 played like an old super 8 movie in his mind. He could see the mobs of people rushing in and out of his store. He shoved his way into the doorway, hoping they would see it was him but they were a frenzied bunch. The only thing they saw was opportunity. They wriggled around him before he was totally overwhelmed. He fell out of the store and soon stood motionless in the street. He now could only observe from a distance. They were the people to whom he once extended credit, people he gave penny candy to their children, young men and women he offered work in the store. They were now running with armfuls of his merchandise--food, clothing, the cash register. He screamed at them. He called them by name but no one responded. He wanted them to hear his voice and remember, remember who he was, that he was one of them. Sadly, it came to him, he realized, he had become--nobody. *Where were the police? Were they all on the next block fighting it out with the MOVE people? Wasn't there anyone to help him?* As the fire blazed on Osage Avenue, a smaller one started in his store. He summoned the strength to run back in as it began to quickly rage out of control. He saw a young man stuck underneath the ruptured counter, struggling to move. He reached over the broken counter and grabbed him by the collar. Getting the boy to his feet he looked him in the face. It was the Anderson boy. As the smoke swirled around their faces, the Anderson boy

4

grabbed a handful of cigarettes from off a dislodged rack before dashing out of the store. Mr. Parker was stupefied, standing motionless until the increasing heat pushed him to exit. Stumbling onto the sidewalk, all he could do was watch. Watch his work; his dreams go up in flames. The neighborhood was up in flames. His whole world was now up in flames.

He looked down at the dozen discarded beer cans on his steps and lawn. He didn't care. He thought of all he lost, the respect of his wife, the control over his sons, his store, his son James. There was nothing else.

But there was. He staggered to his feet and looked up at his bedroom window. He still had his pistol; no one could take that from him. He flattened a can with his foot and staggered inside.

ELLIS

-1999-

HE WAS IN A small, dimly lit café, no name but familiar. He was wearing his favorite navy blue, double-breasted suit with the bright red silk tie. Most of the café was cloudy save for the beckoning exit sign. The music was low but he could hear a voice haunting him. Grinding away softly in his ears was the hypnotic rhythm of Lisa Fischer's "How Can I Ease the Pain". He sat motionless. The room moved to bring objects into his view. A complete revolution brought his sights back to the door as a strong erotic aroma filled his nostrils. In the doorway stood a faceless young lady with the attitude and body he savagely desired. Naked and entwined, they fell onto the floor which now became a bed. He could see that his eyes were closed as he drowned in the deepest pits of passion. She drained him of the pains and trials of life and he smiled endlessly as they left his body. They lay still on the bed. Abruptly, a hand touched his shoulder. His vision altered--his smile vanished. It was Clarissa.

Jolted from his sleep, Ellis raised his head and focused on the clock. The morning film faded to reveal the remaining seven minutes before the alarm was to sound. He had the dream again. Although it was the same dream from the last three weeks he couldn't recall any of it once he woke up. It simply felt the same. Whatever happened in the dream excited him. That's all he could retain. He buried his face into his pillow to hide his expression. With one eye, he watched the clock's digits change minute by minute. 6:08...6:09...6:10... 6:11... 6:12...6:13...6:14. Ellis leaned up and shut off the alarm just as the first signal sounded. He wanted to be quiet, not to disturb, but it was too late. He felt a stir from the other side of the bed. She mumbled softly with her eyes closed, still semi-sleep.

"Go back to sleep Clarissa," Ellis's voice was low and direct. "You have another hour to go."

"You want some pudy-pudy?" Clarissa was awake and alive. She rolled closer to Ellis, brushing her bare breasts against his arm. Her nipples sent the signal that she wanted to start her day out properly. The sound in his ears caused his eyes to roll back in his head. Earlier that week she had her hair braided and embroidered with beads on the end. They clicked with each twist and turn of her head. The sound got under his skin.

"C'mon baby. You want some of this here pudy-pudy?" There seemed an eternal pause.

"Yes babe." Ellis surrendered. He didn't need the argument. Not now. Not today. As he moved to kiss her, he planned a lovemaking schedule; a minute of kissing, some fondling, then finishing with record-time intercourse. The finale would be approximately five minutes of holding or until she fell back to sleep, whichever came first. He performed and ended his show with two minutes to spare. Rolling off of her, he wondered if he was a strong lover or if she was just tired. In the end it didn't matter to Ellis, as long as she went back to sleep.

Ellis was now free to officially begin his day. His routine was so--so routine. Mornings, weekends included, were so familiar that he moved through them with unconscious fluidity. He began with brushing his teeth. After gargling, he applied a hot washrag to his face to soften his stubble. He smoothed shaving cream onto his face and neck. The warm spray of the shower awakened him. He felt ready for the day. It was a Monday so Ellis opened a new razor. He shaved using the same razor pattern since he began shaving. He washed slowly, preparing his mind for the business of the day. After drying, he strode naturally through the master bedroom, crossing the hallway to the ironing room to plug in the iron. He re-entered the bathroom, rolled on deodorant, splashed on cologne, rubbed in a dab of pomade and tied on his wave cap. He grabbed a fresh pair of briefs and a v-neck undershirt from off the shelf in the closet. There, he also secured his clothes for the day. Gray slacks, white shirt, burgundy-paisley tie, black belt, black socks, and the black loafers. All of this was carried to the ironing room where the shirt was pressed and the remaining clothes were put on, except for the shoes. He waited until he was downstairs in the kitchen to put them on. He prepared one of his usual breakfasts: scramble eggs and scrapple. He watched the Today Show intermittently as he moved from the cabinet to the stove to the table. He missed old Bryant Gumbel but Ann Curry was easy on his morning eyes. The ritual ended with a blessing of the food. The sun dropped several beams of light onto his forearms and chest. Ellis smiled.

Clarissa entered the kitchen just as Ellis was finishing the dishes. He looked at her but didn't stop washing the frying pan. He could tell she was losing weight from the way her robe drooped on her body. He didn't say anything. He didn't want to hear her redundant plea for attention by complaining that her weight loss program wasn't working fast enough. Clarissa's goal was to lose thirty-five pounds. She was only eight shy. Ellis felt she looked fine but what he felt didn't matter.

"My moms called last night." Clarissa moved to the refrigerator and found a small can of grapefruit juice hidden behind a bowl of mashed potatoes. Ellis took a deep breath and closed his eyes. He made fists underneath the suds in the dishwater. The tensing of his face came and went so quickly that Clarissa didn't catch it. He knew why Clarissa's mother was calling and it made his stomach hurt.

"You mean your *mother?*" Ellis was always bothered when Clarissa used her street lingo.

"She wants to me to come up for that visit." Clarissa sipped her juice. This conversation was no stranger to Ellis.

"You know the only thing that's going to happen up there is a fight between you and you brother. Always does, always will!" Ellis took the deli meat from out of the refrigerator.

"It's not all like that. You know she wants me to see my father."

"That's what it is?" Ellis drew a knife from the butcher's block and like a surgeon, operated on a Kaiser roll. "All I remember from last month was me standing outside listening to the two of you having a swearing competition." Ellis put the newly sliced bread down on the counter. "In fact, I don't think you ever got around to seeing your father that time."

"That's just how we communicate." Clarissa watched him meticulously make his lunch. He had the two slices of bread, side by side, the meat and cheese added in the same order as all of his previous lunches, the swirl of mustard, topped off with a sprinkling of Italian seasoning. "I want you to come with me again." Ellis paused for a moment. "I think my family is finally warming up to you." This too was a repeat conversation. He resumed his ritual. He placed all of his lunch items into his satchel. "It'll be fine. All you have to do is be quiet, let me visit my pops, listen to us talk, get something to eat, then we're outti." Clarissa tightened her robe with a strong jerk. "Well...he is my father. Besides, I should suggest that my moms live with us here. I think she would like Philly. What do you think?" Clarissa reached over and lowered the volume on the television. Ellis took a Tastykake Krimpet from the pantry and added it to his lunch. Clarissa watched him. He was as silent as the muted Matt Lauer on the screen. This is normally how their discussions ended, just as he finished making his lunch. At 7:15 Ellis was picking up his briefcase and was in the doorway to the garage.

"We'll talk about this tomorrow night." Ellis's hand was on the doorknob.

"Why tomorrow night?" Clarissa knew why.

"I have a meeting tonight."

"You always have meetings. Can't you skip it tonight? I want to go out to a nice restaurant. Maybe a movie. No, no...a club!"

"Clubbing? Please Clarissa! You know I can't miss this...especially not for clubbing...it's a work night." Ellis propped the door open with his foot and grabbed his set of keys from the hook by the door. "No Clarissa...Friday, perhaps... not tonight." Ellis could hear the sucking of Clarissa's teeth.

"Go on!" Clarissa spread the attitude on thick. "Go on to your little thing tonight."

"I said we'll do it Friday."

"Go!"

"Well, I'll see you when I get in."

"I'll be sleep!"

"Good night then!" Ellis fell silent as he forced himself to move slowly towards Clarissa.

"I see you're not wearing that watch I brought you! Not impressive enough for your co-workers?"

"I have to go."

He kept his briefcase in one hand and his lunch in the other so that he wouldn't have to embrace her. He leaned and kissed her gently on the lips. No response. Ellis retreated to the garage. He placed his things into the trunk of his midnight '80 Jaguar XJS. He gripped the steering wheel and exhaled. On his next breath, he reached up and clicked the unit attached to the visor and opened the garage door. He didn't bother to look and see what kind of day it was. It didn't matter anymore. It was ruined.

HAPPY MOTHER'S DAY

-1985-

"WHEN WE GONNA eat? I'm starvin' like Marvin!"
Max snorted as he scrolled through the radio stations until he stopped at WDAS. He jerked and jostled his arms and legs, copying the dance steps of New Edition while mouthing the song Mr. Telephone Man. It was less than a minute before Kenny walked over and switched the small transistor radio to a news station.

"What you go and do that for?"
Kenny walked away without a word and found his place back on the floor. The other brother, James, downed the remainder of his soda and shot the empty can into the wastebasket.

"When I get out of here the first place I'm gonna hit is the courts. They have to be missing my talents down there." James gathered several other pieces of trash and banked one after the other into the wastebasket. "There's money to be made."
A quiet voice rose from the corner.

"You know dad says you're not supposed to be hanging out at the park."
James arched a balled piece of paper at his youngest brother, hitting him on the top of his head.

"Dad don't know what's up and you need to mind your business and keep that corner warm."

"Didn't Pops say to be quiet?" Kenny lashed out. "So just be quiet. Damn! Is that so hard for all y'all?"

"Why we gotta be cooped up down here all day? Can't we go out back or something?" Max went to the basement window and looked out. Their father had reinforced the window with an old blanket to darken the room or in case something came through. Max pulled back the duct tape so he could see outside.

"Seems like everything has stopped. We should be all right." No sooner had Max finished his sentence, a hail of bullets could be heard from outside. The boys dove onto the ground.

"Ellis? Ellis? Are you all right?" Kenny duckwalked over to the corner where his youngest of the brothers huddled nervously. "It'll all be over in a while. Don't worry about it. Dad says we'll be safe down here." Ellis heard his brother's words but his fast-pumping heart told him something else. *More bullets.* He inched further into the corner, wishing that he could crawl behind the furnace and be free from all of the madness. Once again, the shooting stopped. The three older boys went back to what they were doing. Ellis remained where he was, secretly nursing his fears and wiping the moisture from his eyes. He knew that the shooting was not going to stop--ever.

Since the early morning the day before, the neighborhood had been a battleground. Over two hundred police surrounded the house on Osage Avenue. For those watching their televisions, and especially for the residents, it seemed that the shooting went on forever. For almost twelve hours, the echo of thousands of rounds battered the ears and fears of the Parker family. In between the drum roll of bullets rose the scratchy sound from police bullhorns calling for surrender. An ever increasing volley of gunshot was the response. Ellis's father kept them in the basement, not knowing what was going to happen. From the small transistor radio on his workbench, Mayor Goode's voice was heard, "...intend to seize control of the house by any means necessary..."

Mrs. Parker crept down the steps periodically to bring sandwich fixings and cans of soda for the boys, ever worrying that they could be stuck down in the basement for a week, maybe longer.

"If this is control, I'd hate to see chaos!" joked Max. Kenneth whirled around and glared. The sounds of the endless rounds drowned out the dire prayers of Ellis's mother. While they ate, Ellis sat quietly next to her as she rocked, calling upon *sweet Jesus* to bring this madness to an end.

"Sorry for such a lame Mother's Day." His mother simply kissed him and told them all to get some rest. Ellis lay next to his brother Max and soon succumbed to sleep. The sounds of the bullets lulled him away like a perverse rain shower.

Suddenly, as soon as it started, it was over. A dead stop. It was the space devoid of sound that woke Ellis up. The absence of noise was unusual for his neighborhood. No sirens. No voices over the megaphone. No people in the street shouting. Perhaps he was dreaming. As if everyone in the world had disappeared except for him. *Am I all alone?* A faint smile was drawn on his face. *All by myself,* he thought. *No fighting. All I can eat. No chores. No big brothers.* It was the sting in his nose that yanked him back into the reality of the room. He kicked his brother's leg.

"Maxi!" Ellis said in a low voice. "You farted and it stinks!" Max rolled over on their shared mattress without waking up, letting loose one more burst of gas. Sitting up, Ellis looked around. The light in the laundry room offered meager illumination but it didn't matter, he knew the layout of the basement all too well. He and Maxi were in one corner, James and Kenneth slept across the room on their own bed of blankets. All of them had been up since the shooting began and sleep finally overtook them, even though it only late in the afternoon. It didn't matter; his brothers were deep sleepers. Day or night, it would take a lot to wake them when their bodies told them it was time to rest.

Ellis tried to lie back down but soon felt an unexpected swelling in his underpants. Slipping his hand into his shorts, he slowly began massaging himself with the myriad of thoughts of girls from high school. He wanted to get up and get a little lotion from the basement bathroom but he couldn't leave the moment. Losing himself in his own silent moaning, he didn't discern his internal hum with the pulsating whisper that passed by their small basement window. In his mind he was with Carmen or Paula or Jackie, it didn't matter, he was almost there. Suddenly an explosion-- outside!

Before Ellis and his brothers could get out of their beds, their father bolted down the steps into the basement.

"You boys all right?" Not stopping to hear their answers, he backtracked, skipping steps, to the living room, threw up the window, and stuck his head out. "Those bastards! What they go and do now?" Ellis knew there were a couple of "theys" his father could have been talking about, but who? Before he could ask his father the question, Mr. Parker dashed to the kitchen while Maxi and James had their heads stuffed into the quickly shrinking window frame. Ellis tried to join the mash of bodies but was quickly pushed out of the way by Kenneth. He could hear their scattered voices questioning, pondering, cursing, and shouting to people who now began to fill the streets.

"I'm going down to the store. You all stay here!" Ellis's father barked his orders as he moved to the front door.

"I'm going with you!" Kenneth shouted. In one circular move, his father turned his head, pointed to all four boys, sternly shouting.

"Keep your asses here in this house!" He whirled back to the door, and without missing a beat, was gone.

"What's going on?" Ellis asked as he tried again to find room in the window.

"World War Three!" snickered Max.

"Will you shut up?!" Kenneth barked.

"Look!" James pointed to the horizon. On the next street, licks of flame began to light the evening sky. Shouts of terror, anger, and confusion from all directions filled the night air.

"I've got to see this from the front steps." Kenneth and Max agreed with James and raced through the door. Ellis was mesmerized. He stayed, transfixed by the now yellowish-orange glow and the rising black column. As he sucked his next breath, he watched the flames greedily consume one house, then another, then another. He wished he were dreaming. Feeling the cool stickiness of his shorts against his skin, he knew he wasn't.

WORD ON THE STREET

ELLIS AND HIS MOTHER sat transfixed at the television in the living room. The events on the next block were now in their home. Ellis sat near the screen, as if trying to reach in and touch the many recognizable faces from his neighborhood. Mrs. Parker sat riveted as if was staked between the real and the surreal. She could smell the swirling smoke just outside their window. She could hear the sirens, the crackling of the fire, the screams of the crowded streets but stayed fixed on the screen. She knew that if she ventured out of doors she would become part of it all--and she wanted to keep it all an image. The front door burst open.

"Yo y'all! You've got to see this!" Maxi ran panting into the living room and dove onto the couch, knocking the contents from off the already wobbly coffee table. "It's 100 percent pure maddness out there." Maxi wiped his forehead on the arm of the couch.

"What? What?" Ellis was too curious to be restrained by the limitations of the television. He wanted to go outside but his mother told him to remain. "What's going on out there?"

Maxi pushed past Ellis and put his finger on the television screen. "I was talking with my man Freddy. He was out there all day. He said that cops was all over the place...everywhere. Then they kinda quieted down and moved back a little. So he thought it was gonna be over and them MOVE people would come out and give up or something. Next thing he says a helicopter comes flyin' over and drops a bomb right there." Maxi began tapping on the screen. "That's the ka-blooey we heard." Maxi then bounced to the front window, drawing their attention to the sky. "So then he says that folks started shootin' again and nobody was goin' nowhere. But with all of the shooting, the firemen couldn't get up there to put out the fire. The MOVE house caught on fire...then the next house…then the next…Ma…it was one after another…both sides of the street. I heard that there had to be fifty or more houses going up in smoke."

Mrs. Parker shivered at the thought. Ellis asked softly, as if he didn't want the world to hear his question.

"Anybody get hurt?"

"Man…you burn down a couple of city blocks and you know somebody's takin' a loss." Maxi looked at his brother quizzically. "Freddy said that people tried to get out the MOVE house but the cops rained so many bullets down on them they ran back inside. Them folks got did!" Maxi could see the look of disbelief in his mother's eyes. He changed his tone. "I did hear that there were some kids in the building but I don't know what happened…you know…like I said…it's crazy out there."

"So where are all of those people going to live?" Mrs. Parker's voice was enough to rise above the confusion. "You're talking hundreds of people." The three were quiet as the sounds of urban mayhem assaulted their ears. Their sense of disbelief was validated by the voice of the news commentator on the television. Mrs. Parker wanted to close her eyes and say a prayer, a prayer for the losses, for the lives, for her community, but she couldn't close her eyes and take her attention from the screen.

"The city should take care of the people…" Ellis' words trailed off with the sound of the front door opening. The strong smell of smoke announced the figure. Now standing in the room was Mr. Parker: smoky, dirty, and sweat-stained. His face was of stone and anger. He tied his eyes straight to Ellis. His words heaved from his throat.

"City take care of what? Those bastards burned down my store and nobody's doin' shit to help me!"

SYLVANIA

-1999-

SYLVANIA WAS ALREADY deep into her step aerobics by the time the clamor of the trash truck sounded outside of her Nicetown apartment, signaling six-thirty had arrived. She followed the instructions of "Dancin'" Debbie Carson on Channel 57. Debbie was the only morning aerobic show that used urban 'jams' as pace music. Halfway through the show, Sylvania left Debbie but kept the pace as she moved from her bedroom to the combination living room-dining room-laundry room-kitchen. She grabbed a lemon-lime sports drink from the refrigerator, taking several sips. With her thirst satisfied, the yellow-sticky on the corkboard came into focus.

> Interview at PowerCat
> Mon. 9:30
> One Liberty Place
> See Devon Hunt
> DON'T BE LATE!

Sylvania looked at the backward faced clock that hung over the stove. It was now moving towards seven o'clock. She knew she would have to leave the apartment by at least eight-thirty to make it downtown by nine-fifteen. She opened the cabinet and took out one foil pack of cherry Pop-Tarts and dropped them into the toaster. She chugged down the remaining juice and switched on the small radio she kept on her counter. She had a Technics upright stereo system in the living room area but the speakers were shot. Even if they worked, Sylvania would rather start her day with this small, outdated radio. She received it as a present from her father to help her get up and ready for elementary school. Touching the switch always brought forth a soft memory of her father. She lost him when she started middle school. It was one of her most treasured items, in fact, her only one. It only picked up one station, POP 93.2. She didn't mind. POP played a heavy rotation of Top 40 songs. As soon as the toaster ejected the pastry the phone rang. Sylvania knew who it was immediately. She quickly threw the pastries onto a paper towel and fumbled with the phone, all the while maneuvering her way onto the barstool by the counter.

"Twist?" Sylvania had gotten the phone by the end of the second ring.

"What took you so long? I told you I would call as soon as I got in!" The voice on the other end of the line sounded exhausted and excited.

"So, what happened?"

"You know what happened girl! Why do you think I'm just gettin' in?"

"You're wild, Twist. Out of control. How long you known Caddy?" Sylvania finished off one of the pastries and began picking the frosting from off the second.

"Don't matter. I know him good enough now. He's just like my favorite chicken wings...*extra spicy!*" They both fell out in great spirits. By now it was seven-thirty. Sylvania was watching the clock but the juicy details of the conversation could not get her up from off the stool. It took a commercial from the Philadelphia Unemployment Commission to break up their conversation.

"Look Twist girl, I've got to go. I'm gonna be late. I'm not even dressed yet."

"And you're probably stank from them exercises. Hey, meet me for lunch today at the Gallery, next to Corndog on a

Stick." They said five more minutes of 'good-byes'. Sylvania raced to the shower.

Sylvania was at the bus stop by 8:13. She had just missed the 8:08 but luck had it that a second one arrived at 8:16. She concluded the first one had to be maxed out. After flashing her SEPTA Transpass, Sylvania made her way to an empty seat about four rows back by the window. She had to squeeze her five-foot-five frame between an old man and the seat in front of her. She winced. The old man wasn't going to move and she knew it. Her buttocks brushed up against his chest and shoulders as she shifted her way into the seat. She resolved not to let this faze her. *Probably the biggest thrill he had in the last fifty years...toothless buzzard!*

As the bus began the journey downtown, Sylvania dreamed of the day when she could purchase a car. On that blissful day, she wouldn't have to put up with the old men and young boys. She would avoid the comments received when she walked. All the nonsense about *draggin' wagons', plump and juicy', and ' Misses Mean Jeans* would be stopped. She sighed as she thought about the time she almost had to slap some ashy-faced joker because he tossed an old 80s line, "Is that Jordache or just yo ass!" *If a brother can't have any respect for a sister, can't he at least be creative?* If she landed this job, she would be able to start saving, and after a year, maybe apply for a loan. She smiled when she saw her own reflection in the over-sized mirror of a passing glass truck. Although the image was slightly distorted, she could see her pretty cocoa brown skin and her hair cut. Although it was a week old, it still looked fresh. *I'm no Halle but* damn *I know my hair sure is!* She pulled a compact from out of her Ziplock makeup bag and checked her eyes. They were bright and alive. Her lipstick was just enough, especially for someone who hated to wear make-up. Slowly she closed her eyes and thought about her other plans. If she got this job she would quit her counter girl position at the donut shop and consider getting a two-bedroom apartment in the East Oak Lane. One room would be the bedroom. The other had numerous possibilities: guest room, or an exercise room, or even a sewing room. She would even learn to sew.

"Broad and Market!"

The bus driver's announcement coaxed her into opening her eyes. She looked out the window and soaked in the atmosphere of the business of downtown. *It would be so nice to work down here.* Her silent prayer rose with her as she prepared to get off the bus. Her stop was next. She got up and squeezed past a high school boy who had gotten on five stops earlier. As she rubbed against him, she saw him huddle up with his friends located directly behind them. Realizing the time, she ignored them and stepped to the rear exit. Her finger gently pressed the signal button for her stop so not to break her new stick-on nail. The bus stopped but the door didn't open. Sylvania pushed on the bar but the door still did not give.

"YO! BACK DOOR!"

The driver and several passengers whirled to look at Sylvania but she stood there, unconcerned with the stares and whispers. The light over the door indicated the release. She stepped onto the curb. The heat from the bus's vent opened her senses. Trash rolled down the street like urban leaves, soon to be crushed underneath the focused feet of nine-to-fivers, making their way to coffee vendors and cubicles. Buildings stretched to blot out the sun, casting shadows onto blank faces strapped with mental blinders or buried in newspapers. Trucks, taxi horns, the creaking platforms of window washers, the clip-clop of police horses, and beckoning calls in all languages from street vendors--the sounds of the concrete and steel ecosystem echoed from skyscraper towers to sewer grates. Beyond the grit and grime, there was an excitement, a pulsating jolt of energy on every street, in every alley, surrounding every doorway. Downtown was where it all happened, where people went to make things happen. She absorbed it all. There was a life here, a life that now enveloped Sylvania's spirit. The city was both a wonderland and wasteland. Whatever it was it would be her destiny. The squeal of the departing bus returned Sylvania to her purpose. She looked at her watch and knew she had better get stepping. She knew exactly where to go and merged into the currents of the busy.

It was 9:23 when Sylvania reached One Liberty Place. Standing in the grand foyer, she was confused. At first glance it seemed that Druer International occupied every floor. Closer inspection of the directory revealed PowerCat--Administration Offices were on the 12th floor. Her anxiety meter raised a notch at the sound of the opening elevator. She stepped in with the knowledge that something big was on the horizon.

"What floor Miss?" A sandy haired courier was standing next to the control panel. He carried only a small envelope in one hand. With his free hand, he was prepared to press a button.

"Twelve please," Sylvania smiled. She wanted to be perceived as very professional to anyone and everyone in the building. Since she didn't know who was who or who knew who-- she had to be cool.

She walked through the glass doors marked PowerCat, Administration 300. She had only taken two steps before a tall, lanky man approached her. She took a quick inventory of his attire to get a feel for the kind of people that worked at PowerCat: Brown broughams, brown slacks, white shirt, suspenders, and a matching bowtie. His glasses were the type that Malcolm X popularized. His only jewelry was a watch with a brown, reptile-skin strap. Before the receptionist could speak, the man in brown slinked next to Sylvania.

"May I help you?" The man removed his glasses as he spoke.

"Yes...yes, good morning. I'm here to see a Mister Devon Hunt. My name is Sylvania Lee. I have a nine-thirty appointment with him." Sylvania looked at the large clock over the company logo on a far wall. It was nine-thirty exactly. She sighed inside.

"Please have a seat. I'll let him know." The man escorted Sylvania to a leather couch. As he walked away, he passed a male co-worker. They stopped and the man in brown whispered into the second man's ear. They ended their engagement by shaking hands playfully. The second man took a sneaky glance at Sylvania before slithering around the corner. Sylvania knew what was happening. If she got the job she would squash any nonsense before it even began. As for now, she would sit quietly. She needed the job.

"Thank you for your time, Mr. Hunt." Sylvania smiled as she was escorted to the main office doors by Devon Hunt. Glancing quickly at the clock, the interview didn't feel like more than 15 minutes although 50 had passed. "I hope my skills and talents can be used at PowerCat." Devon Hunt smiled.

"We'll be in contact with you in a day or two. There are a couple of people we want to look at. Thank you for considering PowerCat as a place for employment. Enjoy your day." After the doors closed behind her, Sylvania quickly peeked to see if Mr. Hunt was the like all of the other guys, checking her from behind as she walked away. He wasn't. Mr. Hunt was talking to the receptionist. Sylvania cursed her paranoia. She was relieved that Mr. Hunt had class, something that she hadn't witnessed in a long time.

Riding in the elevator to the street, Sylvania evaluated the interview. It began with the timed typing test, which she passed with flying colors. Following the typing test was the proof of knowledge of several software programs. That was somewhat trickier for her since it has been a while since she did any direct accounting work. Although she was confident that she did well on that portion. Most programs worked the same so she hoped her scores in that area were strong. The last part was what she dreaded the most--the personal interview. In the small room was Mr. Hunt, the man in the brown, and an older Hispanic woman from Human Resources. They asked her questions about customer service, her work ethic, and some others designed to trip her up. *I handled myself in there* was her last thought before the doors to the elevator opened. Sylvania was proud that she controlled herself for not going off on brown suit. For the entire time of their session, his eyes moved from her breasts to her thighs and back to her breasts. *That's why he didn't have any questions for me.* Sylvania shivered at the thought of him. She knew his type, the old dude at the club. She giggled at how pathetic he really was. *I should get a call.* When she took him out of the equation, she felt that she had been recognized for what she had to offer and not for what she looked like. It felt good. It was a great feeling and she was determined to keep it for the rest of the day.

Sylvania soon found herself standing on Market Street. Checking the time she had a couple of hours to kill before meeting up with Twist at the Gallery. She figured on doing a little window shopping on Chestnut. As she started towards shops she heard, "Damn baby, you got any room in tham jean for me?" She didn't bother to acknowledge the asinine inquiry. *"Can't that fool see I'm not even wearing jeans?"* Although the weatherman called for a sunny day, the clouds of her life rolled back in quickly. Sylvania took a deep breath and picked up her pace.

JUICE

THE TIME SLIPPED THROUGH Ellis's mind as he looked at his framed diplomas--five minutes--ten minutes. Prominently placed above his desk hung the lightly faded bachelor's degree in finance from West Chester University. On the cabinet atop the 1996-97 files sat his MBA from Penn. Together, they represented the only two pieces of evidence of any accomplishments in his life. Not that being the lead Finance Manager at Druer Financial Corporation was any less an accomplishment; on the contrary, it was a recognized prestige. Business Journal listed Druer as one of Philadelphia's top 25 companies. In this past quarter, the company out-performed its peers by over 13%. A lot of the success of the company was due to Ellis's financial strategies, unfortunately the level and quality of his work continued to be underappreciated by one person: himself.

Ellis worked without a word. He rarely commiserated with the other executives or members of the financial section. Morning coffee was at his desk. Unless it was a business meeting, lunch was at his desk. When he used to smoke, he would walk around the block rather than *catch a quick one* on the loading dock. In time, he became invisible to most, if not all, of the staff, except for two. Winsome -*I'm just two steps away from retirement*-Bennett, his administrative assistant, who prepared all of his reports for the board. Winsome had worked at Druer since 1966, only her second job after high school. "'I've worked for many, many money movers and you're like all of them…bizarre!" Winsome joked with all of the staff but didn't seem to be able to break through to Ellis even though he was cordial, polite, accommodating, and demonstrated his appreciation every year with thoughtful birthday and Christmas presents. When out for a hip replacement, Ellis sent flowers to her at Jefferson Hospital and sent a couple of restaurant gift certificates to her husband so he wouldn't starve while Winsome was bed bound. She liked working for Ellis though there was a mysterious air about him. She knew one day she would figure him out. The other person who interacted with Ellis the most was Henry Morris from Human Resources. He went by Hank. To Winsome, they had a Cain and Abel relationship. Ellis' interactions with Winsome were warm and welcoming. Hank was a different story. He was an intruder. Hank was a competitor. He always wanted to know what Ellis was working on, who he had just talked to, how his meeting with the chief went. Hank had the need to know what was going on with Ellis. While this bothered Ellis, he never said a word, never complained. Even when Hank co-opted a couple of Ellis' ideas to the board as his own, he remained silent. To him, his ideas weren't anything outstanding but Hank saw something else, precious gems to be pilfered. Ellis was respected and his opinions were encouraged by the top brass. Hank was all show, all talk, and all glad-handing.

"Mr. Parker?" Winsome's voice came over his desk speaker. "Mr. Parker, Mr. Morris is here to see you." Ellis closed his eyes and placed his head in his hands. He could hear Hank's smugness over the speaker.

"Tell him to wake up, I'm coming in."
It was impossible not to hear Hank caught up in his own world. Ellis reached over and tapped the button. "Send him…" Before he could finish his sentence, Hank was already in the office, fingers pressed against Ellis's picture window.

"What do you need Hank?" Just having Hank in his office gnawed Ellis to his core but he kept a quiet composure. "I'm kind of busy right now.

Hank straightened his tie and continued to look out the window. It was no secret. Ellis knew that Hank was envious of his office. When Mr. Morgan provided Ellis with the office Hank made it known around the water cooler that the space should have been his. Hank noted that from this vantage point he could see across toward the 30th street station, the post office, and most of the University of Penn. Through his fake smile, he said that West Philadelphia looked like the place to live. The rows of homes interspersed with trees, all divided so nicely by the El train. It was quite a sight from that height. Now, at ground level, he related a different story. The trash, the bums, and the traffic--it all sickened him. Hank knew that Ellis was from that area so he reveled in sharing that he enjoyed his quiet hideaway in Ardmore. It was a commute but he didn't have to *deal with the underbelly of the city when he put his feet up at night.*

"Look Ellis..." began Hank, "I have things to do myself so get Winsome to set us up another meeting. I'm hitting a round at the Cricket Club at St. Martins so let me say this quick." Hank took a seat at the small conference table adjacent to the window. "You know the boss is thinking about expanding operations to either Chicago or Los Angeles. He wants impact projections and I don't have time to work on them." Ellis sat silent. This was not a new conversation. Every project they were to work on together became his responsibility. "So check this..." Hank began his familiar ramblings, propping his feet up on the window ledge. "We need some numbers that support the expansion. I can see myself making that move to LA...especially as the VP." Hank swiveled in the chair and looked straight at Ellis. "Let's do this as a team. You get the paperwork together, I'll make the presentation. Sound like a plan?" Ellis felt a groan in his throat. He didn't believe it was time for the company to make that kind of move but it was clear that the change was in the wind. LA did sound exciting but inside his stomach, Ellis felt a large stone drop. He knew he wouldn't or couldn't go to LA. While Clarissa would leap at the move in a heartbeat he thought about his mother and brothers. He didn't think he could leave them. Through the swirl of images in his mind he nodded affirmatively to Hank who immediately bolted out of the office, the links awaited him. Ellis shook his head, opened his planner, and penciled in his latest project.

When Ellis looked up again, it was a quarter to one. The office area was quiet. Most of the people in the suite were good about taking their lunch at noon. Ellis didn't mind. He liked the solitude of the empty office, as well as the notion that if he did decide to go to lunch, most people were just getting back. The thought of his sandwich invaded his mind, slowly becoming more and more unappealing. He considered going out to one of the local restaurants, the Gallery, or even Reading Station. His train of thought pulled in, on time, to its usual station. It was his own strict voice telling him not to waste his food. *You brought it, you eat it!* It wasn't really his voice; it was the voice of his father. Here, almost a dozen years later, the words of his father had successfully morphed into his own. He didn't know why they were still there and he didn't know how to be rid of them.

-1985, September-

Ellis stood up from the table and proceeded to the refrigerator. Retrieving the orange juice, he poured himself a second helping. As his lips touched the rim of his glass, he heard his father.

"Ellis, you just don't get it, do you?"

Momentarily confused, Ellis continued to drink. In between swallows he responded.

"Get what? Just drinking some juice." Ellis was a smart fifteen year old boy but not smart mouthed. Still, he had a way of responding that annoyed his father. His mother warned him to keep his quick responses under control, especially with his father.

Conversations like the one this morning was commonplace but this one was a little different. He could hear something in his father's voice but couldn't put his finger on it.

"You just don't get it!" Ellis's father repeated his statement. Now Ellis was really confused. He looked to his mother who lowered her eyes and continued to sip her coffee.

"What are you talking about dad?" Ellis tried his best Eddie Murphy voice to relieve the rising tension in the room. It was met with a haze of tension. Ellis's father stood and pointed to the bottle of juice.

"That's what I'm talking about! Guzzling all of the juice. You know that there are other people in this house and there's not enough to go around!" Ellis looked at the almost full bottle as he tried to make sense of his father's remarks. In his mind he asked himself if his dad was kidding. This had to be a joke but his father wasn't known for his humor.

"Dad, there's plenty enough for everybody."
Four months earlier, the city dropped a bomb on the house across the street. On this day, Ellis's comment was the bomb that ignited the kitchen. Now standing, Ellis's father moved to reach for the juice container.

"This, this has to last us until the end of the week." Frustration poured out like a bottomless bottle of orange juice. "Don't you remember that night when they blew up Osage Avenue? You remember that don't you?" Ellis's dad's questions neither invited nor required a response. "Remember all of the people in the streets out of control? You remember that night our store was looted and burned?" Ellis felt numb. He wanted to put the juice down. He wanted to spit it back into the glass. He wanted to pour it back into the bottle. "Yeah, now you get it, don't you?" Ellis's father left the kitchen with one last parting word. "We don't have what we had anymore because we live on the wrong block.

Enjoy!" Ellis looked to his mother, who quickly began gathering the morning dishes.

"Get ready for school." That's all she had to offer. As Ellis gathered his book bag, he forced down the last drops of the soured beverage.

-Present-

Ellis found himself looking out his window. The clear skies opened the western side of Philadelphia to him. If he had a pair of binoculars, he would be able to see the beginnings of his childhood neighborhood. Slowly, Ellis clasped the drawstrings and closed the drapes, closing out the view, the city, and the past. It was time for lunch but he didn't feel like eating his sandwich. He would find something different today--at least that was his hope.

LUNCHIN'

SYLVANIA HIT THE GALLERY food court at the height of the lunch rush. Single tables didn't exist--the lines to each of the sixteen eateries were at least twenty deep. She remembered Twist's instructions and squeezed her way through the masses of high school students, business people, tourists, shoppers, and other assorted bodies, eventually making her way to the Corn Dog on a Stick counter. She stood there and looked around. No Twist. If there was ever a poster child for *C-P* Time, Twist was its supermodel. She was great for making plans and chastising others who held her up. When it came to being somewhere agreed upon, time answered to her. Sylvania felt the growling in her stomach, announcing that the toaster pastries were fully digested. She gazed at the monolith of lemonade in the center of the floor, opened her bag, and retrieved her purse. Hidden behind her transpass were three one dollar bills, a five, and a coupon for a 1.00 off at some Italian food place in Cheltenham. She found an opening in the line and scooted her way to the counter. Several people behind her cursed but she wasn't fazed. She was hungry. *C'mon y'all, it's only Corn Dog on a Stick, it ain't Bookbinders.*

"Can I hep you please?" The young man behind the counter grinned, revealing a mouth full of gold teeth. Sylvania cringed.

"Nothing...never mind." Sylvania stepped away just in time to hear the familiar *Yo Syl!* Twist was bulldozing her way to Sylvania, waving and smiling. Twist grabbed Sylvania's arm and led her towards the Chinese Food counter. Twist ordered the bar-b-cued spare ribs platter and a drink. Sylvania selected the rice and broccoli special. They circled the food court once before finding a table.

"So how'd it go?" Twist sipped her Coke in long, quick draws--her meal came with free refills.

"Check this out. I know I can handle the work but this one nasty-ass dude was stripping me with his eyes the whole time." Sylvania tried to use the chopsticks but her stomach told her to stop playing and reverted back to a fork. "The other guy was about business, straight up. Good questions, looked me in the eye, and when I was leaving, he wasn't all checkin' me. Like I said, all business."

"Was he fine?" Twist started on the ribs.

"Well...h'al yeah he was fine!" They toasted with their drinks, cracking up loud and hard. Twist handed Sylvania a napkin for her face.

"You think you'll get the job?"

"I hope so. It's up to them now. I can't stand working at the donut shop. I have got to get out of that hell hole." Twist snickered while fanning her face.

"What's so funny?" Sylvania was puzzled.

"You said *hell hole* and you work at a donut shop." Sylvania chewed her food blankly. "Hell hole...donut...a donut has a hole...forget it Syl." Sylvania finally chuckled. "Seriously, I know you impressed them. You can type damn near a thousand words a minute...you can type, can't you?"

Sylvania attempted to explain the job was much more than typing but Twist was up and heading towards the Chinese Food counter for her refill. She wasn't surprised to see Twist bogard her way to the front of the line and thrust her cup at the counter. Twist had a way of always getting what she wanted. She had an attitude that didn't restrict her. She had a way of saying whatever was on her mind. Whenever it was ready for it to come out, it came out. She went where she pleased, dressed however she wanted, dated whomever caught her eye. In many ways, Sylvania wished she could be more like her. If she was, she would have told the man in the brown at PowerCat not to mess without waiting until she got the position. Even if she had Twist's attitude, she knew she wouldn't. She needed the job that bad.

"You need to stop daydreaming and start checkin' out some of these goodies up in here..." Twist appeared back at their table. "That reminds me. Tonight is ladies' night at the Idyll. We gots to be up in there."

"I thought you'd be seeing Caddy tonight."

"You the only one worried about Caddy. Like I always say, and you know I do, it's the smart woman who keeps an extra man in her purse." Sylvania had heard that philosophy of Twist's so many times she was able to mouth it along with her. They were filled with a merriment that those around them couldn't understand. Sylvania enjoyed her time with Twist. They had become more sister-like over the years. When times were good, they celebrated together. When one fell upon hard times or had the proverbial broken heart, the other was there to console or 'cuss' the dog of a man out.

"Alright," Sylvania began collecting her tray, "What time do you want me to be ready?"

"Ladies are free until 10:30. I'll come by and get you around 9:30. That should get us in just as things are jumpin'." Twist stood up, leaving her trash on the table.

"It's a plan." Sylvania stood with her tray in her hand and felt her shoulder collide with someone's elbow. She tried to maneuver her body but it was too late. She heard the crashing of a tray and saw the leaves of a salad tumble around her feet. Embarrassed, Sylvania was now facing a well-groomed, smartly dressed man. He didn't seem bothered by the event even as he watched his can of soda roll away, disappearing under a table.

"I'm sorry," Sylvania began apologizing. "Let me replace your lunch." It was after she said that she remembered she only had three dollars left in her purse.

"Don't worry about it." The man smiled as he wiped bits of croutons, cucumbers, and salad dressing from off his pants leg.

"You sure it's all right?" Sylvania awkwardly helped the man clean himself up.

"He said it's all right!" Twist looked at her watch. "Later girl, I got to get back to work. City Hall ain't workin' unless I'm workin'." Twist gave Sylvania a hug and was soon off.

"Everything's fine," the man paused, "May I sit here? I still have my soup."

"Sure, it's all yours." Sylvania reached over and picked up Twist's tray. The man sat as he placed his soup on the table.

"Who needs a salad?" He smiled gently at Sylvania. "It's for rabbits anyway."

"I'm really, really sorry." Sylvania apologized again and tried to catch up with Twist who was already out of the food court. As she walked, she reflected on how cool he was about the whole situation. *Most brothers in Philly would have gone off, especially being dressed so nicely. He got it going on, that's for sure.*

OFF THE MENU

ELLIS REACHED THE ESCALATOR leading down to the food court. It had been years since he last ate at the Gallery. Most of his business lunch breaks were spent either at Smith and Wollensky, Bookbinders, or Le Bec Fin with clients. He favored the anonymity of Rothstein's Deli. Except by his order number, no one there knew him. The lunch meetings at the other restaurants were phony. It wasn't his time. He was only a proxy. He was shaking hands for Mr. Morgan. He smiled, mustering half-hearted displays of hilarity at tired jokes for Mr. Morgan. At the end of every meal he would say, "Let me take care of the check." To him, it was as if his mouth moved and Mr. Morgan's voice came out. Today would be different. He welcomed this change. He knew, deep in his heart, he could never escape what bothered him but as he entered the eating area he felt there could be a chance for something--something new.

He surveyed the court. It was packed. People of all backgrounds milled back and forth; eating, talking, howling at jokes, and pushing. Standing at the threshold of the congested eatery he observed the people who moved in a crowd, in pairs, and then there was him. At each of the counters stood people of diverse occupations: bankers, street workers, students, secretaries, jewelers, business representatives, even a few homeless people who had gotten past the mall security. Ellis took a deep breath and joined them all. He took his time deciding what he would have for lunch. It had been a long time since he made a decision for himself, by himself. All of his decisions in the last three years had to be approved by either Mr. Morgan or Clarissa. Whether it was the hiring of a new staff member or getting a haircut, the final word always belonged someone else. Out of habit, he headed towards the deli counter. No. Today he would change his menu. Each counter offered a dish he knew he would enjoy. For the moment, he felt really good. As he continued looking, a young man walked by with a fresh chef's salad piled high on a plate. Ellis made up his mind and made his way to The Garden Spot counter.

He ordered the Caesar salad-French Onion Soup combination and a Frank's Black Cherry Wishniak soda. He didn't know what a Wishniak was but whatever it was, it was good. It didn't seem as if there was a single seat in the food court. Ellis was a little thrown off because by now the lunch crowd should have thinned out. He stood like an explorer between a table with two young ladies and one with three young men. He balanced the salad and can of soda on his tray while holding the hot soup in his other hand. He about-faced slowly. Without warning, he felt a sudden push on his elbow, causing his tray to tip. Ellis tried to catch the tray which only made matters worse, spilling the salad back onto his pants. The can of soda managed to zigzag around other patrons' feet and roll underneath a neighboring table. The young boys at the table in front of him looked up. They loved this, something to point at and ridicule. For the next several minutes the incident was the focus of their conversation.

"I'm sorry," the young lady began apologizing. "Let me replace your lunch."

Ellis looked the young lady into the eyes and could tell her apology was genuine. It's better that it happened here by himself than with Clarissa. If Clarissa was with him she would have made a scene. Not this time. A spilled salad would not be the source of the ruination of his day. Ellis couldn't believe the young lady going into her pocket book. Not the norm for the women he knew.

"Don't worry about it." Ellis smiled as he wiped bits of croutons and salad dressing from off his pants leg. He tried to wave the young lady from trying to help him clean himself off but it was of no use. She appeared truly sorry and embarrassed for the entire situation. The other young lady had already begun to leave and coaxed her friend to do the same.

"You sure it's all right? I could get you another drink." The young lady cleared off the rest of the table and told Ellis it was 'ok' to sit down. When he looked up to thank her, she was gone.

Despite the reason for their sudden and short interaction, he found her to be refreshing in his world of demanding and demonstrative people. Ellis decided to forego his soup and purchase a small meal from a hot dog cart on his way back to the office.

HOLE

IT WASN'T UNTIL AFTER two when Sylvania entered her apartment. She heard the phone ring and dashed into the kitchen. She fumbled with the receiver but it was too late. She knew that it was probably Twist making sure she was still on for clubbing. She lumbered from the kitchen to the bedroom and flopped face first onto the bed. She hated this time of day. As the commercial said, *Time to make the doughnuts!* She dreaded having to go to work even though she had put in for a half day. When she thought about her training and skills it made her sick to think of serving doughnuts, coffee, and juice. To make matters worse, she was generally stuck on the evening shift, when all the creepy creeps of the city come out--and they all have a sweet tooth. Sylvania stopped counting the number of times the store was about to be robbed, how many times she witnessed people relieving themselves on the side of the building, and the frequent drug deals taking place while in line for a cruller. She rolled over onto her back and stared at the Gerald Levert CD cover on her dresser. *Maybe he'll come in and take me with a dozen.* She forced a smiled. The job helped to pay the rent and some of her bills but was still short when it came to the end of the month. She closed her eyes to lock the feelings away. Whenever she felt defeated, she didn't cry, she would hold it in and faint a smile. Her mother had taught her that when she was ten.

"What are those tears for?" Sylvania's mother stood in the doorway with the dishrag in one hand and the broom in the other.

"Tammy won't let me go to the Ice Capades with her." Sylvania's words were broken by incessant sniffling and swallowing.

"So what you crying for?"

Sylvania was confused. She knew why she was crying. She never had to do this with her father.

"I'm asking you again, what the tears for?"

"Cause I can't go, that's why?"

"Let me ask you, are the tears getting you to the Ice Capades?"

"Nope!" Sylvania poked out her bottom lip.

"Crying doesn't get a soul anywhere. Now, you can stand there and waste your time crying or you can do something else." Sylvania stood there, her arms crossed. Her mother continued. "If not, other folk will find something for you to do." She thrust the broom into Sylvania's hand. "Go sweep the basement, that'll take your mind off the Ice Capades." Sylvania dried her eyes with her sleeve and descended the steps to the basement.

Slowly Sylvania stood up removed her interview outfit and searched the closet for her uniform. She found her smock next to the black suede mini she decided she would wear to the Idyll. She hated she had to wear the stretch, double-knit slacks--always too tight and attracted too much attention. She fished through her dresser drawer and found the regulation hair net. She had an hour before she had to report so she closed her eyes and said a silent prayer for her interview.

"You must've had the *all-you-can-eat* special down at the deli, Ellis. It's almost 2:30." Devon called to Ellis who was had just reached the third floor landing. "Something wrong with the elevator?"

"Nothing's wrong. Can't a man walk up the steps after lunch?" Ellis walked past Devon. Druer Admin was on the eleventh floor, two floors above Devon's office. The only reason Devon would decide to utter a word to Ellis was if Hank told him so. It was well known that Devon was the heir apparent to Hank's social empire, even if it was only existed in his mind. Street translation: he was a flunky.

"I was talking to Hank. He's killing them on the links. I should have gone with him."

"Yes, you should have," Ellis thought. He continued on the stairs.

"Hank says that you are handling some big project. Looks promising for him...oh...and for you too. So I guess you better get back to work, huh?" Ellis reached the next landing. He could still hear Devon's voice calling to him. "If a fossil like you can walk up 14 flights of steps, you should work out with Hank and me sometimes. You might be able to hang!"

I should be hung if I ever did that. Ellis picked up his pace. Entering his office, he said hello to Winsome as he set his mind to the litany of tasks that awaited him. He had three hours to go before his evening meeting with Mr. Morgan and a couple members of the board. It was a standard meeting--mostly listening and eventually offering the perfunctory recommendations. He would be finished by 8:30 or 9:00. No chance of Clarissa being asleep when he got home.

The sound of weights clanging against the floor echoed throughout the room. Devon sat at the bench press and toyed with the seventy-five pound weight. His chest, bare and cut, glistened in the low light. He moved the bar above his head slowly, tensing the muscles in his arms until the veins were visible. He lowered the weight just as slowly, feeling the tension in his pectoral muscles. It hurt and that felt good to him. *If you ain't hurtin', you ain't workin'!* It was one of the many catchphrases that Hank showered on his apprentice. After three more repetitions of ten, he stood and moved to the full-length mirror. He admired his physique. *Damn I look good!* It had taken him two years but he had the washboard stomach that made so many jealous at his clubhouse pool. He moved his pecs one at a time, to a beat that only he knew. He did a number of the classic body builder poses and admired himself with each one. He angled himself to look at his butt. He flexed. *True buns of steel!* He heard the door open.

"Man, get away from that mirror before you get sucked in." A large figure stepped into the room.

"About time you got here Hank, I'm cutting my work out time today short so I can get my head tightened up. I'm starting to woof and I have to be right for the weekend." Devon shook Hank's hand. Hank stood six-foot-four and weighted more two hundred and fifty pounds. Unlike Devon, who considered himself God's gift, Hank just considered himself God.

"I got hung up on the course talking to this fool about a deposition from a year ago. I tried to tell him to forget about it and to be cool but the clown continues running off at the mouth about his reputation. You think I'm worried about his rep...his wife maybe but the hell with his rep. Blew an hour of my day...but look, I'm here. Go put two hundred on the bar so I can get warmed up." Hank stripped down and changed into his workout clothes. "You'll see what it takes to be the total package."

If any man were to ever portray the character John Henry in the movies, it would be Hank. Based on appearances, if one had to decide corporate executive or a mason worker, the mason worker would win hands down. Listening to him was another story. When with Devon or his other friends, he is one of the boys; in the office, a walking management textbook. An academic standout at Temple University, Hank entered the world of business with a vengeance. His track record for bolstering small companies, turning them into market competitors, had businesses from across the country recruiting him as if he was Patrick Ewing coming out of Georgetown. Not only did this swell his bank accounts, his ego expanded as well. He looked and played the part of the modern *Buppie*: elegant townhouse, leased BMW, and, of course, ladies on the string. He shared another catchphrase with Devon, *You don't order a plated meal when there is a free buffet?*

"So how's the gig going?" Hank rested between repetitions

"I'm not moving up like I planned. I made myself know to the bossman today but I don't think I made that much of an impression." Devon sat down on the rowing machine but didn't row.

"If you want to move up, you've got to make a move. I didn't become senior project manager at Druer by letting things slip by me. You have to see the problems in the office and take them straight to the top. You have to make them think you feel more for the business than your supervisor. Their bottom line is the dollar and those in power don't care who they have under them as long as they produce." Hank finished and sat up. "You know that Ellis in my office? Well I got that sucker working on projects that are going to get me that VP slot in LA. That's what you've got to do in your shop."

"I hear what you're saying. One of my supervisors messed up good today. I let the boss know I was there to fix the problem but I don't think it impressed him."

"Don't tell him you were there to fix the problem, tell him that you fixed it!" Hank let the bar slam down on the carrier for effect. "Just keep letting your man slip and you'll slide right in." Devon smiled. He knew exactly what he had to do. He began rowing faster--faster. As if he had a new destination in mind.

The smell made her sick. Six months ago, Sylvania enjoyed a donut or two as part of her breakfast-workout routine. She had favored the vanilla cream. Now, they made her sick when serving them to customers. She gets sick watching the customers eating the doughnuts. It sickened her to tie on her doughnut apron. Now, at three-thirty in the afternoon, she was sick of coming to this place. She had rent to pay but she was thoroughly sick of it all.

"Sylvania, take care of the counter, I'll be in the back." Mikal, her manager was sniffing the air as he pushed past a stack of boxes. He always acted as if he smelled gas whenever he wanted to sneak a drink. "Do you smell gas?" Sylvania groaned just in time to catch three young men entering the store.

High school idiots! Sylvania's face dropped into a scowl. She hoped Mikal would hurry up just in case these boys started *playing the nut role.* Two of the boys approached the counter. The third leaned on the cigarette machine by the door. The boy with the Cazel glasses spoke.

"What you got good up in here slim?"

"It's all right there." Sylvania pointed to the racks of doughnuts on the wall but saw that his eyes were set on her chest.

"Is your phone number up in there? I can't quite see it." He took off his glasses and huffed humorously. He stretched out his hand, palm up, on which the second boy slapped as if on cue. At that moment, the third boy moved to the counter, pushing the first one on the shoulder.

"Look man, she ain't interested. Let's pull up." The first boy whirled around.

"Stop buggin' me man! If you wanna roll...then roll! I'm workin' right now!" The first boy reset his attention back to Sylvania.

"Now, what's it gonna take to get them digits?" Inside, Sylvania was burning up. She had been on duty less than two hours and this marked the beginning. After these *ignorants* leave the mothers of the little league teams will arrive with their incomprehensible orders. Following them will come several of the local police at shift change. *They don't act any better than the high school boys.* The evening rounds out with the neighborhood derelicts staying until the next morning, slovenly singing dismal tales of the lives they never had. Eight o'clock could not come fast enough.

"Hey! I'm talkin' to you!" Sylvania's mind bounced back to the boys at the counter. The second boy chirped up.

"Look man, she ain't payin' you no mind. Here comes the trolley. I'm gone!" The third boy walked quickly to the door. The boy with the glasses sucked his teeth.

"All right then…give me two of the glazed, two jelly, and three creams and hurry. Don't make me miss my ride!" He began digging into his pocket. Sylvania quickly bagged up the doughnuts.

"Three dollars and forty-five cents please." Sylvania spoke firmly.

"Three forty-five? It's high up in here!" The boy with the glasses looked at the second boy.

"Just pay her man. There's the trolley now." The third boy now had the door open and was on the way out. Suddenly, the first boy snatched the bag from Sylvania's hand and bolted out the door. The second boy was close behind, laughing hysterically as they ran through the door. She watched the three of them dash down the street and out of sight. It was the third time somebody made it out of the store without paying since she worked there. The smell of cheap alcohol tugged at her nose. Sylvania looked toward the rear of the store. Mikal was in the doorway.

"How much did they get away with?" Sylvania could tell he was on his way to being intoxicated.

"Three dollars and forty five cents."

"You know that has to come out of your pay?"

"I know."

"Can't you tell when someone's about to rip you off yet?"

"I'm not even thinking about that. I'm just trying to sell doughnuts."

"Well, maybe this three dollar and forty-five cents lesson will help you spot thieves in the future. Now that all of the action is over, why don't you wipe down the counter? I've got some unfinished business in the back to take care of." Mikal mumbled more something and disappeared into the rear of the store. Sylvania thought how ironic it was that Mikal would use the word *future* when speaking about the store. She knelt down underneath the counter and grabbed the bucket with the wash rags in it. Reaching in, she felt something tickle her fingers. Jerking back, she watched two roaches fall from off her hand. *"Damn!"*, Sylvania thought to herself. *Damn! Damn! Got-damn this place makes me sick!*

It was a shift of long hours for Sylvania. The spills, the complaints, the leers, the insults, and aggravations by Mikal, all came to a crashing halt when the clock read 8:10. It was 8:20 when she stepped onto the trolley and 8:47 when she reached her stop. She was inside her apartment at 8:59 and picked up the ringing phone by 9:10.

"I'm on my way over! Be dressed! Remember, ladies night only lasts until 10:30!" Sylvania was tickled. She knew Twist would be determined to get to the club before she had to pay. She was cheap like that.

She hung up the phone and undressed on her way to the bathroom. It was 9:38 when she finally stepped out of the shower and 9:40 when Twist knocked on the door. Sylvania opened the door and stepped back. Twist threw her leg forward and began her entrance. She modeled her ensemble.

"Dang girl, don't you know what time it is?" Twist pulled some gum from out of her pocket.

"I'll be ready in five minutes." Sylvania hurried back into her bedroom and dressed. She could hear Twist from the other room.

"I better not have to pay a cover because of you making us late."

"It's only ten dollars."

"I'm not trying to give up any dollars. Not for cover, drinks, or nothing. You know why?"
Sylvania looked up and saw Twist in the doorway. Twist had a serious look on her face. She slowly extended her hand, bringing together her thumb and middle finger. In a motion full of fluidity and purpose, her arm rotated, with her index finger pointed towards the ceiling. As she spoke, her arm traveled clockwise.

"Because I am one broke-ass, free-loadin', coupon-clippin', moochin', stayin' one jump ahead of the landlord, lady of the new millennium...fully equipped with thick thighs and bedroom eyes!" There was a long pause as Sylvania waited for Twist's hand to finish its revolution, concluding with a loud snap of her fingers. They both broke into deep soul-sister rejoicing.

It was past 9:45 when Ellis noticed the sea of flashing red lights in front of him. He had just left the expressway and began heading north on Route One. He could see the brake lights of the cars ahead of him thickening and concluded he better detour if he didn't want to be stuck for who knows how long. He exited at Wissahickon Avenue with the hopes of picking up the One later on. He had not been in this part of town since his teenage years and it had changed--dramatically. More abandoned buildings and less light. Many of the points of reference he used as a teen were no longer there. A glance in the rearview mirror, it came to him suddenly with an ironic veil of humor that he was lost. He realized he was smiling broadly. He could smell the TastyKake factory which allowed his nose to be his guide. He gained some bearings but he was still lost. After about fifteen minutes he ended up on Broad and Erie. His memory regained its confidence and began to repaint the layout of the area in his mind. He knew which way to take. He was never really worried. In fact, he wished he was still lost. It was an excellent excuse for getting home late. Clarissa would have been watching television or sleeping. He could have gone straight to bed and avoided any conversation. Now he would be home in twenty minutes or so. He turned on WDAS and began humming along with the radio. He felt a chill when the song *Wildflower* came on. It had been a long time since he last heard it but he remembered all the words, especially the spoken part. He sang along as he wondered who his flower really was.

You see, you're like a flower that blooms in any season, that's why I'd like to say you're my flower baby."

After the song ended the DJ announced the party happenings at the Idyll. Ellis suddenly realized he was right there, right around the corner from the Idyll. An unexplained force moved him into the left turn lane. Sitting at the light, he thought about what he was getting ready to do. His face fell as his hand grasped the turn signal. Ellis prepared to move out of the lane and back into the mainstream of traffic. Unfortunately, the brightness of the left turn signal and the blaring horn behind forced him onto the side street. *I'll just drive by, get a peek at the place then head on home.* Ellis felt better about that decision and proceeded down the crowded street. He slowly noticed how beautiful and free the people looked as they left their cars and walked swiftly towards the club entrance. The men were dressed in suits, both casual and conservative. The women in skirts, pant suits, and some outfits Ellis couldn't describe. Suddenly, without warning, a car screeched from out of a parking place several car lengths in front of him. A feeling of confusion came over him. He could park for a minute, go inside, listen to a little music, and be home in no time. Clarissa wouldn't know the difference. He gripped the wheel and slowed down. He took several deep breaths and put on his signal. He started into the space but his mind was quickly flooded with Clarissa's voice. The clock on the dash read 10:25. He knew what he was in for if he got home any later. He disengaged the signal and moved away from the space. He drove to the corner and made a left. He knew how to get back to Route One. He drove home. Not once did he look back. It wasn't in his nature.

PASSING TIME

ELLIS PRESSED THE BUTTON on the side of his watch...10:57. He slowly pulled himself from out of the car and headed for the door. He depressed the button and stood there as the garage door slowly descended to the floor. He repeated the time to himself the time as he put the key into the door. He turned the key only to find the door was already unlocked. He opened the door slowly and walked through the kitchen into the living room. On the sofa by the door, Clarissa was fully reclined, watching television. Ellis knew what this meant and took a deep breath. Reaching the sofa, he leaned over.

"How was your day?" He only kissed her cheek.

"Do you know what time it is?" Clarissa sat up quickly, arms folded, her eyes glaring as if awakened from one of her dream dates with Denzel.

"It's something after ten."

"It's almost eleven! Where have you been?"

He twisted the truth. "Traffic on the expressway was tied up. Haven't you been watching the news?" This statement was his trump card. Clarissa never watched the news. She could watch Hard Copy, Maury, Inside Edition, Geraldo, and Judge Judy. She never seemed to be able to watch anything of substance. If it was gossip, she was well informed. If it was serious, she was clueless. While Clarissa chewed him out for being late, he went into his 'zone'. He could look at her and seem to be part of the conversation, but in reality, his mind would drift to other places.

-1987-

Pine Street, West Philadelphia, has always been Ellis's home. All of his brothers were born in the small two-level house. At that time, the Parkers were one of the few Black families in the area. With connections at the shipyard, Carl was able to buy his way into a partnership with a white co-worker and opened a corner store at the end of his block. It was the fortunate misfortune of Carl's friend being caught red-handed with a red-head which led to a pending divorce. As he quickly dissolved his assets, he sold his share of the store to Carl for fifteen dollars. It was that turn of events that helped to establish the Parkers as an important family in the neighborhood. His little store stocked everything: candy, health and beauty aids, magazines, and tools. Whatever one was looking for, Parkers Corner had it or would get it for you.

With wife Lynn, Carl knew in his heart that he would establish a chain of corner stores throughout the Philadelphia area, maybe even into Delaware. Many evenings were spent dreaming as their first two boys were born. Those dreams were poisoned with the construction of a new A & P supermarket less than a mile away. At first, Carl's customers tried to remain loyal but as time passed, it was easier and cheaper to buy everything from the A & P. Although he didn't go out of business, Carl's establishment was reduced to a corner store on life support, limited to selling loose candy, soda, and water ice. As the neighborhood changed, his customer base transitioned into a lower economic class who turned a landmark into a hangout. Unable to get any support from the city's urban assistance program, Carl watched his dreams shrivel, fade away into a distant memory. Slowly, his jovial personality began to match his storefront; hardened, defaced by life, with his soul now in disrepair.

The man who once greeted the boys with treats from the store now was bitter, miserly, and a destroyer of dreams. The store, once a symbol of independence became the impending prison for Ellis. His two older brothers, Kenneth and James, were plopped into the business after they dropped out of high school.

Max, Ellis's closest in age brother, also dropped out of school and joined the store, just in time to take the place of James who had become a certified member of the streets. Ellis knew for a long time that he didn't want any part of it. When he wasn't at basketball practice or working on the family car, he was stocking-- actually, dusting the store merchandise. He recalled the day he shared with his father his plans to possibly join the Navy.

Carl stumbled into the kitchen, inebriated and breathing heavily. Ellis and his mother were seated at the table reading papers and brochures. Carl started to pass through but stopped. He dumped himself into one of the kitchen chairs.

"What's all this mess?"

"Just some information about the Navy. I thought I should check it out." Ellis held the brochure up to show his father but it was quickly slapped from out of his hand.

"What's damn Navy gonna do for you?"

There was something scary in his father's voice. His mother rose and moved to the stove.

"I...I don't know but I wanted to go and just talk to them." Ellis stammered. Mr. Parker stood, opened the refrigerator door, took out a beer, messily chugged it down. Once finished, he wobbled back to his seat. Carl was furious. He was not going to let anyone else in the family abandon his dream. Lynn tried to referee but neither gave way.

"What the hell you wanna go and do that for?" Carl crushed the can in his hand.

"I have to figure out what I want to do and I think the service will do that for me," Ellis said with a well manufactured confidence.

"Do for you? What's wrong? I can't do that for you? I thought I did. I gave you boys something the world will never give you--opportunity."

"Dad, that store isn't my opportunity." Fearing the direction of their conversation, Lynn braced herself. "That store is like a cage!" In an instant, Ellis felt the sting of the crushed can across his cheek. Carl tried to rise but stumbled back into his chair.

"Forget it! Forget him! Forget all y'all!" A second attempt and Mr. Parker was up and stumbling toward the front door. "Goin' to the store! You…you bedda get your head straight before I get back!" He turned with a look that was a combination of anger and shame. Ellis was transfixed by his father's bloodshot eyes. He wanted to stop him from leaving but an eerie feeling tightened all of his joints, restraining him from acting. In a moment, his father was gone. Ellis looked to his mother who was gripping the stove. There was blood on his cheek but Ellis refused to wipe it. He bolted out the back door.

Ellis walked the streets for most of the day and into the evening. He had never really signed up for the Navy, only picked up a brochure at the A & P. The voice that told him to take a stand against his father was now rising. This scared Ellis. He was normally the one who followed his parent's requests without question. Ellis was the dutiful one. His brothers were different. Kenneth, James, and Max could always get away with disobeying father. The oldest, Kenneth, was just a stubborn bull, with the hide to match. Beatings, punishments, and other forms of restrictions didn't bother him. He only cared about strength, so being sent to his room meant he could do push-ups in private. He was also a young man churning with anger. Something was forever seething in his soul. By the time he was sixteen, he was bigger than his father. He would leave the house for days before retreating to his room upon his return, bloodied and cursing, without question from anyone. His father would never admit to being afraid of Kenneth but the family could tell. Ellis tried to talk to him but the smell of alcohol meant he was to be left alone. Soon he never left the room, except to get a fix. He became a shell.

Max was the handsome one. 'Little Mack' Max was what the other fellas in the neighborhood called him. In the beginning, he was the attraction for the store. Max brought in the girls, who in turn brought in the guys. Max helped make the store the place to be, for a little while. It wasn't long before he finally understood what all the fuss was and soon he became full of himself. The store became a waste to him. There were lots of girls and being behind the counter was sucking up precious time. It didn't take long before Max stopped coming to the store, stopped going to school, and stopped coming home when expected. He acquired new friends--friends who peddled the pleasure of the streets. Max had found his new hang out and any street corner would do. When it came to money, Maxi became the breadwinner in the family, dropping cash on his mother's table once a week for groceries and bills their father could no longer provide. Mr. Parker was rendered mute by his son. Never asking where the money came from was the only way to accept it.

James was Carl's favorite. A star athlete in middle school, James brought neighborhood pride to the Parker home. A basketball player is one of the most beloved on the block. Mr. Parker looked to him to elevate their lifestyle when James would be drafted eventually by the Sixers, Lakers, or Celtics. He had lots of plans for his son. Regrettably, James had his own. A good player is one thing; an undisciplined player is another. He was removed from the varsity team in his sophomore year of high school, failing to come to practice and make the grade. For James, this was fine as it provided him the time necessary to gamble his talents at playgrounds across the city. Quick cash and tragedy was his story, another dark chapter in the life of Mr. Parker.

By the age of twelve, Ellis was the sweeper in the store, by thirteen, he stocked the shelves, and by fifteen, Ellis took over the register. His mathematical abilities made him a natural for calculating tax when the register wasn't working, giving accurate change, and analyzing the receipts of the day. As time progressed, along with his father's drinking, Ellis was running all of the aspects of the store, bookkeeping, ordering, and finances. He did all this while maintaining good grades and participating in Junior Achievement periodically after school.

He used his sleeve to wipe his face. The blood was drying but the wound still burned. It burned because he knew he had to go back home and tell his father the Navy thing was out but that didn't mean he wouldn't try to be free. This was his day. Today! There were so many times he heard his father shouting through the liquor about being a man. So, here it was, his day to claim it, to defend it, to be it. With resolve and a new strength, Ellis began to make his way home.

The wail of the siren was nothing new to him. Ellis would hear sirens in his neighborhood both day and night but this time it was different. With every step, the sound stayed in front of him, getting louder. As he passed the boarded up front of the old Parker's Corner store his feet turned into lead weights. The red flashing light of the ambulance began licking his face, mesmerizing him. He could make out Kenneth in the doorway of his house holding back his mother. Two people were missing, his father and Max. Ellis tried to run but couldn't. Had the street life finally caught up with his brother? An argument over a girl? Had it out with the police? Some stupid machismo flexing? It could be anything because Max was into everything.

"What happened?" Ellis turned to see a gold Camaro IROC-A pulling close to him. In the back seat, Max sat with two young ladies. His face had the same desperation that Ellis felt inside. Anxieties accelerated. *Where was his father?*

"I don't know. I'm just getting home." Ellis didn't know if Max heard him. The car streaked off before screeching in front of the house. He could see Max bound up the steps to his mother, causing him to misstep. Kenneth caught him easily. One minute he felt as if he was a hundred miles away, the next second he was standing in the way of the paramedics.

"You'll have to get back." The larger paramedic began blocking Ellis until he was pushed out of the way by Kenneth.

"That my brother." In the next instance, he watched as two more paramedics walk in slow motion from the house, down the stairs, to the open doors of the ambulance. They were carrying a gurney but Ellis's mind refused to make out who was lying there. The face was a blur of blood stained bandages and confusion. Finally, words escaped his mouth.

"What happened?" His vision cleared as he heard his mother's voice.

"After you left…you know your father and his moods…he said he drove his last son away…he left for a while…Later I saw him drinking outside…then he came in…he went to his room and grabbed his gun and…" Uncontrollable sobbing took her over.

"We're taking him to Penn, one person can ride with us." The paramedics held the door open as Kenneth lifted his mother into the back of the ambulance. The doors shut and the vehicle sped off.

That evening, the brothers sat quietly after they returned from the hospital. In his thoughts Ellis spoke to his father. *"It's my fault.*

It will never happen again." That night both their father and the Parker's Corner dream passed away.

In the spring of 1989, Ellis was finally back in stride, extending his senior year at West Philadelphia High. His mother had gotten a part time position as a teacher's aide with the Philadelphia School District. Ellis was pleased. It was good for her to be around all of that life in the classroom. Kenneth became the latest casualty of America's War on Drugs and was put under the care of his Aunt Daliah. Max found his place in the world of pimping and rock cocaine. For Ellis, he now had more time to devote to Junior Achievement and basketball. He had made the varsity team as a walk-on. Usually after practice, Ellis would shoot a couple rounds before going to his part-time job at a local auto shop.

"So what happens after graduation?" Ellis didn't notice the counselor, Mr. Williams, standing on the side of court.

"I don't know," (swish), "I guess I'll start working full time."

"What about college?"

"What about it?"

"Have you considered it? Your grades reflect you could handle it."

Ellis stopped shooting for a moment and pondered the question. He resumed his free throws.

"I never really gave it too much thought. Besides, college costs too much and--"

"And what?" Ellis didn't have an answer. He knew there was some value to college.

"I thought so. Anyway, you have a little skill with the round ball. Stop by my office on Monday and I might be able to help you out." Mr. Williams had the reputation of putting a little extra effort into students he thought had potential. Now this was some news he could share with his mother.

It was the curiosity of college that carried Ellis to Mr. William's office on Monday, just curiosity. The conversation was short and to the point.

"A friend of mine heads up the admissions office at West Chester. You heard of it. Small college outside of Philly. It wouldn't be far from home. Good school to get you prepped for your MBA or Ph.D. or some other advanced degree." Ellis had the look of surprise. "Have to think about your future Ellis. Anyway, he asked me if I knew someone who had decent grades, decent basketball skills, and the potential to make it in college. I thought of you...interested?" Mr. Williams leaned back into his chair. Ellis could see a note pad on his desk with a list of names. Only one above his had been crossed out. There were at least six below. He thought for a moment. He had never heard of West Chester nor saw himself as someone who could ever attend college. Mr. Williams brought the pencil closer to the notepad.

"How would I pay for it?" Ellis shifted from one foot to the other.

"You could receive a partial scholarship for the first year. If your grades are good there's some help available for you. Now, if your grades are very good, you might be able to go to school for free."

"What would I have to study?"

"The choice is yours." Mr. Williams put the pencil down and grabbed a sheet of paper from the corner of the desk and handed it to Ellis. "Here's a list of the majors they offer."

"Man I don't know what to pick." Ellis handed the sheet back to the Williams who in turn looked out the window. He rubbed his face, pondering his next question.

"What are your brothers doing nowadays?" Ellis shook his head. He knew that Mr. Williams had known all of his brothers, knew their potential, but more importantly, knew the answer to his own question. Ellis began to get the picture--and it scared him.

"So what I gotta do to go?"

Mr. Williams smiled and grabbed another stack of papers and handed them to Ellis.

"Take these, fill them out, and return them to me. Don't worry about the application fee, that'll be taken care of. When you bring the application back, we'll talk about the SAT's."

All the way home, Ellis read and re-read the application and the description sheet of West Chester. With each step, he began imagining himself on campus, in the classroom answering all of the questions, making the winning game shot, being the big man on campus. He slowed his pace when he reached the steps of his house. He felt an uneasy and eerie chill wrap his body. He knew where he was but sensed some place different. He saw a figure in the doorway and knew immediately who it was.

"Dad..." he heard the shakiness in his brain. "I need to do this." His father's image stepped from the shadows and sat down on the steps. Ellis heard his voice with a clarity he never knew was possible.

"College? How are you going to have time for college when you have your mother and brothers to support?" Ellis knew that his part-time job was about to go full but even still that wouldn't be enough to support the family. Max would drop a couple of dollars off to his mother every now and then. As much as his mother hated to take the money, the mounting bills caused her to continue to turn a blind eye.

"You promised me that you would not disobey me again. I need you here." Ellis looked at his father's face.

"This is my chance Dad. I have to take it."

"You let me down son." With that, the doorway was clear and Ellis felt familiar again.

The topic came up at dinner and Ellis shared the gist of Mr. William's conversation with his mother. Although she was visibly excited about the prospect of one of her sons going to college, she remained reserved with the thoughts of paying for her son's education. Kenneth stood at the stove, listening. His face was expressionless as he waited for their conversation to finish and his mother could start serving dinner. Ellis explained while there might be scholarship for both his grades and basketball, he pieced together a plan where he would wait a year or two, work a while before going to college, when things got easier around the house. There was a tap on the back window. Kenneth looked, opened the back door, and left. As the talk between mother and son continued, Ellis caught a glimpse of his brother Max, or at least his stylish clothes. Their eyes locked and soon he noticed Max waving him out.

Ellis stood near the trash can shivering in the cold evening air. Max dug his hands deep into the pockets of his leather trench. Kenneth, tank-topped, didn't feel the cold.

"Yo El man, I ran into that Mr. Williams today and he tells me that you got doubts about goin' to college and shit." He started to light a joint, remembered where he was, and put it into the band on his hat. "You know we can't be havin' that."

"College costs too much...besides, I promised Dad that I would stay and help out."

Max stepped closer to his younger brother and put his hand on his shoulder. "You don't need to help out baby bro...you need to get out." His fingers now began to dig into Ellis's skin. "Pops always had you under his thumb, livin' out his dreams. Damn man, wake up and look around. You see anything around needed to be helped out?" Ellis jerked away and began to walk back to the house.

"Who are you to come off telling me what to do?! You bailed on Dad, Mom, all of us years ago. Yeah you drop Mom some change when you want but you're not here for the daily." Ellis turned and grabbed hold of the doorknob. Before he could turn away, a massive collection of fingers wrapped around his wrist. Looking back, he saw Kenneth's massive forearm, which lead to biceps, shoulders, and eventually to his face. Kenneth was not known for talking but he uttered a quiet, "Listen to Maxi."
Max removed his shades and looked Ellis squarely in the eyes. "I'm not sayin' that what I did with my life is right. Look at us man, I'm in the streets and I know I ain't never comin' out. Jimmy's dead…and Kenny here…well, you and I know he ain't all here." Max gave Kenneth a quick glance before bringing his attention back to Ellis. "See, he don't even know what I'm talkin' 'bout." There was sincerity in Max's words. "All I'm saying is that if you want to honor Dad and his dream for us…and I mean his real dream…you need to go…go to college…go do something. It's going to be a while before you believe it but you better get started before you get stuck here." The honk of a horn signaled for Max to put his shades back on and proceed out the back gate. Kenneth walked past Ellis and opened the door, holding it for Ellis.

"I wish I could do college."

BULL & HORNS

"RIGHT THERE! Get it! Right there!"
Sylvania pointed frantically at the parking space. Twist waited only a moment, allowing the ambivalent driver in front of them to clear the space before she swerved into the spot, just avoiding the parked car in front of her.

"Whereat you learn to drive? Sears?" Sylvania slowly released her grip from the armrest and quickly opened the door. Before she could set a foot onto the ground, Twist pulled her back into the car.

"Where you goin'?"

"I'd like to get inside before ladies night ends." Sylvania readjusted her jacket. Twist yanked the rear view mirror to get a look at her hair. She began teasing at it with a small comb.

"You just going to go in there without checkin' yourself?"

"That's what ladies rooms are for." Sylvania pushed the car door open again.

"Girl, you ain't been out in so long you don't even know what's up." Twist fingered gloss onto her bottom lip. " You gotta look tight when you walk in the door. You neva know who's gonna be walkin' by. It just might be Mr. Right for tonight!" Twist gave herself the seal of approval and opened her car door. "Let me tell you something. I should be drawing a salary because looking this decent is a full time job. Just like you got yourself together for your interview today, you're going to be interviewed tonight! That's for real!" Twist tugged at the waist of her white skintight jeans and stepped into the street. Cars screeched to a halt and horns blared, she didn't care. She was working. Sylvania looked at herself in the reflection of the car window. What did she have to prove? She looked all right. Her clothes were fitting right. Although there was still a trace of *eau de doughnut* on her, she smelled all right. She guessed it would be an all right night. Cautiously she entered the street.

"That'll be ten dollahs each!" The bouncer didn't bother to look at either of them. In his hand he held a thick wad of fives, tens, and twenties. He began to unfold them to receive their payment.

"The ad said it was ladies night tonight." Twist looked the bouncer straight in the chest.

"It was...until 10:30...and now it's 10:45. Ten dollahs each please."
Twist stood her ground; Sylvania watched anxiously.

"Hold up, the ad on POP 92.3 said it was ladies night...until eleven. I got it on tape from last night's Smooth Grooves show." Sylvania was confused for only a moment until she knew what was going on and was soon caught up in the wake of Twist's typhoon.

"Ladies night, no cover until eleven...that's for true!"

The bouncer shifted his 265 pound frame to see how many others might challenge him.

"Well, I'm sorry but..."

"Sorry?" Twist was now on her tippy toes looking directly into the man's chin. "That's false advertisement then." Sylvania stepped up to the bouncer's chest, speaking directly into his tie clip.

"According to consumer code..." Sylvania quickly looked around as she spoke. The woman behind her nodded supportively. "... consumer code 40-d, any advertisement, whether broadcasted, televised, or printed, must be honored else the provider face strict financial penalties and the chance of license revocation. Do you have a phone where I can make a complaint?" Sylvania frantically looked around for a phone. Even above the music, they could hear the labored breathing of the bouncer. Twist sniffed the air.

"Syl, is that weed I smell? That's that killa weed.

"Look ladies, we just got our liquor license back so we don't need no trouble. In fact, I do remember something about eleven o'clock. Go on in and have a good time." Sylvania started in but Twist blocked her.

"Sylvania, he's forgetting something." Both Sylvania and the bouncer looked puzzled. "The ad said a free drink coupon to all ladies." Without hesitation, the bouncer reached into his pocket and retrieved two coupons, giving them to Twist. Slowly, Twist turned and paused before proceeding into the club.

Clubs opened and closed routinely in Philadelphia but the Idyll stood as a landmark for students of the 'old school'. Unlike many of the newer clubs complete with laser light shows, neon, game rooms, and fog machines, the Idyll maintained the atmosphere of an old basement party. It had a tarnished mirrored ball, a few spotlights, mismatched tables and chairs, a small dance floor, and a kitchen that served meals like somebody's country mama was burning up the stove in the back. The ambiance is what kept the people coming back. The Idyll was located on the edge of North Philadelphia, right on the corner of two major intersections. If you didn't have a car, one could easily get there by bus, subway train, or taxi. If you really had a jones for partying, you could walk with the hopes of getting picked up on the way. Everybody who was anybody in black Philadelphia jammed tough at the Idyll. Doctors, athletes, politicians, media personalities, city workers, the unemployed--it didn't matter. It was the commonality of wanting a good time that kept them coming back to the Idyll. It was the place to be!

Twist pushed her way through the crowd and found a seat in one of the booths. There was already another young woman seated, waiting patiently for one of her friends to return. Twist lit a smoke and nonchalantly stared at the dance floor. The young lady stopped a passing waitress and ordered a small drink. It was a showdown. This booth, prime seating for watching or cuddling, only had room for two. Sylvania stood outside the booth and watched the two ignore each other. Three songs later, the young lady gave up, grabbed her drink, and moved on, flicking Twist off--to which Twist responded with a scrunched-up face and a "Step off...ski-zank!"

"Come get in here girl!" Twist waved frantically. Sylvania beat it into the seat next to Twist, all the while sniggering. "I thought that heifer would never leave...with her vinyl wearin' self." They slapped palms and ordered drinks. The place was packed with women and doubly with men--good looking men. There were some ugly ones but the goodness just swallowed them up. Most of the men were dressed in suits or jackets. There were a few homeboys dressed in outfits they thought were presentable to attract but it didn't work for either Twist or Sylvania.

"Yo, can I get this dance?" Sylvania looked hard at the man and forced a yawn. She turned back to her drink. Twist sneered. "We don't like this song."

"I ain't asks you! I asks yo girl." The man smiled, showing two gold teeth in the upper right hand corner of his mouth and one in the lower left. Sylvania almost choked on her drink. After a day of dealing with the worst of the worst at the donut shop, she didn't want to invest the strength to tell him to move on. Collecting herself, She kept her eyes on the table, hoping that one of the top shelf brothers in the place would just walk over and push this one back into the dumpster from which he oozed from out of. Ironically, she did like the song that was playing. Inside her body was moving to the beat but outside she remained aloof and uninterested.

"C'mon pretty thang, let's do this!" The man's ashy hand extended to receive Sylvania's but sure as the striking cobra, Twist shoved it out of the way.

"You don't get the hint! We're not interested, beat it!" Twist looked hard and tight into the man's yellow eyes. The smile that was on his face dissolved.

"I knew it, I spend all my money and I can't even get a dance. You simple bit..." At that moment, Twist rose up from her seat in between his syllables. He caught himself. "Y'alls women," he continued, "come here and just profile...like you ain't tryin' to meet nobody." The man took a step to leave but Twist got the last word.

"Naw bruh, we just ain't tryin' to meet you." Twist was brash and her loudness carried the man away on a sled of shame.

"I never thought that grimy grill would ever leave." Sylvania scanned the room, "Making me miss a good dancing song." Twist finished her drink in one swallow.

"The free drinks are always the weakest. C'mon girl, I'ma go get us some tasties." Before Sylvania could open her mouth Twist was up and walking across the dance floor. She had a presence that parted the crowd in a way that even Moses would be a bit envious. Sylvania lost sight of Twist as the exuberant crowd filled in behind her wake. She sat there as another song she liked played came on when a distant baritone voice caught her attention from behind. Not wanting to be obvious, Sylvania began scanning the room from the opposite side until she caught sight of the voice. The attractive vibrations emitted from a handsome, well-groomed man. His skin was dark, like a concord grape, shining beautifully like a polished stone on display at the Art Museum. He wore a tan single-breasted suit that seemed tailored just for him. It was hard for her to see the rest of his outfit from her angle but if it was anything like what she could see, it was right on time. She realized she had been looking too long because the turn of his head brought the two into eye contact. She turned away but not fast enough. The voice stopped talking to one of his friends, gave a quick handshake, and turned his attention towards the cubbyhole. *So far, so good.* Sylvania mind raced as she quickly finished her drink. She could feel his presence consumed the cubbyhole's archway. She looked up. From within the beard appeared a warm, inviting smile. She giggled with the thought that this man must've been a ventriloquist because she did not see his lips move but she swayed to the baritone voice that asked her to dance. Sylvania didn't want to seem too eager or desperate--so she hesitated. All of her life, opportunities have slipped through her fingers due to her hesitation. She knew it, she understood it, cursed it, but never tried to do anything about it. Tonight was no exception. Before she could respond, Twist and two bammish looking men were jamming themselves into the now cramped cubbyhole.

"Scuse me cutty!", said the one with the open collar exposing a lackluster chain with a bull's head on it. The bearded baritone moved quietly to the side. Sylvania, slow to speak, watched the man with the voice fade away into the crowd. The other man with the leather vest looked at Sylvania and announced, "I'm ready to do the do!" Sylvania didn't know what he was going to do but was damn sure that she wasn't the one that the doing was going to be done to. She couldn't tell which guy was with Twist because both of them were checking her out from head to toe. The one with the bull had the bodacious audacity to dip down under the table to take salivated gander at Sylvania's legs.

"Oh my lawd!", he exclaimed as a waitress handed him a pony sized bottle of malt liquor. "Ain't no stick, it's awlll thick! Baby here is fully equipped!

"Preach rev, preach!" Leather Vest gave his friend a pound on the fist and leaned over, muttering a liquor-laced nothing in Twist's ear that made her lick her lips gleefully. A song with a heavy bass downbeat boomed. Twist and the Leather Vest rushed the dance floor. It wasn't long before Sylvania could see the two lock hips. She held her breath after catching sight of the man with the baritone voice at the coat check, preparing to leave. Sylvania thought about rushing over to say something until she was brought back to the present by a tapping on her leg.

"Check this Sylia."

"The name is Sylvania."

"Yeah, I can dig that...you named after the lightbulbs?" He rubbed his mouth like most players do as a way to express a whole lot of nothing.

"No, I wasn't."

"Well, check it, before we dance, let me just say that...and I hope you don't take any disrespect baby to what I'm about to say..." Sylvania was weakening quickly. "So, let me say this...I think that you are a meaty...beefy kind of lady...and I mean that in a sexy way."

Sylvania was startled by the boldness of the Bull.

"Beefy? You callin' me fat?" She started to leave but the Bull blocked her path.

"Aw girl, you know, that's what I like!" Sylvania felt a twisting in her stomach as she watched him wipe the drool from his chin. Sylvania rubbed her temples. *Was that supposed to make me feel special?* She looked at her watch--11:45. How much longer would she have to be here? She had an agreement with Twist that if nothing jumped off by eleven-thirty they would leave but looking at her on the dance floor, she knew she was stuck. Sylvania suddenly realized that the Bull was still talking and abandoned all hope that he would get the hint she wasn't interested.

"C'mon Selena, let me get this dance, all right?" This was the third time Bull had asked her but the first time Sylvania heard

him. The music was fast and she figured that she could see if there
were any other men in the place that caught her eye. Sylvania
walked slowly to the crowded dance floor with the Bull close in
tow. So close that he pushed up against her back twice, offering a
sly *excuse me* each time. Sylvania found a good spot and turned to
begin dancing when suddenly the music changed and the tempo
slowed. Sylvania wanted to cry because she knew what was next.
She felt the hands of Bull pull at her waist.

"This is the cut!"

The song, *Reasons*, began playing. Up until now she loved the song
but now she hated it. She hated it for being too long, she hated it
because everyone--especially the Bull--thinks they can sing it, she
hated it for the strong baseline which the Bull used as a metronome
for his pelvic thrusts. Sylvania suffered for the rest of the dance.
The Bull laid his unshaven face on her cheek. She could almost
taste the malt liquor on his breath.

"…kissin' and huggin' and holdin' you ti-i-ight..."

The Bull dropped his right hand lower onto her hip. His other
hand pulled tightly on her lower back.

"...after the love games have been played..."

He tried a dip but Sylvania refused it.

"...la la la la la la la la la la la la la la la la la la la la la la la..."

Bull sensed the end of the song was near. He arched his back,
pulling Sylvania so tight that she could hardly breathe, rubbing his
engorged self in a rhythm that only his body could hear. In disgust,
Sylvania pushed herself away.

"What's up Saliva? What's your problem?" The Bull
followed her off the dance floor. Sylvania reeled around.

"My problem? I got a problem? You're out there trying to
sex me down on the dance floor like I'm the last piece you're ever
gonna get...or the first ever had? And you ask me if I got a
problem?" Sylvania was now at the coat check.

"Look, I was tryin to let you know how I feel..." The Bull's words trailed away into nothingness. Sylvania put her coat on and started past the bouncer. On her way out the door, she turned, eyes pierced, and threw her final venom at the Bull.

"The least you could have done was get my name right! It's Sylvania...like...like...like the light bulbs!" She pulled the door hard behind her and stomped across the street. There was a cold wind, but she could not feel it, at least not until her hand clasped the near frozen handle of the car door. She took a deep breath and turned back to the club. *Twist has the keys.* She dreaded the thought of returning back to the club but what could she do? She was stopped by the bouncer when she reached the door.

"Sorry miss, but you ain't get your hand stamped before you left." Sylvania was too mad and too cold to waste time and he saw that, indicated by his quick step to the left. She walked straight to the edge of the dance floor, beginning her search. It didn't take long. There was some form of house music playing and Twist was dead center on the floor between Leatherman and the Bull. She took a deep breath. "TWIST!" Twist's head turned and saw Sylvania flagging her over. After a few words to the men, Twist danced over to Sylvania.

"So what happened with you? My man says you didn't like him."

"Let me have the keys to the car."

"You ain't got to marry the brother. It's all about having a good time."

"Let me have the car keys please."

"Look, Smooth and his friend said they would to take us to Waffle Place for a late night snack, you with it?"

"Where's your purse so I can get the keys to the car?"

"You can ignore the brother later. Let's just keep'em happy, get the quick grub, then kick it home."

69

"I'm going to ask you one more time. The car keys!?!"
Reluctantly, Twist walked over to the coat check and dug into her
pocket.

"Here! Now don't leave. And don't run all the gas out!"
Before Sylvania could respond Twist was back in the center of the
dance floor returning to her Bull-Leather Vest sandwich.

Sylvania sat quietly in the car as it hummed, sputtering
periodically. Several flakes of snow began to fall on the window,
quickly melting. She turned on the car radio but didn't find
anything to make her feel better. She returned to the doldrums of
the space. She awoke at 1:40 AM to the rapping on the window.
She leaned over and opened the door. Twist stuck her head in
quickly.

"Look, I'm getting a ride with Smooth. Take my car. You
can pick me up tomorrow. I'll call you. Later!" Twist shut the
door. From the rearview mirror, Sylvania could see Twist getting
into a late model Toyota. She turned on the lights and headed
home. What a waste. What a waste of a night. What a waste of an
entire day. What a waste of a life.

CHURCHIN'

-1965-

"WATCH THE BABY WHILE I get my things together?"

Lynn Parker shimmied past the boxes marked dishes and retrieved her purse from the hall closet.

"Can't you?" Carl Parker was finishing his scrambled eggs and coffee. "You might have to change him or feed him or something."

"Forget it!" Lynn slung her bag over her shoulder and walked quickly to the baby's room. "Just get ready. This boy is getting baptized today!" Carl chomped down hard on his toast, remembering his agreement to have his baby boy Kenneth baptized before he turned twelve months, which was now two weeks away. As a child, Carl hated going to church. Like most of the young boys growing up in Greensboro he would have rather been trying to catch crawfish in the nearby creek than the Holy Ghost. He told himself that when he was old enough he wasn't ever going back into a church.

"Carl? You ready?" His wife's voice reminded him of the promise he would not be able to keep. "Service starts in thirty minutes."

"We'll get there in time. Pine Street Baptist is just a couple of blocks down." Carl rose to brush his teeth and finish dressing.

Since moving to their new home and trying to get the store off the ground, there always seemed to be too many things to do and too little time to get anything done. When their son Kenneth Carl was born, Lynn insisted he be baptized before his first birthday. Carl found himself so engrossed in his new business that the first six months of his son's life flew by. They had visited a couple of churches recommended by some of the women in the neighborhood. Their first stop was the Mother Bethel African Methodist Episcopal Church. Carl voiced his concerns immediately.

"It's too far away and the name is too long."
After their visit he added that the service was too long as well. A couple of weeks later, they attended a service at Bright Hope Baptist Church in North Philadelphia. Carl found the service to be lively but the building to be too *fancy*. Carl knew they would expect a full collection plate each week. What made him cringe the most was the press for the members to be involved in city politics and activism. *I have enough to worry about...no time for all this political mess.*
One afternoon in the store, the pastor of Pine Street Baptist Church stopped in for a soda and a pack of cigarettes. His conversation with Carl was so down to earth that the invitation to visit was easily accepted. Pine Street Baptist turned out to be the kind of church that Carl could go to—periodically. It was large enough where he could almost disappear. It was conservative--not a lot of shouting and *falling out* as with other churches. Carl even liked the choir. They sang their songs in a style similar to the Mormon Tabernacle Choir which he enjoyed watching at Christmas time. *I can understand the words...not all that gospelly screechin' and screamin'.* The service also was consistent. It never seemed to run long, another positive which secured Carl and the Parker family as future members.

-1999-

"I can't believe that after all these years we've been together, this is my first time going to church with your family." Clarissa was fidgeting with her shocking pink hat, adorned by a large bow and three pink plumes. "Oh, this is going to be ferocious!" The hat matched her shocking pink almost mini-dress, leggings, and shoes. Ellis watched from a distance. Clarissa just knew she was the fifth friend on the cover of McMillian's *Waiting to Exhale*--but from where he sat, it was quite clownish. "Now, what's the name of this church again?" Clarissa was putting the finishing touches on her make-up.

"Pine Street Baptist." Ellis flipped through the Sunday Philadelphia Inquirer, not really looking at anything. "Did you know that in the last ten years the Spirit Ambassadors…that's the choir… earned three Grammy nominations for their musical productions? The choir attracts people from all over the city and even some from Camden." Ellis could hear Clarissa responding positively. "The Pine Street Baptist choir isn't real big…it's about sixty vocal members plus musicians…but they're good…real good."

"I can't wait." Clarissa adjusted her dress in the mirror. "Pine Street Baptist Church!" She said the name of the church slow and with the convicted accent on the *Baptist*. "I just might have to catch the Holy Spirit up in there today. You know how the Baptists do." She paused for a response from Ellis but none came. "Anyways, I hope the choir does one of those church roof-raisin' numbers. I'm going to be doing like this." Clarissa began to rock back and forth before breaking out in a step that Ellis mentally described as a cross between Riverdance and the Funky Chicken.

"Let's go. We'll meet my mother on the front steps." Ellis turned just in time to see Clarissa fanning herself.

"Hallelujah!"

Ellis and Clarissa pulled into the gravel parking lot across the street from the mammoth structure of Pine Street Baptist. Black people of all hues and complexions, outfits fancy and simple, in cars, cabs, or walking, greeted each other in the warm Sunday morning sun. Two deacons stood by the dual sets of double doors, shaking hands and kissing cheeks as parishioners entered for a morning full of glory.

"There she is, right over there." Ellis slipped his hand onto Clarissa's arm as he guided her across Pine Street and over to his family. As they walked, Clarissa fired a shot of words, stinging his ear.

"How come you're not wearing the watch I brought for you? You need to show your moms how much I take care of you." Their faces turned to smiles as they neared the Parker family.

The first to approach was Ellis's brother Kenneth. He walked slowly, trance like, into the street and was sternly called back to the curb by their Aunt Daliah. When the two finally reached the sidewalk, Kenneth threw his arms around them, giving a kiss on the cheek to his brother.

"Kenny, you look sharp today!" Kenneth's tight fitting suit was a little high around the ankles. It was Kenneth's favorite suit.

"Real sharp", Kenneth replied as he smoothed down the sides of his jacket. "Mama says sharp as a tack." After being released from Kenneth's grip, Ellis greeted his Aunt Daliah.

"Where you been boy?" Daliah's kiss smudged a deep burgundy on Ellis's shoulder. She always wore too much make-up. Consequently, so did everyone else who came in contact with her.

"Just working." Ellis moved Clarissa into position. "This is my lady friend, Clarissa. Clarissa, this is my aunt, Daliah."

"Hey now girlfriend!"
Though there were a couple hundred people in the vicinity, Clarissa's comment produced an uncomfortable stillness.

"No! You're his girl friend...I'm his aunt." Without missing a beat Daliah turned to *good morn*ing a couple of parishioners.

Well mom, it's your turn. Ellis braced himself.

"Good morning Clarissa."

Clarissa bounced the cadence of a 2AM televangelist. "Oh it is Mrs. Parker...it is."

"I'm glad you finally joined us. You know this has been our family church since the boys were just that." Mrs. Parker looked Clarissa up and down.

"You like my hat?" Clarissa adjusted the hat on her head. "The feathers are all that." Mrs. Parker just smiled.

"Well...it's you." Ellis gave his mother a sheepish glance and she shrugged her shoulders.

"Well, let's get inside," Aunt Daliah motioned, "I don't want anybody sitting in my seat. Come on Kenny."

Ellis and Clarissa walked up the stairs first, followed by Mrs. Parker, who was whispering to Kenneth. Ellis strained to hear what was being said but was unsuccessful--except for Kenneth's loud response.

"She look like cotton candy!"

Clarissa scanned the program. "When does the choir sing?"

"The choir sang as they walked in."

"No. I mean really sing. That first song was just some lame hymn. You know, when they gonna start be-bumpin' gospel-style?" Ellis took a deep breath.

"Well, they're going to sing an anthem after the minister's message." Clarissa was quiet for a moment before she started tugging at Ellis's jacket.

"He's going to be shoutin' it up, isn't he?"

Ellis smiled. "Just you wait and see."

Clarissa held herself with excitement. She had seen and heard fiery black preachers on television and in the movies, unlike the reserved white ones from her home town. She loved how the

.

.

congregation would sway back and forth, humming and moaning, followed by shouts back to the preacher. At her childhood church she had to be quiet. She wanted to be a part of that, and now, this morning, she was ready. It was time.

The minister opened with a prayer followed by a short verse. *Jesus keep me near the cross...there's a precious fountain...free to all, a healing stream...flows from Calvary's mountain...*

"Testify!"

Ellis's neck almost snapped as he watched Clarissa jump up from her seat and point to the minister. He felt all eyes on him as he heard the murmurs among the congregation began to rise. Her boisterousness reminded him how quiet and reserved his church was--very reserved. Clarissa didn't seem to notice or care as she clapped, shouted, and felt a spirit that seemed suddenly awakened. Ellis's mother leaned over to offer a firm susurration.

"What is she doing? This is not a Methodist church!"

It was too late. By the time the choir begun their slow, melodic rendition of *Nearer My God to Thee*, Clarissa was in the aisle. The ushers, not used to such showing out, weren't sure what to do with the fully animated white woman. They cautiously followed her as she spastically approached the altar. The choir continued singing the hymn in their envied eight-part harmony but Clarissa didn't hear that. She was no longer in Philadelphia but had been evangelically transported to a small church located in some backwoods no-name town. The sixty member choir had become a group of twelve, garbed in faded and frayed robes--sweaty, screaming "amens" and "oh lawds" in the blistering heat of the summer sun. There were no hymnals to be held, as they screamed every song by heart. Their fingers and palms, raised to the heavens, were blistered by the sanctified pounding on the life worn tambourines. Pine Street's electric organ faded away to become a decrepit piano, held together only by faith and the master's word.

The blind pianist banged on the dulled chipped ivory keys. His music called down the full rush glory, shaking the very foundation of the church—from the floor to the ceiling, from wall to wall. While inside the church the air conditioning maintained a comfortable seventy-two degrees, Clarissa just knew that the congregation was outside, underneath a revival tent, cooling themselves furiously with fans adorned with pictures of Jesus and Martin Luther King praying, eyes gazing heaven bound. Even as the minister stood stoic at the front of the church, Clarissa saw an unbridled preacher vociferating the name of *Great Gawd Awlmighty* as he flailed a dog-eared bible over his head, calling down fire, brimstone, blessings, and victory. Clarissa was in church that morning--just not Pine Street Baptist.

Church ended noticeably sooner than normal. Outside, several parishioners wished the Parker family well, as they haughtily wished Clarissa a blessed day.

"Oh y'all, I like this church! It was real!" Clarissa beamed as she walked over to where the family parked their cars. Mrs. Parker stopped and slowly turned.

"Clarissa child, you should visit other churches. Share their experiences." In a flash, her eyes were fixed on Ellis, who avoided direct eye contact. "Ellis would be more than happy to do that…wouldn't you Ellis?" Ellis opened his mother's car door and suggested they go to Bookbinder's for brunch. He didn't have anything else to say.

EASY PICKINS

DEVON AND HANK MADE their entrance into the upper bar area of The Promenade. Hank, like a pecan-colored statue of marble, moved slowly. He stepped with purpose, never wanting to seem rushed or anxious. His presence was a magnet for the fine brown eyes in his vicinity. His charcoal gray suit was a beacon with ladies fluttering furiously about him like moths. With all of the attention on Hank, Devon was not to be outdone. Even at six-one, he was not dwarfed by Hank. It was his boyish face that tipped the scales of attractiveness in his favor. He had what one girl in high school called *lovers lips* and *pillow-talk* eyes. The two purposefully moved at such a tempered gait they seemed to simply materialize at the bar. The bartender nearly dropped a carafe of white zinfandel when he turned and saw the two sitting there.

"A Kaluah and Cream", Hank dropped a crisp twenty onto the bar. He turned, not pressed whether someone snatched it or not.

"Hennessy," mouthed Devon. He too dropped a twenty and turned to face the crowd. A well endowed, braided beauty in a tight red business set brushed past Devon, allowing the full of her pelvis to lightly, yet tellingly, brush up against his knee. She smiled at him but the nonchalant expression on his face let her know she should keep moving.

"You must be wearing your booger-magnet cologne tonight." Hank held his nose. He reached behind him and felt his glass. The bartender was pleasantly surprised to see that he had not even taken his change.

"Women must think I'm an equal opportunist." Devon turned back to the bartender and motioned for a second glass. The two watched the upscale crowd on the dance floor, moving to the melodies laid down by the dee-jay. The Promenade was the home of the black elite of Philadelphia. It wasn't a private club but the favored patrons were socially screened. Steps to becoming a member were straightforward. A current member had to bring your business card to the management. After a careful review of employment, position, and reputation, one would receive a phone call, an invitation to enjoy a complimentary visit. Prior to the visit, a current resume, the completion of their application, and informal interview was required. The rationale of the Promenade was to create and maintain an extensive networking database of Black Urban Professionals. Non-members knew the truth; it was a weeding process--referred as the new millennium brown bag test. Many have tried to *sneak in the back door* but after a few phone calls were made, the ejection process was only the beginning of the humiliation. Management was savvy enough to know when you were trying to be what you weren't.

Hank favored the Promenade, one of the few social scenes he frequented in Philadelphia. There was a deity. It satisfied the rawest passion he held, the need to be known, respected, but most of all, desired. When he was in eighth grade, he was known as Hank the Tank, an overweight lumbering ox. Hank endured the teases and taunts of the other kids in his classes. When he entered high school he had hoped things would change. They did, but for the worse. At Masterman, he became the invisible fat boy. While the other teens were using their free time to meet with the opposite sex, Hank, shy and unsure, kept to the books. His father encouraged him to try out for the football team but after one hit, he resigned to the fact that his strongest muscle was located somewhere behind his eyeballs. After those four long years in the gulag called high school, Hank entered Temple University. It was there the transformation took place. His thinking was sharp and quick. His uncanny memory and research abilities shot him to the top of his class each year. He focused his time and energy on honing his power of speech, persuasion, and strategy. In the halls of the Temple, he became Hank the Tank again, but this time he was an intellectual machine to be reckoned with. It was there he firmed his physique to Herculean specifications. After earning his masters in business administration with an emphasis in management, he was quickly picked up by the prestigious downtown Philadelphia firm, Druer. They recognized his consultation skills in building successful small businesses when he was with the Philadelphia Small Business Incubator. In the end, he had achieved everything he had been denied in his youth, fame, respect, money--and women. He was Hank the Tank--and he was rolling over everything.

He spied a firm, tall, bespectacled, young lady sitting with some friends. He raised his glass, catching her attention. Motioning toward the dance floor, she understood his message and nodded. Hank watched the young lady giggle in the ear of one of her friends.

"Don't hurt nothin' man!" Devon slapped Hank on the back as he rose from his seat.

"If I don't come back, give my change to charity because I'll be making a donation personally tonight." Hank met the young lady half way on the floor, and even though the song was an upbeat pace, he initiated a slow dance with her. In a minute, Devon could see his hulking friend's frame swallowing up the lady.

Devon amused himself. He remembered meeting Hank right after his arrival at PowerCat. Devon, too, was from Philadelphia-- *North Philly*. He spent most of his formative years in a small row home and served as an acolyte at the Church of the Advocate. His father, a postman, wanted only the best for Devon and enrolled him in the famed, Chestnut Hill Academy. Devon earned a full scholarship in music to Florida A&M but his father was adamant that a black college would limit his success. Liquidating his pension, Mr. Hunt paid for the full four years at Princeton, in cash. Promising to repay his father for all of the sacrifices, Devon studied like a maniac. Following his father's accident, the family changed--he changed. After his first year of college, he found his relationship with his mother stagnated and eventually flat lined. Confused by the myriad changes in this life, the pain drove him deeper into his own world. Devon hardened himself, thinking only of material gain and selfish satisfaction. He hated others who seemed to have that one thing in life he lacked--happiness. Devon had plenty of empty relationships, always a new car, and a townhouse in Society Hill but in his heart he remained unsatisfied.

Devon's venture into the building's health spa was not for health reasons. It was vanity that drove him to work out. From across the room Hank watched the smaller man attempting to press his own weight on the Universal. Devon's struggling made him howl out loud.

"What's so funny?" Devon stopped long enough to talk.

"Yo man, I'm not laughing at you. I'm just reminded of my early days on the machine."

Devon looked at the overly developed man. *He's on the juice!* Devon extended his hand but Hank ignored him and strolled over to the full length mirror and admired his forearms.

"Damn man, you could have pipes like these." Hank continued on about himself and Devon listened quietly. He knew he already had the good looks but he needed a tighter body. Hank eventually turned on his personal infomercial about how he could help Devon. The two of them stopped talking and exchanged names, occupations, and other information until a young lady entered the health room. She had already changed from her business attire to her workout outfit. Her honey brown skin accented her bronze two piece aerobic set. She walked over to the Stairclimber and limbered up with stretching. The music from her headphones officially started her workout. The four eyes of the two men watched her bulbous hips as they stretched and contracted with each motion. Hank was hypnotized as glistening sweat beaded up on her neck, trickling down into the small of her back. He licked his lips. He could just taste it. The engorging in his shorts put an idea into his head. He looked over at Devon who appeared to be thinking the same.

"Let's see what you can do with that!"
Hank watched Devon go to work. He was a master instructor taking on a young precept. He could not hear their words but he could read what was going on based on her facial expressions. First she was peeved because he had interrupted her workout. Her face showed little curiosity, as if he had something possibly interesting to say. A moment later her lips pouted and her eyes closed. Hank knew Devon was losing it unless he said something pretty spectacular. The young lady reached out and shook Devon's hand and got back to her routine. Devon returned to Hank.

"I'll save you the embarrassment." Hank reclined on the bench and began his press regiment.

"I'll get the next one." Devon tried to save face.

"You ever go fishing?" Hank spoke to the rhythm of his reps. "You can either fish with a hook or with a net. You went after her, using your hook...and she got away." Hank finished his first set and sat back up. Flexing his pecs, he continued, "Now me, I go where there are plenty of fish. All shapes and sizes...and I cast my net." He motioned with his hands around his chest. "I can then cast out all the ones I don't like and keep the best. Now that's fishin'!"

Devon was quiet. He had never felt defeated like this before. He looked at Hank with a respect he now desired. Hank knew this and returned to his workout, satisfied that he had secured a pupil to pass on his wisdom.

Devon's mind returned to all that made the Promenade. He admired the décor. It was the confluence of glass, steel, and aquariums teeming with exotic fish that told him that this was a place to be admired, not touched. Voices rose and fell as he passed one of the semi-private billiard rooms. A tray-bearing waiter offered several options of champagnes and wine in smoky fluted glasses. He chose a white wine and took a long slow sip. He was casting his net. It was only a few seconds later did a walnut-skinned beauty in a midriff and form fitting pants sway to the beat in front of him. Devon spied Hank giving him the "thumbs-up". Devon was happy that his teacher was pleased.

SOURED

SYLVANIA SURVIVED ANOTHER LONG day at the donut shop. It was past ten when she stepped through her apartment door. The only light visible was the flashing red of the answering machine. *You can wait until tomorrow.* She began peeling out of her coffee stained smock. She piled her clothes in the combination living room-kitchen-dining room. She smelled like the shop and couldn't wait to take a long, peaceful bath.

Sitting on the edge of the tub, she started the water slowly, letting it cascade over her hand with a warmth that made her smile. There was a certain peacefulness that came with bathing. She walked naked and quickly to the kitchen. Quietly she cursed herself for not having any Bath and Bodyworks products. For now, dishwashing liquid will have to do. *What the hell, its lemon scented!*

The hint of Roberta Flack's *Oasis* floated in from the kitchen as she submerged her body into the soothing water. Relaxation lowered her defenses and a wave of sadness crashed over her. Her mother was right. She could have had more. Here she was, twenty-five and living in a proverbial phone booth. Forget having friends over, if she really had any other than Twist, but she didn't even want to be there herself. Lifting her hand through the fading bubbles, she looked at her fingers--no ring. Not a single one: no wedding, not one for engagement, not even a promise ring. It might have been Stevie's *Ribbon in the Sky* on the radio but it was her mother's voice in her head. *You need to stay with that Kelly Hunter. That boy is going places.* At that time Kelly Hunter was corny--"a straight-up nerd". He was nice to Mother but a bother to Sylvania. Every neighborhood had one: The boy who would run errands for your parents, shovel your walk without being asked; the boy who always had the homework assignments. Mother thought he was special, sweet, and smart. Sylvania thought he was annoying, boring, and needed to bother some other family. Of course, in true teenage rebellious fashion, Sylvania had her eyes, heart, and soul set on Kervis Calloway. Kervis was older, had a scar below his left eye from a shattered bottle to his face, and was rumored to have fathered a child back in the ninth grade. *Ohh!...but he was hot!* The worst thing Sylvania's mother could do was tell her to stay away from him. That only pushed her faster into the back of his uncle's customized conversion van. Sylvania's defiance blinded her to the sweetener Kervis was laying down on her. The first time he entered her it was painful.

"Let's do it like I talked about...turn over!"

"Can we do it regular-style first?" Sylvania felt the van heating up.

"Damn girl...I thought you was a woman. Just get on your knees!" Kervis' strong hands forcefully guided her to the floor. Not knowing why, she soon felt a swirling sickness in her stomach. Excited, Kervis was rushing and tried to jam his way in. Not wanting to appear immature and inexperienced she remained quiet, fighting the pain that now shot throughout her body. She turned her face from the carpet and looked out the port holed-window with the hopes no one would see her.

"How that feel baby?" Kervis grunted a few other sentences but twenty seconds later, he rolled onto the floor and told Sylvania it was time to go. At their next encounter Kervis brought some lotion and rubbed a dab onto his erect manhood. "Go in greasy, come out easy!" Sylvania thought his *cute* sayings were another jewel in his crown of charm. As they would say in the streets, Sylvania was *turnt out*. She began sneaking out of school, lying about where she was going, and eventually leaving her home at night for the momentary rendezvous. Sylvania stopped breathing momentarily when she thought back to when Kervis wanted her to *put it in her mouth.* After about five seconds of having his pubic hairs caught in her braces, he gave up on the idea. Memories of Kervis Calloway caused Sylvania to convulse with a sudden chill, splashing the water. Grabbing towels to dry the floor, she remembered all the reason why Kervis wasn't the one, why her mother was right, and why she concluded that she had nasty habit of picking the wrong man.

The truth came to light one evening when Kervis told Sylvania to come to a party. She was told it would be the usual scene: in the basement, music, dancing, some snacks, and the old folks sitting upstairs. When she arrived, she knew it was something else. She knew she should have turned at the door but there was Kervis in a Rick James Tank Top. He pulled her close and tongue twisted her until she heard the door shut behind her. The party was on.

Sylvania sat on the sofa uncomfortably although Kervis had his arm around her shoulders and a quart bottle in the other. She recognized some of the other males in the room but didn't know them. There were a couple of other girls in the room as well but not enough to evenly match up boy-girl. After another thirty minutes of watching Kervis and his friends drink heavily, Sylvania had the feeling in her gut that she should go but when she rose to leave...

"'Sup baby, where you goin'?" Kervis' words were slurred.

"Home." Sylvania tried to be strong. "It's time for me to go."

"Home? C'mon now."

"I got to go home. My mom..." Kervis grabbed her wrist and pulled her roughly back down to the sofa.

"How you gonna leave now? We just gettin' started." Sylvania noticed that most of the couples had left the room, leaving two more boys seated across from her. One was passed out but the other, Trev or something, was eyeing her as he had been all night. Only now, his eyes were lazy, bloodshot, but alert. This was the first time she heard him speak.

"Yo Kerv, you need some help with that?" Sylvania had heard Kervis say time and time again that she was his girl and that he would *beat down any fool that stepped to her.* Hearing words like that made her feel good, feel special. But tonight, he said something different, something that screamed she should have listened to her mother.

"Yeah man, you can help me out…and help yourself." In the moment he finished the word *yourself*, he pushed her down on the sofa and began to pop the buttons from her blouse. As she fought his hands, she felt another set beginning to tear at her belt and zipper.

"Turn that freak over! She got much ass!" Sylvania could hear Kervis laughing. Terror filled her bones as she kicked violently at Trev. She felt two hard stinging slaps on her face. The trickling of blood from her nose brought forth a renewed strength. She took a deep breath and screamed. Even with Kervis' hand on her mouth her fear echoed throughout the house.

"What's goin' on down here?" It was one of the other girls. "Kervis!…Trev!…Leave that girl alone. Y'all know she ain't down with all that!" Kervis shouted *shut up* to the girl. That's all Sylvania needed. With their attention now on the other girl, she summoned her remaining strength and kicked Trev off her. Kervis sat up.

"Go on Syl! Don't nobody want you're ol' dry-ass pussy." *Fits of laughter.* Sylvania didn't stay to hear any of the other comments. In a fluster, she covered herself as she ran out to door and down the street.

Sylvania entered the house the same way she left, quietly through the basement window. She crept upstairs, stripped down, and went into her bathroom. She kept the light off because she didn't want to see what she looked like. She didn't want to see the foolish face in the mirror. She wet a washcloth and wiped her nose and face. Taking the compress to bed, she curled under the covers, seeking sleep, hoping when she woke that it was all a bad dream--more foolish hope from a foolish girl.

Sylvania's fingers dipped into the conditioner and applied the cream gingerly to her scalp. She was tired and knew she had another day of job searching ahead of her. She thought about the advice from Twist--to just quit her job. *Nothing makes you find a new job like desperation!* That was too risky. Twist lived her life that way but not Sylvania. She needed the stability, any kind of stability, good or bad. A terrible job was a job. A small apartment was a place to live. A no-good man was a man. That was how she lived her life. She wanted, needed a change but didn't see it ever coming--not for her. After wrapping her hair, she turned out the lights and headed for her bedroom. In the dark, she saw the red flashing of the answering machine. *It might be Twist bragging about her latest love romp.* Sylvania decided to listen, to put a funny story in her mind to help her sleep. Her finger depressed the button and a woman's voice came over the speaker but it wasn't Twist's.

"Good afternoon Ms. Lee. This is the offices of PowerCat. We would like to offer you the administrative assistant position. Please return the call if you still have the interest. Please call..."

Standing there in the dark, a light finally illuminated Sylvania's life, though small, it was a light--and that was good enough for her.

TAKE A TIP

"YOU READY?"

Ellis called from the kitchen. He hated being late for dinner, especially when it required a two-week advanced reservation. "Clarissa?" There was no response. He could hear her moving in their bedroom but it was as if he was talking to himself. "Remember," his tone was cautious, "You wanted to go to Smith and Wallensky's." Ellis didn't want to go out. This was his peace offering for when they visited her mother the previous week. He knew there was going to be a blowout and could have avoided it but what happened happened. His thoughts were interrupted when Clarissa entered the kitchen. Except for her soured facial expression, she was still as beautiful as when she was back in school. Time added a little here and there but she was still a head-turner when out at the mall or company functions.

"You need to stop rushin' me. Goodness takes time...you know that." Throwing her head back in self-wonderment, Clarissa pointed to the door. "Let's go!"

The ride to Smith and Wallensky was quiet, the way Ellis preferred it. He decided to take the East River Drive to Center City. Aside from several cyclists, the traffic was light. This was more relaxing than taking the expressway. It was also an opportunity to see Boathouse Row from the front, rather than the lit-up back which was better known. He and his brothers would cut through Mantua, walk over to the Schukyll River, and throw rocks and trash into the water. In the dark, the boathouses would reflect perfectly on the water as the ginger bread houses to which they were famously referred.

They weaved through Center City, making their way to the Rittenhouse Square area. Approaching the corner of 21st and Walnut, Ellis began slowing down.

"What are you doing?" As if from out of a trance, Clarissa became aware that Ellis was looking for a parking space. "Just drive on up and get valet service!" She focused her attention out the passenger window. "Damn! You're so cheap. It's like this everywhere we go. Can't we just roll up like the big ballers we are...for once??" Ellis couldn't get to the valet stand fast enough. The red jacketed young man ran around to open Clarissa's door. "Now that's what I'm talkin' about!" She abruptly extended her hand for the young man to assist her from the car but that was an old school gesture he wasn't familiar with--so he just stood there. "You ain't gonna help a sister out?" A funny smile crept up on his face as he stammered.

"Oh yeah...my bad." After assisting Clarissa from the car, the young man waited for the keys from Ellis.

"For your troubles." Ellis gave the young man a ten dollar bill.

"No trouble sir. Anytime!" The young man quickly returned to station waving the bill in another red-jacketed face.

"I said we should roll like big ballers...not throw money around like one. That was worth a dollar." Even though Clarissa's voice was loud, he could hear the young man's comment--*too late for that homes*, followed by muffled chuckling.

"Let's get inside." Ellis took Clarissa by the arm and led her toward the door. He had lost his appetite.

Smith and Wallensky was a standard in the Philadelphia's dining scene. With its panoramic view of Rittenhouse Square and a classic steakhouse menu, it clearly was a major player in the impeccable dining experience, attracting both politicos and the new hip social scene. With its grand fireplace, coveted private dining rooms, and extensive wine list, Smith and Wollensky was the experience to be experienced. The primo touch was the main dining room. Tables of two's and four's--all tucked away in their own private area, another reason why Philadelphia's politicians and those with seedier backgrounds appreciated Smith and Wollensky--discretion was always on the menu.

They were seated on the far side of the restaurant, next to one of the fireplaces.

"Can y'all turn that on? It would be so romantic." The waiter paused for a moment at Clarissa's request. It was summer. Ellis cut his eyes to the waiter. Although he didn't possess ESP the waiter could hear what Ellis was thinking. He smiled at Clarissa.

"Not a problem Miss." He leaned back behind the fireplace, turned the gas release knob, and engaged the switch. "Will that be all before your drinks?" Clarissa smiled and Ellis ordered. He knew this was going to be a big tip night.

"So Ellis", began Clarissa as she started in on her shellfish bouquet. "When you gonna be made VP? You've been with that damned company for almost seven years. They should be giving you that by now. Hell, you keep them afloat, out of trouble, and you know more than any of them other stiffs in your office." Clarissa crunched down on a celery stick. "Hand me the salt."

"There's been some talk about opening the LA office but I don't think I would be interested."

"Not interested?" Clarissa shook the salt furiously onto the celery and proceeded to talk fast between the chews. "LA would be the bomb! The beaches, the weather, hell, you know we gonna see some celebrities."

Ellis fiddled with his salad.

"We did see Frankie Beverly in front of the Academy of Music. Remember that?"

"I'm talking about movies stars. We could get invited to those parties. I'm talkin' big timin' it."

"It's expensive there. We couldn't afford…"

It was this point in the conversation that frustrated Clarissa. Ellis could always find a reason to say night air was bad air. She knew that the reason why he didn't excel further at Druer's was because of his own self-depreciation. It was she who forced him to apply for the position at Druer's years ago. He had just started his M.B.A. at Penn. His stellar performance in the program caught the eye of one of his professors, a close friend of a member of Druer's board of directors. He shared with Ellis an opportunity to get in as one of their financial accountants but Ellis declined. He had already signed on with the General Accounting Office and felt that he had to honor the commitment. This infuriated Clarissa. The GAO was a nice government job with a level of security but the Druer job--*now that would be the move*--fancy dinners, rubbing shoulders with a lot of fat cats, trips, and the shopping. She knew that she had hit the jackpot. She hounded Ellis for more than two weeks until he submitted a letter apologizing to the GAO, rescinding his acceptance. A week later he had his interview at Druer and on the spot he became a junior finance accountant.

"We'll be able to afford it 'cause you'll be paid. Just have them add a house to your offer. They'll do it. As much as you do for that company! Don't let me tell…" Clarissa's comments were cut off by the waiter's presence. Ellis was glad it was time to order. "And how come you're not wearing that watch?"

OPENED

BEING A BALL PLAYER had its advantages. Even riding the bench for most of the games his first year, Ellis found a kind of popularity he'd never experienced before. Being a jock was great but add to the mix his exceptional performance in the classroom, everyone knew there was a new catch on the small campus--and it was Ellis. In the fall of 1989, Ellis was one of 110 black students on campus, with the majority of them being female. Of the males, most of them were on the sports teams, with the remaining dozen on scholarship for various programs. It was a nice tight community of brothers and sisters who supported each other when problems arose in the classroom, on campus, or in the local community. They were like a family--except when it came to the taboo topic of dating.

The season was over and they ended with a 6-19 record. No playoffs. Secretly, Ellis was glad because of the number of projects he had due at the end of the semester. Most of the other players didn't share that sentiment. Ellis could hear his father's voice when he thought of the possibility of going home with failing grades. *I told you that college was a waste of time.* His father's voice weighed heavy on him most days. He had his own room, the food in the cafeteria was great, but most of all, he had a freedom like never before. What should have been a fantastic experience was always overshadowed by those thoughts of his father.

Ellis was in the library on a Wednesday evening. Most of his friends were back in the dorms watching television on the lobby big screen but Ellis knew that if he wanted to go on the weekend road trip to *catch ladies* at Lincoln University he had better get his paper researched and written by Friday afternoon. He hadn't noticed his name being called, maybe because it was all but a sigh.

After the third time he looked up and couldn't discern who had called his name.

"Ellis."

There was that song again. He surveyed the tables in the room. There were singles, couples, and groups. He had to be dreaming. Maybe it was his father's voice again.

"Oh, Ellis."

This time there was a collective giggle that accompanied his name. He zeroed his sights on a table of young white ladies with their heads huddled together.

"What?" Ellis knew they were playing. This happened often. The black girls on campus would walk right up and say, *What's up?* or start a conversation but the white girls tended to be coy, almost to the point of being silly. "Why you keep calling my name?"

The redheaded one spoke up.

"My girlfriend wants to meet you." Ellis let loose a long exhale. *Not now.* He had too much work to be messing around and listening to someone talk about how bad the season was. Ellis continued to ignore the girls until he noticed a shadow fall across the papers on his desk.

"Look… I'm not trying to be rude but I got to get this work done. You can dig that?" Ellis finally looked up and paused. He had met a lot of white girls in this past year but he had never seen this one. There was something about her that captured his attention. Her hair was long and blonde but had a curl to it that made him want to reach out and touch it. She was tall, well endowed in the chest area, which he liked. She also had a complimenting waist, not too big or wide but not too small either. She didn't have much of a butt, definitely not like the sisters, but it was a little more than average, more like a hump or a lump. Even though it was cold out, she wore a plaid pleated skirt that settled just above her knees, revealing a leg length that, as he surmised in his mind, *could be worth the trip*. Before he knew it, she was seated next to him.

"Do you know how to type?"

"Yeah I know how to type." Ellis didn't know how to type.

"What's your wpm?" He didn't know what that meant.

"Perhaps I can type your papers for you." The young lady slowly extended her fingers in front of Ellis's face. Ellis knew what was going on but still asked.

"What you want to do that for?"

"Because," she started with a long sigh, "You're on the basketball team and have done so much for the school. Why shouldn't I do something nice for you?" Coach warned him about situations like this but the inflation in his sweats blurred the advice.

"True dat. What's your name?"

"Clarissa...but my friends call me Clarissa."

"Well, how you doin' Clarissa?

"Oh...we're not friends...yet." Their playful conversation went on for another twenty minutes until Clarissa convinced Ellis to come over to her suite--for typing lessons. By the end of the evening he called her Clarissa--several times.

Ellis and Clarissa moved from being sex partners to an actual couple by the beginning of his junior year and her senior year. The reputation of *bagging a Becky* provided him status among his fellow ballplayers but among the *sistahs*, he was *sellout athlete number 180*. Not that he was the 180th brother to date a white woman exclusively but that he did a 180--turning his back without even giving them a chance. That's how they felt and that made it real. All that didn't matter to Ellis. Even though Clarissa's grip on his life was tightening little by little, he didn't mind. It felt good to have someone concerned about his whereabouts, fixing him meals, typing his papers, showing up during and after practice. He figured that's what girlfriends did. Besides, he was getting sex on the regular--nice freaky sex. The kind he had heard guys talk about in high school but knew wasn't happening. It was for real now; head after practice, hand-jobs in the library, and lap dances during meals. She would even drop him a couple of twenties each week just for *incidentals*. She had him and it felt good. Life was sweet. Toothache sweet.

TEA LEAVES

THERE WAS A KNOCK at the door.

"Sylvania, would you get that?" It was the third Sunday of the month and Sylvania's mother, Wilnonia Lee, was hosting her sorority's monthly tea. The Mondaine Madames of Tau Beta Lambda prided themselves on high achievements--the achievement of marrying well. This afforded them the opportunities to perform large scale community service and other charitable events but most importantly, the finest socials in the tri-state area. The tea was a bold move for Wilnonia, as she was positioning for the highest office of her chapter, the Grand Empressio. For years she sought the position but was constantly relegated to being the chair of one committee or another. There were bigger, more impressive names in the circles of elite Black Philadelphia and the Lee name hadn't arrived. At least, not yet.

"I got it!" Sylvania shouted.

"It's *I have it* or *I'll get it!*" Wilnonia, in a hushed shout, provided grammatical correction to her daughter. She hoped whomever was on the other side of the door didn't hear her daughter. It was little things like that, the social faux pas, could take her out of the running at the next election. Sylvania opened the door and admired a stately, mature woman draped with a fox stole.

"Good afternoon Mrs. Carter-McCloud. You look stunning this afternoon." Sylvania knew she had to play the game for her mother's sake. Mrs. Carter-McCloud walked slowly into the Lee home. She looked around as if she was a home inspector, taking in every piece of art, the placement of furniture, and especially, the arrangement of family pictures. She didn't say a word until she was seated.

"Do you own a pet?" Sylvania looked at Mrs. Carter-McCloud quizzically. "Do you?"

"No. Why?" Sylvania was curious. She had a cat when she was growing up but that was decades ago.

"I have allergies and I don't want to be sneezing all afternoon." Sylvania smiled as she walked out of the room, snickering with the knowledge the fox was a faux. *Oh, the airs we breathe!*

For the next twenty minutes, grand looking women of all shapes and sizes paraded through the doors of the Lee home, a dozen in all. The women sat about the living room, sipping tea, coffee, and sparkling fruit juice. Not being a member, Sylvania was relegated to the kitchen. She didn't mind. Their chatter about fashion shows, debutante balls, and fundraising held no interest for her. *Hell! I'm trying to just make rent each month.* She did notice how the women treated her mother. They weren't actually talking to her, they were talking around her, watching her, testing her. This really was an interview for the position and Sylvania wasn't sure how her mother was doing. Each time her mother came into the kitchen to refresh someone's drink or the platter of hors d'oeuvres, the conversation of the group deadened to a hushed chatter. Upon her return, they were all smiles and compliments. As the afternoon waned away, Sylvania was gently awoken from her sleep by the harmonious voices of the women singing their sorority hymn:

..sisters of the world together we will strive
for long as Tau Beta Lambda is our guide...

Mrs. Carter-McCloud was the last to leave.

"Willy, your house and your hospitality was impeccable. It was truly a treat this afternoon. We must get together soon."

"We should," started Mrs. Lee. She drew a long breath. "Perhaps my daughter can join the sisterhood."

The split-second pause felt like an eternity. Mrs. Carter-McCloud adjusted her coat.

"Where does she work again?"

They shared a ceremonial kiss on the cheek and the flailing fake fox tail followed Mrs. Carter-McCloud down the walkway and to her car.

Back in the kitchen, Sylvania and her mother worked to return the house to normal.

"Mama," Sylvania spoke as she washed the glasses. "Why do you put up with all that bougie bullshit?"

"You know I don't go for that kind of talk in this house...and your father didn't either." Mrs. Lee continued putting the dishes into the rack. It wasn't worth the argument but Sylvania harped on the topic.

"Alright, alright, but why do you let those ladies come into your house, give you the up and down, and hope they give you something you rightfully deserve?" Sylvania moved onto the silverware. "Seriously Mama, you put many years into TBL and you never got elected president..."

"That's Grand Empressio!" The correction came without Mrs. Lee turning from the dish cabinet.

"Grand Empressio! Got it! But check this; all the years you served on all those committees, directed those fashion shows, run the book drives and what-not...it's like they ain't recognized you yet." She pulled up a stool by the island in the center of the kitchen and sipped on her now watered down lemonade. Sylvania looked hard at her mother and wondered. She wondered why they were so much alike--both searching for an acceptance that would never come. She knew it would never come because the acceptance would first have to come from inside. Her mother didn't have it to bring it out and Sylvania knew she didn't either.

Downing the small corner of her drink, Sylvania dropped the subject. "So…you been out on any dates?"

"I'm too old to date…and really too old to talk about my private business with my daughter." Mrs. Lee hid her smile. It was a long time since she and Sylvania talked like this, even though she was serious about not discussing 'grown folk' with her daughter.

"Come on Mama, a good lookin' woman like you has to have the old school gents lined up outside." Sylvania admired how well her mother took care of herself. At 5'1", Mrs. Lee was well proportioned and exceptionally maintained. Her skin was smooth, almost flawless. The weight gained over the years brought a new beauty to her frame. In fact, if there was anything that Sylvania wished for was to be as well preserved as her mother. Mrs. Lee's beauty still mesmerized men of all ages when purchasing fruits and vegetables at the Italian Market. Like mother, like daughter.

"I guess your father ruined me for all other men." Mrs. Lee sighed as she picked at the German chocolate cookies that were left over. "That's why the sorors are so special to me. You understand, don't you?"

Sylvania leaned over and kissed her mother on the cheek. "You're still the catch of the day!"
Mrs. Lee smile faded fast.

"By the way….can you help me out with my rent this month?"

OH DADDY!

THE SKY HAD JUST opened, raining down a warm, steady stream of droplets. It was an amazing sight watching the clouds move across the horizon so quickly. Dots of water peppered the windshield as Ellis and Clarissa pulled onto 76 West toward Carlisle, Pennsylvania. He slowly put in a jazz compilation CD although he knew, today, there would be no arguing over the music, at least not until the ride back. The drive was somber. No talking, no incessant popping of gum, no rap magazine references, just a sad, filling silence. When the traffic eased as they passed Valley Forge, Ellis glanced over at Clarissa, taking inventory of her appearance. The first thing he noticed was that her hair was out of the braids and down, falling over her shoulders. It was also back to its natural brown. Her make-up was subdued as well. She was wearing a paisley sun dress, stocking less, with black flats. The last time Ellis saw that dress was on their previous trip to Carlisle. To him, the dress was a signal--the return to the only time she *kept it real.* Clarissa moved to scratch her cheek and her nails, once long, painted, and adorned with metallic pieces, were now trimmed and painted clear. Clarissa was someone different now; a metamorphosis from ghetto fabulous to now--a plain Jane.

It was early afternoon when they pulled into the Lakeside Park Terrace. Ellis laughed inside as he did every time he visited this place. There was no lake to be beside and no terraces to look from. The only truth in advertising was the parked trailer homes. He didn't mind visiting trailer parks like this. To him, they were simply projects on wheels. After passing several rows of adorned and 'tricked out' double-wides, they reached lot 77. The trailer was a dingy yellow but the front porch was new. A couple of the screened windows were patched with duct tape and the small garden in the back flourished with roses, tulips, and other beautiful flowers. Years ago, Ellis had seen this home as one of the flagships of the trailer park but over time, the needed care wasn't there. Ellis parked next to a three-toned 1984 Mustang. Before he could say anything to Clarissa, she quickly exited the vehicle and climbed the three steps to the door. Clarissa's finger depressed the doorbell but there was no sound. A couple of neighbors looked in her direction causing Clarissa to turn her face. She started to knock but before her hand could touch the door a young girl opened it.

"Hey y'all! Clara's here!"

Ellis enjoyed this singular part of the trip. Unfortunately, the moment didn't last long. The breaking loose of hell was just around the corner. He was smart this visit and brought a couple of reports from the office to keep him occupied.

"Bout time you got here. We almost gone now." The girl stepped forward to give Clarissa a hug. Clarissa put her arms around the young girl and slowly pulled her close.

"Hey there Bitsy. How are you?"

Bitsy looked up and with her missing-a-front-toothed smile, "Everthings all right. Mom-Mom's in the back room watching TV, Big Joe's at the shop, and Big Paw's waiting for us at the joint." Bitsy giggled as she ran to the back of the trailer, into the room with the television. Clarissa looked around. Nothing changed. Except for a few new pictures on the wall, the place looked exactly the same as when she left for college eight years earlier. Her mind drifted back to the days when she used to sleep in the room that now had the television. There were some good times here; Mostly when Daddy was out, or working, or over at his girlfriend's trailer. Then it hit her--the pungent stale smell of Camel cigarettes.

"Hi Mama."

"Him wit ya again?" Clarissa's mother limped into the room. Still in her bed clothes, she leaned over the sink, cleared her throat, graced it, then ran the water to rinse whatever landed near the drain. "So you showed up. Good." Mama took two more steps before dropping onto the well-worn recliner. Clarissa looked at her swollen feet, ankles, and legs, evidence that she hadn't been taking care of herself. The smell of cheap gin made its way through the cigarette odor. "Y'all know your daddy don't go for your boyfriend at his res-dence." Clarissa started to speak but was cut short. "You bring him round each time when it's supposed to be family." There was a loud rumbling outside the side window. Immediately, Bitsy came charging from the back room.

"Big Joe! Mom-Mom! Big Joe's here!"

"You'n stop that runnin' in here before you break my good china. Ellis conjured one thought, *the only thing from China in this place was the Dogs Playing Poker print over the sink*. Ellis's eyes were quickly pulled to the burley biker entering the trailer. His salt and pepper hair was pulled back into a pony tail. His body filled the frame of the door. As he extinguished his cigarette on his boot, he looked over to Ellis first and eventually to Clarissa.

"What should I call you? Clara? Clarissa? Cleo?" The air in the room was still. Then it was broke by his gruff guffawing. "Girl, I'm just bustin' your chops. Come give your brother a hug." Clarissa felt her spine compress as he wrapped his arms completely around her. For a moment, a smile appeared on her face, until her brother spoke. "You still gotta bring that around?"

"Joe! Please!" Her face hardened as she stepped back from her brother. "Every damn time we come here it's the same thing!"

"Mama, tell her to watch her tone in my house." Mama adjusted herself in the chair. "We supposed to be here on family business and you bring him on in here each time." Mama lit another Camel.

"This ain't yourn house Joe. This my house!"

"I'll be in the car." Ellis turned and exited the trailer. There was a chill in the air. Slowly looking around, he tried to understand Clarissa. *Who wouldn't want to escape this? To put all of this behind them.* Changing her name back in college was her first step. Clara was too plain for a Central Pennsylvania woman who desired the flavors of city life. The rain prompted Ellis to get into the car. He turned on the radio but the reception in the area was limited. He sat, humming lightly, as he thumbed through the report, not really reading. He knew what they were talking about in there. It partly sickened him. Not because they held such feelings but that he held his tongue. He wouldn't stand for talk like that among his co-workers but here with the understanding of the nature for the visit, he didn't want to add to the distress. As the windows on the car fogged over, he began envisioning the drive home.

"Look, let's just get ready to go. Daddy's waiting." Clarissa tried to change the subject. Mama looked at the clock over the stove.

"Clara's right. Joe, hep me up so I can get dressed. Bitsy, get your mom-mom a drink." Joe leaned over and with a slight grunt, strained to lift his mother out of the chair.

"You should stayed home and helped me take care of mama and daddy. Runnin' off to the city ain't helpin' none of us." Joe smacked his pack of Marlboros and lit one. "We got plenty need round here."

"Ellis works to help me send money back here."

"He ain't doin' nothing special. I got a job too and I lay plenty of cash on the table."

"Joe's right." Clarissa's mother opened a drawer, fishing for a small bottle of pills which was now empty. "Hey Joe, give me ten dollars for my prescription."

"I ain't got it now Ma. Thursday."

105

"You can do better than that out there any day Clara. That boy...what's his name?...you know...Shep's son..."

"You talking about Beasal?"

"Yeah...he got a good job down at the plant. Driving them machines down there and makin' a good chunk-o-change. He's still single. Got a nice room in his family's place." Joe returned, rinsed his hands in the sink and dried them with the window curtain.

"Ellis is a good man. He's an executive at a finance firm. In fact, they want to make him a vice president and move him to LA."

"Louisiana?" Joe scratched his head.

"California, fool." Joe moved to look in the cabinet. He found a bottle of Jim Beam. Grabbing a plastic cup, he poured himself a taste.

"So Clara, you need to loan your mama some money. You can see she's ain't livin' like Donald Trump."

"I send what I can. I'm only working part time...." Clarissa knew where the conversation was headed.

"You there livin' with him and he don't give you any money to take care of your mama? I know he gives his mama money all the time." Clarissa wanted to leave but she was there for an important purpose.

"It's his money and he does what he wants with it. He takes good care of me and that's all to that."

"Are y'all ready to go or not?" Mama came from the back. Dressed in an old flowered dress that was fraying around the waist, Mama adjusted her wig and put the pack of Camels in her purse.

Bitsy stood by the door. "Can I ride with Clara...please?" Joe didn't answer. Mama slapped him on the arm. "Answer your daughter, she talkin'!" Joe shook his head. Bitsy bounded out of the trailer toward Ellis's car.

"You need to be takin' better care of her Joe. I ain't gonna be here forever. Mama pushed past Joe. "Now go get your daddy's truck." After a brief period of time, they were all outside. The rumbling of the pick-up echoed throughout the trailer park. Clarissa stood there as her mother struggled down the three steps. She cursed when Joe wasn't right there to help her into the cab of the truck. Clarissa looked around. Among the sea of trailers she saw her past. She saw what could have been. She often heard Ellis talk about how he loved his hometown. She didn't have one. She had this--and she hated it.

It reminded Ellis of a warehouse, adorned with a couple of potted plants in the front. This was his third trip to the Carlisle Heights Arms Convalescent Home. He hoped there was a way to remain in the car but deep down he knew he couldn't. He was here to support Clarissa. As the five of them entered the building, Ellis held his breath. The first time he visited, it had a strong, pungent smell of oatmeal. The second time, it was something like peanut butter. He didn't know what to expect so he entered hoping it was something he could tolerate for the next hour. The lobby brought sadness to Ellis. There were about a dozen elderly people, most in wheelchairs, lining the walls of the hallway, medicated and despondent. Seeing their life-worn faces and bodies impacted by the generations caused him to surmise that they were waiting--waiting for some attention, waiting for some family to come visit them, waiting for angel of death to stop procrastinating and get to work.

Ellis made it as far as the reception desk before he took a breath--broccoli, overcooked broccoli. The family walked down the hall, with Bitsy peeking into each room as she passed by. It was as if the vigor of her youth could be detected. Elderly men and matrons raised their heads, waved their hands, or simply followed her with their eyes. Some rooms had family members, others with nursing staff, still most were only visited with images from the television. As they rounded the corner, Bitsy turned into room 112.

"Big Paw!"

Clarissa's father was sitting upright in his chair. Bitsy knew better to jump in his lap but threw her arms around him and squeezed tight. His arms wrapped gently about her shoulders. Mama leaned over the two of them and kissed him on the cheek.

"You doin' all right there Ansel?" Mama fixed the pillow behind his head. "Is it warm enough in here for you?" Mama asked the usual questions, ending with *I got a surprise for you.* "Guess who's here to see you?" Ansel slowly lifted his head and a strange smile struggled to form over his face. Clarissa moved out from behind Joe and embraced her father. As she leaned over, she was catapulted back in time to the days when her father was the strong mining man and she was his favorite little girl. He would come home covered with coal ash but that didn't stop her from running and jumping into his arms. After he spun her around she too would be covered in ash, leading to the *daily cussin'* by Mama about getting her clothes dirty. This was their special fun; the two of them together, inseparable--until the day of the accident.

It was the Friday of Clarissa's eleventh birthday. One of the travelling carnivals had come to the neighboring town of Mechanicsburg. All day at school, Clarissa's mind was a million miles away from the math, English, and playground gossip. This was the day her father promised to leave work early, pick her up, and take her to the carnival--just the two of them. The clock above her teacher's desk seemed to cease to move after the lunch hour. She was already struggling to understand the book, *Jonathan*

Livingstone Seagull. The period lumbered on she found herself reading page 41 while the rest of the class was on 78. The admonishment dispensed by the teacher when asked to read the next paragraph dematerialized like an exorcised spirit at the sound of the bell. Quickly packing her books, she dashed through the hallways and out the front door, hawking the line of cars for her father's pickup. It wasn't there. She figured he took the time to shower at the mine before coming, so she found a spot on the front steps and waited. Nearly twenty minutes went by before she noticed a flurry of activity in the house across the street from the school. The house next to that one had a woman bolt across her porch and into her car. Clarissa's mind was trying to piece together what was happening as cars sped past her, all in the same direction. She could hear people shouting from inside the school but the words were not discernible. From out of nowhere, she heard the deep roar of a motorcycle. The sound was familiar enough for her to look up just in time to see her brother Joe speeding down the street and when he caught sight of Clarissa, weaved smoothly onto the sidewalk.

"Geet on Clara!"

"You know Papa says I can't ride on your bike without a helmet." Joe's face was flushed and sweaty, as if he had run all the way over. "Shut up and geet on the bike girl. Ain't you heard? There was an explosion at the mine!! Pop's hurt!"

Clarissa lost her breath. She couldn't move. She knew she had to get over to the mine, get over to her father, but she couldn't stand, much less lift her leg over the seat. She could see Joe's mouth moving, telling her to get on the bike but the sound didn't reach her ears. She felt him grabbing her arm, causing her to drop her book bag, spilling the contents onto the ground, but still her body resisted. It wasn't until she heard his next set of words that returned her to a functional consciousness.

"Gawd-dammit Clara! Geet on the fuckin' bike!" Clarissa knew something real was happening. In the next instance, she was on the back of the bike and the two of them were weaving down the back roads to the mine.

Clarissa never went to that or any other travelling carnival. The explosion had caused a portion of the mine to collapse, trapping her father and three other men for six days. Though they pumped fresh air into the devastated section of the mine, the denseness of the debris made breathing almost impossible. Two men died, one man survived miraculously with a broken hip and arm and the loss of one eye, but Clarissa's father slipped into a coma and remained in a vegetative state for more than six months. When he was finally released from the hospital, he suffered from deficient memory disorder, unable to remember anything beyond the day of the accident, free from the mine but trapped in time.

Mama motioned for Joe and Bitsy to leave the room.

"Let's go get a snack and let Little Clara spend some time with her Papa. That was the signal. Clarissa had experienced this time alone before but still shuddered as she knelt beside her father.

"Hey Clara..." Her father's voice was soft and distant. As if she was listening to an old recording. A seventeen year-old recording she had fully memorized.

"Hey Papa." A tear formed in her eye, which she quickly dabbed with her sleeve.

"You know, after work today, I have a surprise for you...just for you."

With a quivering voice, Clarissa took her father's hand. "What we gonna do Papa?"

"You wanted to go to that carnival? Well I'll pick you up from school. Just you and me so don't tell Joe or your mama, okay?" Ansel reached out to put his hand on her head, slowly stroking her hair. "You want a hot dog or a hamburger?"

Liquid emotions began streaming down her cheek as she answered. "A hot dog…with mustard…no catsup."

"Oh, you just have to try it with catsup…that's the best." There was an animated smile on his face--a smile from long ago. "And we're going to ride all the rides. Don't worry about getting sick…that's part of the fun."

Clarissa closed her eyes, trying to hold back the flood.

"I don't worry about that Papa".

Ansel slowly leaned back in his chair, drawing a deep breath. "I'll see you after school then Little Clara." As he drifted off to sleep, he blew her a small kiss. "Remember, don't tell your mama…you know how she get." Clarissa rose and sat on the edge of her father's bed. In an instant she was crying uncontrollably.

The ride back to Philadelphia was silent.

KISS THE GIRLS

THE UNITED BROTHERS INCORPORATED 1998 annual gala was the stand out event of the summer. The media buzzed Columbus Avenue. On this evening, the Aquaphila Convention Center, the newest addition to the Delaware River Waterfront, was filled with successful, determined, and influential black men of all hues, clime, and complexions--and then there was Hank. Devon spied him by the bar as he entered the reception room. Hank had invited him to the affair and told him with unquestionable specificity to come solo. He understood why. There were many, many single, beautiful women in the room. What young, single, black woman wouldn't want to be in a room full of a significant number of educated, professional, and available men? It wasn't like shooting fish in a barrel but a sister could stick her hand in and pick out a good one.

"Devon!" Hank's voice rose above the crowd. "Over here!" Devon made his way over to the bar. "Glad you made it homeboy! Tonight is the night you lose your virginity!" Hank grunted heartily, washing down the remainder of his Kaluah and Cream.

"Come on Hank", Devon signaled for the bartender. "Now you know a fine-ass brother like me gets his." With the bartender at their attention Devon ordered the house white wine while Hank motioned for a second Kaluah.

"I'm not talking about that." Hank leaned back onto the bar and swept his hand slowly from one side of the room to the other. "I'm talking about all of this." As Devon sipped his wine, it was apparent that he wasn't sure what Hank was talking about. "Let me ask you this Dev...are you going to the Delta convention next month?"

"The Delta's? The sorority?" Devon gave Hank a strange look as his voice had a slight tinge of agitation. "What are you trying to say?" Devon now regretted the *fine ass* comment.

"Calm down. You're uptight because you don't see the whole picture." Hank motioned for Devon to walk with him through the crowd as he talked. "Here we are at the premiere organization for solid, smart, and successful brothers, right?" Devon shook his head in agreement. He had tried on two occasions to get put on the invitation list and still, with his credentials, had not received an offer. On this evening, he was a guest of Hank. The two ascended the stairwell leading to the mezzanine level balcony. Hank turned their attention to the ballroom floor below. "Check it, Dev. There are almost 700 hundred plus members here tonight. Of that number, approximately 180 of the tickets sold as couples. Another one hundred fifty tickets were individual tickets for members. That leaves almost 200 tickets for non-members." Hank pointed. "I would guess about fifty of those are comped…you're included in that number. That leaves about one hundred fifty for single women who are looking…looking for me…looking for you." Devon smiled slightly. Hank continued. "Now, don't get too excited. Remember the scientific principles of attractiveness. Of that 150, fifty percent are the straight up ugly ones…waste of space. Then there are those who might be worth it if the night doesn't go right. Might have a nice body but need grill work. They represent about thirty percent. But the cream of the crop…the beauties…now that's twenty percent." Hank continued to climb to the top of the stairs. Looking back out again at the crowd, Hank offered a caveat to his observation. "Don't be fooled…even the 20 percent requires trimming. After you weed out nasty attitudes, the gold-digger factor, and church girls…you're only looking at 10 percent or about fifteen choice opportunities here tonight." Hank clasped his hand and leaned onto the railing. "You have a lot of competition here tonight my brother!" Devon ran the calculations through his mind. Looking out at the guests, he could imagine all of the single men...as well as some married brothers on the sly...scooping up the 10 percent...leaving him with the scrappish remains. A question popped out of Devon's mouth.

"So what does this have to do with the Delta's convention?"

Hank shook his head teasingly. Again, he found the joy in enlightening Devon, just as the Emperor delighted in turning Anakin Skywalker to the dark side. "Flip the script and go and be that ten percent...Mr. Fine Ass!"

A moment passed before a light switched on in Devon's head. Hank turned and strolled away. "I'm going to take a leak. See you at dinner. Table six." Devon's cherry was busted.

It was close to eleven-thirty when Hank returned to the reception area. With a buxom brown-skinned beauty on his arm, he scanned the room, seeking out his protégé. The room had couples and small groups of those who strayed away from the dance in the ballroom. The beauty asked Hank for dance. He instructed, *just wait right here.* His eyes now focused squarely on Devon who was standing quietly at the bar. Hank intercepted.

"So Dev, how's it going my man?" Devon was caught off guard. He hadn't expected to see Hank so soon--and alone. Hank smiled, moving his eyes, motioning to the doorway.

"Another one down. Looks like the odds are against me tonight, huh?" Devon fidgeted uneasily as the bartender moved an apple cosmopolitan towards his hand.

"There's still time." Hank grinned slyly. "I'm only holding onto this one until I find one better. If this is it for the night, it'll be alright." Devon's face gleamed as he tasted his drink. As they both moved away from the bar, the bartender called to Devon.

"Sir…your mojito."

Devon whirled around with a cautious look. He dropped a couple of bills to thank the bartender and picked up his second drink.

"So you did score tonight." Hank threw his arm around Devon's shoulder, almost causing the mojito to splash. "See, I left you something."

"Nothing like that. I'm talking to this fella from the Mayor's office. He's telling me about how they plan to expand the waterfront on the Camden side of the river. Good information to take back to the office."

Hank shook his head.

"There's a time for business and a time to get busy." He waved for the beauty to join him. "Brother, it's time to get biz-zzy. I'll see you Monday."

Devon watched Hank squeeze the beauty around the waist and head for the door. He knew that she was in for a wild night. Turning, he carried his drinks back to his table.

"Here's your drink. I guess the next round is on you." The well-manicured gentleman cradled his drink in his hand and drew a long swallow.

"It'll have to be the next time. I have a meeting tomorrow afternoon and I need to tighten things up in the morning." Reaching inside his suit jacket, he retrieved a small, gold case. Opening it, an ornate business card was taken out. Devon read the card, *Cary Glass*.

"Call me." Cary extended his hand and the two exchanged a few additional departing pleasantries.

Devon decided to have one last drink before leaving. After two sips, he realized he was in the sights of the peanutty-toned beauty who had flirted with him earlier that evening. She moved in slowly, allowing her form fitting dress to begin its hypnotic spell on the men she passed. Devon gave her body a very indiscrete appraisal. Sashaying to his side, she spoke in a low, intoxicating tone.

"I've been watching you all night and here we are…at the end." Without having to look, Devon could sense the moistness of her lips. "Are you capable of giving me a ride tonight?" Devon wasn't fooled by the play on words. He took his time to finish his drink before responding, knowing she wasn't going anywhere-- alone. The eyes of the men in close proximity were on Devon; Eyes of admiration, eyes of jealously, waiting to see how he handled the situation. Devon was cognizant of the public review.

"A lovely like you wouldn't come to a function like this without her *own ride*." Peanutty smiled, bringing her face close to Devon's ear. She lightly licked him as she spoke.

"Here's my phone number and address…" She scribbled her digits and her name on a bar napkin. "I'm going to go get my car…I'm on the second level. My place isn't far from here. I know you won't have a hard time keeping up with me." With that she turned, allowing her bulbous rear to accent her comments, which took the breath away of the remaining men. "I'll take it slow and easy for you." She murmured her comment without turning back to Devon. A collective exhale took place followed by a series of *dammmnnnnns!* One man walked past and patted Devon on the shoulder.

"That's money in the bank right there, playboy!"

Stepping out into the cool evening, Devon had the feeling. It came on strong and needed to be satisfied. He reached into his pocket for his keys and felt the napkin. Retrieving it, he looked at the name--*Desire T.* He didn't know if that was her real name but it didn't matter. He had a taste for something new. Something was definitely tempting his sensual palate. He walked to his car. As he passed a trashcan, he tossed the napkin in.

TWO STEPPIN'

THE LINE EXTENDED INTO the hallway and down toward the receiving dock. Having a guest chef in the building's cafeteria was always an appetizing delight but a bane for those who had to return to their desks within the hour. The monthly culinary special was a combination of pain and pleasure for the employees of One Liberty Place. The flavorful smells of Beef Wellington surrounded Ellis's nostrils; the line to the dining room deadened his senses. He worked his way past the deadpan faces and made it to the main door. Just outside on the sidewalk was a young woman he recognized from the floor below. She was talking loudly into the lobby phone.

"You just met him and he's over for some afternoon delight?...You too much Twist...I heard that...I guess I'm having lunch alone."

Ellis had seen her on a number of occasions, stepping into the elevator, waiting in the common areas, on their way in, and each time there was something about her that caused him to gaze at the whole of her. He had not spoken to her--until now.

"Can you think of anywhere else to eat besides the Gallery?" Ellis could not believe that he had said something. Not once in all the years he was with Clarissa had he ever considered lunch with a different woman other than for business, but today, this moment, he was suddenly unleashed. The woman turned her attention to Ellis, paused a moment before returning her attention to the phone.

"Enjoy your lunch Twist. I'll get back."

"I'm sorry for interrupting your phone call..."

"No problem...I was just saying..."

"I was just wondering...with the crowd inside..."

"Yeah, the line is too long for what little..."

"I was just thinking…I'm sorry…I interrupted…"

"No, it's cool. I was just talking…"

Seconds turned to moments as the two stood there, catching each other's pupils. Suddenly, both lost the pangs for lunch but their hunger grew for getting to know each other. Ellis extended his hand.

"My name is Ellis…Ellis." Her hand glided easily into his. It was then Ellis finally heard what he had secretly desired for some time.

"I'm Sylvania…I know…you don't have to say it…

"Say what?"

"Something about my name…"

"It's a very nice name…unforgettable."

Sylvania was taken aback. Most of the men she encountered either raised an eyebrow or cracked a snide remark in reference with her name--if not just mispronounce it all together.

"Sylvania? Hmm. Let's see how your whole name fits together." Ellis smiled gently as he waited.

"Fits together huh? Okay, how's this? Sylvania Marcel Lee." For some reason, Sylvania knew that Ellis would find something exceptionally pleasant about her name.

"Whoever named you was a poet. I think all names should have a rhythm…a natural flow." He repeated her name, almost singing it. It was as if Sylvania was hearing her name for the first time--and it did sound beautiful.

Neither knew who made the first move but soon they were walking down Market Street talking about their names.

Their lunch was simple. A non-descript deli for sandwiches and coffee. Sylvania, for the first time in a long time, felt at ease. She didn't suspect that this man Ellis was out for an easy lay. Her *spider sense* was usually jumping at this point but today her whole body was calm yet excited. Here she was, with a very handsome professional black man, eating a grilled chicken salad, and talking about her favorite movies. Most of the men Sylvania ever dated slobbered conversations that centered on sex. *What's your favorite slow jam? Ever watch a porno movie? Yo baby, ever tried raw oysters?* Sylvania thought that one was a joke because most of the brothers she knew would never eat raw oysters. They liked their food cooked.

"I'm going to have to go old school on you and say...Claudine...with James Earl Jones and Diane Carroll," offered Ellis.

"Claudine?" Sylvania almost choked on her soda. "Where did you see that...the Smithsonian?" Ellis squinted as he bit into his pastrami on rye.

"What's so funny? That was a good movie."

"How about one from this millennium? Like Boomerang with Eddie and Halle.

"I give you that. Boomerang was pretty good." Ellis wiped a dot of mustard from his lip, "But if you ask me...I never thought that Eddie should have ended up with Halle. His character didn't deserve her. The other guy should have gotten with Halle. You know, the friend...not Martin but the other guy. I can't remember his name."

"I can see that. Okay, hit me with another one...and it has to be in color and a talkie." Sylvania beamed as she responded to her own humor.

"I'm old but not that old. Okay, try this one...and don't say anything." Ellis took a quick sip of his coffee. "Let's make this a little more interesting. Here's a line from the movie. Let's see if you can guess it." Ellis strained his voice to raise an octave. *"Wait! That's not Lake Minnetonka!"*

For a moment it was quiet--which was soon cut by a sudden rise in frenetic laughter. Sylvania reached out and slapped Ellis's hand playfully.

"You didn't just do that! That's the worst Prince imitation I've ever heard." They talked a while longer before realizing the deli had almost cleared out. "I don't know about you but I have to get back to my desk." Sylvania rose, putting her money on the table. Ellis motioned for her to take her money back as he tried to finish his coffee. Sylvania counter-motioned and her money stayed on the table. Ellis nodded and added his funds to the pile. Their pace was quick as they headed back to their building.

The two continued their pleasant conversation as they walked down Arch Street. Passing an alleyway, a disheveled young man appeared. He was seated on the ground, leaning slightly against a dumpster, wrapped in a worn blanket; his hand extended an empty drink cup in their direction.

"Spare change?" His voice was low and gravely. His bloodshot eyes and stench of cheap liquor put the both of them on alert. For Sylvania, he represented the customers she used to have to call the police on almost every evening. For Ellis, he represented the person many of his friends of his neighborhood turned into. For both of them, he was someone they wanted to avoid.

Ellis slowly moved between the man and Sylvania. He paused and checked his pockets. He didn't have any cash left, just plastic. Sylvania continued on down the street.

"Hey!" The man shouted after the two. "Hey! Let me tell y'all something! I know it's nice to be important...but it's important to be nice." The man's words sunk deep into Sylvania's core, severing the nerve that held her patience. Without speaking, she made a tight arc and walked back to the man. Ellis stopped and quickly caught up to her, not knowing what she was going to do. He could see in her face that she wasn't returning to offer some *spare change.*

Sylvania stood within breathing length of the man. "Let me tell you something…if you can look up…you can get up!" Without a second breath, Sylvania was moving back up the street. Ellis paused for a moment and gave the man the look of, *what can I say?* Seconds later he was by Sylvania's side.

"Shoot! Let me make sure I don't piss you off!" Sylvania stopped and Ellis could tell she was shaken.

"I'm sorry. I shouldn't have gone off on him like that. It's just that where I live there are a lot of brothers with potential who just think school is corny, work is lame, and getting' high is all they need to do. Then one day they wake up and they're bummin' for change. I'm not trying to preach but when I see brothers like him, I just say to myself…what are you gonna do? Hell…what am I gonna do? If I could do more for him, I would. To keep it real…I'm still working on myself."

Ellis didn't interrupt. He could hear in her voice the paradox of truth. She wanted the best for her fellow man but knew that there was very little she could do for him. They walked the last block, bringing their conversation back to the two of them. Rounding the corner, they had returned to One Liberty Place.

Reaching the elevator, Ellis depressed the button and motioned for Sylvania to get into the car when the doors opened.

"Aren't you going to get in too?" Ellis shook his head.

"I usually take the stairs after lunch."

"That's a lot of stairs."

"The steps don't bother me. Thanks for a pleasant lunch." Suddenly, Sylvania's hand kept the door from closing. She leaned out and smiled.

"Speaking of steps…do you know how to two-step?"

Entering his office area, Ellis passed by Winsome as she sorted the afternoon mail.

"Did you have a good lunch Mr. Parker?"

Ellis slowed but didn't stop. When he reached the doorway to his office, he turned.

"All things considered…today I had a great lunch." Winsome had never seen Ellis smile so broadly.

"That's good, Mr. Parker."

"You said it, Winsome." Ellis walked over to his window and removed his jacket. He scanned the panoramic view of the city. The clear blue sky was accented by lush greenery that reached beyond the rooftops of the homes in West Philadelphia. The beautiful architecture of the 30th Street Station shined, serving as a link between the past and the present. His eyes caught sight of the El train as it began to slice the landscape into two attractive halves. He allowed himself to absorb it all, trees and towers, stone and streets, movement and history. It had been a long time since he thought about what a beautiful city Philadelphia was.

A week passed and it was time for the quarter reports. Ellis finished revising the numbers and was confident the board members would be pleased with the growth of investments as per his recommendations. With the volatility of foreign markets, he had impressed upon them to focus on growth in American companies. It turned out that not only was that a good financial move, it made for easy promotions with the PR department. Patriotism was gold!

Ellis's thoughts were interrupted by the grating sandpaper of Hank's laughter. The reception area was an easy twenty feet from his door but that didn't matter. The cacophonic cackle of Hank was almost as irritating as his presence. Slowly, Ellis walked over to his office door, easing it closed. He knew why Hank was there-- *to strategize for the board meeting.* Translated, that meant he was fishing for a way to upstage Ellis and position himself for the vice presidential slot in LA. Not that Ellis was sure if he wanted the position for himself but for some reason this afternoon, he didn't feel like handing it to Hank. His phone rang. Once. Twice. Quiet. He was comforted that Winsome would understand that he was not to be disturbed. Not even the bosses, Mr. Morgan and Clarissa, were granted "stroll on in" access. The juvenile sounds of Hank drifted into nothingness. Winsome was his sentry, a true *no password-no entry* kind of person, providing him the premium of solitude; A solitude from Hank, from Clarissa, from the rest of the world. Solitude--not quite peace--but a healthy dose of solitude which was enough for him.

A light knock drew Ellis from his monitor. He couldn't believe it. Somehow Hank convinced Winsome to allow him in. Ellis hesitated but could faintly hear Winsome's cautious voice. The door opened.

"Mr. Parker? I'm sorry for the interruption."

"Yes?" Ellis's voice was low. If Hank was right behind her, he wanted a moment to gain some composure.

"Mr. Morris found his way in?"

Winsome scrunched her face. "Mr. Morris is long gone. You should know by now that if I tell somebody that you're busy, then you're busy! I don't care how important people are or how important they think they are--you're my number one priority!"

Ellis smiled an apology. "So what's up Winsome?"

"I shouldn't give it to you now...but here." Winsome handed Ellis a small envelope.

"What's this?" Winsome answered before he could look inside.

"Two tickets to the Tri-State True Stepper's Ball."

"You're reading my mail now?" Ellis chuckled as he inspected the tickets further.

"I read all of your mail. This was put on my desk while I was in the ladies' room." Ellis noticed Winsome was grinning a little more than usual.

"What?"

"I hope you're going to go. The TBL knows how to throw a function in the junction!"

"Well, I'll think about it. It will depend upon my schedule...besides they were probably dropped off by Hank." Ellis spied the waste basket.

"Listen Mr. Parker. First, you need to put your schedule on the back burner, get on the floor, and shake off some of your troubles. Second, who cares if Mr. Morris or the Tooth Fairy dropped the tickets off. They're yours now. Go on and enjoy!"

"I just don't want to be beholden to anyone."

"You're the one *be holding* the tickets." Winsome smiled as she left the room. Ellis closed the door and again was soon looking out at the city. The script on the tickets lent an air of sophistication...*sponsored by the Mondaine Madames of Tau Beta Lambda*. He knew of the organization but didn't know of any of the Mondaine Madames personally. As he reached for his jacket, he was still curious as to where the tickets came from.

Ellis thought about Winsome's words as he drove down the expressway. It wasn't until he reached Lincoln Drive that he began to consider attending. When he turned onto Greene Street he figured Clarissa would enjoy herself.

"Clarissa!...Hey babe!...What are you doing tomorrow night?" The house offered no signs of life. Ellis forgot it was the second Friday of the month. She was gone for the weekend.

SEDATIVE

SHE AWOKE TO THE numbing of her arm.

"Hmmph…get up! You on my arm!" Twist nudged the hulking body next to her. "Come on…" She couldn't remember his name. "Dude!" The man next to her rolled over, belching as his stomach flattened on the bed sheet.

"Wha'…" He raised his head slowly. "What time is it baby?"

Twist knew that the only place he had to go was home to his live-in. As she rolled her eyes the rest of her head followed and faced the clock.

"It's almost six." She felt the heaving of his body move against her buttocks.

"Lemme get a little…for the road." He reached over with one hand to grope Twist's tender breasts, pushing the other between her legs. "This'll get you nice and wet." Twist ambivalently surrendered. She didn't have any plans. The weight of his body rose and pressed for forty-five seconds, concluding with a long huff.

"Damn baby, that'll keep a smile on my face awwlll day!"
It was a blur. His clothes were on just as the door closed behind him. In the quiet echo of her apartment, Twist rose slowly from the bed and made her way to the shower. She needed to wash the funk of what's-his-name off of her body.

Later that afternoon, Twist found herself sitting at the small table in her living room. In her hand was a small, crinkled card. Even after reading the card for an eleventh time the message didn't change; *doctor's appointment the next day.* Pulling her robe closer around her body, she laid the card face down and reached behind her to the shelf containing a row of assorted liquors. Without really looking, she grabbed the half-filled bottle of strawberry Cisco. Three tumblers passed her lips before she looked at the appointment card again. She could feel the liquid pacifier taking effect. She smiled. She knew she would miss the appointment in the morning. She missed all of her appointments this way. Whatever the doctor had to say to her would just have to wait until she had the strength to hear it. For now, the only thing she wanted to hear was the filling of her glass.

It was next day noon when she opened her eyes. Slowly raising herself from the floor, Twist felt the appointment card in her hand, which she began to crumple.

"Lord...!" She called out, "I'm not dead yet! My ass is still here!" Her eyes began to water at the same time her stomach sought relief. "I'm still he....." She slumped back down onto the floor, into the pool of vomit. A sad smile was on her face. "I'm still here."

It was four in the afternoon when she opened her eyes again. She felt her sticky body fluids under her arm and in her hair. She could also feel that her robe was wet around her crotch. Unfazed, as this was not the first time, she rose to bathe. The remainder of the afternoon was spent cleaning herself, her floor, and fixing a light dinner. As the evening sun disappeared into the hills of East Falls, Twist felt a depression rising as her hangover subsided. What would make her feel better? She knew what she had to do. She picked up the phone.

"What up?" The gruff voice on the phone sounded preoccupied.

"Hey Caddy, what you up to?" She held her breath.

"Nothin'. What you want?" There was a long pause. She wanted some soft talk. Some romance. Someone to tell her that she was desired. Someone to tell her that she would be alright. Someone to make her feel safe. That's what she wanted but she knew better.

"Some good dick."

That's all she was getting -- and that was enough.

TETE-A-TETE

SOUNDS OF SMOOTH JAZZ station WRTI surrounded Devon as he drove to Chestnut Hill. His new Seabring moved easily down the potholed Germantown Avenue. It was four o'clock on a Saturday afternoon. The weather was balmy enough to put the top down but Devon didn't trust to do that in Philadelphia, even if he was at the edge of the city. The vibration of his phone tickled his chest. Devon knew who was calling but there was no need to answer. The restaurant parking lot was on his left.

It was his first time to Cin-Cin. He thought it to be a nice recommendation for a late afternoon lunch as he favored the out of the way restaurants. A young Asian lady met Devon as he entered. She checked his name off the reservation list.

"Right this way, sir," the young lady motioned. "Your guest is already here." Devon took a deep breath and followed the young lady to a secluded booth on the far side of the restaurant. Straightening his tie, Devon reached the table and placed his hand on the shoulder of the person already seated.

"How are you Cary?"
Before standing, Cary smoothed his moustache and took a quick sip of his water. Once face to face, they shook hands firmly. Devon continued to look around before focusing his attention on the restaurant.

"This is a fantastic place. I've driven through Chestnut Hill hundreds of time but I never knew this was here." Devon smiled as he took his seat. Cary pointed to highlight interesting pieces in the restaurant as he spoke. "It's a nice fusion of Asian and French cuisine. I'm glad I could introduce it to you." The waitress arrived.

Cary perused the drinks menu carefully.
"I'll have a Shanghi screwdriver... and my friend..."

"I need something sweet…what do you recommend?" Cary winked at Devon then returned his attention to the waitress. "He'll have a hibiscus bliss." The two sat back as the waitress walked away.

"So…you doing alright?" Devon started the conversation. His finger slowly circled the rim of his water glass.

"I've been fine…oh…before I forget," Cary reached down under his chair. "As promised, here are the spec sheets of the properties acquired by my firm. You should find them very beneficial." Their conversation centered on additional mutual opportunities for their businesses. For Devon, what intrigued him more was the fitted shirt that Cary was wearing. He shook his head to refocus on the business possibilities but soon the smell of Cary's cologne wrapped around his nose, teasing his senses.

"You seem preoccupied." Cary's words were more statement than inquiry. Devon returned his mind to the conversation and he felt it was time to change the subject.

"So", Devon began as he sipped his drink. "You from the city?" The conversation flowed along the surface as the waitress returned for their orders. Cary leaned forward.

"Order for me Dev."

Devon scanned the menu quickly. His cheekbones lifted to reveal an attractive smile. He pondered a moment then addressed the waitress.

"Good…I'll have the crab cakes and my friend will have the Peking Duck salad. We'll start with the shrimp and water chestnut appetizer." The waitress jotted down their order and disappeared. They continued on about school, work, and travel until the smells of their lunch interrupted their conversation.

"How's your salad?"

There was a long pause before Cary responded.

"You do a lot of round the block talking Dev. Why don't you ask me what you really want to know?"
Devon stopped chewing the small piece of crab cake and swallowed hard.

"What are you talking about?"

"You're too smart, too insightful…and too cute to play coy." Cary returned to his salad. "Business is business but we could have accomplished this via courier and phone." Devon shifted uncomfortably in his chair, sipping his water thoughtfully.

"Sometimes we out-slick ourselves." Cary reached across the table, taking Devon's hand. Devon wasn't sure of how he was feeling in the moment. There was fear but at the same time comfort. It was as if a veiled part of his being was now exposed-- minus the guilt and shame. In that brief moment, he felt at peace. He relaxed. Cary's long fingers trailed gently across Devon's fore and middle fingers. The sensation moved from his hand, up his arm, down his spine, and straight to his midsection--causing him to shift in his seat. Looking past the delicacies of the table, he began to gaze into Cary's soft brown eyes--until a familiar voice took over his consciousness: it was Hank. Devon quickly pulled his hand away.

Cin-Cin's parking lot sat off from Germantown Avenue. Devon felt a bit more comfortable as they left the restaurant. Cary leaned against the Seabring. He was quietly taking in all of Devon. It was apparent to Devon that Cary was comfortable and confident--knew exactly who he was and what he liked. He didn't say a word when Devon withdrew his hand, retreating from Cary's affection. Devon was convinced that he wasn't Cary's first pursuit. He was now feeling uneasy and confused.

"Look Dev. I'm sorry for pushing up on you like that? I just thought…well, I just thought."

The only thought that ran through Devon's mind was for Cary to step away from his car and let him roll out.

"No biggie," lied Devon. "I'm somewhat flattered. It feels good to be appreciated." Moving toward the car door, Cary picked up on the hint that Devon wanted to get out of there.

"Hey, no hard feelings, okay Dev?" Cary extended his hand. Devon felt that in order to get on the road, he should at least be cordial. He clasped Cary's hand. In the next instant, the two were face to face. So close that Devon could feel Cary's warm breath on his cheek. "All I want you to do…," whispered Cary, "…is to be yourself. Not what your family wants you to be. Not what your friends want you to be…or any domineering co-workers." With that, Cary picked himself up from off the car and walked away. Devon jumped into his car, driving quickly into traffic.

"What was he thinking?" Devon began cussing Cary out in his mind. Reaching a stoplight, Devon began rubbing his eyes. Slowly he brought his hand down to his nose--it was there he stopped. He took a deep breath. Cary's cologne was in his hand. He inhaled deeply. It seemed like an eternity until the bus behind him blasted its horn. Devon pulled over and reached inside his jacket, retrieving his cell phone. He dialed.

"Hello?" The voice on the other end sounded both relieved and happy.

"I don't know why I'm calling you." Devon's phone was slipping in his now sweaty palm.

"You might not know why…but I knew you would."

FEEL THE BEAT

MRS. PARKER OPENED HER front door. Ellis stood in the doorway. Leaning in, he kissed her softly on the cheek but his mother quickly hugged tight her youngest son.

"Why didn't you just use your key? Making me miss my show." Their chatter was whimsical as Ellis followed his mother into the kitchen. Finding a seat at the table, he looked about the kitchen of his youth. The room almost looked exactly the same as when he left home. There were a couple of new appliances, microwave, and a new phone but the Formica floor, the cabinets, the lighting, and curtains seemed to have avoided the passing winds of change. His father had promised to renovate the kitchen but time, alcohol, and depression made for other priorities.

"You look nice. What brings you by? And where's what's her name?" Mrs. Parker poured a cup of coffee, offering it to Ellis.

"No thank you…and her name is Clarissa Mom. I don't know why you don't like her. All she does is try to fit in."

"Well, she's trying too hard. If she would just be herself…a simple white girl…I could deal with that but she comes off like she grew up right here on this block. I don't even like the way the home girls act around here so you know I can't handle an import."

Ellis put his head down on the table.

"So what did you come over for? It's already past dinner. Your girlfriend isn't with you so she didn't make you visit. So what's happening?"

Ellis picked his head up and began to play with the plastic fruit in the basket on the table.

"I received two tickets to the Tri-State Steppers Ball. I don't know if I should go."

Mrs. Parker sipped her coffee.

"You mean to tell me that a college graduate with an MBA, who lives in one of the nicer sections of the city, who works downtown in one of the fanciest buildings for one of the best companies, and drives some collector's car can't make a decision on whether to go to a dance or not? Your brothers might not make the right decisions for their lives but they all could solve this one."

A bubble full of funny slowly rose from his belly to his throat to his mouth. His mother joined in.

"No…what I'm asking is do you think it's appropriate for me to attend the dance without Clarissa?"

"Do you think it's appropriate to have her all laid up in your house without being married…or having a real job?"

"Touché! Let's not get into that. I'm just asking…."

"Well, where is she? What does she say?"

"She's not home. She has been taking off every month or so to visit a friend. I don't put any pressure on her because when she comes back she's in a better mood…for a while."

"And you allow that?"

"She says it's a girlfriend of hers…besides…I don't run her. She has her life…"

Mrs. Parker moved her chair closer to her son. Reaching out, she took his hand from off of the plastic apple and held it.

"Elliston. Listen to me. I'm not going to be some old meddling mother but let me just say this. You have been so responsible since you were a small child. More responsible than we should have expected…but with your father's problems…your brother's nonsense…you were the steady and consistent person in the family. You're a good man…a good person…that's why I get like I do with Clarissa. She's alright…a little annoying…but I admit she has a good heart. All I'm saying is that you have missed out on a lot of life. You don't take vacations. You don't treat yourself to nice things. You do what Clarissa wants even when you don't want to do them. You have a pretty good life but you're living just a little. You should be living a whole lot more. Especially with her running off doing her thing...you should go and do yours. I'm not saying disrespect her but it's just a dance."

The two talked a little more and by 8:30, Ellis was standing in the doorway giving a goodbye kiss to his mother. As he walked down the steps, he heard her voice but didn't respond.

"I will tell you this. If your daddy was going out of town to meet up with his "friend" I can guarantee I would be at the Tower Theater trying to meet Marvin Gaye."

The traffic was moving briskly on 95 South into Wilmington. Thinking, Ellis realized that he had only really visited Wilmington about three times in his life; once for a wedding, another for a graduation, and for the funeral of a former Druer board member. He eased onto King Street and continued south. Following the numbers, he began looking for a parking space. Without Clarissa, he knew he could find a spot on the street and not have to pay a valet. He spied one on the opposite side of the street. He weaved past a bakery truck and secured the spot.

The lobby of the ballroom was a blinding splash of color and style. Leaning against a wall was a man in a bright red, Chinese-collard suit. The woman he was whispering to toyed with the four pair of gold buttons that served as the pathway to his pleated pants and fire engine red Stacy Adams. Across the hallway sat another with an unlit cigar held gently in his teeth. His eyes were hidden underneath the oversized brim of his hat, which was of the same design and material as his classic Zoot Suit. Many of the couples matched their outfits from head to toe. Ellis had to smile when the man in the lime green suit escorted in the woman in the bright yellow dress. There were plenty of hugs, hand-slapping, cheek-kissing, posing, and posturing. One thing for sure, if there was a place to have a good time, this was the place and these were the people.

Ellis approached the reception table. Two well-dressed women were seated, taking tickets and stamping hands. He handed them his ticket. The older of the two women motioned to Ellis and stamped the back of his hand with the scripted *TBL*.

"Here's your ticket for the door prizes. We'll be drawing later on this evening," spoke the younger one.

"But you have to be present to win!" The older woman instructed without looking at Ellis. To the contrary, the younger woman was looking at Ellis and liked what she saw.

"I'll tell you this Marjorie, he'll be here for the prizes." Ellis just smiled. He began to walk into the dance but whirled around and backtracked to the table.

"Oh yes, I have an extra ticket here." He handed it to the younger woman. "Perhaps someone may need it."

"Who sold the ticket to you?" She was curious.
Ellis smiled.

"They were a mystery gift. I really don't know."

"Oh that's so nice." The younger woman grinned,

"Well…have a good time."

As soon as Ellis was out of earshot, Marjorie opened the ticket receipt book.

"What's the number on the ticket Renee?"

"His was 216."

Marjorie moved her finger down the list of ticket numbers in her book. "It looks like those tickets were sold by Willy Lee. I wonder what she's up to?" Renee's eyes followed Ellis until he disappeared into the ballroom.

"I don't know about all that..." Renee stood, lightly touching her hooped earrings, "...but I'm going on break."

Marjorie didn't blink. "You better sit your butt back down and keep collecting tickets. Like you said, he'll be here."

The River's Edge Ballroom had been transformed from an empty shell to an impressive array of decorations, twin mirrored balls, and tables filled with sophisticated people of varied ages and dress. It slowly became clear that the Mondaine Madames of Tau Beta Lambda were serious about their social events. The live band was preparing to go on while the DJ finished his mood setting music, keeping the true steppers on the floor. Ellis was tickled by an older couple who commanded the parquet. The man, looking to be in his 60s donned a fedora and a three-quarter length pin-striped gold suit set with matching shoes. His lady, around the same age, was his feminine mirror image. In her hair was a gold flower that also matched her dress. The two twirled, dipped, and stepped in and out to the music. When the music finally ended, the room erupted into thunderous applause as the two of them took bows, making their way back to their table. Accolades and acknowledgements continued. Ellis reflected back to his mother's words, *they were living!*

A passing waitress offered Ellis a glass of complimentary Champagne, which he refused.

"Do you have any Ginger Ale?" She referred him to the bar. There he secured his drink and continued surveying the crowd. He watched an elegant, silver-haired woman approach the front and with a single wave of her hand dropped the music to a lull. As if on cue, a younger man appeared by her side to escort her onto the stage. A hush fell over the ballroom.

"Good evening", she began. Her pacing and diction was clear and deliberate. "I AM Madame Evelyn Carter McCloud,

Grand Empressio of the Mondaine Madames of Tau...Beta...Lambda...Tri-state chapters." An ear-piercing squeal rose, was held, and dropped off sharply from the many members of TBL. "I would like to thank everyone for joining us this evening. You all look so beautiful and I want you to know that so far this evening we raised ten-thousand-seventy eight dollars for the Elmwood Girls Club, but I know that by the end of the night we will do much, much better. Remember, this is our special charity and we must let everyone know that the T-B-L serves the community oh-so-well!" The crowd acknowledged her statement with applause. "Now, I'm not going to talk long because the Tri-State *True* Steppers Ball is why you are all here..." With that proclamation, Mrs. Carter-McCloud proceeded to talk for another ten minutes on the virtues of the TBL, their work in the community, and how elegant she and her executive board looked. She summed up her comments: "...So I have said enough. What we like to do now is to make sure people feel comfortable on the dance floor...so I would like to call Madame Catherine Thompson-Worthy and her husband, Dr. Ronald Worthy, to offer some beginner steps for those who may not know how...please enjoy!"

The band leader turned to the audience and announced the next set would be dedicated to those who were novices at two-stepping. The two gold-suited dance instructors took to the stage. As the music rose, couples, both eagerly and timidly, found a spot in front and slowly went through the basics of Chicago-style stepping. Being unsure of himself, and not having a partner, Ellis simply nursed his soda and moved back onto the wall. About the third round of instructions, a sudden and soft voice broke his thoughts.

"If you can scope it out, you can turn it out!"

Ellis turned to find Sylvania approaching. Whatever he might have remembered of her from their lunch was paled by her beauty this evening. Ellis found himself comparing her looks. At the office, she had the required presentation: simple pantsuits, white blouses, and neat hair. Thinking back, he may have seen her once or twice before their lunch encounter. She might have had the same outfit on, at least that what he thought, but tonight, she was someone new. He noticed her eyes. They sparkled with each glimmer of the mirrored ball, clear and inviting. His attention was then drawn to her whole face. Her smile brought a charm to her entire presence. Now he noticed--really noticed her hair. Though he was used to long blonde curls, tonight he marveled at her short, highlighted, razor cut which emphasized her facial features delightfully. Her beauty was right there and that's where he stopped.

"Sylvania," Her name tasted good flowing across his tongue. "You must be the steppers ball ticket fairy. Thank you." He extended his hand to shake but Sylvania offered a warm embrace.

"I thought you would like them...so...why aren't you out there?"
Ellis rubbed his chin, thinking of his awkwardness.

"I guess because I don't know how...besides...take a look at me...I don't exactly fit in." Sylvania put her hands on her hips as she sized Ellis up.

"What are you talking about? You look very nice."

"That's what I'm talking about...just nice. Look at the men on the floor. That's style."

Sylvania agreed with his assessment.

"Let me tell you something Ellis. Most of the men out there are just like you...businessmen, lawyers, doctors, and whatnot. For them, this is dress-up. It's a chance for them to relax...put the job behind them...and be what they want to be...men enjoying the evening with their women. You want that too...don't you?" Sylvania turned and looked out on the dance floor. The lessons had come to a close.

Ellis wasn't sure of what to say. The band struck up their rendition of James Brown's *The Boss*. The opening lead guitar licks released the floodgate and couples swarmed the floor.

"Well, you can't do it by holding up the wall. I'm sure there's a beam or a nail taking care of that." Sylvania grabbed him by the arm and guided him toward the crowded dance floor. Ellis knew it was useless to argue and soon the two were standing on the outskirts of the raised parquet floor. "So...you ready?" Sylvania began swaying to the music, preparing to launch into her steps.

"I'm sorry...really...you're going to have to show me how to do this." Sylvania paused. She could see that Ellis was nervous.

"Let me show you...it's easy." Sylvania stood next to Ellis and eased her hand around his waist. "Now, it's easy. Watch me. First, with your left foot, take a step." Ellis was nervous but was determined to try. "Next, bring your right foot up next to your left...now, slide your left foot back...(*watch me*)." Ellis asked to start over but Sylvania was determined to turn this man into a stepper. "Here comes the only tricky part...bring your right foot over and then step back and cha-cha for the next two beats...that's the basics."
Sylvania worked with Ellis for the entire song but as far as Ellis was concerned, he might as well as been playing Twister. The next song offered promise, the band whipped up the Electric Slide. Ellis' confidence returned. Soon he and Sylvania were in the center of the room, clapping, celebrating, and acknowledging their ever changing side partners. It was appropriate this event was called a ball--because Ellis was having one.

After two more slide-style dances, the two found a seat toward the back of the ballroom. Ellis waved over the server.

"What would you like Sylvania?" Before she could answer, a whirlwind reached their table.

"She'll have a White Russian...just like me...you can handle it, can't you?"

"Twist!" Sylvania took one hand and shielded her eyes with exaggerated embarrassment. "Ellis, this is my best friend Darlene...but we call her Twist." Ellis rose up from his seat and extended his hand. Twist took his hand and flipped her hair back.

"Check him out Syl...this one has a little class...standing for a lady an' do."

"You should always expect more." Ellis returned to his seat. When the server arrived he ordered drinks for Sylvania and Twist. For himself, this time he requested a ginger ale and orange juice.

"Slow down money," joked Twist. "Remember, you're driving." Ellis didn't mind her teasing. He was already feeling good and a little silly talk wasn't hurting anything. "Hey Syl...I saw y'all from across the room but I was too busy with this guy from Cherry Hill. He was a little stuck on himself but still gets points on the cute factor...told him to call me and I'll see if I answer." Twist dominated the rest of the conversation. With each drink, Twist's voice found the competition with the band to be less and less. Three drinks later, she began to bring others into her rants. Sylvania tried to calm her down but that only caused her to become more animated. This attracted the attention of some of the older women of the TBL.

The mood of the ballroom shifted from fast and funky to a slow rhythmic tempo. The lights, timed just right, fell just enough for couples to find their way either back to their tables or into each other's arms. Ellis noticed Sylvania had become quiet. If Twist was still talking, he didn't know. He was tuned into Sylvania's quietness. She was looking off in the direction of the dance floor but at nothing in particular. He watched her head and shoulders find the heartbeat of the music. Through the dimness of the room, he could see the fullness of Sylvania's beauty. Their conversation had revealed her inner spirit and intellect but now, the faintness of light unveiled the completeness of her womanhood. He gazed at her, soaking up her features; marveling at her stature--her legs, her arms. He watched her breathe as if he was introduced to a new idea. He wanted to ask her to dance. Twist had left the table and was on the floor with a similarly drunk young man. Ellis could hear in his heart to go for it, to hold her for a moment, to indulge his senses in her scent, in her aura.

"Sylvania!"

The voice did not belong to Ellis. Their heads turned in unison to see Wilhelmina Lee and Mrs. Carter-McCloud standing at their table.

"Sylvania...may we talk with you for a moment?" Sylvania's mother's voice was reserved, not wanting to attract any additional attention. That was Mrs. Carter-McCloud's job.

"Look at your friend on the dance floor...damn near having relations...in front of all of our guests...how vulgar!" Sylvania and Ellis's attention was bee-lined to Twist. Mrs. Carter-McCloud was right. Twist was certainly packing it in on the floor and didn't care who was watching.

"This is a classy affair and we're not going to have it soiled by some Fox Street trollop. Willy...have your daughter get her friend." Ellis could feel the air in the area tightening up.

"I could go get your girlfriend while you talk with your mother." Ellis appeared at Sylvania's side. "Mrs. Lee? My name is Elliston Parker...and you have a lovely daughter...now...excuse me." Looking quickly, Ellis spied Twist now dancing alone off to the side. Before Mrs. Lee could respond, Ellis was gone.

"I have to go to the front for the door prize drawings," began Mrs. Carter-McCloud. "So I expect you to take care of your daughter and her...ass-sociate." Without waiting for a response from either woman, Mrs. Carter-McCloud stormed off, crossing the dance floor to an awaiting group of elderly women who quickly surrounded her.

"I told you not to invite Darlene," began Mrs. Lee in a measured tone. "You know I love her but this isn't the place for her...especially since you know I'm being reviewed."

"She's not the only one lit up here tonight Mom...look around." Sylvania took a deep breath. She didn't want to fight, not this night. It was going so well and looked to have the potential to take an even better turn. "I didn't want to come to this thing anyway. I don't like the way they treat you...especially that *mad Cow-ter-Mc-Cloud.*" Mrs. Lee hushed her daughter as she looked around frantically; making sure no one heard.

"Look, they're starting the drawings. When this is done, we'll all go." Mrs. Lee slowly regained her composure and smoothed her hands down the sides of her dress.

"I came with Twist." Mrs. Lee took a deep breath. There was a quiver in her voice.

"Sylvania! Please! This is important to me. This is all I have. So please...let me have it." As she turned toward the crowd, a manufactured smile formed on her face and with her head held high, she moved toward the drawing table positioned at the front of the ballroom.

Sylvania took a seat in the closest chair. She knew how much this meant to her mother. She knew of the sacrifices her mother made since the days with her father. She never complained, not when things broke, not when money was tight, not even when their car was repossessed. If she ever felt frustrated, she never verbalized it. If there was one thing she knew about her mother it was that she had a reservoir of strength that helped her face all manner of adversities. Sylvania finally recognized that her mother's desire to ascend the ranks of the TBL required her support. Another thought crossed her mind. If her mother became the next Grand Empressio, perhaps she would finally gain the dignity and respect amongst the membership.

Sylvania's train of thought was derailed by shouts and applause. She started hearing the numbers being called. She stood to see her mother holding up a large ornate basket--and cringed at the grating voice of Mrs. Carter-McCloud.

"...this next basket was donated by the law offices of Reynolds, Rankin, and Bell. As you know Madam Lavinia Mayer-Bell is the wife of Curtis Bell...he's a divorce attorney...I have his card ladies." *Pretentious laughter.* "This basket is overflowing with goodness. It contains a flavor wheel of English cheddar, assorted seasonal fruit, a stick of summer sausage, honey-mustard to dip the specialty pretzels, a bag of chocolate covered raisins, and a pint-sized bottle of sparkling cider." After the ceremonial *oohs* and *aahs*, Mrs. Carter-McCloud lowered her hand into the basket and drew a stub. "The winner of this beautiful gift basket is 6-0-3-9-4-1." A flurry of heads scanned their tickets. A low murmur of deflation settled over the room which was soon broken by...

"AWWW YEAH BAY-BAY!" Heads turned to see Twist moving roughly through the crowd, dragging Ellis behind her. "Out my way y'all...the champ is here! I'm the winner, baby, I'm the winner!" As Twist approached the table, Sylvania could see Mrs. Carter-McCloud's face stiffen...as well as a sliver of glee appear on her mother's.

"Let me get my prize," continued Twist. "I ain't never won nothing! Thank you Jesus!" The crowd crowed broadly as Twist stepped to claim her basket.

"Let me see your ticket first," snapped Mrs. Carter-McCloud. "I have to validate it."

The drinks still had a hold on Twist.

"Sister, I don't care if you validate, violate, or discombobulate...I'm just here to gets mine." Twist handed Mrs. Carter-McCloud the ticket. She looked intently at the numbers. Mrs. Lee winked at Ellis who worked hard at keeping a straight face.

There are times in life when words flow like water. On this evening, they were like large globs of cooled fish grease as they rose from the throat to the lips of the Grand Empressio Evelyn Carter McCloud.

"We...have a winner." Ellis stepped forward and retrieved the basket from Mrs. Lee. Before he could turn, Twist thrust her hand through the decorative cellophane and grabbed an apple.

"This is right on time...a sister gots to get her grub on." *An explosion of laughter.* Twist bit hard into the apple. Mrs. Carter-McCloud moved away from the microphone and hissed discretely into Twist's ear.

"You are so uncouth in your presentation." Twist took another bite, chewed, and leaned back with words only for Mrs. Evelyn Carter-McCloud's ears.

"If you act right, I'll let you have the sausage...you'll know what to do with it." With that, she took Ellis by the arm and two-stepped her way across the dance floor toward the door, all to the beat of raucous laughter and applause.

Mrs. Lee stood impatiently in the lobby. She watched the exchange between Twist and her daughter but could not hear their conversation. That didn't matter; she was fluent in body language. She could read that Sylvania was pleading for Twist to leave but it was apparent that Twist had other plans--and that plan, a tall, lanky

El DeBarge-type who was just coming out of the men's room. He simply smiled and took a seat away from the two ladies. He wasn't worried, his night was set. The conversation between the two concluded.

"You ready mom?" Sylvania was putting on her coat. Her mother took a deep breath and held it. "Well? You're the one who wanted us to leave?"

"So is Darlene giving you a ride?" Mrs. Lee was clearly agitated. "If not, I'll take you but you know that means I'll have to drive halfway across the city."

"So what do you want me to do?" Sylvania huffed as she shifted from foot to foot. "You can see that plans have changed."

"I said I'll take you!"

"I don't want to put you out." Sylvania knew that if she took her mother's offer, it would be a long ride back to North Philadelphia, especially having to hear her mother point out everything that went wrong this evening. She weighed the option and the ride with her mother didn't seem worth it. Sylvania felt she didn't have any other choice.

"If you feel comfortable," a voice spoke up. "I could give you a ride home."

The two women turned to see Ellis slipping into his trench. With all that was going on between her, her mother, and Twist, Sylvania had forgotten all about him.

"Where do you live?" inquired Mrs. Lee. Ellis shared where he lived, what direction he would take, and that he expected that Sylvania would call once she arrived.

"I guess it's up to Sylvania...but I told her I would take her." Ellis turned to Sylvania, awaiting an answer. *Could this be it?* Sylvania's thoughts raced through her mind. *This guy...No!...this man seems to be the real thing...handsome...polite...respectful...handling his business...but...* The doubts began to creep in and backfill her thoughts. *Why would he come to a fancy event like this alone? Is this all an act? What would he see in a person like me? What if he's only after one thing? He hasn't acted like it...maybe I'm not his type...or anybody's.* Sylvania looked to her mother but received the *what-are-you-looking-at-me for-look.* She knew the decision was hers.

"Okay mom," she began. "You go on home. I'll ride with Ellis." Mrs. Lee gave Ellis one last long gaze.

"Thank you for coming. I'm sure you enjoyed yourself."

"I most certainly did! Thank you very much." Ellis shook her hand gently and escorted her to her car. Sylvania and Ellis waved her off and soon found themselves driving north on 95 toward the city.

The dead air rubbed Ellis like a dirty contact lens. He could see that Sylvania was still having the argument with her mother in her head. She sat, facing forward, arms folded tightly against her chest. Ellis never really understood the relationship daughters had with their mothers. He saw the same with Clarissa and her mom. Their love was full of fire for each other. One moment it was an argument--the next it was swapping recipes. One moment they couldn't stand each other--the next minute they had such a need for each other that no one else mattered. They could see each other and consider themselves perfect strangers but let a word pass and they become perfect reflections of one another. Ellis thought about his relationship with his mother. Never did he raise his voice, even when she was wrong. When she said how she wanted things to go, that's how they went. He revered her wisdom, her patience, and her love. He had her on a pedestal that only a son could construct. Perhaps that was the difference with daughters, they see themselves on the same pedestal--and there's not enough room. *Who knows?* He thought to himself. His father's words became very clear. Once, during his sophomore year in high school, he walked into the middle of one of his parent's arguments. His mother stormed out, leaving his father stewing in his easy chair. The two males locked eyes and after a couple of swigs from his longneck, his father said, "Don't spend your time trying to figure out a woman, go build a bridge or a skyscraper, it's easier!"

For Ellis, it was a strange twenty-two minutes. For once, the silence he normally favored made him uneasy. It wasn't until they passed through the town of Chester did Sylvania speak.

"Mind if I turn on the radio?"

Ellis nodded. He expected to hear some hip-hop or rap so he prepared to turn the volume down. To his pleasant surprise, Babyface's *Whip Appeal* filled the space within the car. Sylvania hummed softly along.

"So you like old school?" Ellis really felt his age, acknowledging his favorite music was now considered *old*.

"You might call it old, I call it *classic*." Sylvania adjusted her body in the seat so that she was turned slightly toward Ellis. He tried his best to keep the impression that his eyes were glued to the road but with each passing patch of light, he caught a glimpse of her legs, her chest, her lips, and her hands, drawn especially to her fingers which lightly tapped the head of the stick shift to the rise and fall of the rhythm.

"This is a beautiful car." Sylvania took in the entire vehicle. "You keep it very nice. I'm afraid to open this piece of candy." Ellis told her it was okay and opened the ashtray for her the wrapper. "Do you only use it for special occasions?"

"Not really...I only drive it to work when I know I'm working late or have errands to run. Normally I take the train in. The station is about six blocks from my house. I try to walk as much as I can."

"I try to exercise but not in my neighborhood. If you go for a run it's because someone is chasing you."

"I know what you mean. I grew up around 62nd and Pine Street. I did a lot of running when I first started high school. Usually my brothers…" Ellis' words were interrupted by a squeal.

"I'm sorry but this is the *cut*." Ellis recognized *Real Love* by Skyy. They both were quiet as they approached the city. Against the clear night sky, the Philadelphia skyline was a romantic series of colossal dominoes, dark and dotted, intimidating and inviting, shadowy and still. As the highway rose, the two of them were dancing a cerebral slow dance. Deep within their own spaces they were holding each other tightly, ensnared in personality and perplexity, curiosity and knowledge, desire and destiny. With each passing song, the two lightly chattered, only as a way to give their lips something to do other than what they truly longed for.

Before they knew it, Ellis was turning off the expressway onto Broad Street marking the end of their dance. Sylvania thought back to the time the she was given a ride by a past date. Just like now, she was close to her home and the 'gentleman' pulled over on Broad Street and told her that she could walk from there. *Didn't want to get lost on the side streets to her apartment.* Sylvania knew this when she hinted that *he wasn't going to get lost all up in her body.* Here she was; same street, same neighborhood, and same situation. She took a breath.

"When you get to Kerbaugh, make a right." It seemed like an eternity but she smiled when she hear the tic-toc of the turn signal. She weaved Ellis through the next couple of blocks to her apartment on Bott Street. Soon they were idling at her doorstep.

"Sylvania?" *Here it comes…the old-can-I-come-up-for-a-minute?* Sylvania weighed all of her options. *First things first…get out of the car.*

Ellis continued.

"I had a good time tonight. I'll wait here until you get inside." Sylvania held her surprise and calmly responded.

"I had a great time too. I'll probably see you on Monday…if you're getting a late lunch."
He gently patted her on the shoulder.

"You got it." With that, he exited the car, moved around to her side, prepared to open her door but she was already out. Sylvania wanted to give him a hug, perhaps give him a kiss. She even expected him to try to *steal a quick one.* The only thing to happen was that he watched her enter the apartment. Once all the way in, full of warmth and relief, she latched the door.

My lord!

LOOTED

MR. MORGAN PONDERED THE new information. The members of executive team were aware of the anxiety that draped the boardroom. His eyes were transfixed on the screen. There were many questions but no one dared break the surface tension established by Mr. Morgan. Standing in the front of the room, Ellis stood firm. He had presented his facts as realistically as possible. He was confident his information was correct but knew they would be hard to swallow. These were difficult times. One of Druer's fiercest competitors was thrust to the brink of bankruptcy by an up-and-coming company just six months before. Mr. Morgan knew the days of the giants were fast coming to a close. This was the time to seek out new ventures, new areas of growth, and new markets.

"Is that it?" Mr. Morgan's question reverberated through the room like the backfiring of a truck in a tunnel. Ellis slowly looked to his left and spied Hank shifting uncomfortably in his seat. He began to sense the next statement from Mr. Morgan and what it could mean for his own future. Hank could taste that same future as well and that hunger brought forth an internal Pavlovian reaction, a craving to receive the delicacies of Mr. Morgan's vision. A normally cool and calloused titan, Hank had the anxiousness of a child on the eve of Christmas. To the contrary, whatever was to come from the lips of Mr. Morgan wouldn't make much of a difference to Ellis. Whatever or wherever Ellis was to do his work that's where it would be done. In his heart, he wanted to hear that the numbers indicated a need to stay normative. He hoped there would be no need to grow, to move or branch out. Most of all, the word from Mr. Morgan would be all of the reasoning necessary to offer to Clarissa. She would argue against any of his decisions to the ends of the Earth but a simple--*that was Mr. Morgan's decision*--would end all conversation on the matter.

"Ellis...." All eyes moved to Mr. Morgan as he spoke. "You and Hank did an outstanding job presenting strategies for new directions for Druer. The time has come to build the next generation thanks to your supportive ideas and forecasts. Here's what I believe is our next move...."

"Cali? For true?" Clarissa came alive at the dinner table. Ellis tried to rein her in.

"Don't get too excited. Mr. Morgan said he wanted to make the move to California...but he didn't say when...or who." Ellis began to pick at his salad. He was hoping for a quiet dinner but he knew that wasn't possible once she asked how the meeting went. He thought she had forgotten all about it since they last spoke about it at Smith and Wollensky's. She did see him working on his report--those activities bored her. She liked TV screens and movie screens, not computer screens. The lure of the sunny beaches of LA were more than enough to keep this project on her mind.

"You need to tell that Mr. Morgan that if he wants things run right out there then you're the man to make it happen!" Clarissa held her baked chicken-speared fork in Ellis' direction. "And the salary has to match too. I'm not going out there so we end up living hundreds of miles from the ocean. We need to have a nice beach front place that's large enough to host some parties."

"What if he picks Hank? He's a contender." Clarissa stopped chewing.

"I can't believe you are even bringing up his name!" She quickly wiped her mouth with her napkin. "That stuck up poser! He got no game!"

"Mr. Morgan thinks so."

"Mr. Morgan thinks so," mimicked Clarissa. "You wanna know the reason why that Mr. Morgan is all up on Hank?--You! You have been propping up that punk since you met him. He's all talk and show. He ain't nuthin' but a front! If you left the company today, he'd be gone in three months...and that's counting the weekends."

Ellis stood and turned toward the kitchen sink. He wanted the running water and the clamor of the dishes to drown out her voice. It's not that she wasn't speaking the truth; he just didn't want to hear it and she knew this.

"Bust suds all you want black man but I'm gonna give it to you on the real!" Clarissa stood right next to him. "Good thing you're not wearing that watch I bought you because you would have ruined it messin' with those dishes when you should be messin' with those people at your job!" There was a drying cloth on the counter but she didn't touch it. "You let that fool advance on the sweat of your work. I don't know how you can go to work every day knowing that he can lay back in the cut and still succeed while you're up there busting your hump. I can't believe it. After all I have done to support you and build you up...I don't know why I put all this effort into you. You ain't changed since I first met you." Ellis looked up for a moment, only to have his eyes return to the suds he was *busting*. "Man, it's like you don't care. You don't care if you're recognized for you work. You don't care if you get used by that beefed-up buster. You don't care if you rise or fall...." Clarissa's words drifted into Ellis's psyche and soon buttressed against the deepest keystone memories.

-1986-

The flood of people leaving the City's mobile Office for Community Relations filled the intersection of 62nd and Pine.

Patrol cars equipped with antsy police officers moved slowly into position, expecting disorderly conduct from the unsatisfied residents. Billy clubs and teargas were in hands reach for many of the officers, ready to be used. The day was ruined for the police. The people congregated for about five minutes before dispersing on their own.

Following the fiery destruction of the homes on Osage Avenue, the City convened several meetings with the residents to discuss and outline the plan of action to restore them to their homes and compensation of their property. Already distrustful of "the system" there were too many questions for the city and too little answers for the residents. The meetings progressed over days and weeks with promises made by city officials--which turned into clichés of human comedy. *What we're going to do* turned into *what we would like to do* and finally into *what we can't do.*

Among those walking away from the meeting were Ellis and his father. Without speaking, they soon found themselves standing in front of their now boarded up store. With each breath pushed out by his father, Ellis could smell the strong stench of cheap alcohol. Not sure of what to say, Ellis asked the first thing that came to mind.

"So what did they mean by *ineligible?*" The question plummeted like the bomb which had dropped on the homes on Osage Avenue. Ellis knew he had ignited the powder keg of rage in his father. He watched the long fuse flicker, beginning with the rigidity in his father's posture. The fuse sparked and moved passed the tautness of his hands. Ellis watched the remaining piece of fuse contort the already angry face of his father.

"All that time you spend in those books and you don't know what the word *ineligible* means," spit Mr. Parker. "Well here's a lesson you ain't gonna get from this tired Philadelphia school system." Mr. Parker found a foot long stick and picked it up. Ellis felt his legs prepare to move until he saw his father turn his attention to the store's boarded window. Each statement was accented with a blow to the plywood on the door. "Ineligible means that because the store wasn't damaged by the police action, we don't get no help in fixing it up <*wham!*>. Ineligible means nobody cares that the big stores killed my business <*wham!*>. Ineligible means that I wasted my time trying to make something of myself <*wham!*>. Ineligible means that I'm just a broke, black man with nothin'! Nothin'! <*wham!*>. In between the swings and fury, Mr. Parker heard his son say that the family loved him. Breathing hard, he stopped swinging and looked to the sky. Mr. Parker's face moved from anger to shame to sadness to a white-hot anger. He looked deep into Ellis' presence and let loose his guttural proclamation. "Love made me think I could be somebody! That I could own something!" There was a loud crack as the stick splintered in his hand. "I wasted my time loving all of you...you...your ma...your brothers." Mr. Parker whirled around as if he was looking for something, grasping at a life that escaped him, reaching for a dream that refused him. Ellis tried to hold him but was thrown off. The *woop-woop* of the police cruiser returned reality to Ellis' consciousness. One police officer stood opposite Mr. Parker, his arm poised at his weapon. The other was on the radio calling for backup. Mr. Parker didn't see them. All he saw was the cinderblock that was once used as a chair outside of the store. Mr. Parker grabbed it. The officer's words warning him to put it down trailed off into nothingness. With his last ounce of life, Mr. Parker threw it at the store, causing a split in the door. The second set of police had arrived and soon three officers had Mr. Parker on the ground. They ignored Ellis' plea to take it easy on him. By the time he was put into the backseat of the cruiser, his face was swollen and bloodied. Before the door closed, Mr. Parker looked to his son and the emptiness of his being filled Ellis' understanding of manhood and life.

"Don't love nothin' or nobody."

-Present-

"I'm just wasting my breath talking to you!" Clarissa sat down in a huff. "You don't seem to care about nothing...forget it!" Ellis was now drying his hands with a paper towel. He looked at Clarissa. For the first time, he could hear the truth in her words. She was right about the many times he bit his tongue in executive sessions when his work was credited to Hank. He realized that he didn't speak up because he didn't respect his own worth. He was a man without value. It had nothing to do with Hank. Deep down, he knew Hank was all wind and smoke screen. Through all of the years he catalogued Hank's vulnerabilities but did nothing to exploit them.

"You know Clarissa," said Ellis as he pulled a chair close to the table. "I see what you're saying. I think I need to make some changes." Clarissa folded her arms tightly against her chest.

"I'll believe it when I see it...cause that's a whole lot of changing." With that, Clarissa whirled out of her chair and grabbed the phone from the cradle. She punched some numbers and waited. "Hey DeNeisha...whatcha doing tonight?...Want to go check out that new flick, *The Hurricane*?...yeah...the one with Denzel...I'll drive over and pick you up...in about forty-five....later." Clarissa put the phone down, gave Ellis one last look. She shook her head as she walked out of the kitchen. Always to have the last word. "Change? I dare ya!"

BRETHREN

ELLIS SCANNED THE DANISHES, pondering which to purchase. With Clarissa away for another weekend, he didn't feel much like cooking. Stopping at the Wawa Food Market, he decided to order a small Italian hoagie, just enough to hold him through the remainder of the day. He caught a glimpse of the baked goods and decided to treat himself. After hearing his order number called, he decided on the cherry.

"Eating like that's going to weigh you down." The voice was vaguely familiar. Ellis whirled around and looked the elderly gentleman in the face. It took a couple of seconds before memories completed the picture.

"Mr. Williams?...Mr. Williams!" Ellis put down the Danish and the two men offered each other a warm embrace. "Man Mr. Williams...it's been too many years."

Mr. Williams stepped back to admire Ellis. "You look great young man. What have you been doing with yourself?"

Normally, Ellis didn't speak on his accomplishments but being in the presence of the man who had helped shape his future, sharing his life history was very easy. Mr. Williams beamed as if Ellis' life journey had been his own. The conversation shifted to Mr. Williams. Long retired from the school system, he now resided in Bowie, Maryland. He was in town for a reunion with friends from his neighborhood and high school. The need for a pack of cigarettes initiated their chance meeting.

"So, how are your brothers?" Ellis was stymied. He hadn't thought this question would arise. It wasn't that he didn't know how his brothers were doing; he just didn't want to say. He wasn't ashamed; he was sad. It was a sadness he would now share with a man who believed in all of the boys from the neighborhood.

This was a man who acted in their best interests, ever seeking a positive future for all. He was also a man from the streets so he understood the weeding process society performs so well. Ellis wanted to avoid talking about his brothers but he owed this much to Mr. Williams. He wanted to shape a story of attempts at triumph but only the truth would form. The integrity of their lives had to be preserved, regardless of how misled their lives were. He opened his mouth and their life stories were shared, tarnished frames and all.

His brother Kenny was the one. As a young child, Kenny was the brother to look up to. He was strong, had a presence, but most importantly, he was fair. When the other brothers fought over toys, food, chores, or the television, it was Kenny who was the referee. No one could say he played favorites or forced his will for his own sake. He was also willing to sacrifice himself for his brothers. Ellis recalled once when the four of them went downtown to go to the movies. After purchasing movie tickets, popcorn, soda, and other snacks, they realized they didn't have enough money for everyone to get home on the El. Kenny made sure his younger brothers had their fare and put them on the train. Their father ordered they were to come home together but Kenny didn't want his brothers walking down Market Street--nothing but trouble at that time of night. They argued but soon they boarded the EL and he walked home alone. Upon his arrival, their father, enraged for breaking his rules, gave Kenny a severe beating. The brothers tried to apologize to Kenny but he said it was alright. *If I can't take a beating for my brothers, who can I take one for?*

As time passed, Kenny found a place for his strength in the streets; and the streets welcomed him. A neighborhood nightspot hired him as a bouncer which soon turned into a bodyguard for a low level gangster. As his pockets filled with money, so grew his taste for wine and drugs. He quickly slid deeper into the world of weed, coke, and Angel Dust--with dusting eventually holding him the tightest. Kenny never knew how unpredictable dusting could be--and never would. The people in the neighborhood saw the change that slowly transformed him. It started with severe hallucinations, hallucinations which prompted violent episodes of rage. A madness so bad that even his block-level boss didn't feel safe with him around. As he continued to use his decline steepened; his speech slurred and jumbled. What was once a sharp mind had become a blank screen. Unable to function on his own, Mrs. Parker's sister, Dahlia, offered to take him in as her own son had succumbed to drugs in the streets. Now a hulking child, Kenny spent his days in the parks on the swings or at home held in awe by the television. Ellis saw the look on Mr. Williams face but he continued.

No one could tell a funny story like his brother Max. Maxi, as they called him in the street, had such a command of language that he could break up a party or start a fight. When it was the craze to *play the dozens*, Max could launch into a litany of mama jokes to the point where the victim would either retreat in shame or throw a punch. At the house, Maxi was the one who got under their father's skin the most. He could turn words, phrases, and reprimands on a dime. Even his mother held back giggles while Mr. Parker's anger thermometer rose until it burst. Ellis loved to be around Maxi as they watched cartoons and evening programs. Maxi could imitate characters or offer alternate conclusions to situations presented on the television. Aside from Mr. Parker, everyone found him funny. Everyone--except Kenny. Kenny didn't like silly.

After dropping out of the tenth grade, Maxi took his gift of gab and charm to the corner. His skills of persuasion helped him become a great *round-the-way* salesman. Stolen jewelry was his specialty, although if it was movable and had enough profit, he had his hands in it. By the time he was twenty-one, he moved from knickknacks and watches to Kimmie and Cassandra, peddling their flesh all throughout the West Philadelphia area. He worked with an iron fist laced with a laugh track. His jokes soon became the veil of the monster he had become. He liked his new lifestyle, fine clothes, cars, and he always held court with men, young and old, who looked to him with jealous eyes.

One set of the jealous eyes belonged to another pimp who felt this rising star was too much for this part of town. No one knew for sure who *snitched* but a phone call to the police was enough to dismantle his operations and send him away for eighteen years. Maxi lost everything--except his smile.

The story Ellis shared about James was short, much like his life. Mr. Williams knew James had the talent with the round ball, not quite pro-level, but could have used it to get into college. Unfortunately, James didn't have patience. He wanted things right away. He had skills but was undisciplined. He didn't like rules. When he played ball, he was all style--which the neighborhood playgrounds loved. It was there he learned he could make a little money by wagering on his talent. Unfortunately, he found he could make more money by wagering on his misrepresented talent. When a target found out that he had been taken by James, the response was quick and James was found behind an Acme Market, a single bullet to his skull and his hands broken.

Except for wishing Ellis well, Mr. Williams was quiet. He knew their stories. He could have substituted a host of other names for Ellis' brothers. He knew there was a line of new, young men and women in the streets, preparing to do much of the same. Twenty-five years ago he would have offered a speech on what the community should be doing; what politicians should be doing, that parents should stand up and be parents, how teachers should teach, but most of all, that young people should be more responsible. Twenty-five years ago his blood would be boiling in his veins to hear stories like to ones Ellis just shared. Today, that anger was gone, that passion subsided; the concern was now comatose. He picked up his pack of cigarettes and smiled at Ellis as he turned to leave. There was still hope but he had long put down the mantle for someone else to carry.

Ellis exited the store. Before he could take a step, he heard a husky voice.

"Hey man, can you help a brother out?" Seated by the door was a disheveled man. He stretched out a worn drink cup that held a collection of assorted coins. Ellis answered the man in his mind. *I always wanted to...but I couldn't.* He handed the man his food and made his way home—his appetite gone.

GARBAGE DISPOSAL

STANDING OUTSIDE THE DOOR, Sylvania could hear the vacuum cleaner running in the living room. Although she spent a lot of time at her mother's house, she still knocked--at least that's what her mother expected. She rapped on the door with more force than usual, knowing her mother would have to hear above the noise. After a minute or two, she heard the decreasing whine of the vacuum, then footsteps.

"Come on in...and hurry...I don't want the rain blowing in the house." Mrs. Lee opened the door just enough for Sylvania to squeeze through. She continued talking as she quickly closed the door behind her. *Who knew these ladies could make such a mess.* Sylvania surveyed the room and identified the grazing trails of the *Mondaine Madames of Tau Beta Lambda.* Discarded cups and saucers, half eaten hors d'oeuvres, chairs in disarray, and forgotten meeting notes strewn around the living room. Mrs. Lee returned to vacuuming a dark spot on her beige carpet, running the cleaner over and over to no avail. Though she was concentrating on the dogged stain, Mrs. Lee's eyes were glued to Sylvania as she wandered into the kitchen. It didn't take long.

"Aren't you going to help me clean up?

Sylvania came out of her zone. Looking down she saw that she had finished off the tray of ham cream cheese pinwheels and half of the Swedish meatballs. She ignored her mother's look of disbelief.

"Hungry?"

Sylvania shook her head *no* but her swollen cheeks proved different. Eventually, Sylvania came up for air.

"So ma, when you gonna put your hat in the ring and run the *TBL?* You've been a member for as long as I remember."

Mrs. Lee took a small cloth and began brushing crumbs from off the coffee table.

"It's not the length of time…it's about the work you put in."

"Or how much money!"

Mrs. Lee knew exactly what Sylvania was insinuating. She cut a *watch-your-mouth* look at her daughter though she knew the truth. The Carter-McCloud name carried a lot of weight in numerous social, political, and business circles in and around Philadelphia. Five years ago when Mrs. Evelyn Carter-McCloud decided to become a sister of *TBL*, the organization knew they would have a leg up on the other sororities in the city. With Mrs. Evelyn Carter-McCloud as a member, the *TBL* began to have their fundraising letters responded to generously, to have top city officials and dignitaries speak at their banquets and socials, and increased attention and turnouts at their events. Mrs. Evelyn Carter-McCloud was the injection the *TBL* needed--but it came with a side effect.

At best, Mrs. Lee could barely tolerate Mrs. Evelyn Carter-McCloud. At worst, she hated her. For the sake of her place and future with the sisterhood, she kept her opinions to herself and placated as necessary. These feelings were lodged deep in the back of her throat and seeped its sickening poison when Mrs. Evelyn Carter-McCloud opened her mouth or when Sylvania opened her mouth about Mrs. Evelyn Carter-McCloud.

Mrs. Lee coughed up some of the poison, landing it squarely on Sylvania.

"You need not worry about my sorority business and worry about taking care of your own!" Sylvania's jaws locked. Her appetite was now gone. The urge to leave was strong but she saw that her mother was positioned between her and the door. Sylvania straightened herself in the chair and fired her first salvo.

"I got a new job and…"

Mrs. Lee intercepted and fired back. "Does it pay enough so I can stop underwriting your rent and take care of myself for once?"

"I pay my half for rent!" Sylvania tried but Mrs. Lee had responses on reserve.

"Half hell! Not when you come here and borrow money for groceries and those silly outings that you and Darlene go to…the…the…I brought your tickets for the Stepper's Ball and that Darlene had the gall to cut the fool! You think she would have the decency to treat me, of all people, with a shred of respect!"

Sylvania could feel the rage and agitation radiate from her mother's being, boiling the frustrations within her.

"Respect? You're worried about respect? Come on mom! I'm the only one it seems who gives you respect. You let them *TBL* biddies disrespect you…in your own house! Why should they see you as the next president…queen…or whatever the title is? You got the snack thing sewn up tight!"

Without warning, Mrs. Lee's nose was a mere fraction from Sylvania's.

"When the money from your father ran out, it was many of those *biddies* who helped me find work, helped me get my certification. A lot of clothes you received when you were younger came from those very same *biddies*!" Mrs. Lee stepped back and threw the cloth, hitting Sylvania on the stomach. "Now you know--so act like it!"

"What I'm tired of acting like is you're the only one taking care of somebody. I take all your *I'm lonely* calls because you must be too ashamed to call your friends. I told you that you need to get out there but you don't. You're scared!"

The voice escalation to personal attacks rose in a one to one ratio.

"If I didn't have to take care of you…"

"I really don't need you…"

"Then why are you here…"

"I don't know why I hang around here…"

"Don't ask for help of any kind…"

"Leave me alone!"

The last sound heard was the slamming of the door--save for the stifled cries of two hurt women.

ICHIGOICHIE

DEVON'S BEDROOM WAS STRIPED with morning light. The sun, streaming in from the east, tickled his eyelids as he lay in a haze. He could smell the cinnamon tea brewing in the kitchen, signaling the commencement of his morning regiment prescribed by Hank. He began with thirty push-ups, rolled over to complete one hundred crunches, and finally, with the use of his armed-chair, thirty dips. Hank instructed that by just doing these three simple exercises each morning, his body would wake up and the *blood will be pumpin'*. Although Hank was right in this respect, Devon worked out this morning with a different purpose in mind.

He sat in the corner of the sofa with a home decorating show on mute, the *Sunday Morning Slow Jams* on Pop 93.2, and the Sunday Inquirer spread out in sections across the sofa and coffee table. Devon looked at the time--10:22--and he hadn't received the call. He tried to focus his mind on the business section but his eyes were drawn to entertainment, the theatre offerings. There were a number of good shows in town and the opportunity for last minute tickets a strong possibility. He had seen *Elephant Man, Top Dog/Underdog, Phantom, Dreamgirls,* and a host of other spectacular theatrical productions. He also enjoyed the many performances at the Academy of Music, mostly the Philharmonic Orchestra. He couldn't wait for the new Kimmel Center to open. When the announcements for advanced memberships were made available, Devon didn't hesitate to secure his. Devon enjoyed going out but was uncomfortable with the looks when he attended the shows alone. To avoid this, he would invite a young lady to accompany him with dinner or lunch included. He made sure it was understood that it was not a date so when the performance was over there was no *encore*. He used to invite his mother to the shows but his father always provided the excuse as to why she couldn't make it. He stopped asking her after *The Lion King* tour.

The ringing of his phone caused a surge of warmth throughout his body. He quickly tasted his tea.

"Hello?"

The voice on the other end brought his temperature back down.

"Your mother and I missed you at church this morning."

"I took a break this morning." Devon could tell his father put his hand over the mouthpiece of the phone but he could still hear what was being said. His father didn't know how to use the mute button. <*He said he took a break this morning.*>
His father returned his attention to Devon. "Your mother says the Lord doesn't take a break."

"Tell her...tell her that I recall that on the seventh day the Lord rested." <*He said that on the seventh the Lord rested. You heard that?*>

"She says you shouldn't be talking smart about the Lord. That's blaspheming!"
Devon prayed for the call waiting signal but none came. "I'm sorry. I wasn't joking about the Lord...never mind...are we still on for dinner? <*We still having dinner tonight?*>

"Your mother is shaking her head yes. Come by around six. <*I'll ask.*> She wants to know if you're bringing a guest. If so, she says she has to bring out the good dishes."

Devon walked into the kitchen, holding his mug with the remains of his tea. He swallowed it as he answered. "I'll let you know around three. Is that okay?" <*Is three okay to let you know?*>

"She said that will be fine <*What? Okay.*> Is it going to be Roxanne? She liked Roxanne."

"Dad, I haven't spoken with Roxanne in two years. Tell mom that if I bring a guest, she will be delighted." <*No on Roxanne. You'll like his new date>.*"

Devon started to argue the concept of date when his phone beeped. The warmth returned.

"Gotta go Dad. I'll talk to you later on." As his father repeated to his mother, Devon switched over. "Hello?" His voice was soft and controlled.

"Devon," began the voice on the other end. "Let me apologize. I wanted to call you sooner but today is my grandmother's birthday and I had to call her and wish her well. It takes time as she doesn't hear or understand that well nowadays." The mercury in Devon's thermometer now read "sizzlin' hot" as he sat on the floor in front of his fireplace.

"I understand perfectly Cary." Devon was filled with the memory of Cary's cologne. "My grandparents passed away when I was younger. I sometimes envy others who have their grandparents at this age."

"It is something special. She lives outside of Dallas in a nursing home. I wanted to talk to her before she went to church. She turned ninety-two and still makes it to church every Sunday. She doesn't have Alzheimer's but does have a hard time focusing. I hope to take some time off and go see her soon. It's been a while."

"I'm sure she'll appreciate the visit." Devon launched into the real conversation. "So how are you doing today?"

"Doing well. I still hope you're free. I have a surprise for you. At least I hope it will be a surprise." Aside for dinner, Devon made sure this day was dedicated to getting to know Cary a little better.

"I don't know anyone who doesn't like a surprise every now and then." Devon was now stretched out on the carpet.

"So...what's the next move?"

"Can you be ready in about an hour? I'll swing by and pick you up."

"Is there a certain look required? Jeans--casual--formal?" Devon sprang up and made his way to his bedroom.

"Keep it casual. It's kind of cool out so perhaps a light jacket or sweater." Ideas raced in Devon's mind. He could tell it would be outside but it definitely wasn't the mall or anything like that. He was sure it included a nice meal--perhaps a bistro or other kind of sidewalk café.

"Looking forward to it."

Arrangements were made and Devon prepared himself. He began with a warm shower and washed with his favorite body wash, *Noir*. As warm water streamed, he felt his body respond to his thoughts of Cary's voice. *Not now...save it for the real thing.* Devon rinsed himself with cold water and shivered as he stepped out to dry off. He looked at himself in the mirror. It had been a long time since he could look deeply into his own eyes. For years, he could only glance, peering from behind the shroud he had created for himself. As he moisturized his skin, he felt free--alive, real. In a couple of minutes, he would share time with someone and not hide his feelings, not blur his words. Adding the sheen to his hair, he saw himself as the butterfly breaking free from the chrysalis he spent years creating in response to his middle school teasing, the questions and rumors in high school, the loneliness of college--but worst of all--the prayers of disappointment sent up by his mother. Looking into his own eyes, he could see that they were as clear as the truth: He could see the truth that had been locked away in the *no one understands* storage bin. Today would be different. As he stood naked before himself he was ready to do the same to the world.

His brown slacks were accented by the tan turtleneck shirt and camelhair jacket. While tying his shoes, he heard his phone buzz. Hopping on one foot, still tying, he answered. "Yes!"

"You sound like your running. Are you ready?" Devon sat surely on a nearby chair, goose bumps alive on his arms.

"I'm all yours."

"We'll see about that. I'm outside of your place."

Devon soon found himself seated in Cary's car. Except for a few books on the back seat, the car looked showroom new. Devon smiled when he inhaled--that scent--just as he remembered.

Their conversation was light as they cruised down the Vine Street Expressway. Devon could hardly contain himself. Cary looked great. Admiring the blue blazer that complimented the yellow striped v-neck sweater, Devon smiled. The entire ensemble, complete with his watch and simple silver chain, accented the jeans and casual shoes which, to Devon, made Cary look as if he just stepped from off of a runway.

A sign flashed as they rounded a turn. "Philadelphia Zoo, next exit, one mile". Crossing the Schuylkill, Devon surveyed the area. *I can't believe we're going to the Zoo. I know he said casual but the zoo is a little too casual. It might have worked in Rocky II as a date...* In that moment, Devon realized he was on a date--an official date--and in that moment the zoo no longer seemed mildly repulsive but a place to spend time and learn more about Cary--and himself.

The car continued past the Zoo exit.

"I have to ask, where are we going?"

Cary smiled. "I thought you said you liked surprises." His hand patted Devon's leg gently. "Hold on, we're almost there. In fact, from this point on, you should close your eyes."

"Close my eyes?" Devon looked at Cary, who never took his eyes off of the road. "Serious?"

"It's all part of the surprise. Now, go ahead. If you don't have a piece of cloth, grab one of the books and place it in front of your face. Hurry!" Devon was mildly tickled by this childish game but something about Cary made him want to enjoy the amusement. He leaned back and grabbed a white book with large black letters. Before he closed his eyes, he read the cover, *Parable of the Sower by Octavia Butler.* Devon felt the turns, indicating they had left the expressway.

"So what is this...a book on spirituality? My parents filled me with plenty of parables." While he talked, his eyes remained shut.

"Not quite...it's a novel by this sister. One of the few, if not only, who write science fiction. Social commentary wrapped in sci-fi...here we are."

Devon felt the car come to a stop. Cary told him to keep his eyes closed until he retrieved him from the car. It was only seconds before Devon felt Cary's hand guide him from the car to what felt like a wooden gate or fence. "You can open your eyes now."

Devon read the sign. *Shofuso Japanese House and Garden.*

"Is this your first time here?"

"This is a nice surprise. This is my first time. I've heard of it but that's all." Cary took Devon by the arm.

"Then let me be your guide." The two walked close down the stone path, admiring the walkway adorned with Flowering Plums, bamboo, azaleas, and other imported plants. With each step, he felt as if he was being transported through time and dimension, as if they were now in Japan of old. The two came to a wooden bridge and marveled at the brilliantly colored Koi fish swimming to and fro in the pond. Further up the walkway, Cary pointed out the statue of Jizo, sharing the history of the Buddhist deity associated with the salvation of small children. After marveling at the sculpture of the rocks and plants they found their way to the doorway of the Japanese House, at which they removed their shoes.

It was peaceful. Cary motioned for Devon to sit. Cary seated himself across from him. Cross-legged and with eyes closed, the two, together in peace, allowed the environment to fill them with tranquility. Time was lost as the soft songs of birds and the breeze filled their senses. The sun was moving across their faces but it went unnoticed. Other patrons to the Japanese House may have entered the room but the equanimity of the two men remained. It was Devon who broke the silence.

"Would you like to have dinner with me this evening?" Cary remained still. Devon couldn't see any indication that his words were heard--not a flinch of his eyes, his breathing was slow and tempered. In all, it appeared that Cary was somewhere else. Devon shifted in his seat and leaned close to Cary's ear. He would whisper, letting his voice drew Cary from his tranquil trance. In the instance that his lips moved to form Cary's name, his world was awoken. A new light illuminated the fogged feelings that rested just above his sensibilities. Like the tingling tickle of a static shock, a new truth was revealed--and it was satisfying. He was free.

Cary could feel the warmth of Devon's breath moving closer to his ear. In a movement, both quick and smooth, he brought his lips around to meet Devon's. Cary could feel there was no resistance--only resuscitation. Cary could taste the awakening of who Devon truly was on his tongue. Was it one second or one minute? Neither knew--nor did it matter. Cary leaned back slightly, just enough to let the words trickle out.

"Only once in a lifetime...the chance of a lifetime...every encounter a treasure...do not pass off the chance of the encounter."

Devon opened his eyes wide. He held his breath long enough to take in the sweetness of Cary's words.

"That was beautiful."

"You're beautiful."

As Devon leaned in Cary asked him about the dinner invitation.

"What dinner?"

HOUSE OF STRAW

ELLIS' THOUGHTS FOUND THEIR way to his dining room table. He had fixed a bowl of tomato soup but it went untouched. The television was off. So was the radio. The noiselessness was different. Unlike the times when Clarissa wasn't speaking to him, this moment told a story. The story of Clarissa not being here was the punch line. He didn't know where she was.

It started six months earlier, following a visit to her mother's. There was the usual arguing for a day or two but by the end of the week something different happened. She said she was going to the movies with a friend, and like normal, Ellis didn't question with whom, when she would be returning, or even what movie they were going to see. Two weeks later, she announced she had to go to visit a friend in DC. This was the beginning. For the next several months, every two weeks, Clarissa was on board a train from 30th Street to Union Station to visit her nameless friend. What touched the fingers of his curiosity was that she never talked about *her friend* after the weekend. She did come back feeling better, even pleasant, but by the next weekend the normal Clarissa returned.

Ellis looked at their portrait on the wall above the sofa. Although they were looking lovingly into each other's eyes, the picture did nothing for him. He didn't smile nor did he turn away. The picture didn't make him mourn her absence nor did he celebrate his solitude. The air was free of her nagging, but again, no easement in the peace. He felt nothing.

Night fall came quietly. Ellis forced himself to think about this relationship--this arrangement. For years, he wished something would happen to change its course but changing course would suggest movement. The Clarissa and Ellis show had not changed its script since the 1980s. Like images splashed on a cave wall, any novice archeologist would be able to tell their story after a cursory review. Ellis wanted to change that, but then again he didn't. He needed stability. He liked knowing what was coming next. At home and at work he knew what hassles and headaches awaited him.

There were times he wanted to leave her. To wake her up in the middle of the night and announce he would be gone in the morning. Times he wanted to leave work and keep on driving, to say without interruption or interrogation that this would be their last dinner together. There were also times he prayed she would not walk through the door, or that he'd find a note by the bed stand, on the refrigerator, the toilet handle--somewhere some sign that she was done and gone.

If he did leave her, he felt he would be no better than the throngs of men who walked out of relationships without trying. He would see himself a failure. He was never much of a *ladies' man*. How could he be one? Clarissa was his only--love wasn't the word--the only woman he had been with and he never really saw himself with anyone else--at least until now.

He continued wondering, only this time, if she was to leave him, what would that mean? He couldn't satisfy her as a man? Their moments of intimacy had changed with time. It wasn't pleasure, it was duty. He knew that his mother would be pleased if she was gone but deep down that she believed that Clarissa was his motivator. It was true. Ellis knew that his success at work was due to her incessant pushing for him to go for new opportunities. The two women in his life made him who he was. His mother polished him--and Clarissa finished him.

Ellis sat in his bed. He looked at Clarissa's pillow. He didn't know what he wanted: to go, to be left, to stay, or to be stayed with. He needed to make a decision for himself but he didn't know how. Maybe Clarissa found an answer for herself. As for Ellis--he was standing at the fork in the road and found himself stuck.

He finally made a decision. He turned out the light and went to sleep.

VISITING HOURS

"DO YOU WANT TO stop for coffee? Something?"
Same questions--different month. Ellis paused, hand poised on the gearshift. He waited, like the month before, the month before that, and for the past ten years. It wasn't patience that made him wait nor was it apprehension. He waited because it was the only salve he had for a broken heart.

"No! Let's just go." Mrs. Parker's words guided Ellis' hand and he put the car in drive. There came a sadness masked by pride and prayer. Prayers sent up for years that never seemed to reach the tender ears of an almighty; prayers unceasingly given with welled eyes and a tired tongue; prayers with offers of self in the place for a miracle. Even though the eons proved themselves deaf, Mrs. Parker always found one more prayer in her ragged rusting chest of hope.

The two made small talk as they managed their way through the Sunday morning traffic on Market Street. They reminisced on the stores that used to be; the superstars who never were, the lives that were now lost. If there were ever such a thing as *good old days--old* was now the way of their world.

While his mother was conversational, her voice was subdued and direct, no variation from the topic, not wanting to give rise to the malignant seeds of her saddened soul. She ushered a strong sigh as they left the expressway and passed the unusual Lightning Bolt sculpture at the foot of the Ben Franklin Bridge. It served as the marker of the beginning of reticence and melancholy. Ellis tried his best at humor.

"Good thing you only pay the toll going back to Philly. You couldn't get me to pay a dime to go to Jersey."
Mrs. Parker smiled slightly at the attempt at humor.

The sign broke their conversation into little pieces of silence: *Riverfront State Prison.* Though they tried not to look at it, the weather-worn sign was emblazoned into the minds of both Mrs. Parker and Ellis. The two stood in line with the gathering of other inmates' friends, loved ones, and attorneys. No stranger to the process, Ellis left his wallet in the trunk of his car, only carrying his driver's license and keys on his person. Mrs. Parker carried a simple purse which contained only her license and a pack of tissues. The line inched forward as each person was subjected to a full search--bags, pockets, shoes, hats, everything. Periodically, the screening process ejected a person from line because they had a record of their own, did not have the proper identification, or hadn't registered in advance for the visit. The Parkers were well prepared as they had plenty of experience. Once cleared, the group was led down a long corridor with the understanding that no one was to talk. The eerie patter of feet on the concrete floor bothered some of the first time visitors but Ellis knew how long the hollowness would last and he counted it down in his mind. They reached the larger metal door with the small glass window. Again, they were screened as they were directed to find a place to sit down in the next room.

The buzzer sounded, issuing in a parade of orange jumpsuits; a flood of wild afros, braids, and bald heads. Old men and young men forced to grow old--walking with their heads up, like brash princes of their enclosed kingdom. Others walked with their heads down in sadness and shame. Some came with noise seeking attention, others in silence with thoughts of regret and absolution. Ellis caught a moment of sorrow looking at the sea of mostly black men, representatives of the forty-five percent of the national incarceration rate. They arrived to waves of hugs, kisses, handshakes, and headshakes; some to meeting children for the first time, some to children they've seen but did not really know, and some to girlfriends who held fast to the dreams of their long awaited release. Time constraint required them to launch into the sharing of stories, problems, questions, and frustrations. This was the Parker's monthly visit and for the last one-hundred twenty months nothing had changed.

Ellis watched his mother find a seat in the crowded room. Her face was stolid, as if crafted by an artisan with the perception to interpret the essence of pain and loss. The sounds of people in the room reuniting with their loved ones passed by her ears, allowing her a moment to be indifferent to the troubles of the world around her. She was waiting for the familiar, the invariable memory of the child who once held her hand as they crossed the street. That child now crossed the room.

"Yo maaahh!"

The memory was broken. Half strolling, half skipping, Max came into view with his officer close behind. Wriggling through the crowd, Max reached for his mother, hugging her before she could attempt to stand.

"Maahhh you look gooood!" Their embrace spanned the length of a single heartbeat before the guard asked them to separate. Max copped a frustrated look. "Damn man…it just my mom." The office walked on as if Max hadn't said a word. Max called after.

"You ain't got to diss her like that." Max returned his attention to his mother. "Sorry ma, that's how they do here." In no time Max transformed into Maxi. Leaning into his mother, he asked how people were doing back in the neighborhood, how Kenny was getting along, about what's changed. He wasn't really interested in his mother's response; he just wanted to hear her talk. Her voice began to soothe the rust that had corroded his spirit. Her tone, her inflections, took him back to a day when he could leave his room and walk into a kitchen filled with laughter, broiled pork chops, and annoying brothers. He touched her hand and was transported to moments sitting around the television watching shows like Eight is Enough, Roots, and the Love Boat. With a turn of her head and he saw a young mother helping him with homework. He warmed at the thought of her voice calling him to walk her to the store. Her slight smile returned memories of when she brought him his first three piece suit down on South Street.

"I'm getting close to getting' my GED. You'd like that."
Mrs. Parker smiled. He had said the same in '96, '94, '91, and '89.

"When I get out I'll take care of some of them things around the house I know you need done."

There was a mighty strength deep within that held Mrs. Parker's body straight and firm as she listened to the words coming from her son.

"I ain't lyin'! I can't be comin' back here no more! I'm up for parole again next year. Gonna show them next time."

Mrs. Parker started to feel for the tissues in her purse but soon withdrew her fingers. She didn't have any more tears to shed. She slowly reached over and touched his hand.

"Yes…you'll show them. Now go talk to your brother."

Ellis felt his brother's grasp around his shoulders. It wasn't as strong as the last time. Max's face was a little more drawn, his weight down as well. In greeting his brother, Ellis could see that he wasn't receiving the kind of dental care needed. Over the past year, he watched his brother's health deteriorate. He knew what it was, it was in Max's eyes: he was still using.

"Like I told you last time, when I get out, I'm gonna do it right…get myself together!"

Ellis wanted to believe Max's words but he knew the truth. If he were released, there would be only two places to go--the streets or mother's house. Neither would be good. The streets would simply be a preamble to the grave. Mama's house would become a haven for trouble and despair. The flash of thought brought an ache to his heart. It would be best, Ellis resolved, if Max just stayed here.

Scanning the room with his ears, Ellis could decipher the scattergun words of the various conversations. He had heard them all over the years; Prayers and promises--complaints and contrition--depression and disillusionment. He knew the faces of the inmates--hardened and cold--reminiscent of the boys from his neighborhood that ended up in places just like this. He took pause to reflect on the number of young men from across the city and state who would no longer enjoy the fullness of life due to their incarceration. He was both saddened and sickened as the room expanded in his mind to represent the exorbitant number of black men incarcerated in the United States; sons, fathers, lovers, and friends--affixed in an abysmal system of which they would be forever infected.

The chilling buzzer announced visitor time had come to a close. From between the goodbye gestures and kisses, Mrs. Parker allowed her arms to release her son back to the living tomb of his lifelessness. They watched the flood of orange backwash through the doors which closed with a resounding 'clack'. They were gone.

The late afternoon sun focused its energy directly on Ellis' windshield. He lowered his visor to see the bridge traffic more clearly. He looked quickly at his mother. The sun was directly in her eyes but she did not squint. He thought he knew what was on her mind but he didn't. Once they cleared the bridge, she spoke.

"Ellis," she sighed as her gaze drifted across the Delaware River. "I'm not bothered by coming here anymore. When I think about your brothers and your father--and you know I love them all dearly--I realize that I have been a prisoner for a long time…and I don't know if I'll ever be free."

MORNING MOURNING

"I DON'T WANT TO go out...not tonight."
Clarissa sat down at the dining room table, kicked off her pumps, and slowly squeezed her hands inside each other. "I just can't do it...not tonight...not again!"
Ellis heard the rising pace of her breathing. Sensing tears, he reached for a cloth napkin. She used it to cover her face.

"What is it?" Ellis was very confused. Clarissa had planned this night two months ago. First dinner at Smith and Wollensky's then drive over to check out an old school R&B revue featuring Keith Sweat and some other crooners from back in the day at the Stand.

"What's wrong Clariss?" Clarissa raised her head a little, revealing her teary eyes.

"We have to talk." Though confused, Ellis helped her to the living room and the two sat across from each other.

"What's going on Clarissa? You're starting to scare me." Ellis leaned forward, trying to hold her hands but they were withdrawn from his reach. Gathering her composure, she took a deep breath.

"I ain't been totally honest with you Ellis. I mean, I've been doing something and I need to come clean." Ellis was in rapt attention. He didn't know what was going to come out of Clarissa's mouth next so he prepared himself. "Remember I told you I was going to see a friend in DC?" Ellis nodded, still waiting for the punch line. "Well, I haven't been seeing a friend at all..." Clarissa's words began to drift off. In his mind, Ellis began organizing his apologizes for Clarissa's shortcomings. He hadn't always been open. He worked long hours. He didn't like her family or the drives out to Carlisle. Most of all, he didn't have the backbone to stand up and be the kind of man she wanted. Ellis put all of these elements together and could see that was more than enough to make any woman step out.

"…So I don't know how else to say it…so here it is…'cause you know I have to keep it real…" Ellis hadn't noticed that Clarissa had stood up, now standing behind the chair. "On the weekends when I was supposed to be…well…I had a standing appointment." Ellis scratched his head as he waited for the news to hit him like a wrecking ball--it didn't. *Standing appointment?* He knew there was a lot of street jargon for having an affair. *Creepin'…steppin' out…Easin'…*even the old standard, *two-timin'* was still in use but *standing appointment* was a new one.

"What do you mean a *standing appointment?*" Ellis felt something rise inside of him.

"Ellis…Ellis…I know but I've been seeing…don't be mad…I've been seeing…a therapist."

"What are you talking about…a therapist?"

"You're not hearing me. There's something wrong with me and I'm trying to set myself straight."

It took several moments and Clarissa washing down two drinks before they were seated close on the sofa. Ellis held Clarissa gently as she burrowed her tearful face into his chest. Quietly he ran his fingers through her long blonde hair. The silence of the night filled the room as dusk found its way through the windows, leaving only the glow of the digital clock to illuminate the living room.

"Turn on the radio", whispered Clarissa, "But keep the lights out."

Ellis complied and a push of a button played a soft and sad tune. Clarissa recognized it, Keith John's *I can only be me.*

"This is a sign for me. A sign that I need to go and find myself."

Ellis held her tighter.

"Things started to fall apart for me after my last visit to my father. I couldn't sleep. I've become more irritable. Most of all, I've started hating myself." Their conversation continued in the dark. Ellis spoke softly.

"We can work this out. Whatever it is."

Ellis could feel Clarissa sit up. In the cross of light and shadow, he could tell she was facing him.

"No. This is for me to take care of. I'm leaving in the morning."

That night, Ellis erupted with passion in making love to Clarissa. The idea of losing the one constancy of his life ignited a level of passion he had not known. It was more than the joining of his body to hers but the feel of her arms, her breasts, her back. It was the taste of her tears as they rolled across her cheeks. He held her tightly as he pressed his face into her neck, tasting her as if this would be the last time. Without realizing it, they moved from the bed to the floor, rolling slowly across the carpet into a sad saturated erotic oblivion. His senses told him to taste her in total. The very essence of her being was now being etched into his soul. He knew that his loving would make her change her mind and that in the morning she would want the satisfaction to continue. It was in that moment the force of his realization of truth and hope left his body.

With the morning sun breaking in though the bedroom drapes, an uneasy feeling stirred in Ellis's stomach. He turned to face her, wanting to ask her not to leave. By the time he realized her pillow lay empty, he heard the front door close.

LONG DISTANCE

THE TRAFFIC ON NORTH Broad was stop and go. Devon realized his mistake in thinking he could get to his parent's house by three on a Sunday afternoon. It seemed that every able-bodied driver was making their way downtown. The traffic going in the opposite direction wasn't any better. By the time he reached West Norris Street it was almost three-thirty. An inexperienced driver provided him the opening to turn left onto Norris. He now entered what he considered the worst part of his trip. Devon slowed; knowing at anytime kids could dart into the street chasing something--balls, each other, the ice cream truck. His right turn onto 21st Street was impeded by a bedraggled man and his overflowing shopping cart. The man, rattled for no good reason, cursed at Devon before pushing his cart into an empty lot. Another left and Devon was on Diamond Street. Memories began to haunt him as many of the storefronts from his childhood came into view. He tried to ignore them. *They were dying when I was a kid...now it's a graveyard.* He looked at the dashboard clock. He knew he should reach his parent's home in a couple of minutes. He made a right onto 22nd Street. As he passed a group of men on the corner, one tried to flag him down--hoping to sell him a t-shirt, some weed, or just bum a dollar. Devon summoned his urban aloofness as he made his last left onto Edgley Street. All he wanted now was a parking space.

Stepping into the street, Devon began to worry about his car. He knew he shouldn't because almost everyone on the block had been there since his childhood days. Perhaps that was reason enough to be nervous. Many of the children on the block were the children-- and grand children--of those he knew from his elementary school.

"Is that you Devon?" A familiar voice rang out as he stepped around his car. He didn't have to look. From across the street, seated on a worn out rocker was Mrs. Jessup--part block captain, part busybody, part church lady, and part rumor mill. Devon reminded himself, *if you wanted to know what was going on in the neighborhood, you talked to her; if you were into something that you wanted to keep on the down-low, better keep your mouth shut.*

"Hello Mrs. Jessup." Devon stepped with caution, stopping in middle of the street. "You're looking well." Mrs. Jessup rose a little from her chair, adjusted her glasses, and fell back onto the cushion with a huff.

"So you in town for that Greek Picnic mess?" Mrs. Jessup knew Devon wasn't one to attend big gatherings like the Greek Picnic. He had told her that a year ago and Mrs. Jessup didn't forget things. This was her way to find out some information.

"No…just here for dinner with the folks."

Devon's answer was the opening for the cascade of prying questions.

"Is that car all yours?"

"You got a house?"

"You married yet?"

"When you gone get married?"

He knew it was time to go when the list of questions moved to probing where she didn't belong.

"So…your father find himself a job?"

"I heard your mother has cancer?"

"People been wondering why you ain't married."

He finessed the questions and was soon waving Mrs. Jessup off as he reached the porch door.

"It's me!" Devon shouted, poking his head into his childhood home. Stepping in, he was immediately hit with the smell of the house--the same cleaning smells, the same food smells, the plants his mother liked, his parents' colognes and perfumes. Next his ears were opened to the haunting sounds of "old-time" gospel music. On this afternoon it was Mahalia Jackson singing *How I Got Over*. The other sound was Phillies baseball. Devon knew his father had only gone to a few games in his lifetime so he committed himself to listening to them on the radio or watching them on television.

He paused his memories as his attention was brought to the familiar sounds of his father's walker--*step-step-clack--step-step-clack*--echoing from the adjacent hallway. Lucius entered the room, nodding approvingly at his son.

"Devon…you made it…good to see you."

The two shared an awkward embrace, partly due to the walker, but more so by their distance. Stepping back, Devon saw an older model of himself. His sights were drawn to one of the many photos scattered across the wall. The photo revealed Lucius Hunt enjoying a lake somewhere in the Pocono Mountains as a teen, revealing a young man of strength, charisma, with a pocket full of dreams. Devon focused on his father's eyes. Even in sepia tone, they sparkled with dreams of being a teacher or perhaps a school principal. His head was a mass of sandy brown curls--an attractive nuisance for the fingertips of women, young and old, wanting to bury themselves in its goodness. His smile told the story that he was happy--and could provide happiness. That picture, with the lake stretching across to the mountainous background, told the story of a young man with a fishing pole in one hand and the pearls of life in the other.

Fast forward to the present, his father was now as faded as the photograph. Gone was the sparkle, the curls, smile, and most of all, the dream. Seemingly long ago, a career with the postal service provided a life for his wife and son but the blinding revelation of the postal truck accident derailed the plans for a second career.

Devon remembered that day well. It was the end of his freshman year of college. He had just gotten home and was preparing for his first summer break. Almost to the door, he was called by Mrs. Jessup.

"Is your daddy alright?"

Devon wasn't sure what to make of the question. He knew she wanted to be in their family business but something was different about today.

"As far as I know…why?" Mrs. Jessup waved him closer.

"I heard there was a bad accident down near the train station. Someone told me that one of the trucks your daddy drives was in the accident a pile up with a couple of cars. Sounded real bad."

Devon went cold inside. He wanted to run but didn't know where to go. His mind raced; into the house, down to the postal office, to the hospital--but which one? He turned his attention back to Mrs. Jessup.

"Are you sure it was my dad and not some other driver?" Mrs. Jessup closed her eyes and clasped her hands as if in prayer.

"They said it was your daddy alright. He might be at Penn Hospital. Check there." Devon ran without another word, bounding up the stairs to his home. "Let me know what's going on…." Mrs. Jessup called after him.

Once inside the house, Devon scrambled to find the phonebook and frantically called the hospital. After several minutes, it was confirmed, he was there. Hanging up the phone, Devon thought he heard the sound of movement from upstairs. He shouted.

"Dad's in the hospital at Penn. I'm going to go see him."
No response. Devon bolted out the house, never to hear the
upstairs bedroom door open and shut.

Devon's thought of that day was disrupted.

" Is he here yet?" The voice came from upstairs.

"Yes. He's right here." Lucius leaned back as he
responded. Movement was heard from upstairs. Devon's father
lowered his voice. "Your mother is still upset for not showing up
for dinner the last time."

"Dad...that was almost a month ago." Devon scratched
his head in disbelief.

"Just letting you know. Just trying to help you out." His
father pivoted and began to make his way into the dining room.
Devon followed.

The table was arranged with the same settings from all of the past
Sunday dinners going back as far as he could remember. The
silverware was highly polished. The plates, saucers, cups, boats--
almost as if they had been untouched. The papered walls held the
framed replicas of oceanscapes and copper-ornate baking tins. The
breakfront contained the second set of plates which had never
been used. Devon hated this room.

Her steps were hard as she descended the stairs. Devon knew
how the conversation would go--it had been the same since college.
He tucked his heart away and looked toward the doorway.

"Has he been to church lately?" Devon looked to his
father as she passed quietly into the kitchen. His father picked up a
fork, wiping it uneasily with his napkin.

"Been to church lately Devon?"

"I've been very busy...but I do take time to meditate."
Mr. Hunt eased down into his chair as he called to his wife.

"Grace...he says he does a lot of meditating...like his own version of church." The only sound from the kitchen was the preparation of dinner. Devon looked to his father, wanting more but realizing this was all he could offer.

A shout came from the kitchen.

"Does he still eat chicken?" Devon closed his eyes, holding his frustration in check. He turned to his father.

"All I said was that I stopped eating fried chicken. I still eat baked. That's what's for dinner...right?" Again, Mr. Hunt called back to the kitchen.

"Devon eats chicken. We're having baked chicken? Aren't we dear? He's just trying to be healthy."

The kitchen door pushed open. Mrs. Hunt backed into the room, bringing food to the table. Devon wanted to offer to help-- to go into the kitchen and assist with bringing in food, fold the napkins, butter the rolls, even pour the juice--but he knew better. Once the food was on the table, Mrs. Hunt looked to her husband.

"Ask Devon to bless the table."

Devon sighed as his father repeated the question. Reluctantly, Devon asked his parents for a moment of silence, blessing the food in their own way. Almost immediately, his mother snapped at her husband.

"Lucius, say a real blessing! Food's getting cold!"

Standing in the small foyer, Devon couldn't remember how the food tasted. He shook his father's hand goodbye.

"Your mother is just having a hard time with...well...you know..." For the first time, Devon could no longer stomach the meal, his feelings, and the *you knows*.

"No dad, there's something about me that mom needs to deal with. I'm respectful, hard working, pretty successful, and just because I don't believe as she does..."

Mr. Hunt dropped his head. The weight on his mind shifted, releasing the truth. "It's not that…Devon…it's not about Jesus or church or your blanket meditation…" Mr. Hunt swallowed hard as he whispered his next statement. "It's because you're a gay."

Devon used the radiator for support. He couldn't believe the words uttered from his father's mouth. *How dare his mother accuse-- suppose his sexuality? She didn't even know him.* Devon composed himself so as not to call attention to his mother.

"Why would she say I was gay?"
Devon's father motioned for the two of them to go out onto the porch. The cooling air did not lessen the heat that now took residence on Devon's head and face. Once seated, his father spoke.

"Devon, I know I'm not as strong as you but you must realize…I am and always will be proud of you…no matter how you live your life. Your mother knew something was different about you in high school. She said she could sense it. I didn't want to believe it because…well…that's not in the plan a father has for his son. We thought you would grow out of it but as time went on …we could see that you seemed to go through the motions with girls. I'm not saying we were 100 percent but we knew something. Once you got to college…we knew something was different for sure."
Devon stood, crossed to the far side of the porch but was conscious of keeping a low tone.

"So what if I was…if that was the case."
Mr. Hunt lifted his head high.

"Son, I love when you come by. I love it when you call. I love your Christmas and other gifts…plain and simple…I love you…for who you are." The warm feeling moved from Devon's face to his heart. Walking back, Devon started to embrace his father but the action was quickly halted. A question sat on his tongue, teetering. *Should I ask? Should I let it go?* The truth was right there. His mother hated him, and his father was, just weak. Just like they had no control over his life choices, he couldn't change his parents. He was who he was. They were who they were. This was his family. The question tipped.

"Dad? Why don't you stick up for me? How mom treats me is right in line with how she feels about me--no mystery there-- but you, I'm your son! You say you love me but you let her treat me like trash! No! She'll talk to the trash."

Mr. Hunt deflated in his seat. The once strong and proud man, fit and fine, was now a man struggling with his health, his place, his purpose.

"I do love you...," he began. "...but I need your mother. She takes care of me. Look at me! I can't walk, I can hardly stand up straight, my vision is failing, and my benefits are eaten by my prescriptions and therapy before I can cash the check!" Mr. Hunt closed his eyes with remorse. "I need her... need her just to survive."

In life, Devon knew, choices are made. Some choices move us forward, others suppress our progress, and others put us in a place where we cease to exist. Devon resolved to break free from that place.

"At the very least, I convinced her to let you come to dinner...."

He hugged his father for a long time, kissing him tenderly on the cheek. As their embrace relaxed, Devon felt the lead weight of his father's whisper.

"Your mother will come around...when you change."

Without a word between them, he walked slowly down the steps and remotely unlocked his car. With trembling hands, he opened the door but was stopped by the calling by Mrs. Jessup.

"Had a good visit with your folks?"
He wanted to shout, to scream *mind your own damned business you rusty old busy-bodied hag!* He wanted to blast to the whole neighborhood that his family treated him like shit and now he didn't give two damns about them. He looked back at the man whom he called dad and in that instance his anger first turned to sadness, finally to pity. He decided to maintain his newly understood facade one more time.

"Yes…" Devon produced a smile. "…had a nice visit."

As he drove toward Broad Street, a sickness in his stomach and head began to ebb and swell. This would be the last time he would see that house and its occupants. At the light, onlookers pointed at his car with question--not realizing that with so many tears in his eyes, he had turned on the windshield wipers.

MOONLIGHT AND ALLEYWAYS

"UH...DON'T YOU THINK you had enough?"

"I said one more! I'm a man, ain't I?"

The bartender leaned over to retrieve the bottle of vodka, pouring a fourth round. Devon cradled the glass in his hand before downing it without regards for taste. After it reached his stomach, Devon wobbled as he stood, bracing himself on the bar rail.

"Where the freaks at my man?"

The bartender turned to tend to another customer. Devon raised his voice. "I said, where are the freaks? It's night time. They're supposed to be out!" Several patrons laughed before returning to their own business. The slurred speech brought the bouncer to Devon's side.

"Say brother, if you don't quiet down I'ma hafta help you take it outside." Through his glazed eyes, Devon sized the bouncer up. Fixing his tie, he leaned back onto a barstool and patted the man on his barrel chest.

"Lemme tell you something. My man Hank would mop up this roach motel with you. No sweat. So you better gone get before I make the call."

Pain shot through Devon's shoulder as his arms were quickly pinned behind him. Customers made a path as the bouncer ushered him toward the front door. Devon spit obscenities and threats which only added to the ridicule as he tumbled out onto the sidewalk.

"Come back when you get yourself together!" The bouncer closed the door, leaving Devon to struggle to get back onto his feet by himself.

"Don't tell me to get myself together...you ain't my mama!"

Devon sat on the curb, stewing in soggy alcoholic anger. He knew how he felt but *who's concern was it?* He could see his mother's face in pooling waters by the sewer drain. *You don't know a damn thing about me!* He kicked his foot into the puddle, splashing the water onto his trousers.

"Looks like you like to play. Wanna play with me?" Devon looked to the scratchy voice. "Come on…if you tryin' to get wet, I can do that for you."

Devon struggled to stand and soon felt two hands help to raise him, leaning him against a car. The too-tight red tube top captured his attention first. His eyes trailed down to the equally tight denim mini skirt complete with battle worn fringes. Through his stupor, he could only imagine the circulation in her legs being cut off by the tightness of the laces that crisscrossed up from her high heels to just above her knees.

"You look like you need something to do tonight." Devon watched the words frothing from her mouth. She looked older, haggard. He could see several missing teeth as she spoke. Though her voice reeked with life and pleasure, there was a weather-beaten aura that surrounded her. Devon didn't know her but he knew who she was. He was conflicted by the simultaneous feelings of repulsion and attraction. She put her hand on his crotch and he took inventory of her chewed down fingernails.

"Come on daddy…show me what you got!"

Show me what you got! A thought staggered into his mind. This was his moment to show everyone *what he got.* The moment to show Hank, his mother, and all of the finger-pointers and behind-his-back whisperers what he was made of. Devon stood as straight as he could and moved close to the woman.

"Yeah, I'll show you something."

"All right then! You can call me..." Devon put up his hand, signaling her to be quiet. He remembered one of the first lessons Hank taught him. *A body don't need no name!*
As they walked down the block she continued.

"Look fella, let's get business out the way. A quickie gonna cost you thirty-five and a *bj* is fifteen extra." She pointed to an alley and the two made a sharp right. "Now if you want to hit it from the back that'll be a straight fifty. Scraped up my knees doin' that once and it took me out of commission for a couple of days."

They reached the bowel of the alley, out of sight of police and others. Devon reached into his wallet and pulled out three crisp twenties.

"I ain't got no change...got that?"
Devon leaned back against a dumpster and grunted an order. "Pop your top." The woman rolled her top down to her navel, allowing the sagginess of her breasts to sway briefly in Devon's vision. For the first time, he realized he was numb.

"Let's get it on daddy. Can't be back here all night. Want me to start with the *bj*? Before Devon could respond, she dropped into a squat and fingered his belt buckle and zipper. The cool air, the smell of her body, and the decreasing potency of the alcohol made way in his mind for a revolution in introspection.

"You alright down there? I could try to get it going but that'll be another five...hand jobs ain't free."

Free!
The word ran circles in his mind. He wanted to be free--and he wanted to be accepted. He realized he couldn't have both.

"C'mon man...relax...let mama be good to you."
The trigger was released. Devon now knew he would never please his mother. He would never live up to Hank's expectations. If he wanted to be free he had to do what he felt was right. He had to

be good to himself. He had to go to those who would be good to him. His head was clear now. He reached down and retrieved his lifeless manhood from her hand.

"What's up daddy?"

Devon put himself back together, placed the money in her hand, and left the alley. He now knew who he was and where he should be. The moonlight broke through the clouds, casting a silvery pathway for him to follow.

"That's right on time! Sixty bucks and I ain't had to get my lips chapped!"

FIRST FLOOR STOP

THE LOBBY OF ONE Liberty Place continued to swell as the lunch crowd returned to work. A disruption in power caused the elevators to become inoperable. The security guard finished his conversation with the mechanic, shaking his head as he prepared to share the news with the anxious crowd.

"Attention everyone!" The crowd of cubicle-bound employees quieted. "The man says that the elevators on this side of the building are going to be out for another twenty or thirty minutes." Grumbles and curses began to rise. "You are welcome to use the service elevator in the back. It's not as fast but you'll be able to get where you need to go." Employees noted how small and dirty the service elevator was. Some resigned to hold their breaths as they rode to the upper floors. Others opted to call up to their offices to inform them that they would be late in returning. Sylvania wasn't sure what to do. Maybe she would find an answer as she let her mind find pause from the moment's events.

For the last three months, Sylvania had worked to prove herself of value to PowerCat. She worked late hours, came in on weekends when requested, and tried her best to offer ideas which would benefit the production in the office. She also put up with the lascivious leering from Ted Stevenson. She knew he was going to be trouble back from her initial interview and since then his actions only worsened. Whenever they passed each other in the corridor, he would lick his lips and comment on how nicely her clothes were fitting. If he was seated in the break room and Sylvania walked by, he accented the atmosphere with a *whew lawd* or *that's it right there!* Sylvania wanted to confront him but she didn't want to risk her job. Ted had been with PowerCat for a long time, a big wig as far as the other people in the office were concerned.

It was a Monday, just moments before the afternoon UPS deliveries. Sylvania left her area to use the lavatory. She stopped by the water fountain, bending to take a sip. Her body jerked rigid when she felt a brushing on her behind.

"Oh, my bad, sweetness." Ted apologized slyly, holding back a smile by chewing slightly on his lip. "You know we work in such close quarters." Sylvania reeled around and pushed Ted, causing him to stumble over a box on the floor.

"I don't know who the hell you think you are!" Sylvania's voice was on fire. "Don't you ever touch me again! Don't even look at me!" Ted regained his stance and stepped toward Sylvania. He spat a low growl.

"Don't be acting all paranoid. Nobody's doing nothing to you. You're lucky to be working here..." Ted started to move closer until he noticed a new figure in the corridor. Sylvania noticed him too.

"What's going on?"

Sylvania's nostrils flared as Ted approached Devon. He was laughing as he put his hand around Devon's shoulder and pointed to Sylvania.

"Man, that girl is buggin'! She thinks somebody's pushing up on her. I apologized to her even though I didn't do anything...just to make her feel better. I think she got a thing for me." Ted gave Sylvania a full once over with his eyes. "You know I'm not down with that type."

Sylvania didn't know what to say. She was so angry words would not form in her mind. All she had were curse words, fear, and a balled fist.

"Talk to her Devon! I got work to do." Ted began to walk away before Devon caught him by the arm.

"Ms. Lee, did he touch you inappropriately?"

Sylvania took pause. *Was this a set-up?* Sylvania knew some staff were being identified for layoffs and perhaps this was a way to get rid of her. She didn't want to be perceived as a trouble-maker or complainer but she knew that if she didn't say anything Ted would take full advantage.

"Well?" Devon stood firm even after Ted shook himself loose from his grip.

"Yes he did." Sylvania breathed out the words. "Not only that, he is constantly staring me down and saying suggestive things. It's been like that as long as I've been with the company."

"That's just a young girl talking Devon." Ted looked at his watch. "Man, I have somewhere to be. Just keep her away from me alright?" Sylvania watched Devon to see his next move. She felt her posture begin to fold as she turned to return to her cubicle.

"Sylvania...come down to my office. Ted, I'll talk to you in a bit." Devon moved quickly. Ted retreated from the corridor but not before turning his face back to Sylvania and quickly flicked his tongue up and down in her direction. Sylvania felt ill as she slowly made her way to Devon's office. She wished she had kept her mouth shut. If she had just let it go she would still have her job. The thought of begging for her donut shop job back made her dizzy.

"Please come in and have a seat." Devon motioned to a chair as Sylvania entered his office. A chill came over her body when she took notice that Mrs. Ortiz from Human Resources followed her into the room. "I asked Mrs. Ortiz to join us as I would like to resolve this as quickly and cleanly as possible."
There was nervousness inside Sylvania which drew the blood from her skin. Shivering, she waited for Devon to speak.

"Marisol, I need your direction on releasing someone from service here. I want it done quickly but correctly. I've been through this before and it ended messy." Sylvania managed to raise her head enough to look at the *Standards of Excellence* plaque stationed behind Devon's shoulder. "I want it clear that there are behaviors in the work place that will not be tolerated." Mrs. Ortiz nodded affirmatively but remained silent. "Sylvania…"

"I didn't do a damned thing to that Ted." Sylvania fired off quickly as her hands tightened on the arms of the chair. "I was just minding my business like always…" Devon rose and moved to the front of his desk.

"Sylvania…I know. I saw the whole thing." Devon turned his attention to Mrs. Ortiz. "I was coming around the corner when I saw Ted clearly brush his groin area on Ms. Lee's buttocks as she was getting a drink of water. I'm sure Ted will tell you it was an accident but the corridor is wide enough to accommodate three people. I watched him turn his whole body so that he could make the physical connection. When I confronted the situation Ted attempted to put the blame solely on Ms. Lee."

Sylvania began to feel even more bemused as she listened. Mrs. Ortiz was writing furiously after Devon asked Sylvania to repeat the other behaviors Ted has displayed toward her. Mrs. Ortiz shared that there had been accusations from other women in the office but none ever filed a formal complaint.

"Are you willing to submit a formal report with my office?" Mrs. Ortiz spoke directly and slowly to Sylvania. "This is not the kind of behavior tolerated at PowerCat but you have to do your part to help bring it to a close." Sylvania didn't know what to say until Devon kneeled next to her, patting her gently on her hand.

"Ms. Lee. I have observed your work here since your arrival. I value you and so does PowerCat. I want you to know that respect and dignity is the inherent right of everyone who works here. I would encourage you to sit down with Mrs. Ortiz and file the report." Devon stood and returned to his desk. "You know what the ironic part of this whole thing is, Marisol? I was on my way to Ms. Lee's desk to invite her to apply to the PowerCats on the Move Managerial Program. It's a good thing I was headed that way or else it would have been a he-said, she-said situation." Mrs. Ortiz stood and asked Sylvania to join her as she left Devon's office.

"Thank you Mr. Hunt." Sylvania could only whisper her gratitude. She followed behind Mrs. Ortiz before being stopped by Devon.

"When you take care of business with Marisol, please come back and see me about the program. I believe in investing in people of value here at PowerCat."

Toward the end of the day, Sylvania heard a string of obscenities words coming from down the corridor. Leaning back in her chair, she saw Ted being escorted out of the office by one of the building security officers. He carried his coat in one hand and a box of items in another. His eyes connected with Sylvania's. Her first inclination was to turn away but she summoned strength from deep within and followed him until he was at the elevator door. Once in, he turned and glared at her before the doors closed. The girl in the cubicle next to her rolled over in her chair and patted Sylvania on the back.

"I can't believe they let him go. He's been with the company for years but was always a kind of icky and nasty. I give it to you girl. It took some balls for you to stand up to him." Sylvania smiled and moved back to her desk.

"Sometimes you just got to grow a pair...know what I'm sayin'?"

From within the movement of the crowd, Sylvania caught sight of Ellis as he entered the building. Quickly, yet discretely, she moved to intersect with him before he reached the steps.

"Hey there two-stepper." Sylvania's voice brought a smile to Ellis' face.

"Sylvania, how are you?" Ellis scanned the lobby, now noticing all of the people. "Elevator down again?" Sylvania laughed. "Well, I'm going to do what I normally do." Ellis pointed to the stairs. "Are you up to it?"

"That's twelve floors."

"Well, like they say...a journey of twelve floors begins with one step."

"Who said that?"

"Somebody whose elevator was broke down." Ellis held out his arm which she playfully linked with hers.

"Let's start the journey."

Reaching the landing of the third floor, Ellis and Sylvania were reminiscing of the antics of Twist at the dance. Sylvania promised to make sure he was on their VIP list for the next year's ball. By the fifth floor, Sylvania began to slow down. Ellis reminded her it wasn't a race and the two of them sat down on the steps until she felt ready to move on. When they reached the seventh floor landing, Sylvania was quiet, allowing Ellis' mind to reflect on how empty his life had become without Clarissa. His weekends had been spent in solitude unless he was visiting his mother. He had thought about going out to opening exhibits at the African American Museum or to hear new jazz artists down at Zanzibar Blue but never did. He knew these were experiences that should be shared.

Sylvania took his hand as she counted down the steps to the ninth floor. She didn't want to give up but the last three flights were daunting. Ellis' hand had a gentle strength that supported her, not pulling her along as she had expected. She knew he had to be late getting back to his office but he didn't appear to be upset or rushed. Neither knew who made the first move but soon their fingers were intertwined by the time they passed the tenth floor. The twelfth floor was in sight. Sylvania looked up the spiral banister and sighed with a happy relief. Ellis had a news flash in his mind. Their time together was coming to a close.

"Here you are Sylvania. Twelfth floor. You did it!" Ellis gave Sylvania a strong embrace as she tried to return the hug and catch her breath at the same time. "Would you..." The notion was stronger than his apprehension. "Would you like to go out with me this weekend?"

He didn't receive a reply. Sylvania leaned against the railing and focused on the floor.

"I'm sorry," began Ellis. "I shouldn't have presumed." Sylvania grinned as she looked up at Ellis.

"I just walked up twelve flights of steps. Give me a minute." Now standing upright, Sylvania offered a breathy smile.

"Sure. I'd like that." As Ellis used one of his business cards to write her phone number on the back they heard a *ding* from across the hall. In unison they looked to see the elevator door open. A group of people piled out and hastily made their way to their respective offices. One of the women waved at Sylvania.

"Hey girl...you should have waited with us." Sylvania began walking slowly toward the door to her suite.

"Not me..." She turned to watch Ellis continue his climb to the fourteenth floor. "...I couldn't wait."

WHISPERS

"GIRL, SO YOU THINK he's all that?" Twist rolled from off of the couch and onto the floor. She slid her legs under Sylvania's coffee table and proceeded to eat her hot wings. Picking, she continued her questioning between chews. "Seriously? He's a high power in your building?

"That's right! Fourteenth floor. Straight up executive." Sylvania sat at the counter dunking her french fries into a pool of catsup. "Got a nice ride and all too!"

"And here I thought he was just another corny dude." Twist's stomach growled, reminding her to get on with her lunch. "He was kind of cute...in a okie-dokie kind of way. I ain't gonna lie, I don't remember much about him. I was a little tipsy at the dance."

"A little?" Sylvania made a face. "Girl, you should have seen the guy you hooked up with...in the light." She snorted as she sipped her Tahitian Treat soda, tickled by the bubbles now in her nose.

"I did...the next day. Said his name was Junior..." Twist knew what she was going to say was funny because she started choking on her lunch. Once composed she quickly blurted out, "His name should have been Goon-yer! Sylvania's room became crowded with their silly assessments of Twist's exploit. "He did the job in bed but when he caught some sunbeams...he was jacked up...lookin' like a black zombie. I beat it out of there faster than you could say *zombro!*"

When they calmed down Sylvania began to clean up.

"Ellis invited me to lunch tomorrow."

Sylvania stopped eating and pointed her meatless bone at Twist lead and struck several poses. "That's right...Bam! An official date!"

Twist applauded her girl.

"A Saturday night all night thang! Go ahead Syl!" Sylvania stopped posing and threw a sly gaze at Twist.

"Oh no...not Saturday night...Saturday afternoon. He invited me to a picnic. He's fixing a picnic lunch and we're going to the park and..." Sylvania's words were cut short when she saw Twist's arms and hands flailing in the air.

"Aw hales no!" Twist struggled to get out from under the table. When she realized it was too much work she leaned back onto the couch. "A picnic? Who are y'all? Yogi and Boo-Boo?"

"I think it's kind of romantic." Sylvania rested against the sink. "When was the last time a man invited you to a picnic lunch?"

"Never did and never will!" Twist folded her arms. "First you tell me he's got it going on and the best thing he can do for you is to slap together a peanut butter and jelly sandwich and have you meet him at the playground? Come on Syl...you gave him free tickets to the dance! He ain't come up out of pocket yet for you."

"And your dates come up out of pocket for you?" Twist was quiet, but only for a second.

"I know my dates are busted...what's your excuse?" Sylvania was quiet. "Yeah, you know I'm right. He comes off like *Happy Days* but he's working on tappin' something just like all the rest of 'em." Sylvania cleaned up the remainder of the lunch. "If he's all front page like you say, he should be taking you to Applebee's or Friday's or something."

It was a warm Saturday morning and the reports called for an even warmer afternoon. She was not only unsure of what to wear but wary of the date itself. Sylvania had picked out a simple short set but right before Ellis was to arrive, she changed to a black sweat suit and sandals. She was pulled into a whirlpool of thoughts. *Why would he want to go on a picnic? Is he trying to avoid running into his high-level friends with me?* She contemplated cancelling the date but she had to see what Ellis was all about. A full report was due back to Twist as soon as she returned home. Skepticism filled the pockets of her intuition when she heard the buzzer, letting her know he was at the front door.

"I'll be right down." Sylvania's voice was flat. She walked down the two flights slowly and paused when she reached the landing before the front door. She prayed that this afternoon would go quickly so she could make up for the day and hit a club. Opening the door she saw Ellis. Instinctually she swooned inside as her greeting was cool and aloof. Even through her sulking eyes, she could see that he was even more handsome relaxed. He had on a Polo shirt, shorts, and a pair of sandals that could almost pass for shoes. He was holding his shades in one hand and extended the other.

"You're looking very pretty today Sylvania…" Ellis looked up to the sky. "But I think you're going to be hot in that today. It supposed to get up to mid-eighties at least." Sylvania took his hand limply, responding dryly.

"So I heard. You ready?"
Ellis was too excited to pick up on Sylvania's attitude. Even with her restrained manner, he still found her to be charming; in fact, he felt he was being exposed to another alluring facet of her personality.

"I hope you're hungry," smiled Ellis.
"Had a big breakfast."
Sylvania walked toward Ellis' car. Once inside, she reached over and turned up the radio. Ellis talked but mentally, she wasn't part of the conversation. As they headed down Broad Street, Sylvania reminisced on the pile of raggedy dates she had over the years. She just knew that this one was going to be the rotten cherry to go atop

the mountainous glob of the wasted time, energy, and total disrespect she allowed in her life. So many to choose from, where would she begin?

She started with Les. He said that he was taking her to a movie. Didn't say it was at the no-named theater just off of Walnut Street that showed films like *She's Gonna Get It*, *Wham-Bam Grand Slam*, and *Drivin' Miss Daisy Crazy*. There was Big Ron. The seemingly strong silent-type she met at the Progress Plaza shopping center. She should have known something was up when he told her to meet him at the Market-Frankford Interchange and from there they would just ride the subway and get to know each other better. How trifling is a man who tries to get his membership into the mile-high club on the subway? She tried to forget Tommy--the one who left her at a club downtown when it was clear *he wasn't gettin' any* after he tried to bend her over the men's bathroom sink. Her stomach tightened when she recalled the Mother's Day with Rahgu. He showed up at her mother's home empty handed and left with a pocket full of CDs, a necklace, and two rings. She should have known, he didn't have a job but always had money which he didn't seem to be able to spend--borrowed money and borrowed love. There were plenty more: liars- stealers-feelers-druggies-drunks-schemers-hustlers-bummers-wannabees-neverbees-dead beat fathers-DL'ers-freeloaders-posers-creepers-beaters, and basement livin' mama's boys.

Sylvania watched Ellis slow down on the West River Drive and ease into a convenient parking space.

"We're here," he announced and proceeded to empty the trunk. Sylvania took her time. She heard him ask if she would *grab the blanket*. Her body now felt like stone as she leaned against the car. She couldn't move. She didn't want to move. Ellis boomeranged back to the car, oblivious to her disposition, took the blanket from the trunk and shut it.

"I'll take care of it. Wait here until I get things all set up." Sylvania fixed the sunglasses on her face and watched Ellis go through his exercise. He rolled out the blanket, placing the picnic basket on one corner and an old boombox on another. From the small cooler he retrieved several small bottles of assorted sparkling juices. He motioned for her to come over. It took all of her strength to push herself from off the car and into Ellis' direction. "Sit on down," Ellis instructed gently as he leaned over to help her. Sylvania refused his hand, causing her to lose her balance and drop hard onto the ground. Ellis rushed to her side but she waved him off.

"I'm okay, let's just get to lunch." As she rubbed her bottom she thought, *I better not have any grass stains or he's going to pay my cleaning bill.* Finally, Sylvania initiated conversation. "So...what's in the basket?"

When Ellis first thought of the idea of the picnic, he started to make his usual lunch but now with a new outlook on life he felt it was time to try something different. A quick call to his mother and in an hour's time he had a menu that was designed to delight both the senses and the palate.

"I hope you like it." Ellis arranged a series of small plates and utensils in a semi-circle around the basket. With the voice of a television travel announcer, he described each item as he displayed them for Sylvania's approval.

"Here we have a short loaf of French bread...or, as they say in the City of Lights, baguette. Next, an assortment of spreads: Dijon mustard, a little horseradish, and Champagne mustard. Your choice of summer sausage or turkey roast. I have an assortment of cheeses to choose from...Brie, Swiss, and Goat. Finally, there are some grapes, two pears, and a melon mix in the Tupperware."

Sylvania felt her stomach curse her for lying that she had a big breakfast. Her eyes were pulled away from the lunch choices to watch Ellis roll over and depress the play button on the small boombox's cassette player. History told her that most of the music played by the guys she dated involved turning off the lights, getting closer and closer, doin' it till they were satisfied, and knockin' boots. There's a message in the music and it was always clear and direct. She paused as the sounds of Grover Washington Jr's *Winelight* sheltered them from the noise of the drive and surrounding park goers. Grover was followed by the likes of Trudy Pitts, Pieces of a Dream, Billie Holiday, Hall & Oates, and Phyllis Hyman. Ellis carefully sliced the sausage and turkey into small pieces and invited Sylvania to enjoy.

History is a prison from which very few escape. Sylvania, a prisoner of her own decisions, of circumstances, of fate, was beginning to hear something on the other side of the containment walls of her own construction. Deep inside, she knew the smile on Ellis' face was not deception. His actions, this picnic, his attention were keys to the shackles that held her bound to the bars of heartache, shame, and self-erosion. She could hear a door being opened at the end of the corridor of confidence but the guards, Self-doubt and Shaded Vision, were the sentinels of admonishment, chiding her not to pull against the chains that held her back. She did tug on the chains as she wondered, how could a man find such pleasure in an outing as plain as this? To purposefully create a space undisturbed by the clatter and clamor of interruptions, booming bases, gyrating bodies, smoke, shouts, and facades. She couldn't fathom that *I just wanted to spend time with you* could be the words that would commute her sentence--but the evidence pointed nowhere else. The warm sun bathed her face as he poured her a drink designed, not to intoxicate her into indecisions and regret, but to simply refresh. Her thirst was diminished as the sound of the cerebral cell door began to open.

The breeziness of his expressions remained as he spilled a dollup of mustard onto his shirt. Inside she knew she was hearing the voice of the warden saying *you're free to go*! When he leaned forward slowly, only to dab the corner of her mouth with a napkin, she could begin to breathe the sweet air of a new-found freedom. A feeling of liberty that allowed her eyes to regain their sparkle, allowed her posture to move from rigidity to openness, allowed her spirit to regain its strength, its beauty, its reason. She now felt a warmness return to her smile. She saw a glow emanating from Ellis as he bit into a grape. She finally could hear the music and its sound waves of tranquility.

Sylvania smiled, leaned over, kissed Ellis on the cheek. "This is a very nice lunch. Thank you." Sylvania felt good all over, except in the pits of her arms. She now regretted wearing the sweat suit.

The balmy winds and the smells of neighboring barbecues accented the conversations of Ellis and Sylvania. They explored each other's past; Identifying similarities from their days in elementary and high school, to the highs and lows of the modern work world.

"Do you have to wear a suit every day?"

"Nothing wrong with working at a neighborhood store...one of the backbones of a community!"

"No, I lost my father when I was very young...didn't really know him."

"Three brothers...one passed on...I'm the baby."

"I'd like to one day own an art gallery and host independent films."

"I would love to be a radio deejay...I know that's crazy."

As the two moved closer on the blanket, a long subdued feeling came over Ellis. His attention was clearly on every word formed by Sylvania's mouth but intuitively he knew he should turn around and to look over his shoulder. He wasn't sure if it was the change in the sounds, the body language of the others in his peripheral vision, or simply street smarts. Whatever it was, he turned slowly; only to find his inklings were right on point. Three young men were coming in their direction and their demeanor was evident they weren't there to enjoy the calming currents of the Schuylkill River. Instinctively, Ellis shifted his body so that he could stand quickly if the situation called for it.

"Check those guys out..." Sylvania's words reached his ears too late. He was well aware of the many possible outcomes from the impending encounter. The play began with one teen staying back from the other two. *A lookout? A distraction? The extra hand when called?* Ellis kept him in his mental notebook. The other two stopped at the blanket's edge. The one in the wife beater t-shirt spit.

"You know what this all about...give it up!"
The second teen's hand reached into the picnic basket, flicking the contents around.

"Y'all need to go somewhere with that dumbshi..." Sylvania's words screeched to a halt when the first teen scrambled around Ellis and stood above her. His hand was poised to strike.

"Tell yo girl to shut it." For one second he turned his face to Ellis'. "I'll pimp slap a bitch with the quickness." The *quickness* was all that he would remember. With a sweep of his arm, Ellis grabbed the ankle of the teen and pulled with a force powered by both anger and anxiety. The young thug landed on the ground hard, hitting his head on the boombox, cracking the case. Sylvania wrapped her fingers around the neck of an unopened bottle of sparkling grape cider and aimed it for the bridge of his nose. Ellis turned his attention to the one with his hand on Sylvania's purse.

214

He leapt up with surprising speed that startled the second thug, as well as Sylvania. He drove his fist into his chest, dropping him to his knees before he could utter a wheeze of lost breath. Sylvania looked past Ellis. The third thug was gone.

"GET THE HELL OUT OF HERE!" Ellis' voice had a power and conviction, telegraphing that this was the wrong day and these were the wrong people. As if on cue, the remaining thugs found their opening and beat their retreat.

Another couple sat with Ellis and Sylvania as they calmed down. Sylvania rubbed ice cubes on Ellis' back and neck while he sat wringing the edge of the blanket. He was breathing hard and his sweating maintained a steady stream into his eyes. It would be ten or fifteen minutes before the couple felt Ellis and Sylvania had calmed down enough to be left to themselves.

"Are you okay Ellis?"
Ellis shook his head, taking a series of quick sips from a bottle of sparkling apple cider. He felt like he just ran a marathon as he began to be able to control his breathing. Sylvania took a napkin and wiped his face again. Ellis leaned his head back and after a brief stretch of time, he began to smile in between breaths. With his hand still shaking, he reached out to Sylvania and touched her shoulder.

"I haven't been in a fight <huff> since the sixth grade<huff>." He squeezed her shoulder gently. "It's a lot more work then I remember." Sylvania smiled and placed her palm on his face. She rubbed his cheeks, squeezing them gently.

"How did you know that fool didn't have a gun or something?" Sylvania shuddered and kneeled down to the ground. "We could have been the lead story on the six o'clock news." There was a long pause. There were no words to be said. They embraced.

Dusk was creeping in as Ellis and Sylvania carried the picnic items back to the car. Popping the cassette from the damaged player, he said a playful prayer and respectfully dumped the machine into a trashcan.

"I've been meaning to get rid of that for years."
Sylvania smiled, "Guess you're ready for a Walkman or something more advanced now." She took his hand and walked Ellis to the car. "You know, sometimes you have to let the past go if you want to move forward."

"Write that down and put it in a card." Ellis smiled broadly as a thought came into his mind. "Speaking of the past, let me show you something...it just might open the door to the future...and you can put that into a card!" The car wheels kicked up gravel, leaving behind an afternoon not soon forgotten.

Ellis turned off the drive and headed up into Fairmount Park. The small streets weaved in and out of the overgrown trees and foliage. At dusk, it was romantic; at night, not a place you would want to break down. After a mile or so, the car rose to meet the glowing dome of Arden Hall and eventually the other sites of the Parkside area. The greenway was scattered with tarnished statues, people picnicking, and winos looking for their next taste. There were groups of teens hanging out on benches, people preparing for the next day by sweeping their walks, and cars headed toward the Dell to see the likes of Terrence Trent D'Arby, The Time, and Lisa Lisa Cult Jam. Sylvania enjoyed this. Riding around the city in a car was a treat, catching pieces of conversations and sights not visible when on the bus or subway. She knew she could do this all night--especially with Ellis.

Ellis pulled the car over to the curb. It was getting dark and Sylvania could see that Ellis was moving quickly.

"You want to see something neat?"

Sylvania could hear an excitement in his voice. The two left the car and walked over to a long curved wall. The streetlight offered an eerie yellowish beam for comfort. Ellis walked over to the wall.

"Sit right here," he said, indicating the stone bench attached to the wall.

Although she had her *street antennae* up for the slightest sense of danger, she trusted him. Once she was seated, Ellis walked away, following the wall to its end, about twenty feet away. He sat down at the other end. Sylvania's "antennae" picked up the *not-making-sense* signal. Her mind wondered what he was up to. *Did he want to see if she would get up and come to him? If so, she wasn't playing that game. Was he going to bolt, jump in the car, and jet? That wouldn't make sense because she knew she was closer to the car than he was.* Other thoughts entered and left her mind until she heard his voice in her ear. Sylvania stopped. She focused. The words were faint. Was she hallucinating? No one ever heard voices after drinking sparkling cider. Cocking her head she heard his voice clearly.

"Sylvania…these are the famous Whispering Benches. If you can hear me, raise your hand." Sylvania lifted her hand. She turned her face to see Ellis nodding his head and grinning. "Go ahead and try it. Just talk normally." Sylvania tried it.

"Okay…I had a great time today…did you hear that? If so, raise your hand." She could see Ellis's hand, waving at her. Sylvania smiled as the words floated into her ear.

"Let me tell you one thing Sylvania. I used to come here as a kid. That's the past. I had a great time with you today. That's the future…I guess what I want to say is that I would like to see you again…if you would like that?" Before Sylvania could answer the sounds of gunshots could be heard in the distance.

"Time to go!"

Ellis heard Sylvania's voice loud and clear and in no time the two were back in the car and headed toward Sylvania's home. Their conversation during their drive was sweet and easy. Succumbing to the hypnotic spinning of rotisserie chicken in the window, they stopped at the Meadowlane restaurant to share a combination platter before finishing their drive down Broad Street.

It was close to ten o'clock when Ellis pulled up in front of her apartment. Sylvania did a quick mental scan of her place and remembered how messy it was. She wanted to invite him up but she wanted to make a proper first impression. Ellis let her off the hook.

"I enjoyed our time together but I promised my mother that I would go with her to visit my brother tomorrow. It's a monthly thing. It'll be a long day so I better get home and get some rest. I'll call you to set our next date…if you don't mind."

At the door, the two were like middle school co-eds anticipating their first kiss. Air filling chatter lasted a minute or so until Ellis leaned over and kissed Sylvania on the cheek. Seizing the moment, Sylvania slowly brought her arms around Ellis' neck and the two lost themselves in each other--until her building's door opened. An elderly man with a suitcase found his way between the two, stopped for a moment, and smiled slyly. They said good night and knew they would be seeing each other very soon--very, very soon.

CHECK, PLEASE!

HANK HAD GROWN TO loathe charity functions. Over the years, his sentiments moved from altruism, to good business, to *too many of these,* to *why am I here?* He stood there, not caring whether the family received a new house, if the community center got new footballs, if the clinic now housed a mammogram machine. All he knew was that he was tired of standing there, smiling for the cameras, shaking hands with recipients, or even hugging them. There were only two things keeping him from walking out. The first was the press. This was good business for the firm and if business was good then Mr. Morgan was happy. If the boss was happy, he was left alone.

The second was the gorgeous woman seated in the second row, quietly waiting for Hank. He didn't know which to pay more attention to--the clock--or her statuesque frame. Even sitting down, Hank could read her curvaceous features and he knew the ending to this story. He slipped in and out of consciousness as the chair or founder or director or whoever droned on about the *goodness and generosity* of Druer Charities...*blah...blah...blah...*

The cool air felt good as Hank stepped out toward the parking garage. The woman held tightly to his arm, looking cautiously at the clouds that had begun to form in the night sky. Hank knew her worry. *She probably paid a couple hundred dollars for that doo...looks good but not my concern.* Hank plotted under his breath. *I'm going to sweat it out later anyway.*

Once settled in the car Hank noticed her mouth moving.

"We going to get something to eat or what?" With the unexpected extension of the program, Hank was forced to rearrange his original agenda. His plan was to spend about forty-five minutes at the program and go straight to his place, lay her out, and when finished, put her into a cab. Now with the program going almost an additional hour, he would have to get her something to eat. Normally, he wouldn't spend too much money on a woman--even one as beautiful as this one--but on this night there was no back up prospect.

"What do you want?" Hank began pulling out of the Ambler Community Complex parking lot and onto Bethlehem Pike towards the city.

"Oooh...what about Dinardo's?"

Hank shook his head.

"Okay, what about somewhere down Penn's Landing?

Again, Hank shook his head, this time adding commentary, "Too far out the way."

She suggested several others with each one followed by a rejection.

"Tokyo?"

"Don't want all that show."

"Hard Rock?"

"Too commercial"

"Ruth Chris'?"

"It's a chain...just like McDonalds." Hank was hoping she would give up but she was relentless. Suddenly, her voice began to annoy him. Against his nature, he knew he would have to feed her fast.

"Hey...!" The woman pointed. "Let's just go there."
Hank read the sign--*Bridget's A Modern Steakhouse*. He suddenly felt tired. She had worn him out. He made a U-turn and coasted into the restaurant parking lot.

The steakhouse was small, as far as Hank was concerned. It was too noisy as well. He smelled the steaks cooking and his first primal instinct kicked in. As the hostess approached, his woman for the evening stepped in front to be led to their table. He caught a full glimpse of her outline as she weaved in and around the seated patrons and his second primal instinct kicked in even stronger. He now knew he needed to eat quickly and get *whatever she's called* to his place. Just as he began to lower his body into the chair, Hank's eye caught sight of something--somebody familiar. He stood up from his chair. On the far end of the restaurant, in a corner, sat two men--one vaguely familiar but the other....

"Welcome to Bridget's...," began the red-headed waiter. "Can I start you two with drinks?"

Hank ignored the waiter. *That looks like my man over there!* Hank needed a break from his future conquest and started toward the men.

"Where you going baby?"

"Sit tight! I'm going to say what's up to a good friend of mine. Order me a Kaluah and Crème and get yourself something. I'll be back in a minute."

The room was dimmed for the evening but Hank's presence cast a shadow on the two men. The first man looked up and offered a cordial nod but wasted no time in returning his attention back to his tablemate. Milliseconds later, the second man looked up and froze. He quickly swallowed the sautéed spinach he was chewing and raised a napkin to his mouth. The first man could see something in his tablemate's eyes and mannerisms. The second man found a small greeting from somewhere and quickly cleared his throat.

"Hank...What's happening?"

"You look like you're ready to get out of here."

Cary finished his Waterbrook Melange and placed the empty glass on the server's tray. "We don't have to stay...I received my honor and now it is all about hobnobbing and pressing flesh." Cary felt

Devon's arm gently wrap around his waist. Still holding his glass of wine, Devon lifted it slightly, acknowledging his friend's recognition.

"Congratulations!" Devon sipped his wine. "Outstanding Alumni of the Year...that's impressive." Taking the plaque from Cary's hand, Devon used his jacket sleeve to polish its face. He read the wording: *Cary Glass, Class of 1994, in recognition of his unselfish support of students and programs of Beaver College....*

"Well...you might not be ready to go...*all this free wine*...but I am. This is just their way to make sure you donate larger dollars at the next campaign." Cary wiggled from out of Devon's grasp and began moving toward the door. Two steps later, the Vice President cornered Cary, introducing him to a young woman. She was the recipient of a scholarship that allowed her to travel and study public health concerns of the indigenous people of Australia. Cary's ears were filled with her stories, which were accented by the statements of gratitude of the VP. Devon stood there, not quite sure of what he was feeling. He could see the joy and excitement in the student's face. He could tell by the body language that the VP knew the college had a friend for life. Even with Cary's casual manner, slivers of personal satisfaction escaped from the inside. It suddenly dawned on him. He now knew what he was feeling. It wasn't just pride, it was more much more. It was love! It had to be. Even free wine couldn't make you feel like this.

"Here you go," Devon held Cary's coat so that he could slip right in. "I'm hungry, let's get something to eat."
The two walked from out the main building and stood facing the traffic.

"I know a wonderful place in Chinatown--the Banana Leaf. The cuisine is Malaysian...you'll love it..." Cary painted a picture. "We could dine on roti canai, mee siam, and some ginger duck lo mee."

"I don't feel like going all the way in town for dinner. Let's just find something close by." Devon dug his hands into his trench coat. Could this be their first argument? Is this the first test of their relationship? Who was to give in? He brought his lips in and licked them slowly. Devon could see Cary draw a breath and prepare to speak.

"Let's just drive around until we find something. I'm not that familiar with this area." Devon was relieved. He reached over, took Cary by the hand, and without the hesitation or surveying who would be watching, he kissed him gently on the lips.

They drove through the small boroughs of Montgomery County, not quite finding anything appealing. After crossing over Skippack Pike, Devon turned the radio down.

"Cary...what's this fascination with Asian foods...Asian sites? It's cool but I'm sensing a theme." Without looking, Cary ran his fingers through Devon's curly hair and rested his hand on the back of his neck.

"My father was in the Navy, stationed in the Okinawa. He met my mother there. She was Japanese. They got married and had me. That's the only home I care to know. After my father retired, my parents decided to stay and let me finish high school." As they passed through Fort Washington, Cary explained how his parents surrounded him with many of the cultural foods, décor, and customs of the country. Eating deep fried squid and burdock roots on a Saturday night was as natural as kids eating pizza over here in the states. That was his life until it came to an abrupt end. Devon could see moisture welling up in Cary's eyes as he brought a pause to his story.

"You don't have to go on if you don't want to." Cary removed his hand from Devon's shoulder and retrieved a tissue from his glove box. As he wiped his eyes, he explained how his parents were caught in a flash flood during the typhoon season. They had left the base to go visit the countryside and the road they were on got washed out. The officials retrieved his mother's body but his father was never found. "Because I was an American citizen and my stateside family was adamant, I was sent to live with my father's sister in Baltimore to finish my last year of high school. She didn't care for my *tendencies*, so when it came time for college, I got as far away from her as I could." Devon watched Cary wipe his nose. His usually upbeat demeanor was now quiet and somber. "The whole Asian theme…just keeps the memories of my parents alive."

Placing his hand on Cary's thigh, Devon knew now that he was even more connected. A door was opened and whatever he would find inside would be treasured.

"Hey!" Cary blurted out. "It's cool! There's a place right over there…*Bridget's*. Let's get out of this car and these memories and eat."

Hank's smile vanished. His eyes became tight and intense. The coolness of the greeting he prepared deadened when he saw Devon holding the other man's hand.

"What the hell are you doing with that guy?" Before either could speak, Hank began putting pieces together in his mind. He now remembered Devon's *friend* from the dance. Devon mentioning him back at the office. Once that guy stopped by to pick Devon up for lunch. Devon brought his name up a couple of times while working out. The tighter Hank's jaws got, the clearer the picture before him became. His brain started to pound with the realization that Devon was lying when they were out hunting women. *Did Devon consider the times they ate together a date?* He flashbacked to their taking showers together after working out.

Was Devon checking him out when his back was turned? Come to think of it, he had Devon rub Ben Gay on his shoulder once--*Damn!* BEN GAY! *Ain't that a bitch!*

"Your friend?" Cary began to rise but was motioned to stay seated by Devon. "Ask your friend if he would like to join us." Hank turned his head just enough to look Cary square in the eye.

"I ain't sittin' down with no faggots!" Hank's voice rocketed above the sounds of the restaurant.

The red-headed waiter had just returned to the main room and watched the entire scene unfold. He explained it to the police thirty minutes later.

"The big man had walked over to their table and just stood there...then out of the blue he starts calling them names like *faggot* and stuff. I moved closer just in case I could help but it all happened too fast. I saw one of the guys, the real cool looking dude, reach for the steak knife but he pushed it out of the way and put the long butter knife in his lap. The other guy...I think he knew the big guy...stood up and tried to calm him down but the big man wasn't having it. The big man then shoved that guy back down into his chair. Good thing there wasn't a window behind him because he would have gone right out of it. Then...like lightning...the cool dude jumps up with the butter knife held in his hands...at both ends...you know...like...like the tightrope walkers hold their balance stick. Anyways...he slams it right into the big man's neck...like like that clothes-line move in wrestling. Big man stumbled back...holding his throat... and said something about *this ain't over.* Next thing you know, he bolts across the restaurant, grabs his date, and is gone. When I turned to check on the other two guys, they had dropped some cash on the table and left out the emergency exit. It was too dark and they were movin' too fast for

225

me to get their license plate." The red-headed waiter gulped down a cup of water. "Oh yeah," he smiled. "I did hear the cool dude say something like *a faggot is a bundle of sticks...and getting hit by a bundle of sticks hurt!*...something like that."

GAMBLER'S EXPRESS

TWIST STOOD AT SYLVANIA'S stove. The salami slices were frying nicely, soon to be cut into small pieces and added to her scrambled eggs. Sylvania fixed herself a plain onion and cheese omelet. After finding two paper plates and packets of sporks, the two sat down for their home style Sunday Brunch.

"What you doing for the fourth?" Twist found words between chews. Sylvania pushed her eggs around her plate. Something was missing but she couldn't figure it out.

"No plans...you?"

"I hear one of them frats is throwing a big party down on South Street. We should be in there!"

Sylvania started to salt her food but she stopped mid-shake. That wasn't it. She turned, looking hard at her spice cabinet: pepper, cinnamon, onion salt--that was all. Sylvania pushed her plate away.

"What's wrong Syl?" Twist asked as she switched her now empty plate with Sylvania's. "Don't tell me you all feenin' for Mr. Pick-a-Nick."

This was the first time Sylvania realized she hadn't told Twist about her date, at least not the whole story. She told her about going to the West River, what they had to eat, the knuckleheads, but that was all. The date had ended so nicely she didn't want Twist to spoil it with criticisms, jokes, sarcasm, or simply playing it down.

"He's away this week and won't get back until the weekend." Sylvania got up, taking the two empty plates to the trash. "I guess I'll just hang out..." Both of their heads turned with the ringing of the telephone.

"I bet it's your mom…probably going to invite you to the house for the fourth. If she's cooking, let's go there first then to the party."

Sylvania did not respond to Twist. Her mind was squarely focused on how to avoid her mother's July fourth picnic without hurting her feelings more. Sylvania knew there was still a lot of unresolved pain from the last blowout. Sylvania's voice was monotone as she answered.

"Hello?"

Twist watched Sylvania's face morph from a flatland to a terrain of excitement. She tried to restrain herself but Twist could tell something was going on. Twist tried to interject the question *who* but Sylvania continued hushing her.

"Yes!" That's all Sylvania said. In a dazed state, she hung up the phone slowly.

"Who was that? What? Yes to what?"

Sylvania got up, returned to the stove, and began fixing another omelet. Whatever she was missing, she'd found it--plenty of it.

Sylvania woke up early on Sunday the third of July. She knew what she was going to wear. She quickly glanced at the clock. She had three hours to go. For her, this was more than enough time to get ready, it was just anticipation that kept her from falling back to sleep. She fixed a cup of coffee and tried to guess what the day would hold. She flipped through the channels with nothing catching her attention. She switched on the radio and caught the beginnings of the Sunday Morning Slow Jams. Peabo Bryson was first to enter her home, singing *I'm so into you*. His soulful voice set both the mood and pace for her preparation. With her hair and nails done the previous day, she could concentrate on make-up and outfit. Not quite knowing what she would be doing or where she would end up she chose an outfit that was classy yet casual;

something that said *look at me stand here* but also, *I'm ready to move.*
The clock caught her attention again, it was almost ten. When the
hand moved to one minute past her phone rang. Not wanting to
appear eager, Sylvania let it ring twice.

"Hello?"

The voice on the other end brought a swelling grin to her face.
You'll honk twice? Okay. Sylvania hung up the phone and sat hard
into one of her kitchen chairs. *Not again* she thought to herself.
The men she dealt with would usually honk their horns to let her
know she needed to get into their cars. One guy, she couldn't
recall his name, which was good, shouted for her, and when she
took too long, drove off. Here she was again, awaiting two honks.
Something snapped in the back of Sylvania's mind. Tomorrow was
Independence Day. Perhaps this was her day to no longer accept
this kind of behavior from this or any other man. This was the day
to expect to be treated with total respect and a little dignity--open a
few doors, pull out some chairs, and a sincere compliment to
round it out. This was the day!

HONK! HONK!

Sylvania slowly walked to her window and peered down to the
street. She surmised a funeral must have been passing as there was
a limousine double parked in front of her apartment. She looked
for Ellis' car but it hadn't arrived.

HONK! HONK!

Sylvania was taken aback. *This brother must be thinking he's already in to
play the honking game. As if I'm going to run and...* Sylvania's eyes
suddenly locked on the limousine. The passenger door on the
street side opened.

I don't believe it! Sylvania's mind repeated those words as
she checked her face in the reflection of the toaster. She ran back
to the window and started to open it. Her first inclination was to

shout that she would be right down but she stopped, composed herself, and walked out of her apartment--breathing heavily.

"Sylvania, you look beautiful." Ellis turned and opened the car door, holding it until she was fully seated. He leaned in and kissed her gently on the cheek, admiring her carefully coiffed face. He quickly returned to the other side of the car and entered. "Well...are you ready for your surprise day?" Sylvania tried to play it cool but could feel a flurry of butterflies in her stomach. It was fabulous already and the car hadn't even moved out of park.

"This is a bit much for another picnic." Sylvania's words were smooth as they filled the air around him. Ellis loved her smile. He wanted to simply have the limousine idle, taking the moments to soak in her lips and cheekbones; but he couldn't, he had plans.

"I hope you're hungry. I have a treat for both your tongue...and your ears." If these words were from anyone else, Sylvania would have been turned off but hearing them from Ellis assured her that she was in for something memorable. This time, Sylvania told the truth.

"I am hungry...didn't eat a thing!"

The limousine glided along the streets and expressways of Philadelphia. In between their small talk, the two tried their best to out "Philly" each other--pointing out murals, statues, buildings, and other local landmarks and attractions.

"You see that over there?" Ellis brought their focus to a lone standing building. "That's the Roundhouse...a police station."

"You seem to know that well..." Sylvania playfully moved further from Ellis. "Should I get out now or is taking a pretty lady on a limo ride just part of your M.O.?" Ellis shook his head and faked a cough.

"No...nothing like that." Ellis looked at the Roundhouse through the rear window. He held his tongue. *I had to get my brother from there a couple of times.* "It's just the Roundhouse."

The limousine eased onto 95 South and Sylvania was quick to point out all of the stadiums. "I always wanted to go to the Ice Capades in the old Spectrum when I was a kid but times were tight back then." Sylvania drifted to the past but was soon distracted by Ellis' question.

"What would you like to do now? Go somewhere? See someone? Do something?"

Sylvania was overwhelmed by the possibilities of the questions. She remembered the saying, *it's hard to dream when there is no rest.* A billboard splashed with Johnny Gill performing at an Atlantic City casino flashed as they sped by.

"You know, I would love to see someone like TLC in concert. I hear they'll be in town later this month. I'll get Twist to go with me and check them out."

Ellis smiled, "That's a little too new school for my taste...take a look...we're here." So preoccupied with thoughts of what she would like to do, Sylvania didn't realize the limousine had turned, travelled north again, and exited onto Columbus avenue. She looked around and read the sign.

"So this is the famed Warmdaddys? I've heard so much about it on the radio but never found the time to come down." Truth be told, most of the men she dated felt the Waffle Hut was enough--if they sprung for a meal at all. Sylvania started to get out of the car but found Ellis' hand gently pulling her back from the doorknob.

"Allow me." Ellis jumped from out of his side of the vehicle and opened her door. He extended his hand. Arm in arm, they walked toward the restaurant.

The door to Warmdaddy's opened to an intimate sea of beautiful people from all walks of life, enjoying a common experience of mouth-watering delights and finger-poppin' jazz. The room was primarily smaller tables but some celebratory parties had larger ones. Couples seated close to each other toasted with mimosas. Quartets shared bites of beef brisket and creamy cheese grits. Sylvania now understood Ellis' opening question. The delicious smells were intercepted by the soul-tingling singer and her talented trio. As he moved to the fresh omelet station, the young woman at the microphone sang her version of Angela Bofill's *I'm on your side.* Once seated at the table, Sylvania and Ellis shared a plate of low country catfish and a pair of jerk chicken thighs. Ellis enjoyed second helpings of the banana bites while Sylvania rocked to the rhythm, savoring her Cajun shrimp Étoufée.

The two moved to the upbeat sounds, ever complimenting the skill of the musicians and the singer's ability to transform her style from Dinah Washington to Brandy to Aretha to Stephanie Mills. The highlight was her show-stopping rendition of Cheryl Lynn's *Got to be real.* The crowd was up out of their seats for almost the entire song. At the eventual close of her set, Ellis suggested they get on their way.

What more could there be? Sylvania thought to herself as they started back to the limousine. Walking past the other patrons, Sylvania knew people were looking at her, not the usual gawking she had become accustomed, but those who wanted to know--*who's that?* For a second time in her life, she felt special, realizing that both times, Ellis was there.

Ellis and Sylvania chatted about the wonderful food and sounds of Warmdaddy's. So engrossed in their conversation, Sylvania didn't notice the limousine had crossed over the Delaware, into New Jersey, and merged onto the Atlantic City Expressway. The two talked about their favorite restaurants, their favorite foods, music, books, and other topics that kept them in good spirits and unaware of the time. During a lull in their delightful discourse, the skyline of Atlantic City captured Sylvania's eye. She had gone to A.C. when she was younger, before it was what it had become. Memories of the beach, salt water taffy, and over-sized slices of pizza now swirled in her head. Unknowingly, she sighed loudly.

"What happened? Your face just dropped." Ellis shifted in his seat to face Sylvania.

"How do you go to Atlantic City and not walk on the beach?"

"Who said we weren't going to walk the beach?"

"In these?" Sylvania pointed to her shoes. With all of her planning, she couldn't have anticipated this.

"I have that covered." Ellis leaned back and smiled. Sylvania began to shake her head back and forth.

"Don't think you're going to be carrying me all over the beach on your back or something..." Sylvania's mild anxious attitude tickled him. He tapped on the driver's window.

"Make our second stop the first." The driver nodded as the turn signal sounded. Before she could ask, Sylvania saw they were turning into the Atlantic City Outlet.

"Don't tell me..."

He did. For the next two hours, Sylvania and Ellis strolled from store to store before picking out outfits appropriate for the beach. In his own simplicity, Ellis found a khaki beach suit and sand shoes. They loaded their bags into the car and were soon driving again. Memories of dirty beach changing rooms gave Sylvania a chill. If there was one reason not to like the beach, that was it. Once when she was a child, she realized in her bare feet that some people used the changing room as a bathroom. Again, she closed her mouth when she saw the limousine pull up to the front of the Borgata Hotel.

Walking through the lobby, passing throngs of excited gamblers, partygoers, and vacationers, Sylvania's mental Geiger counter began ticking rapidly.

I knew it... Her thoughts began. *There are some brothers who are tricky...others are slick...my man here is slick-ity. He had me fooled when he bought me the outfit but its all clear now.*

They approached the check-in desk. An older woman looked up, welcomed them, asked for the name, and proceeded to search the reservations. *If he thinks he's getting a little A.C. action, he'd better think again. The only thing he's going to be playing with will be a pair of dice.* Sylvania was firm. *I ain't gettin' played again...no more!*

"Here it is Mr. Parker..." The lady looked up and began the process of preparing the room keys. "Two rooms...1515 and 1517...overlooking the bay. Perfect for tonight's show."

"Are you ready?...Sylvania?...Are you ready to get changed?" It took a couple of seconds before snapping back to reality. Inside she was kicking herself. With each imaginary blow from her foot she pushed against the relationship demons in her mind. For as long as she could remember, she had hoped, wished, and prayed for a man to treat her like the queen she believed she should be. Now here, standing next to her, was that man, and with each bend in the pathway, she raised force fields of doubt and resistance. She was so angry and disappointed with herself, it took all she had to cheerfully answer.

"Can't wait!"

They took to the boardwalk first, like teenagers, peering and peeking into each and every shop. They drank root beer floats, devouring oversized slices of pepperoni pizza. Ellis held onto the boxes of salt water taffy, one for his mother, one for her, one for Winsome, and a smaller one for Twist. Sylvania suggested a small one for Twist because she knew it would just get messed over. Arm in arm they watched boardwalk performers and marveled at the distinctive styles of the different casinos. They battled each other in air hockey at the arcade. Reaching the far end of the boardwalk, Ellis noticed Sylvania was getting a little worn out. He hired a boardwalk taxi to ride them to the opposite end. As they rode, Ellis sniffed the air.

"Do you smell that?" Sylvania took a couple of whiffs but couldn't discern what Ellis was referencing. "It's the distinctive smell of the beach."

"The ocean?" Ellis shook his head *no*. "The garbage?" Ellis had her going. "Food? Exhaust? Is it me?" Sylvania grimaced with her final guess, placing her nose close to her armpits.

"Suntan lotion." Once said, a rush of Coppertone and Bain de Sole filled her nostrils.

"Whew!"

"What you're having now is an out-of-culture experience." Ellis chuckled as he took her by the hand and guided her to an unoccupied bench. As they sat, he leaned over and in one swift moment, he removed her shoes. "Now, let's take that beach walk."

For the next hour they weaved in and out of people tanning, kite flying, drinking, sleeping, reading, and running to and from the crashing waves. At one point, they stopped, looked out across the ocean, and gazed at the distant horizon.

"The horizon was in arms reach…"
Sylvania looked at Ellis who had not taken his eyes from off of the horizon. "What did you say?"

"Oh nothing." Ellis pondered momentarily then continued. "It's from a poem I had to memorize in high school. It's nothing." Sylvania tugged gently at his arm.

"Go on…let me hear it."

"I don't know if I still know it." Sylvania didn't say a word but her eyes encouraged Ellis to go deep into the recesses of his memories.

"The horizon was in arms reach
The gray, hazy curtain
Was drawn closed to the ocean blanket
The white caps dove and surfaced
As they raced to the steps of the shore
While periodically…the sun
Peers through stagnant clouds
Looming over a simmering beach
Inorganic life is tossed and retrieved
By semi-violent waves
Of salt and earth and history
While the entire stage of life
Remains silent
To allow this world
To speak its lines that only last
For all eternity."

Their silence was drowned out by the pulsating crash of the waves upon the shore. Seagulls hanging like kites on the wind drifted on the ocean winds, brought a smile to Sylvania's face.

"That was beautiful…is there more?"

"Yeah but I can't remember the rest of it." Ellis turned to face Sylvania. He took her by the hand, gently stroking her arm.

Sylvania watched a cloud drift by.

"Do you ever wonder what's out there?"

Ellis smiled as he answered Sylvania's question.

"No…not really."

"Well, I know what's out there." Ellis guided Sylvania closer to him.

"So pretty lady…what's out there?"

Sylvania leaned up and kissed Ellis on the lips. Her words were carried on the sea breeze.

"Whatever we want."

They ate a quiet dinner at the Borgata's Seablue. They shared a Maine lobster pot pie, eating slowly, savoring bites--savoring their moments together. The fine dining was only matched by their intense conversation. They talked about past relationships, their families, their fears, what made them happy. Ellis took Sylvania's hand. The low light showed a tender beauty who had been wandering aimlessly over the years. He could see in her eyes the timidity held deep within her. He promised as they sipped their beverages to treat her like the delicate flower he so deserved. In that same light, Sylvania could sense here was a man breaking free from his bonds of self-confidence--a man who was now ready to take a step, to dash, to take flight. In the beginning, his kindness and gentleness was strange, a joke, but now she realized it was genuine, a strength, a treasure.

There they sat. Two people finally making their way from out of a maze, confused by the twists and turns of sadness and disappointments; stumped by blind spots of empty apologies; stymied by dead ends of desires and longings. Now they stood outside, perched on the edge of a future of their own design. Like the waning candle in the center of the table, their pasts begin to fade away, allowing room for a new candle's light to burn strong and brightly.

"That was a wonderful dinner. Thank you." Sylvania's words brought a joy to Ellis' face but he couldn't respond. He knew what he wanted to say, what he wished he could say, but found he was afraid to speak. Unfounded caution informed him that if he spoke there would be the chance of derailing what had been a beautiful day.

"Thank you for everything...the beach...the brunch...this was one of the best days of my life." Sylvania moved closer. Her smile told him to ignore his routine mindset and say something-- anything. A few *right* words entered his mind but were interrupted by the ringing of slot machines and rising celebratory cheers. Ellis opened his mouth.

"Somebody's getting lucky tonight." Ellis wished he could take that comment back. The busyness of the hotel lobby fell into a state of suspended animation as a now found himself in a pickle. "I'm sorry. I meant that somebody's getting some...some luck tonight...no...I mean...(ugh)...you know what I mean." Sylvania laughed to let Ellis know she did.

"It's getting late. Let's hit the elevator...unless..." Ellis helped Sylvania from her chair.

"Unless?"

"Unless...you want to hit the casino." Ellis shifted with subtle anxiety.

"No...I guess I'll be heading up...to my room."

"Oh yeah...me too." As Ellis moved toward the elevator he noticed Sylvania was fixed in her space. "Coming?"

"I need to stop by that Essentials store. With this surprise and all, there's a couple of things I need to pick up."

"The hotel has toothbrushes and toothpaste in the rooms."

"Feminine things," Sylvania smirked. Ellis covered his face to hide his blunder.

"I'm sorry." He leaned forward and kissed her softly on the cheek. "Have a good night. I'll call you in the morning for breakfast." The elevator door opened. After stepping in, he turned to see Sylvania still standing, looking only at him. Before he could say a word the doors closed. Sylvania entered the corridor leading to the shops, quickly walking past Essentials.

Ellis finished brushing his teeth with the complimentary toothpaste and looked out the large plate glass window overlooking the harbor. The fireworks would begin soon but that didn't hold his interest. He kicked himself for not speaking up--for not letting Sylvania know what was on his mind. He took a deep breath. *No more!* This was his moment, his Independence Day. If she rejected his advances--*to hell with it!* He grabbed the phone from off the cradle and dialed her room number. *Busy.* He eased into the sofa and allowed the repeating signal lull him back to his usual self. Slowly he put the phone back as he stared into the darkening night.

"Will that be all Miss?" The sales girl totaled Sylvania's purchase. Retrieving her only credit card, Sylvania paused with caution. She had told herself to only use the card for emergencies. It had taken her months to pay off her last purchase, even with the money she borrowed from her mother.

"That'll be it." As the sales girl placed her purchase in the bag, she noticed Sylvania's ambivalence.

"Girl...this is nice."

"Yeah...," Sylvania took the bag from the young woman,"...but this is going to hurt." Before exiting the store, she heard the playful tone of the sales girl.

"You...or him?"

Sylvania entered her room, placing the package on a chair and drew open the curtains. She caught her breath looking out across the bay at the illuminated casinos. In a way they reminded her of the skyline when Ellis gave her a ride home after the dance. Pleasant warmth filled her body. The day had been right and Ellis was such the gentleman--what a Mr. Right should be. The feeling inside that had been with her since brunch moved her to the phone. She nestled it in her hand as pangs of regret began to form. She quickly dialed Ellis' room before they could take hold. The annoying pulse of the busy signal caused Sylvania to return to the window and close the curtains.

Silence is unnerving. The absence of sound brings rise to our surroundings, what we have, what we desire, what may never be. Silence brings the hungering drive of want. It feeds our unmet desires, our unquenchable longings, until we are dizzy from a starvation of our own design. It is a spirit we can neither join with nor exorcise. It fills our air until...

It was a crash before the cursing. After a moment of cautious curiosity, Ellis peeked out of his door into the hallway. Across the hall was a waiter struggling to pick up his room service order. A spilled glass of orange juice, several bottles of beer, and a tray of shrimp was scattered on the floor. Ellis moved to assist before stopping. His eyes locked on Sylvania's, who too had peered into the hall to see what had happened. As the waiter dabbed the carpet, the two smiled, unable to step back into their rooms. The waiter ping-ponged the faces of the two then proceeded to gather up the shrimp.

"You folks have a good night!"
Ellis' words drifted over the waiter as if he wasn't there. "Would you like to watch the fireworks with me?"
Sylvania sighed with relief. *I thought you would never ask.* By the time the waiter secured his cart Sylvania was closing the door to Ellis' room. The waiter pushed his cart with a sly grin knowing fireworks were about to start.

Together they moved the sofa to face the window.

"I'll get the lights." Ellis turned the dimmer, creating twilight of their own. Seconds later, the first rocket burst in the sky. The bright flash found Ellis and Sylvania in a tight embrace. *Boom! Boom!* Cascading golden streams outlined their faces as their tongues discovered the long hidden desires they held for one another. Ellis' long slender fingers, highlighted by the blue and yellow starburst, nervously stroked her cheek, descending slowly to the collar of her blouse before resting on her breast. Sylvania heaved a stuttered breath. *Boom! Snackle! Crackle!* Light faded to darkness as Sylvania's hand explored beneath his shirt. They couldn't hear the next volley as the room was consumed by their breathing.

Sparkling green light flickered just as Sylvania pulled back from Ellis' hand as it found a way to unbutton her blouse.

"Wait!"

Ellis froze. Apologies swirled in his mind as he prepared to deliver the best one. Without a word, Sylvania quickly left the room as she pulled her blouse close to her body. The fireworks continued as Ellis sat dumbfounded on the sofa. His thoughts reminded him this wasn't the time. His thoughts ridiculed his belief that she was the one. He stood and walked to the phone. He formed an apology as he picked up the phone and dialed.

From the depths of dejection came a knock. Dropping the phone, Ellis bolted to the door. A moment of lightheadedness surged in Ellis as Sylvania pushed her way back into the room.

"Come on...I don't want nobody to see me like this!" Sylvania rushed past Ellis and returned to the window. Ellis could only stare. There she stood, by the window, clad only in the oversized complimentary bathrobe.

"You came back." Ellis' mouth fell open as he watched the robe drop slowly to the floor.

"I never left."

A brilliance of purple bathed the room, revealing the curvature of Sylvania's womanhood. His senses were hypnotized by the white lace halter babydoll which covered her delicacies. Her sensuousness was more dazzling than any of the pyrotechnic paintings on the night sky. In his mind came a flash. There she was, the woman from the dream. The one his body ached for. The one he savagely longed for. The one his body and mind responded to on all levels. The woman before him, now bathed in light and passion called to him to become conjoined in pleasure and heat. Ellis' body could no longer wait. He removed his shirt and was holding her hips in one fluid movement. Sylvania tugged at his belt buckle, seeking the release of his manhood--his strength. As he fought to free himself from his tangled trousers, his hands traversed the softness of her skin, crossing from hips to stomach to breasts to her arms. Caressing her shoulders, his fingers came across a surprise--the sales tag. Sylvania blushed but said nothing. Ellis held his breath as he gently brushed the delicate cloth on Sylvania's shoulders. His strong hands massaged her shoulders although his fingertips were numb, evidence that the blood had moved to where it was needed most. She pressed her body to his, sighing as she melted into his grasp. He placed his fingers on her center, feeling her body quiver in response to his touch. She turned, arching her back as she bent into his ready midsection. Ellis reached forward, gently taking hold of her shoulders, and turned her back around.

"I want to look at your beautiful face."

Sylvania leaned her head into him, kissing his chest, trailing downward. Her eyes dropped a few tears onto his stomach. *He's wonderful.*

Neither knew how they returned to the sofa but they were ready to fulfill a lifetime of desires. Sylvania parted her legs and attempted to pull Ellis in but with a swift move, he rolled onto the floor.

"Give me a second," huffed Ellis. Sylvania reached to him.

"What's wrong?"

Ellis double-timed it out of the room and returned twice as fast. As he leaned down to Sylvia, a beam of light exposed an open condom package now on the floor. Sylvania smiled.

"Was that complimentary or you just knew you were going to get some?"

"I picked it up earlier at the mall. No plan...just being prepared." Ellis' last word.

Sylvania's hand snaked its way from his back to his thighs. Taking his hardened power, she slowly guided him inside. A time-stopping exhale and then their bodies sought to establish pleasure's rhythm. The fireworks reached their climax as the two bodies ebbed and flowed to a pulse only they understood. Ellis was a slow, easy lover--savoring the sweetness of Sylvania's moans and sweat. Sylvania hands gripped Ellis' back tighter and tighter as he descended into her love to depths no man had done before. Ellis's hands flowed from her face to just below her midsection, massaging her ribcage with each metered stroke. He found her skin to be supple, a spellbinding texture which furthered his craving. He used this position as the fulcrum to reach further into the abyss of gratification. Sylvania pushed back forcing him to heave an unintelligible whisper from his lips. She felt a scream rise in her throat but it was stifled by the sucking of tongues--allowing only an *ooohh* to escape. Ellis' actions reverted to raw instinct. Without thinking, he thrust his hands past Sylvania's head and grappled the arm of the sofa. Sylvania's hips writhed as she descended deeper and deeper into the growing chasm of the cushions. All was silent, save for the explosions outside and the fiery murmur of their emotions within. In the darkness their pace increased until a deep and guttural groan from Ellis released his remaining essence into the vessel that was Sylvania's love. They remained there, entwined, slightly shivering as the heat left their bodies.

"Hold me tighter", whispered Sylvania. With only part of the moon peeking into the room, Ellis held onto Sylvania, never wanting to let her go.

"Sylvania…you're my flower."

Wrapped in a sheet, they quietly watched the trailing smoke drift away toward the Atlantic. As Sylvania lay with her head on Ellis' chest, he felt the words.

"The horizon has drifted away
The blanket still drawn
The sounds still carry
The hot sand cools
The day has come to a close
And nature's show
Is at its finale."

"You remembered the end of the poem."

"For you," whispered Ellis as he kissed Sylvania long and slow. "Just for you."

On July 7th, Sylvania received a small card in the mail. Seeing Ellis' name in the return address, she quickly opened it. Two tickets fell out. She read the card as she kneeled to retrieve the tickets from the floor.

Sylvania, just wanted you to know I had a wonderful time with you. Perhaps one of the best times I had with someone as far back as I can remember. I know Twist is probably mad that I took you away for the 4th. So, as a peace offering, here are a couple of tickets to see TLC at the Mann. You and Twist enjoy! —Ellis

PULLED MUSCLE

"HEY BABY…HURRY UP in there. I'm getting bored!" The beautiful woman sat on the edge of the bed. Soon she found herself picking at her nails. She looked around the room. It was well put together. Very upscale. Had a woman's touch but clearly, no woman lived here. On the bedpost was a silk robe with the initials HM classically embroidered on each sleeve. She leaned over and could smell the same aroma she smelled at the club. The tingling in her nose reminded her why she was there. "You all right in there?"

"Fix yourself a drink or something." A grunt from the bathroom. Nothing more. The woman found her way to the kitchen and poured herself a glass from the bottle stationed on a marble stand. The taste was both strong and sweet, nothing like the wines she and her friends were used to. She found herself having to sip instead of her usual gulping.

"What kind of wine is this?" She shouted back toward the bathroom. "It is delicious."

"Read the label."

She mouthed something smart at his response. Holding the bottle up to her eye level, she shouted back.

"It says…it says peanut noor or something." There was a pause.

The woman put the bottle down as a shadowy figure stood in the doorway to the kitchen.

"It's pronounced *pen-no na-war*. It's French. It's a red wine grape and this particular brand is very expensive…not the house party swill you're used to. So don't waste it."

The woman admired the package; the broad chest and shoulders, taut stomach, strong arms. His aroma captured her. Clad only in silk shorts, he grappled her arm, pulling her to him.

He guided her quickly back to the bedroom. Once there, he hoisted her as he proceeded to probe the inside of her mouth with his tongue. Her soft murmuring filled his ears as he tossed her onto the center of the bed. As far as he was concerned that was gentle he was going to be. The woman felt the strong hands begin tearing at her clothes. She too was excited and tried to pull down his shorts but he pulled her hands away and soon had her blouse on the floor, minus two buttons. He drooled as he held her down with one arm and began rolling her bra off from the left. She was just as ferocious and she bit at his chest and arms, snapping and licking, arching up and being pinned. Her teasing shrieks, cackling, and panting was only matched by his low groans of pleasure. He began peeling the pants from off her body. He cursed himself because he usually told the women who came to the house to only wear dresses. Now that he was focused on freeing her one leg at a time, she wrestled her way to his back, clawing and kissing. Again, she tried to shove her hand down his shorts and again she found her hand trapped between his arm and chest. *Oh, you gonna make me beg to see it ain't you?* He responded with one move, flipping her over onto her stomach and thrusting the full weight of his body on top of her. She gritted her teeth and howled. She spoke his language. She found just enough strength to raise her buttocks to meet his crotch. She turned her head to speak when the silky shorts fell next to her face. *'Bout time!* She relaxed her hips and waited. She could feel his arm tighten around her waist. The first thrust would be the strongest. She knew this and prepared to have her head slam into the headboard. Suddenly, nothing; the arms around her waist relaxed. The lifeless mass of his body crashed down, causing her to collapse fully on the bed. She could feel the sweat of his heaving chest. Once filled with the eruption of erotic pleasure, the room now was filled with another kind of panting, sounding similar to a child trying to catch his breath from running too fast. She moved her leg out from under his and felt the coolness of his fluids on the satin sheet. She strained to raise him so she could take a breath. She looked back at the floundering giant.

"Damn Hank...that's all you got for me?"

Following the horrors of high school, Hank was convinced his inability to approach girls was due to his over-weight frame. Part was hereditary; some of the other kids teased him by saying that when he stood next to his father, they looked like a capital and lower case 'o'. The other part was his diet: Fried foods, sweets-- anything that tasted and made him feel good. His only true friends were television, snacks, and books. Many hours of sitting, watching, munching, and reading didn't help his ever-increasing weight.

His parents knew his troubles and thought he would make a new start at Temple. Even though he lived in the city, they hoped he would make new friends if he lived on campus. Hank liked the idea. He didn't have to go back and forth from school and see the same guys who tormented him. Living on campus would soon be his opportunity for change. His roommate was a walk on for the football team. Samuel Taylor, better known as Saber, was from South Jersey. He was a sophomore, a transfer from Rutgers. Saber enjoyed the college life--minus the *college* part. His three favorite subjects were football, working out, and the spoils of being a football player. Many a night, Hank slept in the lounge because the coded *piece of tape over the key hole* let him know that Saber was in *class*.

It was a late mid-week afternoon near the end of the semester. Hank was studying for his tests and Saber was on the phone scheduling a couple of young ladies to "help him" with his exams. After hanging up the phone, Saber turned to Hank.

"Say homie...you ain't got no play this year...did you?"
Hank lifted his head from out of his history book.

"Play? What's play?"
Saber fell back on his bed, spitting his thoughts.

"Come on cuz. You know what I'm talkin' about. Play...hittin' the skins...bustin skeet...the poonani...gettin' paid...okay man?...Puzzz-zzzy!"

Hank knew exactly what Saber was talking about and that he had never had any. In the eighteen years of his life, the closest he ever came to *gettin' paid* was at Carlotta Houston's party in the sixth grade. They were playing "seven minutes in heaven" and he was selected to go into the closet with Carlotta. She didn't want to go but as the host, she had to. She gave him a quick peck and even quicker pieces of advice to keep his mouth shut and better not tell anyone what happened. Hank figured that since nothing had happened, there was nothing to tell.

"Look", began Saber. "You been cool about me an' my honies all semester. I bet if you dropped a little weight, you could pull yourself a little here and there. Nothin' like every night but if you worked on your game a bit, you could get some... like twice a month."

Twice a month? Twice a month! Hank thought that if he could get that much action his cup would be running over.

"So dig this, when we come back from the break...you and me...in the gym." Saber picked up his book bag and headed out the door. "I might even give you some patented mackdaddy tips."

Spring of 1989 was perfect for Hank's training. The hawk was out and snow covered the streets made the gym the perfect haven for working out. Saber showed Hank around the weight room, starting him on the indoor track and a series of calisthenics. Hank was as determined to learn as much as Saber was determined to shrink his rotund roommate. In the first semester, Hank dropped twenty pounds and Saber was dropped from the team and out of school. Hank worked through the summer and by the time he returned in the fall, he noticed that he was beginning to get noticed.

It was in the SAC that he met his first. The Student Activities Center was the hang out for many students. Hank was eating lunch and noticed a spectacled young woman peering at him from behind her book. Since this was unusual, he looked around, in case he was blocking her view. She stood and walked over to him. By the standards of his peers, she was very plain.

"You're in my poli sci class, aren't you?" She sat down next to Hank--another first.

"I sit a couple of rows behind you...on the left." Hank may not have talked to the ladies but he had a great mind for details. "My name is Hank...Hank Morris."

"I'm Jontelle Nolan...." From that introduction their conversation moved to friendship and eventually Hank's first sexual venture. He was so excited the moment ended almost before it began. It didn't make much of a difference as this was Jontelle's first experience as well. The two tried again a week later with much of the same results. With no understanding why he performed as he did, he believed it was the fault of her looks--and his. If he could look better, he could *score* prettier women. If that happened, the sex would be better.

As time passed, Hank increased his size, the women were prettier, but things never changed. He went to see several doctors over the years but they all said it was natural. He could learn to control *it*. He refused to hear them. *Doctors were just jealous.* When he looked at himself, he knew deep inside, he hated what he saw.

He hated the middle schooler inside of him-the high schooler-the college boy, and after each workout, no matter what, he had to get bigger, stronger, and the women have to be more beautiful. He was looking for a complete package that seemed always just another workout or another woman away.

Hank called a cab as the woman dressed. "Hey, um…" As usual, Hank hadn't put much thought to remembering her name. It could have been one of a million names. It didn't matter. She wasn't the one. "…a cab will be here for you in a minute. Take you wherever." The woman looked at Hank.

"Hmmph!" After that, the least you can do is pay for my blouse." Holding up the damaged clothing, she scrunched her face. "This ain't cheap!" Hank left the room, quickly returning with two one hundred dollar bills which he tossed at her feet.

"I'm sure you can buy eight of them with this."

As the cab drove off into the night, a tense and frustrated Hank returned to the bathroom to continue what he had started earlier in the evening. He sat on the edge of the sunken bathtub and held his member. Tear drops dotted the back of his hand as it moved back and forth.

SIDE ORDER OF THORNS

"HAPPY ANNIVERSARY SYL!"
Ellis stealthily crept through the front door of Sylvania's apartment before displaying a bouquet of twenty-four pink roses.

"Pink?" Sylvania caught her question but it was too late--it already left her mouth. She didn't want to seem ungrateful. In fact, Ellis might've been the first man to ever give her a rose. The few flowers she received didn't count--the closest she had ever come was from Darnell Puckett.

She had dated him briefly following her first year at the Community College of Philadelphia. She had seen him reading in one of the student lounges. It didn't seem like he was ever preparing for class but he did have a book and that was more than what she was used to when it came to any of the young men she knew. After her class, they locked eyes, and Sylvania agreed to meet outside. Standing on the corner, Sylvania began to doubt Mr. Puckett, until he pulled up in a dark blue BMW. *A book and a BMW...this brother!* They rode around the city for a couple of hours before he found a parking space at the Lakes in FDR Park. It was there they made their way around the bases--stopping at third--since it was a very public place. Sylvania's other dates with Darnell were much the same. He told her where to meet, they'd drive around, make out, and in the end, would drop her off.

On the day of the rose, Darnell instructed Sylvania to meet him on the corner of Broad and Olney and the two drove quickly to the Red Roof Inn in King of Prussia. The promise of sweet talk, the BMW, and dinner at a classy restaurant was enough for Sylvania. Her mother once told Sylvania that time reveals all things. That thought was far from her mind until the two ended up at a hole in the wall eatery called *The Last Noodle*. Sylvania swallowed her true feelings as they entered. No real décor, a smell other than food, and when the grizzled faces at the bar turned toward them she knew the place should have been called *The Last Straw*. Sylvania chronicled the clues as to why she should have turned her heels, flagged a cab, and got the hell out of there, both in the restaurant and the hotel.

Her first clue was no appropriate greeting when they arrived. Once in the restaurant, she realized there was no one to seat them or offer a clean table. In the hotel, Darnell failed to address her comfort. He didn't take her coat, offer a drink, or even a seat. He stepped into the bathroom, and while there, Sylvania peeked into the bedroom and saw the bed linen in disarray. She started to question if he had been there earlier and now she was the second round.

The atrocious service was clue number two. At the restaurant, the waiter was not shy in letting them know this was the worst place to work and eat. He was slow, appeared agitated, and expected a lot more than he deserved. At the hotel, Darnell bemoaned his past conquests—*correction*--experiences. He made it clear that the other women were too young mentally because they refused to "try" his freakish bodily gymnastics.

"Just bury your face in the pillow and let 'Big D' do the rest."

Clue number three: At the restaurant, the experience was more than horrible and the cost of the *Dutch Treat* was too high, the food was overcooked, unappetizing, overpriced, and more than unsatisfying. By the time Sylvania left the hotel, she felt the same. At the hotel, his pillow talk was overblown. His lovemaking was degrading. The only moment of pleasure was her walking out into the lobby and seeing a cab waiting outside. As he ushered her across the lobby he pulled a single pink rose from the vase on the front desk. It was wilted.

Pulling away, she cursed herself. *I stayed at the restaurant because I was hungry. I stayed at the hotel because I was lonely.*

"What's wrong with pink?"
The warning light inside Ellis' head began to blink. He wasn't sure if he understood her question, perhaps he really didn't want to. He knew he hadn't showered Sylvania with gifts the way he did with Clarissa. This relationship was new--a new beginning for how he wanted to be treated, and how he would treat his woman. After the recognition that he and Sylvania were "a couple" he resolved not to do as he did in the past, which included the daily niceties that Clarissa demanded; fancy dinners, shows, the *be seen* events, all of the things he struggled with. Most of all, Clarissa had demanded flowers, for every occasion, for any reason. And they couldn't be just any flowers. They were to be exactly as she wanted them. For her birthday, she wanted yellow carnations. For Thursdays--tulips. Sunday dinner--orchids. Ellis learned quickly.

A year after their first date, Ellis thought it would be *neat* to surprise Clarissa with a small bouquet of flowers to celebrate her landing an assistant buyer position with Strawbridges. At the florist, he struggled to pick out the right arrangement. He looked in every display case, went through two store assistants and three shoppers. In the end, he settled on a wild flower mix. They looked nice and were affordable. He cradled the arrangement as he transferred from the subway to the 67 bus. There was no way they would be crushed, dropped, or stolen. By early evening, he showed up at her Northeast studio apartment on Teesdale Street. Standing at her door, hands still moist from the trials of public transportation, he nervously depressed the click-bell on her door.

"Who!?!" Echoed in the hallway.

"It's me", sang Ellis. As the door opened, Ellis slipped the arrangement behind his back. Excitedly, Clarissa's guarded tone changed to glee as she wrapped her arms around Ellis' neck and pulled him close for a little tongue in cheek. She turned, leading him into the apartment. He watched her whimsy walk with each of the ten steps it took to reach the other side of the room. He just knew the flowers would seal the deal for a quickie before he started back home. With his mind on getting a little *pudy-pudy*, he revealed his gift. Anticipation's schemes deflated.

"Where'd you get that?" Ellis paused. It wasn't the question, it was the tone. In her eyes, the flowers quickly deteriorated into flakes of dejection.

"I thought you would like them."

"Like them? They're not even in season." The small apartment transformed into a gaping chasm.

On the bus ride home, Ellis questioned how he could do better--be better the next time. He knew Clarissa was hard to please but he resolved to learn how. When his stop came, the flowers remained for the rest of the ride.

"Forget it!" Sylvania turned her attention to the counter. The chili she made was now quickly cooling. "Are we going to eat or what?"

Ellis noticed her tenor. It bothered him. Not that they hadn't had times when they disagreed, but they felt like casual conversations--unlike this. Something was brewing and about to boil over.

"I'll eat if you're ready to eat." In an instant, Ellis knew his response was wrong. They had moved from talking to chopping words, with fragments flying everywhere.

"All you can do is think about food?"

"You asked if I was ready to eat?"

"No, I asked you if we were going to eat. Get it straight!" Their verbal projectiles continued. Ellis took refuge across the room, near the door. He hadn't looked at the doorknob but now it crossed his mind. It was right there, no more than a foot from his hand. He could turn, open the door, and be done with these theatrics. He felt strongly about Sylvania but it appeared that what they were working toward was turning into something he had before. It was from within the silence between their escalated voices that Ellis finally heard what Sylvania wanted to say.

"You didn't say a word about the job offer." There it was. Ellis knew this package had to arrive and now it was sitting at his feet. "It's like you don't care."

Ellis cared, only he was the only one in the room who knew it. He had listened to Sylvania pine on about the new opportunity but he hadn't put much thought into it. Not that it was a long shot or that it was in the bag but concerns about moves and changes at Druer found a permanent place on the backburner of his mind. In this instance, he realized he was wrong but the time for apology was not ripe.

"I told you that if I was offered the management opportunity I would have to work at their New York office for six months. After that, I would receive my placement…and that could be either in Manhattan, Chicago, Kansas City, San Francisco…or possibly stay here." Sylvania paced as she pushed the words from her mouth. "Did you hear me? If we are supposed to have something, I would think you would be concerned about us being together and not what we're going to eat tonight!"

"I didn't say anything about food."

"You didn't say anything!"

An argument is rarely a competition but Ellis knew he was losing. He remained silent but kept his eyes fixed on Sylvania's. He knew deep down she was right. Whatever she needed to hear was in him but he couldn't produce it. Sylvania moved closer to the door, leaning on the wall.

"You know, at first I felt that what I was doing was not important. I mean, look at you: great job, your own house and all, and when it comes down to it you're a catch...and I'm just always getting caught up." Ellis tried to interject but Sylvania couldn't hear him. "You just don't seem to care about what I want." Sylvania's eyes moistened but her inner strength held back any release. She knew weeping was a private affair.

"I know you have a hard decision, "Ellis' words began to rise from the dust of her anger. "The decision is yours. It's your life. I respect that." He watched her body language which remained distant. "It's not for me to make...don't you understand?"

In seconds, their postures and room positions changed. Ellis, now on the bar stool and Sylvania, now at the kitchen sink.

"Don't talk to me about *my decision*," continued Sylvania after a short drink of water. "Answer me this...do you want me to stay? With you?"

"Don't put this on me like that!" For the first time since Clarissa's departure Ellis felt anger in his voice. "I need you to make your own decisions!" What he wanted to say would not form. What he wanted to do, he could not act. The shadows of his past were now the specters of present. "All I'm saying is that whatever you decide, I'll support you."

The tension in the room was broken by the clanging of Sylvania's few utensils thrown into the sink. "I don't want your support! I don't need your support!" Sylvania's face was contorted. "You say you respect me...you say that you care...but I need more...I need

257

love!" The package was opened. There it was, at his feet. Would he pick it up? Would he embrace it? Would he nurture it? Ellis knew this was the same question Clarissa asked. It was the same that he wanted from his father, from his life. In that instant, that moment, with the resonation of the vibrations trailing from Sylvania's lips, he realized that it wasn't that he didn't want the package. He couldn't carry it. Somewhere in his soul the shell that had long formed cracked, revealing a truism--fear. He was afraid.

Lies come in all shapes, sizes, and colors but the lies we tell ourselves are cold, devoid of mass and dimension--most of all, they are a distorted reflection of ourselves.

Finally, he said, "I think what we have is fine."

As if carried by spirits of ruth, Sylvania moved silently to the door. The slow movement of her hand hinted to the possibilities of regret only to be overridden by the firm clasping of her fingers on the doorknob.

"I was just making it when I was by myself but now I need more." The door to the end was opened. Ellis wanted to say something but then he was gone.

Sylvania reached over and turned her radio up loud so that her neighbors wouldn't hear her crying.

CHEERS!

THE SEPTEMBER TEMPEST STAKED its claim on Philadelphia. Three rain storms resulted in downed trees and flooding. The chilly air filled Ellis' lungs as he stepped from the Chestnut Hill Local. Not wanting to fight the Friday traffic, he took the train. Except for spots where puddles of wet leaves made treading tricky, his walk was brisk and easy. There were pockets of young children dashing to and fro as he sauntered by the attached houses of Mt. Airy. Soon the rows of homes broke into single homes with larger plots of land. He enjoyed this neighborhood of both professional and blue-collar workers. While its diverse make up made for cultural challenges, it was an exciting place when it came to block parties or the annual festival, Mt. Airy Day.

Hypnotized by the arch of oak trees, Ellis' trance was broken by a rowdy collection of young men near the corner. They perched themselves on or near the wall of large section of land that hosted a modest skeleton of a vineyard. Though they seemed not more than thirteen or fourteen years old, several of them were smoking and one passed around a brown-bagged beverage. Ellis recognized a couple of the young men from the grocery store. One young man motioned to the others as Ellis was approaching. Slowly their postures changed from lazing to one of alertness and preparation.

Ellis' steps became more determined. He rationalized that he couldn't cross the street, a clear sign of fear; he also couldn't run. He would have to put on the facade that he had somewhere to go and wasn't to be bothered. In fact, he wouldn't even make eye contact although he would keep them all in his sights, in case one of them made a move. He was now less than ten feet away when a smaller one nudged the one with the "beverage." He just shrugged, taking a swig from the bottle. As Ellis passed them, a high-pitched voice trying its best to sound manly began the conversation.

"Hey mister!" Instinctively, Ellis stopped.

The one with the glasses and cigarette stepped forward. He appeared to be the leader.

"Don't you drive a black Jag?"

Ellis tried to pull together reasons why this was of interest. Were they planning on robbing him and this was just a ploy to get him to stop? Was this a way to send the message that they knew where he lived? He didn't know what they were up to so all he could do was answer.

"Yes...that's my car."

As soon as Ellis answered, they erupted into a cacophony of cheers, arguments, comparisons, and wishes.

"I told you that was his car. Y'all don't know nothin'," spoke the one with the beverage.

"That car is sweet. How fast it go?" The one with the hat had stepped in front of Ellis.

"You ever race that car on Front Street?" The shortest one stood on the wall, towering slightly over Ellis.

Finally, the one with the glasses told them all to shut up, bringing the focus back to Ellis. "So mister, what you do? I mean, you got this nice ride but now you're walking all the way from the train station. Don't tell me your ride was re-po'ed."

The young men watched the funny smile creep up onto Ellis' face.

"No, it wasn't re-po'ed. Every now and then I rather take the train into work instead of fighting traffic." They looked at Ellis as if he was speaking another language.

"Man...if I had a ride like that I'd be on the road everywhere, everyday, all day!" The leader spoke up, accepting the acknowledgments from his friends.

"You guys know Liberty Place? Just off Chestnut." A few nods. "That's where I work. I'm in finance." He could tell they were impressed, but wasn't sure what impressed them--his job or where he worked.

"So that means you have a lot of money?" Beverage holder spoke up.

"I'm responsible for a lot of money...but it's not mine." Ellis could feel that his welcome was wearing thin as a couple of the boy's attention was drawn to a young lady across the street. He got their names and a couple of handshakes before continuing down the street.

Spritz of rain began to fall from between the leaves of the trees. This was the first time that he could recall that he encountered a group of young men who actually engaged him in a conversation. He knew that he would encounter them again, giving him the opportunity to perhaps build a friendly relationship. Perhaps he would mentor a couple of them. The world could always use another black man in finance. Turning onto St. George's Road, his natural high dissipated. He was startled by the silver car sitting in his driveway. The question wasn't why? More importantly, who?

Ellis approached cautiously. He looked closer at the silver Honda. The windows were tinted but light enough for him see the visage of the driver. The person was reclined in the front seat. *They've been here for a while.* Ellis' thoughts were hushed as he closed in on the rear of the car. He hoped it was simply some teens enjoying themselves with an early evening rendezvous. He would tap on the window, startle them, and watch them speed off, laughing at getting caught. *Tap-Tap!* He watched the shadow stir. It moved slowly to an upright position. The shadow was a woman, he could tell that much. He did startle the driver, he could tell by the frantic motions of face wiping and smoothing of the hair. *Time for you to start the car....* The car did start, but just so that the driver's window could go down slowly. Ellis' ears were the first to know.

"Ellis. It's been a long time." A smiling face leaned out of the opening. Only one word could leave Ellis' mouth.

"Clarissa?"

There was something about Clarissa. As he helped her from the car he tried to figure out what was different. Soon he was looking at her from across his kitchen table. She was the same person yet someone different as well. Physically, he could tell right away that she was taking better care of herself. Her curves were now accented by a tightness that he hadn't seen since their college days. Her hair was back to her natural auburn brown and styled in a modest, conservative cut. All of this highlighted the natural beauty of her face. She had on just enough blush to bring out her cheekbones and a touch of gloss on her red lips, bringing his attention straight to her. Gone were the braids, the beads, the nails, and the bling. When she walked to the dining room table her arms didn't make the *jingling* noise of her old rows of bracelets.

Their conversation rolled freely. Something he hadn't recalled holding with her for many years. They talked about her therapy, her family, and the new car. She was excited about working on her dental assistant's license at the community college in Montgomery County. Ellis talked about his mother, visiting his brother, changes at the office, talking with some of the neighborhood kids; his general health. Neither crossed the relationship bridge.

Time passed and without knowing how, the two were seated on the sofa in the living room. Clarissa's newness slowly became familiar to Ellis. Her voice rose just above the soft music.

"It is so nice to see you again Clarissa." The best of their memories together caused Ellis to smile. He could almost see his reflection in her clear blue eyes.

"I asked you to call me Clara. Clarissa is the past." Ellis was now hearing something new…in Clara.
She perked up abruptly.

"Oh yes, I have something for you." Clara had a new glide to her step as she sashayed across the room to the front door and out to her car. A bright smile lit her path as she returned with a long, stylish bag. Pleasure and sensuality beamed from Clara as Ellis removed the tissue paper. Looking in, he forced a smile.

"Let's celebrate!" Clara reached in and retrieved the bottle of red Bordeaux. Ellis' thoughts were quick and didn't give away his mock appreciation. She knew he didn't drink--at all.

In June of 1992, the wedding of Romulus Hardy to Tiffany McKenzie was the event of the year--as far as Romulus and Tiffany were concerned. Both Ellis and Clarissa had been asked to be in the wedding party. Ellis and Romulus were basketball team members and it was Clarissa who introduced Tiffany to her soon-to-be husband.

The day was beautiful. The bride was forty-five minutes late for the service which only added to the internal seething of her father. His attention was on the number of young black males in their family church. It was kind of comical. Here was her father, who clearly had disdain for black men, was faced with the thought of his daughter serving up *dark meat* every night.

At the reception, Ellis breezed into Clarissa's ear.

"You know, we're gonna be the only ones in the limo when this is over."

Clarissa knew what he was hinting but she wanted to hear his words.

"So?"

"So...can I get some?"

"Some what?"

"Why you got to play? You know what I'm sayin'!" The waiter interrupted their tete-a-tete and served their dinners. Once the waiter had left, Ellis continued. "You gonna let me get some...limo style?"

Clarissa whispered in a low sexy moan. "Limo style...that's new."

From Ellis' freshly licked lips, "That's right...I just invented it!" The groomsman sitting next to Ellis nudged him.

"Cut the sex talk...they're toasting."

All attention moved to the best man. His words were humorous and heartfelt.

"To my man...my brother Romulus and his beautiful Tiffany...many, many, many years of happiness." He raised his glass, signifying others to follow. Ellis and Clarissa clinked glasses with their neighbors and entwined their arms to complete the toast. It took only a second for Clarissa to empty hers. Through the stemware, she could see that Ellis returned his glass to the table-- full.

"Aren't you going to drink that?"

Ellis began to address his dinner. "You know I don't drink."

"Not even a swallow...in honor of your friend? And my friend?"

"They'll have a happy life whether my glass is emptied or not." He could see it in her eyes. Challenging her was a mortal sin. Ellis knew she was about to blow but knew she wouldn't make a scene, at least not here. Clarissa hissed.

"It's tradition! For god's freakin' sake!" Her eyes cut deep into Ellis' tuxedo. "You can forget about any damn limo action...Mr. Inventor man!"

As she opened the bottle, Ellis concluded that the Clarissa of old had passed and a new woman was standing in front of him.

"You're not going to toast to our reconnection?" Ellis shook his head.

"Still don't indulge? That's cool."

"*That's cool?*" Ellis replayed the words over and over in his head. In the past, he would have prepared himself for battle, but today, it was a feather in the wind. After a couple of drinks for *Clara* and a warm glass of cider for Ellis, the two were seated close on the sofa--very close.

"Did I tell you that I missed you?" Ellis heard the honesty in her voice. She inclined closer. "You know, you are the only man I ever really knew." Ellis felt an ease coming over him--he was now unarmed.

"I kind of missed you too." He reached for more words. Her leg was gently touching his. Her fingers started their march to his fingertips, past his palm and onto his wrist. She tickled him. He smiled. As their bodies began their descent into forgotten passions, she whispered into his ear.

"Still not wearing the watch I gave you?"

Time stood still. Her pursed lips, now held in a frozen in time, turned familiar to Ellis. He could hear her now. He could see her. She had changed but her essence was the same. He knew in his heart that she was ready--ready to be loved, to be cherished, ready to start anew--but not with him. His long look into her eyes revealed a new desire, a new face, a face he now longed for.

265

Clarissa sat in her car, hammering the steering wheel with her fists. The idling engine tried its best to drown out her wails but her lungs were stronger. Ellis shouted through the window, hoping to calm her down and get her to stay. She jammed the car into gear. Before pulling off, Clarissa's window opened to reveal the long familiar scowl.

"You're a fool, Ellis! Like always! You're gonna remember this day, September seventh, two thousand-one! When you finally realize what you've been missing!"
The car peeled out in reverse, slid into the street, and was gone, leaving only serpentine muddy tire trails.

"*I do know what I'm missing Clarissa,*" Ellis thought as he wiped the dirt and leaves that had splattered up into his face. Looking up to the clouded September night sky, he sent up a one-word prayer.

Sylvania!

SERVICE CENTER

RESTLESS AND STRESSFUL--that was Ellis' weekend. He couldn't concentrate. Everything reminded him of Sylvania. Everything reminded him of how he'd lost Sylvania. Everything reminded him of how much he wanted and needed Sylvania. She was in his bones. With every breath, he longed to inhale her essence. His ears wanted her laughter. His tongue longed for the taste of her tears. His now useless arms extended to enwrap the memory of her form. His ankles ached from the countless steps of regret. His swollen eyes told the story as they welled and poured with each passing thought of Sylvania. She was lodged in his nervous system. She was flowing through his veins. All of the facts and figures of his job were now pushed aside and his mind was saturated with the solitary features of her face, of her smile, of her breathing, of her living. Restless and stressful--that was Ellis' weekend...because he was in love.

He had become the living dead, unable to feel the world around him. Sunday morning, Ellis awoke, dressed, and made his way to his mother's house. In his dream-like state, the streets of Philadelphia were a blur, an opaque image of a life incomplete. The cars that whizzed past him only added to the vagueness of his new existence. How and when he found himself in the space in front of his mother's home was a mystery. How and when she got into the car and talked about the annual church picnic at the Belmont Plateau didn't register in his mind. The realization came at the end of the service when it became apparent that he and his mother were the only two left in the church. This gave him pause to do what he must do. He reached forward, took a pew bible into his hands, and closed his eyes. Of the billions of prayers offered around the world in that instance, none was more vehemently given than the one of a heart now open and ready to receive the fulfilling joy of love's true balm. With a bowed head, Ellis' heart and mind tried to connect with Sylvania's spirit. The pastor watched them from outside the sanctuary but knew that Ellis was in good hands there with his mother. Deep in his heart, Ellis knew this was the place, this was the moment to find the power to let go of the past and reach with all given strength to claim what he should have held onto. The tears that fell from his closed eyes turned into the rain of the soul as they touched his hands, causing them to clench the Bible with a desperation he had never known before.

When he finally opened his eyes, he felt the sun's rays bathe him as they passed through the stained glass windows.

"Do you want to talk about it?" His mother's words were soft and reassuring.

All he could do was embrace her.

TALK SHOW

IT WEIGHED HEAVY ON his mind all morning. The Monday departmental meeting dragged longer than usual. He streamlined his comments before excusing himself, lying about an international call to be made. He knew he was wrong but double-timed back to his office and furiously dialed. No answer. It had been the same since Friday evening. It was the same all day Saturday. Even at dinner with his mother on Sunday, the periodic attempts yielded nothing but a whirlpool of unanswered rings.

The idea he had conjured on Saturday afternoon popped back into his head. If anyone knew of Sylvania's whereabouts, it would be her friend Twist. From all of their conversations, Twist--more importantly--her antics were a popular subject. He remembered her first name, *Darlene,* but he never knew her last name. She worked in City Hall--but where? How many offices were in City Hall? How many women could be named Darlene? Would she even still be working there? Her behavior would definitely get her fired. These questions flattened Ellis. A pause in his thoughts brought forth a new idea and a sense of inflation. Her behavior would also make her stand out, at least among a certain crowd. Ellis knew exactly who to talk to.

He approached the main entrance and caught the attention of a security guard. The guard, believing Ellis was a councilman or attorney, began to open the employee door, but Ellis waived him a "no".

"I'm looking for the loading dock." Not wanting to know why, the guard directed him to the rear.

Ellis stopped at the top of the driveway and listened. The sounds of delivery trucks, clanging dumpsters, and freight elevators echoed within the heart of the dock area but Ellis was listening for something special, something distinctively familiar, and it didn't take long. There it was; rising above the clamour was the bawdy echoes of urban wildlife. Laughter!

A group of men, mostly black, a few white and Hispanic, seated on crates, boxes, or simply standing, were loud and boisterous. Their conversations were scattered, scathing, savage, and scandalous. This reminded him of the men who hung out in front of his father's store. For hours they would talk about what they would be doing, what they should be doing, where they thought they should be going, but in reality it was just talk. His father was more specific. *They just talkin' shit!* That's what these men were doing--and today, that's what he needed.

At first, the men quieted as Ellis approached. All they saw was the suit. As he neared one by one, they returned to their conversations. No one recognized him. Ellis spoke to the first man.

"Would any of you happen to know a young woman named Darlene? She works here in the building."

The man rifled through his Daily News, indicating he didn't want to get involved. Wasting no time, Ellis passed the question to an older man leaning against a steam pipe. Again, no response. A man from the back, eating from a bag of corn chips, piped up.

"A lot of babes around here named Darlene...describe her."

Ellis was stumped. He had not put much stock into how she looked--she was mostly mouth.

"I can tell you that she's pretty loud," Ellis described. The men erupted into spirited and raunchy examples of women they knew. The man sitting on the turned up bucket gestured to Ellis.

"Half the women in Philly are loud...and the other half are louder!"

The loading dock resembled the Apollo Theatre with Chris Rock stomping the stage. Frustrated with the dockside levity, Ellis considered walking away, a tactic he knew all so well. A flash of Sylvania's smile strengthened him. Ellis cut through the nonsense.

"Perhaps you know her better as Twist." The noise subsided and the men began cataloguing the women they knew. From the back, a young man stretched up his gold-toothed grin.

"Wait a minute...Twist? Yeah, yeah...y'all know her...from records...the records office...on the second floor."

Another added, "Tall, brown-skineded...bowlegged."

"Pops a lot of junk?"

Like the breakthrough between Anne Sullivan and Helen Keller, the information began to flow freely.

"She owe you money, don't she?"

It wasn't long before Ellis passed through the main doors, was on the elevator, and finally arrived at room 217.

"Can I help you?" The elderly man at the front desk, clearly disturbed by the interruption, greeted Ellis sourly.

"Yes, I'm looking for Darlene." Ellis looked around as he spoke. The man turned down his radio.

"Are you from human resources? I've been complaining about her for months. She's always..."

Ellis cut the man's grumblings short. "No...I just need to talk to her"

The man pointed. "That cubicle." He returned to his radio and his mumbling. It didn't matter, Ellis had moved on. Soon he was standing at Twist's cubicle. Looking at her desk he could only image the state of her apartment. Papers and forms in disarray, a portion of a bagel and associated crumbs were scattered near her phone with drink stains imprinted on folders marked *Important*. Ellis now knew why so much city business was stalled.

"What you want?" Twist's voice came from behind Ellis. Whirling around he looked directly at a face full of attitude. It was clear that this wasn't a *Hi Ellis, how are you?* moment. Ellis jumped right into what he wanted.

"Do you know how I can get in touch with Sylvania?" Twist stood silently with only her eyes scanning for who was listening, primarily her supervisor. The coast was clear.

"Look!" She began. Her voice was low but as she talked, it moved like a rollercoaster beginning its ascent. "First of all, you don't know me like that to be coming to my job! Two, you just dumped my girl with no good reason. And first of all, she really loved you but you don't need to know that!"

Ellis was stunned. Not by the erratic style of Twist's statements, but by her veracity. What right did he have to approach Twist, to seek out Sylvania, to expect anything more for his future--their future? He didn't say a word. Slowly, he turned and walked away. With each step he felt the love he harboured slip further and further into darkness. From his disheartened state, he could still hear the caustic prattle of Twist digging into the back of his neck. He also heard another voice. As he passed the old man's desk, the voice of radio personality Patty Jackson was introducing a song: *...sometimes we can be foolish...we can be a clown when it comes to love...but if we learn that we can say we're sorry...we can start over. Come'on y'all...let's live just a little...it ain't easy but it's possible..."*

For once, without hesitation, Ellis stopped, turned, and stepped strongly back to Twist's desk.

"You back? What you want now?" Ellis ignored her. Reaching inside his suit jacket pocket, he retrieved his business card. Handing it to Twist, he spoke calmly.

"Look...I made a mistake. I love her and if you can help me get the message to her, I would greatly appreciate it."

It was a stand-off. Twist wasn't taking the card and Ellis wasn't taking it back. They looked hard into each other's eyes. This was a statement on strength; a statement of a mutual love for one person. The others in the office took notice and wanted to see who would make the first move. In this event, the business of the city really did come to a grinding halt--until the old man shouted from the front.

"Just take the damn card so everyone can get back to work!"

Without taking her eyes of Ellis', Twist slowly plucked the card from his hand and tossed it into the black hole of paperwork on her desk. Ellis offered a quiet *thank you* and walked away. Twist watched him leave the office and turn into the hallway. She waited until she heard the *ding* of the elevator. When she was sure he was gone, she snatched the phone from the cradle and punched buttons. She tapped her foot impatiently until she heard a voice on the other the end.

"Gurrrrlllllll!"

PROEM

SYLVANIA CAUGHT HERSELF DRIFTING off in the elevator as it slowly rose to the seventh floor. One wheel from her roller bag had snapped and disappeared behind a trash receptacle. With her hands already full with two smaller bags, she struggled to get the key into room 732. After the third try, the key card opened the door. At first glance, the room looked extremely comfortable, especially after her seven hour travel ordeal. Beginning with the Philadelphia International Airport, the plane arrived late and all passengers were required to wait for an hour due to mechanical concerns. When it was announced the plane was out of commission, Sylvania and the other passengers were instructed to go to another gate in the next terminal for an awaiting plane. As fate would have it, the plane was ready but the pilot had not yet arrived--another hour. Once she landed at LaGuardia, the next 50 minute wait was for her bags. Sylvania mentioned to an older lady that it couldn't get any worse--but then she caught her cab and soon found herself trapped in the middle of rush hour traffic. She crept along for one last hour until she reached her hotel. The numbers on the cab's meter were so high she offered up a *thank you Jesus* that the company was covering all of travel.

Now in the room, Sylvania took in a deep breath, and felt it in her throat. The air was stale. Dropping her bags, Sylvania searched, found the thermostat, and adjusted the air to high cool. She tried to open the window but it was sealed tight. There was nothing for her to do but give the air conditioner a chance. She disrobed to take a shower. It seemed forever before the water warmed up and then, halfway through, it went cold. As she dried and lotioned her body, she prayed this was the worst of the trip. This interview was important. She had proved herself as management material at PowerCat. To be selected to participate in their PowerCats on the Move Managerial Program was the perfect opportunity. Tomorrow would be her final interview at the main office and she wanted to be fully prepared.

Her growling stomach encouraged her to go out and find something to eat. After giving her hair a little attention, the phone rang. She paused because she had only given her hotel information to two people.

"Hello?"

"Gurrrlllllll..!"

"What's up Twist? I just got in and was on my way to get something to eat..." Twist didn't have time for that.

"You can eat later! Listen! Let me tell you who had the nerve to roll up all at my job."

"Caddy?" Sylvania didn't know who to say. There was a buffet of men to choose from.

"Caddy? Hell naw! If he comes to City Hall it's because of warrants."

"So who?"

"Yo man!"

Sylvania was confused. "What man?"

"You know your man Mr. Elliston Parker? MBA Financial..." Sylvania could tell Twist was reading.

"What are you talking about? Ellis? At your job?"

"That's right! All up in my b-i-business."

"Your job? For real?" Sylvania was still trying to process Twist's words.

"Look, this is how it went down. I'm just minding my business...working hard as usual...then next thing you know...like a up-tight Houdini...he appears right in front of me...demanding that I give up your whereabouts." Sylvania sat up on the edge of the bed.

"So what did you do?"

"I cussed him up and down, right there! I would have cussed everyone out if they said something." Sylvania closed her eyes and prayed.

"Did you give him this number?"

"HALLS NAW! I ain't pressed by him. Shit! I was raised on the corner of Kicksum and Azz."

Sylvania found herself kidnapped by her thoughts. She missed Ellis. They ended wrong. For the first time in her life she had felt comfortable enough to resign herself to another. Maybe the breakup was the price paid for falling in love.

"...when I finished cussin' him out...I threw him out!" As Twist continued describing how she grabbed Ellis by his *played out jacket*, dragged him down the hallway, and tossed him into the freight elevator, Sylvania struggled to muster the strength to ask the one question that poked at her heart.

"Did he say anything about me?" There was a long pause complimented by a disgusted huff.

"He was talkin' all this trash! Trying to run the game on me that he loved you. Believe that mess?"

Sylvania did. She felt a single tear tip-toe down her cheek as the softness of the memory of Ellis echoed within her senses.

Twist kept Sylvania on the phone for thirty more minutes before rushing off for a date with her new man of the week. Sylvania stood and looked out the window. She felt swallowed up by the skyscrapers of Manhattan. She adjusted her plan; after the interview, she would call Ellis to see where thing stood. Her stomach brought her back to the present but before going out, she placed her confirmation note on the mirror.

Appointment with PowerCats on the Move

9:00 AM – 9/11/01

Don't Be Late!!!

MOMENTS OF SILENCE

ELLIS POURED HIMSELF OVER the monthly reports of his directors. They had been on his desk, organized by Winsome, waiting to be prepared for his meeting at 9:00 AM. He arrived at work early that morning with the hopes of leaving after the lunch hour. After his encounter with Twist, he needed time to think about what was important in his life. More importantly, maybe purchase a peace offering for Sylvania--if ever she takes his call again.

"Mr. Parker," Winsome's voice quivered on the intercom. "Mr. Parker, would you come down to the break room?"

Ellis was irritated by the interruption. Looking at the clock, he had ten minutes until the meeting. He depressed the speak button on his intercom.

"I really don't have the time Winsome. I'm due in monthly at nine." There was a brief pause before Winsome's voice returned, reeking with anxiety.

"Please Mr. Parker. The break room." Ellis was reluctant but said he would join her for only for a minute. He didn't like to be late for meetings. Turning the corner, he saw a dozen people trying to stuff themselves into the small break room. They were eerily quiet. Winsome squeezed from out of the crowd and rushed to Ellis. She grabbed his arm, moving him to the front.

"What's going on?" Ellis was surprised by Winsome's conduct. For all of their years working together, he had never witnessed this kind of behavior from her. His attention was directed to the small television seated atop a cabinet. He looked at the screen and saw a building on fire--or that's what he thought it was. The script ran across the bottom of the screen indicated a plane had struck Tower One of the World Trades Towers. Confused voices rose from the crowd, speculating how it happened. *Was it weather? Pilot error?* Some even began to discuss the problem of tall buildings. No one knew and no one could turn away. Seconds passed and someone shrieked.

"Look!"

A second plane streaked across the screen and slashed into Tower Number Two. Rising screams filled the room. *What's going on? What's happening? What should we do? This is madness!* Ellis was as dumbfounded as the others. A few people leapfrogged from the break room to small radios on their desks, tuning to gather as much information as possible. Ellis didn't know where it was coming from but the voice of President Bush was heard throughout the room, announcing that the "United States was under an apparent attack." Following President Bush, the news correspondent came on the screen, updating the insanity to include a plane hitting the Pentagon and one crashing into a field in the town Shanksville, Pennsylvania.

They stood there as the horror continued. The cameras captured the entire moment. As if in slow motion, they watched the Towers collapse atop themselves. Staff members held onto each other, unable to turn away. The image was burned into all of their psyches, engraved upon their hearts to last for the remainder of their memories. As if in a vacuum, all sound ceased. No moving. No breathing. Only the vibrations of racing heartbeats echoed throughout the room. They were there. They were nowhere. It was unreal. It was as real as life would allow. In this moment of silence, life ceased to be.

Almost instantly, the building intercom system chimed-- announcing instructions, simple and direct. *As a matter of safety, we are asking all offices to be closed and all personnel and visitors to vacate the building immediately. Elevators will be disengaged, please use the stairwells with caution...*

Winsome helped Ellis clear the suite, encouraging people to leave their workspaces as they were and begin the 14 floor descent to the street. Once satisfied everyone was gone, Ellis took Winsome by the hand and prepared to leave--until the phone on his desk began to ring. He stopped.

"Let it ring, Mr. Parker. We have to go." There was panic in Winsome's voice. The phone continued to ring. He knew it was an outside call--he let go of Winsome's hand. A voice spoke to Ellis. *That has to be Mom making sure I'm safe.* He motioned for Winsome to go ahead.

"They told us to get out!" Winsome's voice was coated with fear. "Terrorists, Mr. Parker! The President said terrorists!" Ellis knew Winsome's trepidation but the ringing--it wouldn't stop.

"Go on Winsome! I'll meet you across the street at the clothing store." Ellis turned and bolted back to his office. He picked up the receiver and listened for his mother's voice.

"This is Ellis." He tried to sound calm but the confusion was too much. The voice on the other end was subdued and breathy, accented with sniffles.

"Ellis?...This is Darlene...Sylvania's friend." Ellis was speechless. "Ellis...Are you there?"

"Yes...I'm here." Ellis answered quickly. This was not the time to hear that Sylvania didn't want to contact him. He quickly thought that Sylvania's friend would enjoy telling that to him. She probably was unaware of what was going on.

"It's about Sylvania. She's in New York...on an interview."

There was a deathly pause. Twist's words constricted the already knotted muscles in his stomach.

"Her interview was in the towers."

AIRWAVES

...TODAY, OUR FELLOW CITIZENS, our way of life, our very freedom came under attack in a series of deliberate and deadly terrorist acts. The victims were in airplanes or in their offices -- secretaries, businessmen and women, military and federal workers. Moms and dads. Friends and neighbors. Thousands of lives were suddenly ended by evil, despicable acts of terror...

The room was dark except for the blue toned light emitting from the television. Twist shivered, her jittery hands barely holding the tumbler of vodka. The image of the Oval Office faded away as the glass touched her lips. This was the first time she ever sat and listened to the President. His words pierced her eardrums although she was unable to concentrate. She gulped down her drink and picked up the phone, dialing the hotel number Sylvania had given her. *All circuits are busy.* The message was the same. Her only consolation was the next glass. She prayed to a god she had abandoned long ago for all of this to be a bad dream. The cold in her spine reminded her it was real. She called again. The message again. The glass again.

...These acts of mass murder were intended to frighten our nation into chaos and retreat. But they have failed. Our country is strong. A great people has been moved to defend a great nation...

Except for a few employees, the Bally's Fitness Center was almost abandoned. Hank stood in front of the monitor, chest heaving, arms aching. For most of the President's speech, he pounded away at the heavy bag. It was all he could think of doing. He wanted to talk about it but had no one. He wanted to hold someone, this time for his own comfort, but again, he knew that he had no one. Deep down inside he was afraid but the years held emotion hostage in the recesses of his being. He turned to say something to the attendant but she was on the phone with a loved one of her own. Hank was alone and could only do one thing. He raised his fists and continued slamming them into the bag. Punch after punch after punch after punch after…

…Today, our nation saw evil, the very worst of human nature, and we responded with the best of America, with the daring of our rescue workers, with the caring for strangers and neighbors who came to give blood and help in any way they could…

The door to Mrs. Lee's home opened slowly. The face of the Grand Empressio peeked into the room, nodding silently. Mrs. Lee, at her dining room table waved her in. Mrs. Evelyn Carter-McCloud and several other Madames entered. Each approached Mrs. Lee, offering hugs and words of encouragement. One woman entered the kitchen to prepare coffee. Another brought a platter of light hor d'oeuvres. Mrs. Carter-McCloud walked to the television and muted it, as she directed the ladies to join hands. One by one they said prayers for the country, for the victims, but mostly for the soul of Sylvania.

…Our first priority is to get help to those who have been injured and to take every precaution to protect our citizens at home and around the world from further attacks. The functions of our government continue without interruption. Federal agencies in Washington which had to be evacuated today are reopening for essential personnel tonight and will be open for business tomorrow…

They sat huddled beneath a Tussah silk comforter on the floor of Cary's townhouse. Devon sipped his tea as Cary began his second glass of mandarin ginger. Devon's mind wandered to the Zen calligraphy above the television. The candles, lit and scented, sat atop bamboo coasters around the room. Tranquility radiated, creating an oasis in a desert of confusion and fear. Devon could sense anger rising in Cary. Slipping his arm around Cary's waist,

Devon could feel his tension subside and their spirits becoming stronger. This was now a world spinning out of control. From beyond the windows of their refuge all they knew had changed but they were determined to face whatever lay before them--together.

...Tonight I ask for your prayers for all those who grieve, for the children whose worlds have been shattered, for all whose sense of safety and security has been threatened. And I pray they will be comforted by a power greater than any of us spoken through the ages in Psalm 23: "Even though I walk through the valley of the shadow of death, I fear no evil, for You are with me...

In unison, the parishioners of Pine Street Baptist recited the Twenty-third Psalm. Ellis and his mother sat with friends, neighbors, and strangers, seeking divine comfort from the events. The choir provided pastoral inspiration as prayers for families, firemen, police officers, and leaders were sent up in both heartfelt thoughts and emotional shouts. Soon Kenneth and Aunt Daliah joined Ellis and his mother in their pew, just in time for the community prayer. The minister prayed for faith and steadfastness. His words echoed throughout the sanctuary. Ellis' mind was somewhere else. He wanted to believe that Sylvania was still alive. That she was somewhere safe. He hoped she would have tried to contact him. He knew that hearing her voice would ease his heart-- a little more than prayer.

None of us will ever forget this day...

WHO KNOWS BEST

HIS MOTHER PLACED THE cup of coffee in front of him.

"There's something heavy on your heart and the way you avoid it is to worry about work. Truth is...your co-workers are home with their families and friends. They're consoling each other. They know work is important but they also know what is more important." She moved her chair closer and put her arm around Ellis. "Let me ask you this. Has Mr. Morgan called you? To ask why you're not at work? He knows you all will get back together when the time is right. But now is the time to take care of yourself."

Ellis looked deep into his mother's eyes. There lay the principles he had known all his life. A value she had tried to instill in him over the decades but he wasn't ready to hear it until now. He felt her lips touch his cheek gently before she rose to leave the room. The truth had set him free.

"Mom...I don't know what to do. Sylvania was in the tower. Now she's gone. I know deep inside that she was the one for me. I loved her. My insecurities drove her away." Ellis' head dropped to the table into a growing puddle of his own tears. "If I had let her know how I felt...she would be right here...with me."

"I'm sorry for your loss and we'll work through it together," His mother stood tall in the doorway. "Know this: if you loved her she knew it. People argue and get in the way of love, but true love is felt. Will you love again? Maybe not for a while but there's always another chance, another opportunity for you to open your heart and receive the love someone has to offer. There's room in your soul for Sylvania and her memory, as well as in the future for the love from someone else."

Ellis watched his mother turn and exit. He heard her words but his spirit told him that Sylvania was the last, the final one for him.

A quiet prayer left his lips for the safety of his true love but it was quickly recalled as the memory of the destruction of the towers was infected with reality. In that moment, he shivered. From deep within--an anger, a fear, a sadness, and other feelings he could never explain, bonded together and bulldozed its way through his body, through his bones, crushing his hope, stifling his spirit. Ellis' hands clasped tightly around his aching head and screamed. How long and how loud, he would never know. Only one word would be remembered: "SYLVANIA!!"

He collapsed onto the table.

WORK ON IT

IT WAS THE FOURTH day of a changed world. Security for travel increased dramatically. Co-workers displayed a heightened sense of fear of people with whom they once worked side by side. New words entered the vocabulary with "extremists" leading the pack. No matter where you were--city, country, rural areas, and suburbs--people looked to the skies with a sense of anxiety when a plane's engine filled the air.

It was the fourth day and Ellis was beginning to close this chapter in his life. Using a few of Winsome's contacts, he was able to contact Sylvania's mother. Not sure of what to say, the conversation was short but understood. It wasn't the words but the absence of sound on the line that reminded each of them what a special person Sylvania was.

Ellis had driven to work, free of noise. He couldn't listen to another commentator speculate about what would happen next, or hear a replay of air traffic controller transmissions, or absorb yet another person sharing their stories of missing friends and loved ones. He wanted to hear their stories. His heart couldn't handle it.

He stood at the window, looking out at the world. Whatever he used to see out there was now gone. It was now a world without understanding: So much anger, so much fear and fatality, so much sadness. Thoughts of Sylvania swirled about his head but he swallowed them down so he could move on.

"Mr. Morris called this morning and said he was on his way down to see you," said Winsome from in the doorway. "He said it's very important." Winsome quieted when she saw the look on Ellis' face. He was a man who changed like the world he lived in. She could sense he was now a man of loss. For the time he and Sylvania were together, although he never spoke of their relationship, she could tell that he was happy. He would take time off. He was excited to go to lunch and return later than usual. He would ask opinions on small gifts and places to go for dinner. He would hum sweet romantic tunes as he worked at his desk. Winsome knew he was in love but not exactly sure with whom-- although she was sure it wasn't *old girl* from before.

"Tell Hank that I'll see him when..." Ellis stopped. Winsome could feel someone entering the office behind her. She knew Ellis wasn't in the mood and with Hank's rhinoceristic personality, today just might be a battle. Looking into Ellis' face, Winsome could see him tensing up, she could hear his breathing. His hand gripped the window frame. She knew that Hank rankled Ellis but today her boss was coming undone. She knew she would have to usher Hank out and back into the waiting area. Deep inside, she would enjoy this. Turning, she too froze in her place, but only for a moment. Winsome had never met this person but her life's experience told her to do one thing--step out of the way and leave the two alone. Ellis, unable to speak, simply opened his arms and in an instance Sylvania raced to his strong embrace.

"Winsome!" Hank barreled into the office reception area. His voice boomed as he leaned against the reception desk. "It's Friday...I have a 1 PM tee-time...and I need to see Ellis right now!" Without waiting for a response, Hank began to enter Ellis' office. He felt the small hand latch onto his arm as he reached for the door knob.

"What are you doing?" Hank almost choked with the absurd thought that Winsome believed her hand could bar him from opening the door. He could easily flex his wrist and she would become uncoupled. He bellowed arrogantly. "Look, I know you're trying to do your job but I have important things to take care of." Hank turned his attention to Winsome. Her eyes were locked on his. There was a seriousness that weakened him momentarily. Her words stung him like a taser.

"Mr. Parker is busy…He'll call you when he's ready!"

Hank started a smart retort but his senses told him to retreat.

"I'll wait for his call."

Hank backed out of the office slowly, bumping into the door before exiting. Winsome found no need to look at Hank as she returned to her desk.

"You do that!"

RECONNECTION

THEY HELD EACH OTHER, kissing away their mutual agonies. Kissing away the apologies. Kissing away the pain of not knowing. Kissing. They stood for a time undetermined; seeking to understand each other's true needs through their silence. Ellis wondered, as his hands stroked her hair, if he was dreaming. Had his mind conjured her image to ease the self-inflicted pain that seemingly no salve or analgesic could ease. As he tasted her essence, he prayed to God that this was not a divine joke or a penance for a life of love wasted.

Sylvania buried her head into Ellis' chest. His arms held her in the same way a child holds onto a blanket for comfort and security. For three days, her world came to a halt. Her sphere of living imploded, leaving her alone in a sea of frenzy. She, bouncing like a rudderless ship, fought the Sirens that infested her mind with illusions of despair and futility. Whatever infection of doubt and fear that was in her system was now eradicated. Ellis' presence was the antidote. She knew Ellis was the elixir for her fears, for her life, for her love.

"Where have you been?" Ellis could hardly ask the question. They sat at his small conference table. From his mini-fridge, he produced two juices. Sylvania tried to piece the days of uncertainty into a few sentences.

"I was supposed to be in the first tower on Tuesday morning. I had an interview and was determined to get there on time. Unfortunately...or fortunately...my hotel had a power surge which knocked out my alarm clock. I woke up late and then had a hard time getting a cab. I didn't get one until about 8:30. I didn't hear the first plane but I knew something was up by the talk back and forth on the cab radio. Traffic started to slow down and bunch up. We sat for what seemed to be forever until news of the second plane hitting came over the radio. At the moment everything speeded up...people screaming...panicking...running. My cabbie just jumped out of the cab and was gone. I didn't know what to do. It was then I heard a loud screeching noise and I knew I had to get back to the hotel. That's all I could think of...except for my mother, Twist...and you. I don't know if I walked, ran, or stole the cab but I made it back to my hotel just as everything got dark." Sylvania shuddered as her words trailed off. She took several long shaky gulps of her juice and tried to continue. She could only utter a few words. "All those people. All those lives. My God!"

Ellis held her hand tightly.

"They let us stay in the rooms but we had no phones. No hot water. They provided us with some food...but how could you eat with all of the cries...the sirens. I felt some hope when a family who was in New York for the first time finally got in contact with some of their family and they gave me a ride to Grand Central Station. I managed to squeeze onto a train this morning and..." Sylvania struggled to stand. Ellis helped her up, sensing her need to move, to walk back and forth. "I wanted to go to my place...to go to my mother's...but I didn't have the strength...I was too tired...just too tired." She leaned against Ellis' bookcase, running her fingers over the volumes of annual reports. "When I got to 30th Street...I didn't know what to do..." She looked at Ellis as if she was looking right through him. "Then I thought of you. I knew you would be here...you would be here for me."

Ellis' mouth dropped open. "You walked over fifteen blocks. Sylvania...you have to be exhausted!"

Sylvania's words slowed. Ellis tried to react but it as if he was in a dream. He watched her eyes. They went from clear to glassy.

Her head tilted backward as if the finger of sleep brushed her cheek. He watched her body go limp. It took two steps before he was by her side, easing her down to the floor. As he called for Winsome, he looked at Sylvania's face. It was peaceful and calm, as if she knew his arms were where she should be.

SWITCH

SYLVANIA SETTLED BACK IN her hospital bed, leaving the gelatin from her lunch for the nurse to remove. She fumbled with the blanket, seeking the ever-elusive remote control. She couldn't stand another minute of the Jerry Springer nonsense. It used to be funny to watch the parade of train wrecks cuss, hit, strip, and engage in other self-debasing sideshow-isms. Now, shows like this weren't entertainment, they were time wasters. Her time was precious now. She saw her time on Earth as a gift to better herself, to make things better for others, to love and to be loved. With a click, she turned the television off.

She looked around the room, taking in all of the various bouquets of flowers, plants, and cards--mostly from the *Mondaine Madames of Tau Beta Lambda*. Her mother sent a beautiful arrangement of white carnations. Viewing them brought a smile to her face, but the warmest glow came from the oversized Teddy Bear holding the heart-shaped honey pot which read, *Honey, I luvs ya!*

"Are you awake?" A familiar voice and a gentle tapping steered her attention to the door. Mrs. Lee entered the room, carrying in an elegant floral arrangement. "This is from Mrs. Carter-McCloud. She sends her very best." Mrs. Lee kissed her daughter's forehead. She reached over and untangled the cords to open the blinds, letting in more light. "Doctor says you'll be going home after your tests this afternoon. You know you're welcome to stay with me."

"I've been doing a lot of thinking over the past couple of days." Sylvania patted the bed, signaling for her mother to sit next to her.

"We can have this conversation at home, Sylvania." Mrs. Lee clasped Sylvania's hand tightly.

"It's okay to talk about it here." Mrs. Lee was used to Sylvania's walls of defense whenever she tried to offer her any kind of advice, but today, she could hear the peace in her voice. "I need to go back to my own place. To sort out what I'm going to do next. You have been so good and generous to me all of my life...but especially over the past few years....and I never truly appreciated it."

"That's what mother's do."

"But what I did...that's not what daughter's should do." Sylvania sat up more. "You've been carrying me so that I never really had to learn to run...but it's time for me to show you...no...me...that I can take care of myself." Sylvania could see the tiny *mother's tear* rising . "Oh...don't cry Mom." She reached up and wiped the tear as it began to fall.

"That's not it," began Mrs. Lee, "It's just that ever since you lost your father, I've been afraid to let you go. I did everything for you because I was afraid of being alone." Mrs. Lee drew a long breath. "When I thought I lost you, I felt that I had died along with you. I've been thinking about how I didn't do all I should have for you...help instill confidence...a spine for adventure...a sense of ferociousness needed for this world. And I know why. If I had, you would have gone out and conquered the world...and I would be left with my own insecurities."

Their gazes were fixed on the floor, the walls, the windows, everything except each other. Their moment of revelation and peace simmered in the room, marinated, building an aroma of forgiveness, openness, and acceptance. The moment was broken by the light-hearted laughter of Sylvania.

"We should have had written all of what we just said down...would make a great Lifetime movie." The sun, shining through the window, joined them in their amusement.

Mrs. Lee caught her breath.

"I've always been proud of you…and now…knowing that you're ready to do your thing…just know that I'll always be here for you. I love you Ms. Sylvania Marcel Lee."

"I love you too, mom." Sylvania beamed brighter than the sun.

Mrs. Lee rose, gathering her things. "I'll be back to pick you up." She tried once more. "You wouldn't consider coming over…I can have dinner ready. Sylvania nodded.

"That's sounds nice…real nice. I could stand a real home cooked meal."

After kissing her mother goodbye, Sylvania picked up the phone. She depressed the numbers with uneasy hesitation. She could hear the phone ring on the line and took a deep breath when she heard the voice on the other end.

"Who this?!"

Afraid for some unknown reason, Sylvania hung up. Taking a deep breath, she promised to call Twist after she got to her place…tomorrow.

BLIND VISION CLEAR

FIRST RING! SECOND RING! Third...

"Hello?"

"Syl? Sylvania?"

"Hi Twist."

"Girl! Why the hell you ain't tell me you was home? I had to hear it from your moms when I called to check in on her."

"I'm sorry. I just had to get myself together."

"Three days! Three days Syl you been home and ain't call me! Me!?!"

"I didn't know what to say...to say to anyone. I didn't have it for conversation."

"Well here's my conversation! I'm sittin' in front of my TV, watching all this madness and remembering that you up in there. I just knew you were..."

"I know..."

"You don't know! You don't know shit! I'm here..."

"Twist, don't cry..."

"Don't cry? Sylvania, don't tell me not to cry!

"I'm alright Twist. I am..."

"Don't get this all turned around! These waterworks are for me...not you! I'm walking around all this time imagining you falling or burning or something and when I finally can have a funeral for you in my mind...here comes your mother with good news."

"That's it Twist girl...good news.

"You're not hearing what I'm sayin'...you knew the good news...your mom knew the good news...but me...your best friend..."

"I wanted to call you...I just..."

"Heard that!"

Click!

First ring! Second ring! Third ring! (Voicemail)

"Twist. I'm sorry. I was wrong. I was scared. I needed you but didn't know how to do that. Please pick up the phone. After that terrible day I didn't know who I was anymore. All that I wanted was meaningless…"

First ring!

"Twist?"

"No. It's your mother."

"I'll call you back! Twist might be calling!"

"Oh, she just called me a little while ago…" (Beep!)

"Bye Mom! I'll call you back!" (Switch!) "Twist?"

"Of course it's me. Who you talkin' to?"

"My mom. Twist, I'm sorry…"

"I know…I heard your message."

"Please forgive--"

"Now girl. I was just exercising my rights to cop an attitude because I was scared for you. I'm all right now 'cause you're all right now."

"So we're still girls?"

"Sylvania Lee…can't nothing break the two of us up. Not the years. Not a man. Not even your good man. And definitely not when times look like the end of days."

"I'm glad for that. You know I love you!"

"I love you too girl but I do need you. That's why I was mad. There's something I realize I need to do but I know I won't do it unless you're by my side."

"Name it."

"Come over. I'll tell you all about it."

"I'm on my way."

"Syl?"

"Yeah Twist?"

"Pick me up some wings from JJ's…all right?"

"Extra spicy….the way you like it."

Click!

The sun felt good on Sylvania's face. This had been the first time since the event that Sylvania looked upward and didn't expect to see visions of death. The sky, the streets, the people--everything all looked different now. The sounds of children playing, music blaring from cars while being waxed, even the unwanted cat calls from sanitation workers brought to her a sense of normalcy. Today, she was going to see her friend, her ace, her other self. She wasn't sure what she was going to say to Twist. She knew that Twist would insist they go out to a club and see what action they could find. She would demand they celebrate her life and get toasted. She knew that it sounded fun but it was time to do things differently. This was the time to invest in herself. It was the time to invest in Ellis. The message was made clear, tomorrow is not promised--invest!

The aroma of the wings entered Twist's apartment first but it was Sylvania's face that brought the brightest smile and jumping joy. They embraced, wisecracked, cried, and pushed each other into the living room. They became out of breath from exuberance and excitement. Each had become a specter in their minds, not knowing if they would ever share the same space again. But here they were like an opened spillway of friendship and love, flooding each other with the kind of rapture they desperately needed. It wasn't long before the plates, napkins, and cold drinks were on the table. Between bites, Sylvania related her story. To her surprise, Twist was quiet, showing an absorbed attention that Sylvania had never experienced.

Sylvania continued.

"Now, I'm ready to move on with my life. There's something out there for me and I'm not going to get it feeling sorry for myself--expecting my momma to do it for me, to chase after lame men, or let a good one get away. I realized to the fullest that I am here for a reason and I'm making that reason real. It looks like Ellis might be moving to Los Angeles and if he does I'm going with him. Not just to follow the man I love but to start fresh. New opportunities. New perspectives. If I go with him it's because I want to...not because I feel I have to."

Once finished, she saw something in Twist's face she had never seen before--seriousness--as if she was pondering a question she was unable to ask. There were words waiting their turn but no release.

"Twist?" Sylvania put her drink down. "Are you okay? I'm here and I'm fine." Twist released a heavy breath and dropped her head. She wrung her hands together before speaking.

"After what you went through...what happened to all those people...and now with what might be coming next in your life I know I just have to face my own reality..."

"What truth? What are you talking about?" This humble side of Twist began to frighten Sylvania. She knew Twist to be a take-charge, no-nonsense, *it's my world* person, but in this instance she was someone else, a weaponless soldier lost in the midst of battle. "What's going on?"

"I don't know how to tell you this!"

"Say it!" Sylvania leaned forward. "Just say it!!" The rise in her voice caused Twist to summon the courage to release what she had been harboring.

"I'm dying."

RENOVATION

SYLVANIA WAS STUNNED BY the casualness of Twist's statement. "Wha...? You're what? C'mon...what did you say?"

Sylvania stammered as she tried to place subject and verb in the correct order in response to what she heard.

"I said I'm dying." Lighting a cigarette, Twist dumped herself onto her futon. Attempting a smoke ring, she sighed. "I've known about it for about seven years now. After momma passed from breast cancer complications, I thought I should go and get myself checked out." While Twist pieced together her collection of thoughts, memories, fears, and complaints, Sylvania took a visual inventory of the amount of empty and soon-to-be emptied wine and liquor bottles strewn around the room. She knew that Twist wasn't necessarily a *neat freak* but it was clear to her the chaotic state of her apartment indicated something was wrong. She brought her attention back to Twist.

"So I'm at the doctor's and he says something about malignancy and that they would check for that. All I could think of was all that momma went through...all the tests...the chemo...the hair loss...the sickness...her last days."

Sylvania witnessed something she had never seen before. Twist was now sobbing. Sylvania had only known Twist as the confident, brash, bold, and full of *sister-girl-from-around-the-way* attitude but now she was a woman who feared for her own mortality.

"So what did the doctor say?"

Composing herself, Twist looked through her blood shot eyes. "About what?"

"About your tests!" Sylvania's voice telegraphed her nervousness. Twist was her good friend of five years, her only friend. As she waited for the answer, her mind flashbacked to the parties, the lunches, the bad movies, the even worst men, and their infamous bitch sessions. They shared so much. They shared it all and now, the unimaginable possibilities that her friend, confidant, *her sister from another mister* would be gone forever. Sylvania choked as she restrained her trepidations. Twist put the cigarette out in an old bowl of cereal.

"I don't know. When he said they might find something I broke camp when he left to see another patient...and I ain't been back!"

Sylvania's jaw dropped. "What? Twist?!?"

"I didn't need to get the countdown to the grave from him."

"That's crazy!! You should know..."

Twist struggled to stand but once up she produced a small crumpled white piece of paper.

"I'll tell you what I know. I know that I got a lot of life to live in a little bit of time. If I meet a man I like...I gots to go for it. I ain't got time for playing games. If I want to do my thing and it jeopardizes my job...then I'm the next contestant on Jeopardy. See all them bottles...well...I'm gonna finish them and then go get more." Twist's bravado quickly degenerated into a fear laced staccato. "I want to live and laugh and love...Syl...I want to live...I want to live."

Sylvania opened her arms and Twist fell into them. Above Twist's cries, Sylvania whispered there were two things they needed to do--and they would do them together. Reaching for Twist's hand, Sylvania took the small piece of paper.

OF WEIGHTS AND WAITS

HANK CONTINUED MUTTERING TO himself as he lumbered into the weight room. He peeled off his workout shirt and dropped down onto the lateral pull machine. Setting the pin for one hundred seventy-five, he took hold of the bar, set his position, and paused. He sat there motionless for five minutes. He didn't move until his trend of thought was broken by a passing custodian.

He returned his focus to the machine. Bracing himself, he began his workout. With each pull, he cursed the decision of Mr. Morgan. *I can't believe he's offering the LA deal to that weak-ass Ellis (grunt)...Out of nowhere he gets the guts to talk about all the value he brings to the company (ungh)...Where'd that come from (grunt)...Talking about profits...raising bond ratings...acquiring government contracts(hungh)...It's like I wasn't even there (grunt)...Like he grew a backbone overnight(ungh)...complimenting me for assisting him in surpassing the annual goals (grunt)...as if I was his assistant...(hungh)...He had me looking like a punk ass fool in there(grunt)...recommending they move my area under him(grunt)...Damned if I'll ever take orders from him(hungh)...I'm Hank the Tank!*

SLAM!

The sound of the weights crashing down as he finished his repetitions resounded all the way through to the rest rooms. He sweated profusely as he moved to the treadmill. Setting the machine for thirty minutes, Hank began jogging in place. He continued his thoughts of frustration until they were intercepted by a solitary figure entering the room.

"Aw hell!" Hank breathed heavy. The site of Devon made him increase his pace. Devon looked at Hank sideways and made his way to the free weights without missing a step. Hank wanted to say something, to shout *faggot* or some other insult but he didn't. He wanted to jump off the treadmill and *bust Devon square in his pretty-boy face* but only his pace increased. He wanted to retaliate for what happened at the restaurant, what happened in the boardroom, the bedroom, but his wants went unsatisfied. Anger and disgust filled his mouth with a taste that could neither be expelled nor swallowed. When the treadmill slowed to a stop, his body heaved with heavy breathing, bathed in perspiration. Seeing Devon from the corner of his eye, he couldn't relax, he couldn't cool down. His body was charged with hate: hate for Devon, for Ellis, for women, for everything. He walked to the mirror and felt sick. He had to avert his eyes from looking at his reflection. To further his disgust, he turned and looked at Devon who had now finished his workout. Hank's eyes closed to slits of rage. He followed Devon with his eyes from the weights to the door. He knew this was his moment to use his power of language, his arsenal of words to destroy his once prototype, disciple, his apprentice who now turned into a limp-wristed Benedict Arnold. He had to say something but all that he could muster was a single word.

"What?!"

Devon's expression did not change. He bent over, tied his shoe, retrieved his gym bag, and pushed on the door to leave. Halfway through the exit, he paused, and brought all of his attention and attitude to Hank.

"Word has it that they're downsizing your area...perhaps I should ask Ellis about that...I'm sorry...you're supervisor. That's what!" The room was silent. Devon was gone.

Hank turned back to the mirror. There he was--Hank the Tank--the one from eighth grade. He closed his eyes, leaned his head against the mirror, and was absorbed by the loneliness of the room.

COME TOGETHER

"WHERE IS SHE?"

Ellis looked impatiently into cloud-filled sky. "It looks like it might rain soon. We should go inside."

"She'll be here. She promised." Sylvania fixed Ellis' tie and patted his chest. "How do I look?" Sylvania twirled so that Ellis could get the fullness of her new outfit.

"Like a young Angela Bassett." Sylvania stopped twirling abruptly and moved her face close to Ellis'.

"Young? What are you trying to say?" Ellis cleared his throat.

"I'm just playing. You look scrumptious!" He leaned over for a kiss but another hand grabbed him by the cheek. "Ow, come'on ma!"

"You know that's not the kind of talk for the Lord's day...and especially in front of his house!"

Sylvania giggled softly. "You know your mother is right."

"Oh, don't get on her side...anyway...where is she?"

Sylvania looked up and down Pine Street. She wasn't sure if this was going to happen but she remained hopeful. Going to church with Ellis and his family was the idea. A good start at least. Ellis' Aunt Daliah and his brother Kenneth stepped from out of a cab.

"Ellis! Ellis!" Kenneth lumbered over and gave Ellis a strong bear hug.

"Ugh! You're crushing my kidneys!" Ellis laughed. Ellis loved his brother--tight suit, tight grip, and now a big smile. Kenny gave his mother a kiss on her cheek and whirled to embrace Sylvania.

"You're not going to pick me up are youuuuuuu!" Kenny had Sylvania three feet off the ground.

"You're pretty. Ellis got a girlfriend!" Kenneth sang as Aunt Daliah peeled Sylvania from his grip before taking him by the hand and directing him to the church.

"We'll save you all a seat. They're getting ready to start."

Sylvania recovered from her Sunday morning carousel ride. She got serious and nervous at the same time as she spoke to Ellis and his mother.

"Do you think I'm doing the right thing?"

"I'll tell you this," started Ellis. "If she had gone and completed the check-up she would have known they only wanted to see if the spot was malignant and she would have found out it wasn't. She wasted a lot of years being afraid."

Mrs. Parker stepped between Ellis and Sylvania, giving Ellis the evil eye before turning her attention to Sylvania.

"Sylvania, let me tell you this. We're all afraid of things in this world. Some folk, like your friend, are afraid of the truth. Others are afraid of the unknown, or failing, or letting go of a loved one. Some people are even afraid of being loved." She glanced briefly at Ellis. Your friend did what she felt would give her some comfort. Now that she knows the truth, she'll have to realize the comfort she latched onto was worse than what she was afraid of in the first place. But she'll see. The truth will allow her to live her life with a little more light and clarity."

Sylvania caught sight of Twist coming down Pine Street and quickly stopped the conversation. Twist approached the trio.

"What's up Syl? Ellis?" Ellis introduced his mother to Twist.

"Darlene," Mrs. Parker extended her hand. "Welcome to our church. It has been our home for years and now you can consider it yours if you please."

Twist spoke as if she was the shy girl at the party. "Thank you Mrs. Parker. There's a lot on my mind about my life that I have to deal with. Sylvania thought this would be a great place to start. Mrs. Parker nodded.

"I agree as well. Let's go inside."

As Sylvania climbed the steps toward the open doors of Pine Street Baptist Church, she realized that Twist hadn't responded to Ellis' invitation to have brunch following service. To her surprise, she was still standing at the curb, gazing thoughtfully at the church's majestic steeple.

"Come on Twist," Sylvania waved. "Service is going to over by the time you get up here." Her airy disposition drifted away. Twist did not move. "Twist...what's wrong?" Sylvania began to return to Twist but suddenly felt a hand take her arm.

"Let me talk to her. You and Ellis go on in." Before Sylvania could register a protest, Mrs. Parker was standing next to Twist. Sylvania entered the church, not knowing what was going on with her best friend.

"It's a wonderful church." Mrs. Parker's words surrounded Twist who remained in her dream-like state. The sounds of cars, busses, people, and barking dogs had all faded away. Mrs. Parker focused on the faint whisper of Twist's periodic sighs. She didn't need an x-ray machine to see the chains on Twist's heart, chains that needed removing. Instinctively, as a parent, as a Christian, as a woman, Mrs. Parker placed her hand gently on Twist's shoulder.

"When times hit me hard, this is the place I always came to...and still do to this day. Not for the preaching or the choir but for the solace and peace this house represents." Without moving, Twist offered a slow cadence.

"Oh, I know…I know exactly what you're talking about." Twist was finally loosed from her trance. Turning completely to Mrs. Parker, it was clear that the dam holding back her emotions had been released. "But there comes a point in life when the extension of credit on forgiveness gets denied." Twist openly reminisced. "Years ago, one of my cousins told me that my body was a temple…a gift from God. You know I paid her no mind. I gave myself to a lot of people and not once did I ever feel satisfied. Ain't it funny? When I thought I was dying, I no longer cared. I ruined my temple when I thought it was useless. Now that I know different, I'm even more ashamed of my life and how I lived it."

Mrs. Parker could see the pain in Twist's face. The trembling of her shoulders couldn't be comforted, not even by a full embrace.

"All I'm saying, Mrs. Parker, is that I'm not worthy. That building's not for me. You sweep out trash…you don't bring it in."

Mrs. Parker grabbed Twist by both arms, holding her at length.

"Let me tell you something. You might fall from grace but you never fall out of it. You are not the first to feel this way and definitely won't be the last. I'll say this like this. Miss Patti sings that you cannot change who you were but you can change who you are." A sliver of comfort bloomed on Twist's face. "This place…this building…is not a monument to those who are good and holy…it is a sanctuary for those with broken spirits…those who have lost their way…those in need of a little grace."

Mrs. Parker took a step, allowing her hands to slide down to grasp Twist's nervous hands.

"Come and find the peace you have been searching for." Slowly Twist turned, taking a step, taking a leap.

The two walked in silence, passing the marquee that read, *How to make a lot out of life when you're living just a little.* The stairs no longer seemed a chore to climb but a placid route to ascension. As the doors of the church opened, the mesmerizing sounds of the choir guided Twist to a place she had been seeking for a long time.

...Oh for the wonderful love he has promised
Promised for you and for me!
Though we have sinned, he has mercy and pardon
Pardon for you and for me
Come home...

ANCHORS AWEIGH

WARM BREEZES AND SEAGULLS surrounded the gathering crowd on the waterfront. One of the highlights of the Philly Pride celebration was the Saturday night party cruise on the Spirit of Philadelphia. Ticket holders and well-wishers milled among the vendors, musicians, street performers, panhandlers, and information booths. A blast from the horn indicated the approaching ship was preparing to dock. Shouts and cheers filled the air by the revelers in anticipation of getting their party on.

A lone figure stood by the ticket booth. He looked at his watch, at the posted departure time, and back to his watch. He wanted to pace but he remained anchored to his spot. He promised to be standing by the ticket booth and he didn't want to risk being missed. The roar of the ship's engine caused him to look at his watch again. A swell of people approached from the South Street Footbridge. Gazing hopefully at the crowd, the person of his expectations failed to appear.

The ship was fully docked. The gang plank was secured and the crowd morphed into a joyous and excited orderly line. He moved to the ticket window.

"How long before departure?"

"Not soon enough as far as I'm concerned."

As he turned, he caught sight of the cab door opening as it reached the curb.

"Devon! You had me over here about to lose it." The two embraced but cut it short so they could secure a place in line.

"I'm sorry, Cary…I was running late. Car problems…ergo the cab." Devon sized up his shipmate's outfit. *Very nautical.* As the line inched forward, Cary noticed Devon's demeanor. He seemed nervous, looking around, as if there was something or someone bothering him.

"You seem distracted." Cary offered a piece of gum as he opened the conversation.

"I've never been…"

"On a ship? Don't worry…you'll enjoy it"

"Not so much the ship…it's just that…I've never been around…around a crowd like this."

"Is something wrong?"
Devon chewed his gum nervously.

"No…it's just different. My being here is a statement…a pretty big statement."
Cary removed his sunglasses and wiped them with his handkerchief.

"I guess the vastness of your statement depends upon what's bothering you." Cary pointed to the crowd, "Is it this lifestyle?" He put his hand on Devon's shoulder. "Or your life?" They moved closer. "We don't have to go. I'm sure I can scalp these." Cary reached inside his pocket, retrieving the tickets. Devon smiled at Cary and shook his head. He thought of the years of not understanding his feelings as a teen, the years of internal struggles with his self-perceptions, the lies he told his friends, his parents, and himself. The desires he suppressed just to play it safe, just to get along. They moved closer.

He continued looking around. He knew that many of the people in the crowd probably shared the same feelings, struggles and fears. But today, maybe only in this moment, he could see that these people were living their lives one day, one instance at a time, pocketing as many happy moments as they could. Devon found himself at the gangplank. Cary looked to him and extended his hand.

"Ready to take this fantastic voyage?"

Devon breathed in his new life, filling his lungs with a chance to explore a new and wanted horizon. His eyes were now clear enough to see that he was where he should be. He had found a piece of peace.

"Aye-yi, my captain!" They boarded the ship together. "Aye-yi!"

EPILOGUE

"SO WHERE DO WE go from here?"
Ellis could hear Sylvania's words over and over in his head as he
purchased his pretzels from the vendor. Did he have an answer?
Should he? His instinct was to plan, to lay out a future for the both
of them. Retrieving his change, his answer became crystal clear.
He knew his next step.

He quietly moved behind Sylvania who was seated on a bench
outside of City Hall. She had suggested they take a walk through
Center City and stroll through the four grand hallways of City Hall.
She smelled the warm aroma of the pretzel and turned to see Ellis.
He reached his hand to hers. She stood, turned, and fell into his
embrace.

"Where are we going?" Sylvania leaned her head on Ellis's
shoulder as they crossed the six-lane street. Her question was a
soft sonnet in his ear, as if a distant spirit seeking solace. Ellis
stopped once they reached the curb. Looking around, he paused,
and, with a flare of excitement, he threw his arm around her
shoulder.

"I know exactly where we're going! Let me show you."
Moments later, the two found themselves standing in Love Park.
Skateboarders zipped by, performing their stomach-tightening
tricks as seniors fed pigeons that looked too fat to fly. Together
they stood under the Love statue. Whatever was happening in
Philadelphia between the sweeps of the hands of the City Hall
clock ceased to exist. This time now belonged to the two of them.
Ellis leaned in and received a long and soul-satisfying kiss. Their
hearts finished the rest of their conversation.

I wish I could have loved you before...
You can love me forever...

END

ACKNOWLEDGEMENTS

I would like to thank everyone who assisted me in seeing this project through to its completion. Very special "thanks" to Tim Lockridge and Stephanie Lohmann for their time, skill, expertise, and support. Further, thank you to my friends who served as readers and sounding boards.

Thank you to my family for understanding my need for time and solitary confinement. I appreciate their encouragement and confidence in my dreams.

Last but not lease, *thank you* to the City of Philadelphia for being a beautiful backdrop.

ABOUT THE AUTHOR

Guy A. Sims is a true son of Philadelphia. A graduate of Houston Elementary and Germantown High, his travels in and around the city served as inspiration for Living Just A Little, his first novel. A long time writer of short stories and poetry, Guy honed his skills at Lincoln University in Pennsylvania. He lived in many regions of the country over the years but the fond memories of subway rides, City Hall, and hot pretzels always filled his mind.

Guy currently lives in Blacksburg, Virginia with his wife Lisa and their three children, Alyssia, Sterling, Chancellor, and their cat Mischief.